# THANK YOUR LUCKY STARS

## A NOVEL OF WORLD WAR II HOLLYWOOD

### MARTIN TURNBULL

*This book is dedicated to*

***STEVEN ADKINS***

*because there's nobody else I'd want be stuck in an elevator with.*

**Copyright 2022 Martin Turnbull**

All rights reserved. No part of this e-book may be reproduced in any form other than that in which it was purchased and without the written permission of the author. This e-book is licensed for your personal enjoyment only. This e-book may not be re-sold or given away to other people. If you would like to share this book with another person, please purchase an additional copy for each recipient. If you're reading this book and did not purchase it, or it was not purchased for you, please purchase your own copy. Thank you for respecting the hard work of this author.

**DISCLAIMER**

This novel is a work of historical fiction. Apart from the well-known actual people, events and locales that figure into the narrative, all names, characters, places, and incidents are the product of the author's imagination or are used fictitiously. Any resemblance to actual persons, living or dead, events or locals is entirely coincidental.

1

Nell Davenport peeked over the balustrade of the Warner Bros. pirate ship. She watched the white beam from the security guard's flashlight whisk across Stage Sixteen and didn't draw another breath until the murky shadows had swallowed him whole.

Finally, she was alone.

Wartime audiences searching for escape and romance ensured that studios were raking it in, which meant Warners was releasing film after film after film. And there had been no tranquility at Nell's boardinghouse after the Office of War Information had asked landlords to jam two lodgers into each room. Or three, if space permitted. Thankfully, Nell had to contend with only one extra girl hanging damp stockings over her coral-pink lampshade. But now there was twice the competition for the morning bathroom.

The cacophony never stopped. The crowding never stopped. The everything never stopped. Sometimes a girl needed a restful nook to recover her wits—like a cozy bunk on a fake pirate ship after everybody else had bolted for the next streetcar or nearest bar.

Something soft and furry ran along Nell's arm.

She shrank from her unexpected intruder. The tiny photo in her right hand slipped through her fingers and fluttered over the wooden railing and onto the asphalt.

"Dammit, Bucky!" She menaced the studio's ginger tabby cat with her sternest frown. "Of all the pirate ships in all the world, did you have to sneak onto mine?"

Bucky gazed at her. If the *Arabella* is anybody's, he seemed to say, it's Luke Valenti's.

He had a point. If Luke hadn't been hiding out here last month, Nell wouldn't have thought of his bunk as the ideal place to sink into a soft mattress and wonder when she might get a letter from him. She could relive his lips on hers, his fingertips stroking her skin, his breath warming the base of her throat. God, how she loved that. And oh, how she missed it.

"I've got *one* photo of him," she upbraided Bucky. "If it disappears, I'll be on the warpath."

Bucky remained unperturbed. He had seen it all: royal courts, New York slums, Maine cottages, clever sleuths and empty-headed chorines, voodoo doctors and murderous nurses. What could one little script girl do?

Nell clambered down the gangplank and pounced on the snapshot, then tilted it toward the three-quarter moon rising over the Burbank hills.

The day before Luke had left Los Angeles, the two of them had piled into a photo booth because only nitwits kiss their boyfriends goodbye without a snapshot.

She stared at his face in the moonlight's milky glow. Did the Navy give him toothpaste? Was the food bearable? Was he warm enough at night? Until she received the letter he promised, all she had were questions.

She would be happy with a hastily scribbled postcard. *Everything's fine! Thinking of you!* Or maybe she should be patient. He had only been gone a couple of weeks. He was still probably getting settled into the rigors and routines of Navy life while packing his head chock-full of training and information and procedures. But still. He had to know she was missing him something awful.

Fidgety, that's what she was. Maybe a stroll around the studio would help pacify the ants in her pants.

She headed up Viennese Street to Brownstone Street. They didn't have brownstones back in her hometown of South Bend, Indiana, but had they reminded Luke of Brooklyn? Maybe one day he'd take her there and point out his favorite haunts. The last block of Argyle Road, where he'd lift his feet off his bicycle pedals and coast along under oaks and elms. The Bay Ridge Candy Shop, where he'd take her for an egg cream. Then on to Bobo's Bakery at 13th and 54th for the best babka and pumpernickel east of the Battery.

"Yes," she told Luke's photo, "I was listening."

Nobody in his life had paid him the least bit of attention before he had landed in California with fifty-one bucks, three days' worth of clothes, and no way to get home. But he would have caught her eye, even if he hadn't been yelling at Humphrey Bogart. Oh, but that second time, when she'd spotted him at Schwab's, his eyes round as fishbowls . . .

Was it any wonder I plopped myself onto the stool next to you, she thought dreamily, practically cracking the glass counter with my chocolate malted? That way you looked at me, as though you'd fallen overboard and I was the Coast Guard holding the last life preserver.

Overhead, a pair of ducks quacked, their wings silhouetted against the moon, as they headed for the manmade lake where buccaneers fought it out with the King's Navy, ocean liners plied the Atlantic, and brave sailors took on Nazi U-boats.

She turned left at the lake, then left again at Editing, and headed into the two-story office block near the water tower. Warner Bros.' PR department was the length of a football field. It held three rows of identical desks: dark wood, each with its signature green banker's lamp and battered typewriter, and each one strewn with pencils and wax crayons, chewing gum wrappers and overflowing ashtrays.

Nell loved how this place reeked of ink and crayon. Newsprint and burned matches. The sweat of meeting a last-minute deadline. She could almost hear someone shouting, "I've got it!" when he came up with the perfect slogan to sell the latest movie.

*It's still the guy with guts and a gun who wins the war: Gary Cooper in SERGEANT YORK*

*The five most shocking words ever hurled from the screen: CONFESSIONS OF A NAZI SPY*

*From a girl aglow with the rapture of her first kiss to a woman fighting for love: Bette Davis in NOW, VOYAGER*

Nell wondered if she was more of an oddball than she cared to admit. Untold thousands of outfits crowded the costume warehouse. Props had billiard tables and Maltese falcons she could play with. But where did her restless feet point her? To the publicity department, with its drafted posters and newspaper advertising mockups, its address books with the names and telephone numbers of every columnist, magazine editor, talent agent, private eye, and bookmaker in town. And probably a few hookers, too.

Being a script continuity girl had been an interesting job at first, but she had been doing it for three years. Frankly, she was bored. Did it really matter if Jimmy Cagney said, "These tommy guns" or "Those tommy guns"? Who cared if Ann Sheridan announced, "I'll wait until you're out of Sing Sing" or "I'll wait till you get out of Sing Sing"? Filming on Bogie's new picture, *Action in the North Atlantic*, was thundering along, but it was hardly holding her interest.

*Casablanca.* Now, there was a magnificent picture. It hadn't been released yet, but it was plain to Nell that it had all the telltale signs of a hit: doomed romance, exotic location, mystery, suspense. Meanwhile, *Action in the North Atlantic* had a lot of guns and submarines and water, but that was about it. Yawn.

Nell wanted a new job and fresh challenges. With so many fellas away at war, right now was the best time for a gal with a pinch of gumption to get ahead.

She sat at the third desk on the left whose trash can was always filled to overflowing. There was no telling what interesting nugget she might find among the discards. She scooped up the topmost ball of paper and flattened a Western Union telegram.

NOT HAPPY STOP
LEGS LIKE DANCING SPIDER MIRROR STOP
TOMORROW DAWNS BUT NOT WITH KONG
KING STOP
WHISKEY FRISKY RISKY STOP
GEORGE

The only way the cable made sense was if this George guy was drunk—and the Western Union clerk, too. No wonder it had ended up in the trash.

Was it George Raft? He'd been bitter since he'd turned down Sam Spade *and* Rick Blaine. What a stupid ass.

She picked up the telephone and pretended to dial a number. "It's Davenport from Warners PR. I got another one of Raft's nutty rants. Made about as much sense as that Salvador Dali kook. Yeah, that's right. Drunk. *Again.*" She slung her feet on top of the desk. "Your client needs to stop sending these cockamamie telegrams when he's stinko. Okay? Okay!"

Nell slammed down the telephone receiver onto its cradle like the people who crowded this room probably did. She'd bet ten bucks this place hummed all day with jangling telephones, typewriter keys pounding at a gallop, and voices calling out, "What's another word for 'tremendous' that we haven't used on Flynn since *Dive Bomber*?"

She left PR and headed past Duplication to the Recording building. Should she? Could she? Dare she?

No, she shouldn't.

Nell retracted her hand from the door handle as though it were an electric iron. Look what happened the last time you opened your mouth to sing. The entire family had come home early from church and caught you belting a high C. Oh brother, the martyred looks and stern lectures.

She stepped away from the door. On the other side lay forbidden territory.

But still. *But still.*

Nobody was around. Nobody was watching. A peaceful silence blanketed the studio like a snowfall.

Screw it. This isn't Indiana.

A long corridor lay past the small foyer with its stiff-backed chairs and potted ficus. Nell tried the first door and peeked inside.

Jackpot.

The recording studio was square, around fifty feet by fifty feet. Next to an upright piano, a thick pile of papers rested on a music stand.

Complete score for
SHINE ON, HARVEST MOON
Producer: William Jacobs
Director: David Butler
Musical Director: Leo F. Forbstein
Orchestrator: Frank Perkins

Nell flipped to the first song.

"Shine On, Harvest Moon"
Sung by Dennis Morgan and Ann Sheridan
(singing voice to be dubbed by Lynn Martin)

She lifted the sheet music, walked past the empty wooden chairs of the horn section, and stepped inside the booth. The microphone was about the size of her fist, with horizontal bars across the front and vertical ones at each end. It smelled faintly of a floral perfume she couldn't place. Whoever had last stood here sure had poured it on thick.

She dug her fingernails into the palms of her hands. *Why so jittery? There's nobody here to disapprove.*

"The chorus," she murmured to herself. "Four lines, then take off before your nerve deserts you."

She opened her mouth, filled her lungs and sang:

"Shine on, shine on, harvest moon up in the sky,

I ain't had no lovin' since January, February, June or July.

Snow time ain't no time to stay outdoors and spoon,

So shine on, shine on, harvest moon, for me and my ga-a-a-a-a-al."

How different she sounded. So clear! So strong! Not at all like the voice in the living room when everyone was at Sunday morning Mass, thinking she had succumbed to a fever.

Reluctantly, she gathered up the sheet music again. She'd pushed her luck far enough. Anyone might come through that door and demand to know what the heck was going on. She hurried down the corridor and through the foyer. As she stepped outside, a loud clatter echoed off the soundstage walls to her right. Nell froze, choking off the gasp that threatened to fly from her.

Why hadn't she stayed safe and cozy in Luke's bunk on the *Arabella* where security guards wouldn't think of looking? She was a script girl who had no legitimate reason to be romping around the recording studio at midnight on a Wednesday. This was wartime. Spies and saboteurs could lurk in any dim corner.

A grinding sound followed, then a harsh CLANG!

Panic crushed her chest; all she heard was the pounding in her ears and her breath coming in short, strangled huffs. She listened through the crack, but heard no footsteps or tuneless whistling. No flashlight zig-zagged across Stage Ten's ventilator shaft.

*Meow. Meow.*

The ginger tabby crouched in front of an upended trash can and sniffed at the contents spilled across the lane. "That's the second time tonight you've scared the cranberries out of me."

He strolled over and rubbed the length of his body against her shin.

She knelt down and stroked his soft fur. "Did you hear me sing? That long note at the end? Pretty hot stuff, huh? Mother and Father wouldn't approve. Even 'Shine On, Harvest Moon' is the devil's music to them. I couldn't win, could I, Bucky-boy?"

The cat meowed loudly, which Nell took to mean, "Not in a million years. You did the right thing. Isn't it time for bed now?"

She straightened and turned to the mess the cat had made. Lying among the newspapers, chicken legs, and drinking straws, was a handbill with two large words across the top: *HOLLY-WOOOD CANTEEN.*

It was a reference to the pet project of Bette Davis and John Garfield, a canteen where servicemen on shore leave could stop by to get some refreshment, meet glamour girls, and maybe even dance with a movie star. It was opening in a week's time and Davis was recruiting volunteers. *Join us!* it cajoled at the bottom. *Won't you do your bit for our boys and for the noble cause we're all fighting for?*

She folded it up and slid it into her pocket. "Come on, Bucky. It's about time you and I got some shut-eye."

2

*H*umphrey Bogart took the chair next to Nell and grimaced as he pulled at the spongy collar of his life jacket.

"You look like a monk tied into a hair shirt," she told him.

"It's giving me a rash."

"I have some hand cream." She reached into her handbag, which was hanging from the armrest. "Might soothe the friction." The twenty-cent cream Nell had bought at J.J. Newberry featured a watercolor sprig of lavender tied with a pink ribbon. She held it up for him to see. "You could end up smelling like Aunt Hortense at her Pasadena pinochle club. Raymond Massey won't be your greatest fan during this scene you're about to film."

Bogie loosened the canvas straps. "Screw Raymond Massey."

She rounded the back of his chair and knocked his dark blue Navy cap into his lap, revealing his balding noodle as crewmembers prepped Bogie's next scene at the helm of the Liberty ship his character served on.

He sniffed at the air. "Ugh. You weren't kidding."

"Your neck looks awfully red, so this'll probably help. But

won't your wife take issue with you reeking of pretty little flowers?"

"Let's not talk about Madam unless we absolutely have to."

"Then let's not—"

"Last night she cooked up a dinner of fried chicken legs—and then threw them at me, yelling out brands of whiskey."

"What a terrible waste of meat."

"We're a terrible waste of everything." He stayed silent for a moment or two. "How's our boy doing?"

Nell rubbed Bogie's neck a little harder than she needed to. "I haven't heard from him yet."

"I assume you ignored his instruction to not write first and have composed how many letters?"

She replaced the lid on the lavender cream and dropped into her chair. "Eight," she said grudgingly.

He flicked the straps on his jacket. "You know how they say the eye of a hurricane is quiet and still? That's how I saw him."

Nell had worked on six of Bogie's movies, but he'd never confided in her like this. She'd been so caught up in how much she missed Luke that she hadn't considered the hole he might have left behind in anyone else's life. "Am I the hurricane in this scenario?"

He looked at her as though he hadn't seen her in a long time. "What I'm saying is Luke's the type of guy I could turn to when everything got screwy."

"I know what you mean." Nell's response leaked out so quietly she wasn't sure he heard her.

"Even now, weeks later, I keep expecting the little son of a gun to walk into my dressing room or pull into the driveway. Don't get me wrong—nothing pleased me more than to hear he'd been accepted into the Navy."

Nell nodded. Proud enough to bust apart at the seams, Luke hadn't been able to stop smiling the morning she'd waved him off at Union Station. She'd been proud, too—of how she had held back the tears until after his train had chugged away from the platform.

Bogie gave her a look. "Listen to me jaw about missing him. It must be ten times harder for you."

"He'll write when he can." She dabbed at the corner of her eye. "Meanwhile, we're both allowed to miss him."

Bogie pulled his cap back on. "Have you seen those Hollywood Canteen fliers Bette's been plastering all over?"

"All those GIs and jarheads and flyboys will get a kick out of being served cake or coffee by the great Warner Brothers motion picture star, Humphrey Bogart. I guarantee none of them will catapult chicken legs at you."

He threw her a jaded fisheye. "I should volunteer."

"You and me both. It'll give you a reason to get out of the house that Mayo can't argue with," she said, referring to Bogie's wife. "And it'll distract me from thinking about Luke."

The words *I need a favor from you* were on the tip of her tongue, but before she could spit them out, he said, "The *Thank Your Lucky Stars* script for my two-hander with Cuddles Sakall arrived this morning. I'm behaving like every hoodlum I've played in the movies, and Cuddles does his schtick harrumphing and waffling and mangling the English language. It's a fun bit, but it's chock-full of rat-a-tat-tat delivery, so I'll need to be word perfect. Can you help me run lines?"

"I'd be happy to." Nell smiled as she saw the opportunity she'd been hoping for. "As a matter of fact, I have a favor to ask." She looked around quickly; the key lights filled the bridge set with murky shadows dovetailing with the North Atlantic dawn. They'd be ready to shoot again soon. She clamped her fidgety fingers onto each armrest. Bogart was astute at reading people, and she didn't want to come across like a timid ladybug. "Lately I've been feeling a little . . ."

"Lovelorn?"

"No. Well, yes, but no. I need a job that's more stimulating than—" she swept a hand toward the Liberty ship's bridge "—this."

He rubbed his chin like she had seen him do in every one of his movies. "Got any bright ideas about where—"

It was easier to say the words in a single burst. "ThePRdepartment."

Now that she had said it out loud, the idea didn't sound nearly so preposterous. "I'm capable of more than spending all day noting slight changes in dialogue. With half the menfolk gone, if I am ever going to make a change, it should be now."

An assistant approached them. Before the war, the assistants had all been teenaged boys. But this one was a young woman, dressed in a moss-green cashmere sweater and pearls that made her look like a small liberal arts college literature professor who knew more about the Brontë sisters than anyone else in New England. "They'll be ready for you in ten minutes, Mr. Bogart."

Bogie thanked her, then turned back to Nell. "I'm impressed by your get-up-and-go, young lady, but that production assistant, and all the women like her, will be shunted out the door PDQ when the Lukes of this world come home. Whereas," he held up a finger, "we'll always need script continuity girls."

Nell felt like a fool for not having considered that the men would reclaim their jobs. She'd been too focused on how to score a better-paying job. Her father wasn't the type to forgive the two thousand dollars she owed him for the wedding that had never happened, and paying him five dollars a month meant squaring her debt would take another thirty-three years.

Twelve of the sixteen boardinghouse girls worked at the war factories. Over the communal dinner table, they shared stories of riveting bolts into aircrafts and ships, inserting propellers into torpedoes, and mounting artillery onto turrets. They so-so enjoyed the work, but they *loved* proving that women could do as good a job as the men. That was all well and good, but Nell didn't relish the prospect of coming home with matted hair, filthy nails, and scraped skin. Stinking of grease and oil wouldn't be so bad, but two of her fellow boarders had been badly injured in unrelated but serious accidents. One of them, a hardy farm girl from Nebraska, might have permanently lost the use of her left hand.

And even if she did take a job like that, when the war ended, *pfffft!* They'd all be out on their tushes. Then where would she be?

At Warners, though, she could build a career. That's what it all came down to, wasn't it? What careers were open to her in South Bend? Supervising the typing pool at Studebaker or Notre Dame? No, thanks.

"What favor did you have in mind?" Bogie asked.

"Put in a good word for me with Robert Taplinger."

"The head of PR?"

"You and he met with Jack Warner the day before yesterday."

"You *do* keep your eyes and ears open."

"I try." Nell had sourced her intel by seeking out Margie, a wardrobe assistant who was sleeping with Rob, the mechanic who worked on the studio's fleet of cars and trucks, whose roommate was dating Estelle, a front-office secretary.

"Nell, honey, I'd love to help out. Really, I would." Bogie eyed the cameraman, who was returning to his position. "Some issues came up over *Casablanca*'s New York premiere in a few weeks. They want me to attend, so I told them they'd have to pay me for the full week it takes to get there and back on the train. Jack argued that I'd be working on behalf of the studio. I reminded him 'working' means 'actively filming a movie,' not smiling for the newspaper cameras."

"How did they take it?"

"The word 'livid' pretty much covers it. They told me I was stymying *Casablanca*'s chances of hitting it big, which will enhance my career. Yeah, and their bank account, which is all they really care about. So I dug in my heels. You can't let anyone treat you like you're a pawn in their game of chess."

"Did you get your way?"

"Taplinger stormed out, but only because he beat me to the punch. So you see, I'm in the doghouse—make that the basement of the doghouse. I'm not in any position to ask either of those putzes a favor. I feel real bad about not being able to give you a leg up, but you'll have to figure out a way in that doesn't involve their least favorite person in the world."

## 3

Nell laid out a sheet of notepaper and matching envelope on Captain Blood's dining table. Until the setting sun sank behind Stage Eighteen, she'd have plenty of late-afternoon light to see by, but then she'd need the hurricane lamp she had borrowed from Props.

She uncapped her pewter fountain pen and wrote

*October 3rd, 1942*
*My darling Luke,*

She was going to add "wherever you are" but thought better of it. Why sound so churlish? He'd only been gone a couple of weeks, but she already felt like an untethered buoy drifting in an ocean whose shore she could no longer see.

So she comforted herself by writing to Luke, pouring out her thoughts, her hopes, and her fears. Her first handful had been terribly earnest, filled with declarations of undying love and unconditional promises that she would wait for him no matter what, no matter how long. Even she had to admit they were hard to plow through.

So now she leavened them with studio gossip. How well *The Man Who Came to Dinner* had performed at the box office, despite Bette Davis's misery during the making of the movie. How Errol Flynn was rumored to be juggling three different girlfriends when filming *Edge of Darkness*. "Where does that man find the energy?" How, despite sixteen girls toiling seven days a week, the boardinghouse's victory garden was a dismal patch of insipid tomatoes, undernourished bell peppers, and mealy cucumbers. And how everybody was frantic at the prospect of coffee rationing.

*My stratagem to finagle my way into the PR department has floundered. There I was thinking myself so darned clever for knowing about Bogie's meeting with Taplinger and Warner. As the head of PR, Taplinger is the one I need to impress—*

"Don't you walk away from me!" The shrieking voice pierced the evening air.

"Who's walking away?" The second voice sounded like Jack Warner. "I'm merely taking a stroll around my private property. You're only still here because I haven't thrown you out."

Yep, that was Mr. Warner, all right. But who was he yelling at?

"But I'll be damned if I leave here empty-handed."

"Here's a scoop for you: That hat is ridiculous. All your hats are ridiculous. *You* are ridiculous."

Good God! Was Warner yelling at Hedda Hopper?

Nell scrambled to the circular porthole facing Stage Eighteen. Twenty feet away, Warner stood with his feet planted apart, shaking his right hand at one of the most powerful newspaperwomen in America like she was the maid who scrubbed his kitchen floor.

Hedda's hat was an absurd concoction of heliotrope-dyed egret feathers fastened with what looked like barbed wire to a Mexican sombrero that looked as though it had shrunk in the wash. "Tell me what I came here for," she snapped. "You know what it is."

"Not everything that happens in this town is your business, you snooping old biddy."

"Who was the one who called you after that party on Flynn's yacht?" Hopper swung her snakeskin purse off her arm as though she were aiming to shot-put it at his head. "I warned you the authorities were going after him. I even gave you the names of Hansen and Satterlee. I warned they were about to dump ten tons of grief on you."

"I'm not—"

"And who told you to hire Geisler because he's the only defense lawyer who'll get Flynn off those rape charges?" Nell gasped softly. Errol was going to be charged with *rape*? "It sure as hell wasn't the goddamned tooth fairy."

"I already told you how much I appreciated—"

"And now it's payback time."

"The situations aren't related."

Hopper threw her hands out like one of Macbeth's witches. "It's a simple question: Is Bogart ditching that drunken shrew? Those two public sluggers are poison to each other, and that reflects badly on your studio. So give me the scoop on when they're splitting so that we can make it official."

"Bogart's marriage is none of your business." A stilted pause punctuated the air between them before Warner added, "Or mine." But it was a halfhearted, unconvincing afterthought.

"Look who's being ridiculous now," Hopper bit back.

She's got a point, Nell thought.

Hedda had thirty-five million readers who wanted to learn who movie stars were sleeping with, which ones were tying the knot, and who was dumping whom. It was all part of the studio publicity machine's way of keeping their stars circulating in the minds of moviegoers.

Warner crushed his hands into fists. "I know what's going on here!" he bellowed. Good for you, Nell thought. Go down fighting. "You're still pissed about the Dies Committee."

"If he's not leaving Mayo, then he's stepping out with someone. My money's on Julie Bishop."

"Why? Because she's the only dame in that picture?"

"Or possibly Ingrid Bergman."

"You're grasping at soggy straws, Hedda."

To her credit, Hopper didn't flinch. "Word around town is that you've got a swell picture on your hands with *Casablanca*. I can scuttle it with a little plant here, a little squib there, a blind item or two. For instance, 'Is Humphrey Bogart not traveling to New York for the *Casablanca* premiere because he knows it's a dud?'"

"These are peoples' lives and careers, and you're playing with them like they're kiddie toys."

"All you have to do is tell me—"

"NO WITHERED OLD CROW LIKE YOU IS GOING TO SHAKE ME DOWN!" Warner's voice smacked Nell in the face. "I'll be more than happy to throw every scoop to Louella from now on."

"You wouldn't dare."

"Don't push your luck, Hedda."

"And don't threaten me, you tin-pot Napoleon. And furthermore—"

"And furthermore, this discussion is over."

"No, it isn't!"

"It is when I tell you to go fuck yourself. And brace your girdle, Hedda, 'cause here it comes: GO! FUCK! YOUR! SELF!"

\* \* \*

Warner's words were still reverberating in Nell's ears as she walked onto the *Action on the North Atlantic* set the next morning. The picture's director, Lloyd Bacon, clapped his hands to capture the crew's attention. "Mr. Bogart has called to say he had trouble getting out of bed." A ripple of knowing laughter burbled through the gathering: Bogart had woken up very, *very* hungover.

What lousy timing. Did he have to be late today, of all days? After Warner and Hopper had stormed off in opposite directions the day before, Nell had rushed to the pay phone outside the Electrical shop. Nobody had answered any of her six attempts to get through to Bogie, so she had given up.

"While we wait," Bacon continued, "we'll get reaction shots from Hale and Massey. Spray the set with water. We start shooting in ten."

Reaction shots didn't need a script girl, so Nell stationed herself at the elephant door.

Few people in Hollywood had the steel-plated gonads to stand up to Hedda Hopper, but Mr. Warner hadn't hesitated. Okay, so maybe he had his own agenda that had nothing to do with looking out for Bogie's best interests. Even so, Bogie needed to know that Hopper was on one of her high-handed warpaths.

"Can you tell me where Nell Davenport is?"

The question came from a front-office messenger.

"You've found her."

"I'm here to take you to see Mr. Warner."

Nell's bottom lip dropped open. "*Me?*"

The kid raised a hand toward the main administration building, where Warner had a panoramic window that took in his kingly domain. "Right now."

\* \* \*

Nell had imagined Mr. Warner's office to be a vast space with shiny marble walls, sparkling crystal chandeliers, and plush

Persian carpets thick enough to trap a girl's heel. In reality, though, it wasn't much bigger than Nell's boardinghouse dining room. His desk was the usual size, filled with the standard executive accoutrements: pen holder, desk blotter, banker's lamp, and several telephones. Photographs and certificates blanketed two of the four walls, but that was about it.

He looked up from the papers on his desk as she approached. "Miss Davenport."

It was neither a question nor an invitation to speak. She clasped her hands together like a novitiate preparing to take her vows.

"The next time you eavesdrop, I suggest you make sure nobody sees you."

Nell swallowed. Hard. The captain's porthole had been at least ten feet above their heads. It hadn't occurred to her that he or Hopper had the slightest idea she had been there. A clammy heat bloomed across her chest as a silent *What have you got to say for yourself?* frown etched into his tanned face.

"If I could have slipped quietly away, I would have. But the only escape was the gangplank."

"If I won't stand for Hedda Hopper interfering with my plans, I'm sure as hell not going to stand for a nosy little script girl."

"You were shouting so loudly that I couldn't help but overhear."

"You're working on *Action in the North Atlantic* at the moment."

The man had done his homework. "Yes, sir, I am."

"I absolutely forbid you to say anything about this to Bogart. Not a word, a syllable, or even a whisper. If you do—" he jutted out his chin "—I'll see to it you never get a job anywhere in Los Angeles ever again. That includes the war factories. *And* I've got the contacts to ensure that happens."

Nell's knees weakened, and she wished he'd invited her to sit down. But this wasn't a "Make yourself comfortable" type of meeting. It felt more like a subpoena. "I'm sure you have, sir."

"I want you to keep an eye out for Bogie." His softened tone made her blink. "Watch what he's doing and how he's doing it. Look out for his moods, take note of the things he talks about. His wife. His next picture. What he says about his director."

"You want me to spy on him?" If Nell hadn't been so startled, she might have been able to gather enough of her wits to frame her question more diplomatically.

"I wouldn't put it that way." Warner turned away for a moment and interlaced his fingers. When he looked back at her, a softer, more kindly light filled his eyes. Was it genuine, or was he putting on a performance to ensure he got what he wanted? The safest route out of this situation, Nell decided, was to play along. "If you see trouble coming, try to steer him away from it."

"By 'trouble,' do you mean Mayo Methot?"

He drummed his manicured fingertips on the blotter. "Hedda's right. Mayo is a drunken shrew, and that marriage is bound to fall apart. In *Casablanca*, Bogie has proven himself to be a better actor with a wider range than I ever gave him credit for." The drumming fingers stopped. "Tell anyone that and I'll deny it."

"Your secret is safe with me, Mr. Warner."

"He's become a valuable asset," Warner continued as though Nell hadn't spoken. "Hollywood divorces don't have to be scandalous. If handled skillfully, Bogie wins, I win, the studio wins. And seeing as how you've worked on Bogie's six last pictures, you win, too, because that means you'll get to work on his next six."

*Which would be fine if I wanted to work on Bogart's next six pictures. But I'm just a girl. Why would it even enter my head to aim higher?* "They're probably wondering where I am back on Stage Five."

Warner flicked his left hand at the exit. Nell bolted past the secretary, past the secretary's secretary, and didn't stop until she could feel the sun on her face and the warm late-summer breeze blowing through her hair.

## 4

Nell tapped a pen on her *North Atlantic* script, relieved that it was Bogie's day off. She'd managed to avoid him after coming back from yesterday's—what *had* happened in Mr. Warner's office? Meeting? Warning? Threat? He could deny it all he wanted to, but "keep an eye out for Bogie" meant "spy on him." Who did he think she was, Benedict Arnold?

A bell rang out across the stage. "Sam, Dane, Peter, boost the pace with a little more gas," Lloyd instructed. "This is the big scene for all three of you. Make it count."

As the sound guy lowered the microphone into place, Bobby from the mailroom handed her a telegram.

She had always assumed Luke's first communication would be a long letter written in his orderly penmanship. But if all he could manage was Western Union's ten-word maximum, then she'd take it.

She ripped open the envelope and pulled out its contents.

MEET ME FOR A DRINK STOP

NICKODELL ON MELROSE SEVEN TONIGHT STOP
HEDDA HOPPER

Nell's teeth clamped down on her lower lip as Lloyd Bacon yelled, "Action!"

* * *

She could tell at a glance that movie people from nearby RKO and Paramount filled the bar. Their faces were a little bit more animated, their smiles wider, their laughter a touch louder, and their hands often a blur of motion.

Hedda's fascinator looked like a flat-topped derby crossed with a beret. It wasn't the worst disaster Nell had seen on Hopper's head, and it was a darn sight better than the frightful mess she'd been sporting the night of her screaming match with Jack Warner. Which, Nell assumed, was what this summons was all about. She weaved her way through the maze of cocktail tables. *Believe nothing she says. Not a word. Not a syllable.*

Hopper looked up from her notebook and gave a little wave using only her fingertips. "Have a seat, dear." She picked up a yellow-orange cocktail sitting in the middle of the table. "I ordered Sidecars. You like them, don't you?"

Nell slid onto the tall chair and took a long sip. The nip of Cognac braced her tongue, along with lime juice and . . . she couldn't make out the third ingredient.

"It's Cointreau," Hopper said.

It was Nell's first Sidecar. Yowzer, they were delicious!

"Yes." The word slipped out of Hopper like a purr. "I figured you for a Sidecar girl. My legman, Jaik, put me onto them."

"Tell me, Miss Hopper, why—"

"Call me Hedda." There was that purr again. A little too smooth. Too rehearsed. "We're here because I didn't want you to assume that you went unnoticed on the Warner lot while Jack and I were playing out our little drama."

*Okay, so Mata Hari I ain't.* "If that's what you call a 'little drama,' I'd hate to think what a big one sounded like."

"Trust me!" The laugh that bubbled out of Hopper seemed spontaneous, but the woman had been an actress before she got into the assassinating reputations game. "I know it looked as though we were playing to kill, but we joust like medieval knights at least twice a year. What you saw, why, that was nothing special."

Nell didn't know how to respond, so she took another sip. This Sidecar really was scrumptious—but her head already felt as though it were filling with helium. But not so fast that she hadn't noticed how the movie folk surrounding them were sneaking questioning squints in their direction.

"You saw me peeking out of the porthole?" Nell asked.

"Well, *I* did." Hopper drained her glass. "Jack Warner walks around wearing blinders half the time. He'd never have noticed you in a thousand years."

Hopper winked. Nell didn't like it, nor did she trust it. "How do you know who I am?"

"It's my job to know who everybody is."

"But I'm only a—"

"Continuity girl." Hopper tilted her chin downward and looked at Nell with unblinking eyes as though to say, *Oh, you naïve little simpleton.* "Do you recall my visiting the *Casablanca* set a couple of months ago?"

"For Michael Curtiz's fifteenth anniversary party. Yes, sure."

Although Nell wasn't halfway through her drink yet, Hopper signaled the bartender for another round. If the woman planned to get what she wanted by plying Nell with booze, she would be walking away disappointed. "I could tell that the entire cast and crew were under orders to attend. Some of them weren't happy to be there, but you flitted about making conversation, handing out cake, jollying everything along. You're one of those people who likes everyone and whom everyone likes. You had a certain . . . glow about you."

Of course she'd had a glow about her that day! The previous night, she and Luke had gone to bed for the first time. Not only the first time with each other, but their *very-first-time* first time. She had treasured the shocked look on Luke's face when she'd shucked off her clothes before he had unbuttoned his shirt, and had then had to explain how modesty had no place in a household of five sisters.

How tentative he'd been that first time he'd entered her. He barely knew what he was doing—not that she'd had any more experience than him. Back in South Bend, she and Hank Elliott had never progressed beyond a timid smooch on the lips. She saw later, as she looked back on that moment with Luke, that their shared naivete helped bond them together more deeply than she ever imagined.

"And so," Hopper continued, "I made it my business to discover who you are."

"I'm flattered, but why am I here?"

"I don't know about you, Nell, dear, but I find it hard to stay in business, especially in an industry dominated by men."

"Don't they run all industries?"

"It wouldn't be so bad if the ones running the movie industry were smart and intelligent and classy. But look around us." She waggled a hand in the smoky air. "These slobs might order their bespoke suits at Silverwoods, but they're still slobs underneath. Out for what they can get. Protecting their asses and screw everybody else."

The waiter arrived at their table with fresh Sidecars. It gave Nell a chance to mull over Hopper's declaration. She wasn't sure it was true for all men, but she wasn't wholly wrong, either.

Hopper pulled a pack of Marlboros from her patent leather

purse. "I fight for what I believe in. It's how I'm built. I suspect you're the same way, though we differ in a number of ways, I'm sure. But we women know that the world is more complicated than the strictly black-or-white approach men have. It wouldn't occur to them that two women like us could share other qualities."

Nell read "Hedda Hopper's Hollywood" every morning in the *L.A. Times*, and disagreed with nearly every viewpoint the woman expressed. Nell had never taken the pro-isolationist stance, and she saw FDR as a bulwark standing between the Nazi onslaught and American democracy. What could she possibly have in common with this odious gossipmonger?

Hopper offered a cigarette; Nell declined. "What qualities do you believe we share?"

"Ambition." Hopper underscored her statement by striking a match with an arching flourish. "Can you imagine being a librarian, or a teacher, or standing behind the makeup counter at the local department store all day long?"

Inwardly, Nell grimaced; the woman had recited most of the reasons Nell had jumped on the first Greyhound heading out of town the morning of her wedding. On the other hand, Hopper had also described most of the women who had answered California's clarion call. Nell inspected her cocktail; it was nearly gone already. She swigged the remaining dregs and reached for its replacement. Not that she would drink it. Not all of it, anyway. "I can't."

"A smart young woman like you is capable of being more than a script girl." Hopper took a shallow drag of her cigarette. "Ever considered getting into the PR game?"

Nell fought to keep herself from gaping. She had only shared her idea with Bogie. He avoided gossip columnists at every opportunity, which left Nell with only one explanation: Hedda Hopper had made an uncannily accurate assessment of her.

Hopper let out a shrill sound, rather like a rooster being choked at dawn. "I'm terribly skilled at reading people. One has to be when one's livelihood depends on one's powers of observation. I've hit the bull's-eye, haven't I?"

"I must admit you have."

"It took me an inordinate amount of time to realize that being underestimated is an advantage, and we should always play to our advantages." She crushed the remains of her Marlboro into the white ceramic ashtray with the green Nickodell logo. "I made out a list." She slid her notebook over to Nell. "See if you can tell me what they have in common."

*Casablanca*
*Dark Victory*
*The Adventures of Robin Hood*
*The Maltese Falcon*
*Sergeant York*
*Now, Voyager*

"They're all Warner pictures," Nell said.

"And?"

They had different stars, different directors, different screenwriters. Nell had worked on some of them, but not all of them. "I give up."

"All produced by Hal Wallis."

Nell ran her eyes down the list again. By golly, she was right. Wallis didn't stride around the studio lot like Napoleon Bonaparte; his modus operandi was stealthier than that.

"Practically every movie he produces is a hit." Hopper retrieved her notebook. "His track record is almost as good as Thalberg's—and that shrimp was a genius."

Nearby, a trio of studio types now leaned toward Hopper. Nell didn't blame them; she was as curious as they were to see where all of this was leading.

"Why are we talking about Mr. Wallis?"

"Because Hal got his start in PR. Way before your time, of course. But it shows where it can lead a person." Nell studied the smile playing on Hopper's lips—it was more like a smirk, by way of a leer. "If you ever get bored with taking notes, you could do a whole lot worse than the publicity department."

Nell wished Bogie was sitting at a neighboring table. She could ask him, "Don't snakes like her always have a secret agenda? Surely, she's not here to give me a leg up with no strings attached?"

"People who work in a studio publicity department are a certain breed." Hopper canted her head to one side. "As a continuity girl, you've had terrific training to spot when a film is heading off the rails. You can see why, and possibly how it can be fixed, as well as how marketing can hide the obvious flaws. Nobody on the set, oftentimes not even the director, is in a better position to comprehend that."

This was exactly what Nell had thought many times, but had never expressed out loud. Keeping track of the script, she had developed a sense of knowing if new lines worked. Despite its chaotic production, several of *Casablanca*'s scenes had been shot on the fly, which was why she was sure the picture was going to be a knockout. It was like snapping together pieces in a jigsaw puzzle.

But nobody had thought to ask her, so she had kept her thoughts to herself, and yet here was Hedda Hopper, whom Nell neither liked nor trusted, saying those very words.

Hopper snapped her purse shut. "I'm volunteering at the Hollywood Canteen tonight. Apparently, Abbott and Costello need a stooge and I'm it. Thank goodness I'm known for my sense of humor because heaven only knows what mayhem I'm in for. Have you signed up yet?"

"I've been meaning to, but—"

"When those boys see Hedy and Marlene and Judy, the looks on their faces will be worth the aching feet." She plucked a business card out of her breast pocket and dropped it on the table. "In case you'd like to call me. Or drop by. I'm in the Guaranty

Building on Hollywood Boulevard, corner of Ivar. Office seven-oh-two. Must dash. Bye now."

Nell stared at Hopper as she zigzagged through the thicket of crowded tables, leaving her with a vaguely unsettling feeling.

*What the heck just happened?*

## 5

Nell waited until Bogie had turned onto Sunset Boulevard before she asked, "Did anyone tell you that the FBI vets Hollywood Canteen volunteers? We all go through a background check. Even famous ones, like you."

"They can't be too careful these days. Loose lips sink ships, and all that." He flicked cigarette ash out his window. "Are they going to find some corpse socked away in your closet?"

They were passing Hollywood High now. The main building didn't look too different from her old high school. "In South Bend? Hardly. What about *your* closet, though?"

"Oh, sure. I've got a whole gang of freshly desiccated corpses in mine."

Nell was glad that the fast-approaching dusk masked the heat blooming across her cheeks. "I was thinking along the lines of the Dies Committee."

Bogie's foot slipped off the gas pedal; they lurched forward as his Buick lost momentum. "Where did that question come from?"

"I was in the commissary the other day. I overheard a couple of guys—"

"Who?" His sardonic tone had evaporated.

Oh, boy, whatever the Dies Committee was, it sure made him touchy. "Just a couple o' schmoes," she hedged. "Nobody I knew."

Silence, heavy as a sledgehammer, filled the car. Just when Nell thought maybe she had pushed her luck, Bogie said, "Accusations are like wet lollipops: they stick to everything."

As they pulled up at the Cahuenga Boulevard corner, the lights turned green and Bogie swung his car south. A broad sign announced *HOLLYWOOD CANTEEN* in flowing letters made from rope. Servicemen had already lined up, three men deep, along the wooden fence out front. Bogie drove past it and into the employee parking lot. Another sign, similar to the first one, hung over the doublewide doors: *VOLUNTEER HELP ENTRANCE*.

Inside, Nell and Bogie found a woman in her sixties, her hair pulled back in a makeshift bun, seated behind a desk strewn with papers and cards. She looked up at them beseechingly. "Please tell me you've come to volunteer, Mr. Bogart."

"I have." He flashed her one of his movie-star grins designed to disarm and bewitch. "As has my colleague, Miss Davenport."

"I can't begin to tell you how grateful we are to have you aboard. Normally there'd be paperwork to be filled out, but we've grossly underestimated how many people it takes to keep this place going. You can fill out the form at some point, but for now, you'll find a stack of coffee cups and sandwich plates six feet high in the kitchen. Get Jack Benny to show you where the fresh aprons are." She pointed to her left. "All the way to the end. You can't miss it."

As Bogie hurried away, the woman brushed away a lock of hair. "And as for you, Bette's instructions were, and I quote, 'Send me the first able-bodied female who doesn't come across like a delicate hothouse orchid.'"

Nell had seen Bette Davis around the studio lot tons of times, but had probably only spoken a scant handful of words to her. And now this woman was telling her to approach Bette like she was the neighbor down the hall?

The woman flicked a fingernail at a pair of swing doors over Nell's left shoulder. "The main room is through there. She could be at any of the food stations or at the entrance greeting the boys. Brace yourself. It's pandemonium. But in a good way. Or not," she added with a laugh. "You take your chances, dearie."

"The servicemen," Nell swallowed hard, "are they—bold? With taking liberties?"

"If only!"

The deep, gravelly voice that boomed in Nell's ear could only belong to one person. Tallulah Bankhead wasn't as tall as Nell would have guessed. She was willowy slim, though, and had added height by piling her dark hair on top of her head.

"Didn't mean to shock you, darling." She grabbed Nell's arm. "Good lord, but it's a veritable beefcake buffet in there. If I don't watch out, Emmeline here will have to check me into LA General for whiplash."

"Did you finish stacking all the coffee?" Emmeline asked her.

"Yes, ma'am. As well as the flour, and the sugar, which—" she threw out a hand to cut Emmeline off "—I did not steal for personal use." She squeezed Nell's arm tighter. "Isn't sugar rationing the absolute worst, darling?"

"Compared with what those boys will be facing soon?" Emmeline asked.

"Heavens, no!" Tallulah released her grip. "I didn't mean *that*. It's just that now we're all watching every sugar crystal and there's hardly any in the stores and it's—it's—someone please shut me up."

"Make yourself useful," Emmeline said. "Take our newest recruit inside and help her find Bette."

Tallulah hauled Nell toward the swing doors. "You might want to gird your loins. It's a lot." She heaved open the right-hand swing door with her shoulder and tugged Nell through it.

A wall of laughter mixed with whooping and hollering hit Nell square in the face.

Around the edge of the dance floor, GIs and sailors clapped along as their lucky pals paired with pretty girls dancing to Kay Kyser's energetic version of "Ma, He's Making Eyes at Me." Food stations lined the right-hand wall, each one crowded with men. At the table nearest to Nell, Constance Bennett was handing out cups of coffee. Next to her, Ann Sothern was distributing sandwiches and smiles. And at the next table along, Loretta Young was doing her best to keep up with requests for slices of chocolate cake and autographs. The whole place reeked of shoe polish, coffee, and sweat.

These men, so many of them fresh off the farm and small-town Main Streets, all wore the same glassy-eyed determination to have a high time. They were soon heading into God-only-knew what depths of hell. But today, there was cake to be eaten, stars to be met, and maybe, if luck held out, a cutie-pie to dance with.

"Bette's usually doing a million different things at once," Tallulah yelled into Nell's ear. "Where she finds the energy, I have no idea, but she does, bless that determined little chin of hers. I'm due to relieve Ann Sothern and her sandwiches, so I suggest you do a lap of the room. If you don't see her, try the wall of photographs near the entrance. Good luck!"

Nell obediently set off. The main room looked like a barn. Thick wooden beams crisscrossed the ceiling. Broad lengths of red-, white-, and blue-striped material hung in deep loops. A wagon wheel dangled from every other beam, each with five hurricane lamps suspended from its rim.

Nell jostled her way through the raucous crowd of brawny palookas, skinny Jewish boys, and a sprinkling of Negroes. Not long before, Bette had caused a fit of indignation from bigots recoiling from her announcement that "the Blacks get the same bullets as the whites and should have the same treatment." No nightclub in America allowed Blacks to mingle freely with whites, the Cassandras insisted. Full integration was out of the question, and that's all there was to it. But those fearmongers hadn't dealt with the formidable Miss Davis.

Near the gallery of studio portraits of the Canteen's more famous volunteers, Nell spotted Bette in a plaid blouse with the sleeves rolled up, and her hair tied back with a red bandanna. She stood shoulder to shoulder with a women twenty years her senior, who nodded as Bette appeared to bark out instructions. The woman departed toward the rear as Nell approached.

"Emmeline said you needed an able-bodied female."

"Thank God! Follow me."

Bette threw out "Hiya, fellas!" and "Welcome!" as she shouldered through the throng, leading Nell to a door marked PRIVATE. Beyond it lay a small, empty room, twenty feet by twenty feet, and filled with the scent of freshly sawn wood. The wall facing the main room had a large glass window cut into it.

"What is this?" Nell asked.

"Well, you see, I wanted the Canteen to cater strictly to enlisted men. When we win this war, it'll be on the backs of those boys out there, so I aim to give them a night they'll remember forever."

"And you're doing it."

"Thank you, but I hadn't counted on military politics. I've started to field requests to accommodate some of the snootier officers. I don't want the fellas out there to be intimidated by the uniform of anyone higher than a sergeant. So I came up with this room as a lounge where officers could witness the goings-on, but not jeopardize the good time those precious enlisted men are enjoying."

The room could be made quite comfortable with a bit of smartening up, Nell thought. "You might need to think about installing a bar. I know you have a 'No Booze' policy, but officers aren't going to be satisfied with a bottle of soda pop and a plate of Saltine cra—" She cut herself off when a puzzled frown creased Bette's brow. "What?"

"You work at Warners, right?"

"I do, yes."

"What's your name?"

"Nell Davenport."

"Well, Nell Davenport, your suggestion of installing a bar is right on the money." Bette hurried off, motioning for Nell to follow. They exited the room through a door on the opposite wall. It led to an alley where a dozen discarded wooden crates had been piled against a rough brick wall. "Let's stack these into the shape of a bar to see if it takes up too much room. If it does, I'll have to bring in drinks from the kitchen, which is all the way on the other side."

They took two boxes apiece, carried them back into the room, and stacked them diagonally in one corner.

"You'll need to leave room for a bartender," Nell pointed out.

Bette tapped her chin in time to Kyser's rendition of "(I've Got a Gal in) Kalamazoo," which bled through the window overlooking the dance floor. "It'll need to be narrower than these boxes."

"It's awfully warm in here," she went on, "so you'll need someone steadily fetching fresh ice."

Bette swung around to face her more squarely. "What do you do at Warners?"

"I'm just a script continuity girl. In fact, we'll be working together very soon. I've been assigned to *Old Acquaintance*—"

"Don't say that you're 'just' anything. A continuity girl's job is not an easy one, but it *is* vital. Don't dismiss what you do nor how well you do it. Unless, of course, your ambitions lie elsewhere."

"I've tried getting in to see Mr. Taplinger about a job in PR, but he always gives me the brush-off."

Bette nodded sagely. "As with most of life's situations, it's not what you know but who."

The glass in the window vibrated as the throng swarming the dance floor stomped its feet to Kyser's brass section.

"Someone has offered to help grease the wheels."

"And?"

"It's not someone I trust, so I didn't take it any further."

"Smart move," Bette said. "Stick to people who won't knife you in the back. My relationship with Robert Taplinger with runs hot and cold, too."

"How is it at the moment?"

"Fine—although that may change with *Old Acquaintance*. Miss Miriam Hopkins, and all that that implies, so best I strike while the iron is—"

A roar filled the main room like a zeppelin. Bette and Nell rushed to the window in time to see Tallulah Bankhead hoisted over the crowd. She had swiped some poor sailor's white cap and wore it tilted on her head at a steep angle. Throwing her arms out wide, she asked the crowd a question that Nell couldn't hear through the glass, but it garnered a booming cheer.

"I suspected she might be trouble," Bette muttered, "but we need all the help we can get." She rushed out the door without saying another word.

6

*N*ell rested against the bow of the *Sea Witch* movie set and watched Bogie knock back a celebratory whiskey with Alan Hale and Raymond Massey. Hale was telling his long-winded story about making *The Four Horsemen of the Apocalypse* with Valentino. It was the third time Nell had heard it. Not that she blamed him. If she had a Valentino story, she'd drag it out every chance she got, too.

As Bogie listened to Hale's anecdote, he downed his sixth whiskey—and they'd only finished *North Atlantic*'s final shot forty-five minutes before. At this rate, he was going to be tanked before the end-of-production party was half over.

He had mentioned several times to Nell how much he'd enjoyed making this picture, with its action and explosions and yelling. Sure, he'd rather be an actual Merchant Marine than play one in the movies, but if he inspired guys to sign up, it might help to compensate for not being able to serve. But still, if he had been so happy, then why was he slamming down those whiskey shots like a condemned man?

Tristan Bannister sidled up to her.

He worked under the studio's costumer, Orry-Kelly, whose

forte was glamorous gowns. This being a straight-out war picture, he'd fobbed it off to Tristan, who had torn and stained and shredded dozens of military costumes. Tall and slender with alabaster skin and a genteelly exotic air, he had reminded Nell of a calla lily the night Luke had taken her home to meet his boardinghouse "family." Ever since Luke had joined the Navy, Tristan had helped to keep the loneliness at bay.

"How come you're staring at Bogart?"

"Am I?" She tried to feign innocence, but spending years facing audiences who weren't entirely comfortable watching a female impersonator had sharpened Tristan's powers of observation.

"Like Lady Macbeth."

Nell wasn't a fan of whiskey, but she'd found it induced a rather pleasant, floating afterglow. "That bad, huh?"

"I'm surprised Bogie doesn't have holes in his head from where you've been drilling him from afar."

"He's been knocking them back awfully fast."

"Wouldn't you drink if you had to go home and face that gorgon?"

"What if he gets behind the wheel?"

"Oh, Mama Bear, he's been driving home half-loaded for years." Tristan draped his arm around her shoulder. "I have some rather fabulous news. We're going to be working together!"

Bogie was now on his eighth shot. His head wavered as though he were standing in a stiff breeze.

"We are?"

"I'm going to be Orry-Kelly's right-hand man on *Old Acquaintance*. I was thinking that with you sitting so close to Miriam battling it out with Bette, there's bound to be so many fireworks I should make you an asbestos suit for protection."

Strident clashes made Nell's job ten times harder. Antagonistic co-stars were more likely to deviate from the script with a spiteful tirade. Sometimes the venomous rant would be better than what the screenwriters had come up with, and Nell would have to scramble to get it all down verbatim. No simple task when an articulate actress like Bette Davis could deliver her barbed improvisation with a speed that would leave Jesse Owens trailing in her dust.

"Alert!" Tristan whispered out the side of his mouth. "Incoming eyeful heading straight for us."

With his sun-bleached hair and tennis tan, the approaching guy looked nothing like Luke. He did, however, have Luke's earnest air.

"I have a letter for a Miss Davenport."

Nell handed her empty tumbler to Tristan. "You've found her."

"I'm from Zippy Bee Couriers." He opened the battered leather satchel slung from his shoulder and retrieved an envelope. "It's addressed to Luke Valenti." Nell's heart sank. "The security guard was pretty sure you'd sign for it."

The envelope was made from thick, textured paper. The real fancy kind. The return address was a firm called Bell, Amiss, and White, on Sixth Avenue in New York. Nell scribbled her signature on the courier's pad and thanked him. She stared at the envelope as he sauntered away.

"Aren't you going to open it?" Tristan asked.

"You think I should?"

"Luke might be gone for years." He eyed the envelope again. "Whoever Bell, Amiss, and White are, they sent it *by courier*. What does that tell you?"

She steered him out of the elephant doors and into the wan November sunshine, then to the end of Fifth Street, where the masts of the *Arabella* reached into the sky like wooden searchlights.

Pulling Tristan down next to her, she sat on Luke's bunk as she tore open the envelope and pulled out a single sheet. "'Dear Mr. Valenti,'" she read out loud, "'my name is Horace Bell, and I am a senior partner at the law firm of Bell, Amiss, and White. I am the attorney in charge of the estate of Boris Osterhaus. Upon Mr. Osterhaus's recent passing'—oh! He died!"

"Who?" Tristan asked.

"Luke's grandfather." She returned to the letter. "'It's my duty to execute the terms of his will. The Osterhaus estate is extensive and complex, and I felt it unnecessary to burden you with a full copy, although I can furnish you with one should you wish. The relevant portion is the third paragraph of page seventy-three.'"

"This guy's will went on for seventy-three pages?" Tristan whistled. "Who the hell was he? A founding father?"

Nell breathed in to quell the pounding of her heart against her ribcage. Whatever was coming, she sensed it was no trivial matter. "'Mr. Osterhaus bequeathed to you a portfolio of stocks and shares.'"

Tristan clamped both hands around Nell's left elbow. "Is our little Lukey rich, rich, rich?"

The page now shook in Nell's grip. "'Because of the war and the doubt as to whether you have signed up and/or survived, it is necessary that you contact me in order to establish that you wish to claim your inheritance. I should inform you that as of today, November 20th, 1942, the current value of the portfolio is—'"

The number stole Nell's voice.

"You've gone pale," Tristan whispered.

She thrust the letter at him. A shrill whistle blew through the porthole, alerting the *Mission to Moscow* crew on Viennese Street.

*Luke could buy a new house, fill it with new furniture, and park a new car in the driveway. Or he could start his own business. He could do anything.*

Tristan blew a long, sharp whistle. "Thirty-one thousand, nine hundred and eighty-eight smackers."

"It would set him up for life." Nell couldn't manage much beyond a squeak.

"Just think: Luke's walking around with no idea how much

he's worth." Tristan placed Bell's letter in Nell's left hand. "You need to read the rest."

"'Mr. Osterhaus has dictated a deadline for claiming your inheritance. You must contact this office by end of business on December 31st, 1944, or one calendar month after the official end of hostilities, whichever comes first.'" Nell breathed out for the first time in what felt like a week. "That's plenty of time to find him."

"What do you mean, 'find him'?"

Nell reached into a small cubbyhole above the pillow and retrieved her stash of letters—now swelled to nineteen—and wiggled it in Tristan's face. "I keep writing these things, expecting to hear from him."

"You don't think he's dead, do you?"

"We *are* at war." It was the worst possible explanation for Luke's silence. But there could be a thousand reasons for it. She let out a jittery laugh that convinced neither of them. "Luckily, I've got two years before that deadline runs out."

"But have you? The Allies are in North Africa. They'll be on the Continent before long. What if German defenses are as flimsy as our balsa wood sets?"

*I have no idea what situation I'm heading into*, Luke had told her before getting on that train. *Don't write until you hear from me.* Yes, well, that was then. Now she had thirty-one thousand reasons to ignore his directive.

"We've got to find Beatrice," she told Tristan.

It was Beatrice's boyfriend, Captain Keaton Vance, who had cleared a path through Navy red tape like Dr. Livingston slashing through the Congo. He was Nell's best hope of tracking down Luke. Perhaps her only one.

"Beatrice from the old boardinghouse?" Tristan asked.

"Is she still at J.J. Newberry?" Nell slid the lawyer's letter back inside its swanky envelope and jumped to her feet. "If she works the swing shift, she might be there."

"You're going to see if she's there *right now*? It's seven-fifteen!"

"You said it yourself. The war could be over this time next month."

* * *

Inside the Hollywood Canteen volunteer entrance, Emmeline looked up from her ledger of names and squinted. "I don't recall seeing you on tonight's roster."

"I'm not," Nell replied, "but I'm trying to track down someone who works at Newberry's. They told me she's here every Thursday night. Her name is Beatrice Varney."

"Yes, she's here. We're down three people tonight. They're all roommates and have caught a twenty-four-hour bug, so if you could spare a few hours . . ." She offered Nell her pen to jot down her name on the sign-in sheet.

"And what about you, young man?" Emmeline asked Tristan. "Any skills to speak of?"

"I can sing, dance, sew, mend, choreograph, as well as work a spotlight like nobody's business."

"With all those skills, why haven't you volunteered before? Don't answer that. They need help with sandwiches."

"I don't suppose you know where Beatrice is working?"

Emmeline permitted herself a shard of a smile. "Why do you think I'm sending you to the kitchen?"

The kitchen rang with the cacophony of a dozen pots clanging with two dozen pans. Nell had last seen Basil Rathbone in *Sherlock Holmes and the Voice of Terror*. How odd, then, to see him standing at a deep sink, his arms buried in soapsuds and singing "Give My Regards to Broadway" next to Mickey Rooney. With Rathbone towering over Rooney by nearly a foot, the pair looked like a real-life Mutt and Jeff. Nearby, Alice Faye and Sylvia Sidney were carving ten pumpkin pies into generous slices and sliding them onto waiting plates.

Beatrice was a sturdily built girl with a can-do attitude, and Nell had immediately liked her. She waved as Nell and Tristan approached her table, where she had laid out twelve rows of sliced bread. "When Emmeline promised me she'd send someone to help, I didn't imagine it would be you two."

"What do you need?" Nell asked.

"Follow me around the table. After I put two slices of bologna on top of the bread, you can dollop mayonnaise and Tristan can smear mustard."

They fell into an efficient rhythm, assembling a hundred and twenty sandwiches. Nell held off her request until they were slicing each one into triangles.

"I was hoping you might do me a favor."

"Anything," Beatrice replied. "If I can."

"It's Luke. I got some important news today that he needs to know."

"You're not . . ." Beatrice wielded her bread knife at Nell's stomach ". . . are you?"

"GOSH, NO!" Alice and Sylvia looked up from their pumpkin pies. Nell told them it was nice to see them, then returned to the sandwich table. "Might you have a way to contact Keaton? Get a message via him to Luke, maybe?"

Beatrice sighed. "Keaton used to write me every week. Then his letters became notes. And now not even that. I assume his silence means he's working long hours on a highly confidential project. I've learned not to hold my breath." She appraised their handiwork. "We need to get these babies out there before the ravenous hordes start rioting."

The din in the main hall was every bit as boisterous as it had been on Nell's first night. Hedy Lamarr clasped her hands together. "I was down to my last six peanut butter sandwiches. These boys! They are so hungry!" She fluttered her fingers at the servicemen crowding her table; they weren't there for peanut butter.

Nell and Tristan helped deposit the last of the bologna sandwiches onto the table when an ear-splitting "YOU!" cut through Kay Kyser's "Let's Put the Axe to the Axis."

Bette Davis stood with her right index finger aimed at Tristan. "Are you Christian Cannister?"

"It's Tristan Banister."

"Follow me." Bette turned around, then turned back. "You too, Nell."

She cut a broad path through the throng and into her office, where she lifted her right arm to reveal the bottom half of the vertical zipper on her dress, which had been ripped away from the seam. "Some over-eager sergeant from Minneapolis doesn't know his own strength. I'm due on stage in half an hour, but I can't go like this. Please tell me you can fix it."

"Not without needle and thread," Tristan said.

"Desk. Top drawer. Left. Cardboard box." Bette undid the buttons leading up to her throat, then pulled the dress over her head. "I'd do it myself, but that sort of thing is beyond me." She pulled at the straps of her peach-colored slip. "Especially after today."

"Why? What's happened?" Nell asked.

"You've heard about this new movie, *Thank Your Lucky Stars*?"

The picture had a threadbare plot: a pair of theater producers try to put on a charity extravaganza whose sole function was to feature a cavalcade of Warner Brothers stars performing songs and skits.

Bette parked her behind on the desk. "Those front-office dummies have put me into a musical number. Who do they think I am, Ginger Rogers?"

"But surely they're not throwing a complicated song at you," Tristan said. "What's it called?"

"'They're Either Too Young or Too Old.' It's a clever enough song, but I'm scared to death!"

"What does the studio vocal coach say?" Nell asked.

Bette played with the lace hem of her slip. "I've canceled all three appointments. I can't face the awful truth of how bad I am. This picture is a Canteen fundraiser, and it was my idea, so I've got nobody to blame but myself."

"You can't put it off forever." Tristan was halfway around the zipper. "They've started shooting already."

"And besides," Nell added, "you're the queen of the studio lot. You accomplish everything you do at a world-class level, but nobody expects you to be able to do *absolutely* everything to perfection."

"That's my whole trouble," Bette said. "I *am* the queen of the lot, and so I feel as though absolutely everyone expects me to do absolutely everything to absolute perfection."

"I doubt that's true," Nell said.

"It's the way I feel, so I've canceled every session with the studio vocal coach." Bette pulled a bottle of sherry and three shot glasses from the bottom drawer of her desk. Apparently the 'No Booze' rule didn't apply in Bette's inner sanctum. "But of course now I've procrastinated so long, I've stuck myself in a big, fat, juicy pickle."

Words spilled out of Nell before she had a chance to reconsider. "I could help you."

Bette plunked the bottle and glasses on the wooden desk. "You?"

Tristan's needle froze in mid-air. "Can you sing?"

Oh, no. Had she really admitted it out loud?

Nell could still picture the stern frowns on Mother's and Father's faces that awful day they had caught her singing "Summertime" in the front parlor. She had feigned a dreadful headache to get out of church so that she'd have the house to herself. Everything would have been fine, too, except that Father Branigan had taken ill in the middle of his sermon on the sin of bearing false witness. Oh, the irony.

Nell nodded, mute as a shadow.

"Give us a sample," Tristan said.

Kyser's "Put Your Arms Around Me, Honey" bled through the closed office door. That song was as good as any.

"Put your arms around me, honey, hold me tight
Huddle up and cuddle up with all your might
Oh! Oh! Won't you roll those eyes?
Eyes that I just idolize
When they look at me, my heart begins to float
Then it starts a rockin' like a motorboat
Oh! Oh! I never knew any girl like you."

Nell finished her performance with a flourish, sending her hands outward and wiggling her fingers like worms on a fishing hook.

Bette and Tristan wore the same expressions of shock mixed with astonishment.

"You! Are! Fabulous!" Tristan declared.

So much for that vow to not sing in front of anyone ever, *ever* again. Then again, it took a lot to impress Bette Davis, and from the sight of her gaping yap, Nell had done exactly that.

"Where did you learn to sing?" Bette asked.

"Listening to Ella Fitzgerald, Billie Holiday, Bessie Smith, Duke Ellington, and the like." Nell spied the progress Tristan had made repairing the zipper. He was two-thirds done, which meant she only had time for the abridged version. "I come from a conservative family. Very religious. The only permitted singing takes place in church. Anything else is secular and sinful, and therefore taboo. I had to hide Ella and Billie and Bessie under my bed and play their records only when the rest of the family was out of the house."

"But you managed it," Bette said with an admiring chuckle.

Yes and no. All hell had broken loose when the entire family discovered her singing a show tune by a pair of Jewish men and sung by Negroes in *Porgy and Bess*. Father had grounded her for a month, forcing her to miss out on her high school graduation. The valedictorian was a math whiz, but not so great at writing or getting up in front of a crowd, so she had written his speech and prepped him with rehearsals. The whole incident had been a bitter pill to swallow, and one that Nell had no desire to regurgitate.

"I'm no professional vocal coach, you understand, but I'll do my best."

"You've got yourself a deal." Bette took her mended dress from Tristan and stepped into it. "But singing this cockeyed number is only half of it. I also have to jitterbug. And not with some regular Joe Lunchbucket. No! They're pairing me with a real-life dance contest winner called Conrad Wiedell. Where do I even start with that?"

Tristan gingerly raised his hand. "I'm the undefeated jitterbug king of Winnetka, Illinois."

Bette's zipper stopped halfway up its track. "You're *what?*"

"He'll be a strong leader, so all you need to do is get the rhythm down," Nell chimed in.

Bette shook her head incredulously. "I'll be in your debt." She ran the zipper to her armpit and straightened the seams. "But for now, I'm needed up on stage." She charged from the office, leaving Nell and Tristan to trail in her wake. They stuck to the wood-paneled wall as Bette approached the microphone.

"Hello, boys!" she boomed. "Aren't you a lively bunch?" The sea of servicemen cheered. "But if you're too overawed to ask Rita Hayworth or June Allyson or Ruby Keeler for a dance, here's my advice: Don't hesitate! That's what they're here for. And if they're busy, ask any of our lovely dance hostesses. They're not going to turn you down." She made a face at a guy near the front who made a loud scoffing sound. "Even if you think you're a stumblebum with two left feet."

As Bette treated the audience to her welcome speech, Nell's mind drifted to the letter in her pocketbook. What if the Navy had sequestered Luke in a hut on one of Montauk's isolated beaches for top-secret military reasons? Jeez, it sounded like a B-movie program filler that Warners was churning out like those bologna sandwiches.

And what about Luke's uncle, Avery? As far as Nell could recall, he and his father hadn't spoken in years. Did Avery even know Boris was dead?

A booming ovation detonated among the men as Bette introduced Frances Langford and Kay Kyser's band glided into "I'm in the Mood for Love." Tristan nudged Nell's hip. "Does Louella Parsons know who you are?"

"I doubt it." But if Hedda Hopper had noticed her on a movie set, maybe Louella had, too? "Why?"

He jutted his head to the right. Fifty feet away, William Randolph Hearst's frumpy gossip columnist stood shoulder to shoulder with an elegantly dressed gentleman near the donut station. The man's eyes were on Langford. Louella, however, was staring straight at Nell.

She looked away. "Who's the Beau Brummel?"

"His name's Walter Tilford. Set decoration. He did *Air Force* for Howard Hawks. Jesus! Louella's not even blinking. What did you do to piss her off?"

"Nothing—that I know of."

"In that case," Tristan said with a conspiratorial leer, "I think it would behoove you to pay Mr. Tilford a visit tomorrow."

"Do you know what picture he's working on?"

"As a matter of fact, it's *Thank Your Lucky Stars*."

\* \* \*

A three-story apartment house filled the northern half of Stage Seven. It had a double-door entrance, arched windows along the first floor, a fire escape attached to the outside, and a lamppost to the left. A chalkboard sign with the musical number they were about to film, "Ice Cold Katie," sat on the stoop.

Walter stood at a window installing pale yellow curtains. He was a dapper gent, floating somewhere in his mid-fifties, and dressed in a dark gray flannel suit with a burgundy necktie that matched his pocket square.

"Excuse me," Nell said, "do you have a spare minute?"

"These darned things aren't draping right." He fussed with the ruffles at the bottom. "Screw it. Everybody'll be watching Hattie McDaniel anyway." When he turned toward her, he blinked several times. "Oh, it's you."

"I noticed you with Louella Parsons at the Canteen last night."

"And now you want to know why she was staring at you."

This spiffy fashion plate was sharper than Nell had assumed. "She was gawking at me so hard."

He told her to follow him to the back of the set. Puttering with the curtains again, he said, "She doesn't know me from Eleanor Roosevelt, so I was taken rather aback when she approached me after I'd been talking to LeRoy Prinz. She asked me for as much information as I could give her on you. She looked terribly downcast when I confessed that I knew you by sight around the studio, but wasn't even sure of your name. But you should have seen her ears prick up like a jackrabbit's when I told her you're pally with Bogart. That's when she asked, 'Is that Nell Davenport?'"

"How did she say it?"

"Like you were some military spy she'd only ever heard about."

Nell fell against the thickly padded soundstage wall. First Hedda and now Louella? What the—? How the—?

But her lunch hour was almost up. She'd have to run if she was going to reach the *North Atlantic* set in time. She thanked Walter and sprinted to the nearest exit.

Did Bogie keep extra whiskey in his dressing room?

# 7

*N*ell tossed her *Old Acquaintance* script onto her canvas chair and walked to the bookcase in Millie Drake's apartment. In all the time she'd spent waiting for the lighting guys and prop guys and makeup guys and sound guys to give their go-ahead, Nell hadn't ever thought to check what books men like Walter Tilford decorated a set with.

She also had to find relief from the acrimony between Bette and Miriam. It had grown so thick Nell had practically choked on it. The sniping, the upstaging, the distracting bits of business, the intentionally fluffed lines—those two pros were pulling out every bazooka in their arsenals. Quite frankly, it was a bit much and Nell was glad for the chance to take a walk between setups.

The bookcase was built of polished walnut, so it would look expensive on camera. She opened the glass-paneled door and breathed in the musty scent of old paper and fading ink. A medieval design of arched gothic windows covered the spine of the tallest book on the second shelf: *Funk and Wagnall's Student's Standard Dictionary of the English language*. Its slim neighbor was called *My Fifteen Lost Years* by Florence Maybrick. Next to it stood a ten-volume set of smaller books, burgundy with gold-stamped text that read *Pocket Library of the World's Essential Knowledge*.

Nell heard Tristan groan behind her.

"Miriam's gown has a high starched collar with a frill that keeps catching on her wig. Orry-Kelly's busy on a last-minute reshoot with Olivia de Havilland on *Princess O'Roarke*, so he sent me to deal with it." He leaned in for a stage whisper. "Not that I blame her for being all worked up. Bette once had an affair with Anatole Litvak."

"What's wrong with that?" Nell asked.

"Nothing—except that he was married to Miriam at the time."

Suddenly, all the point-scoring made sense.

He watched the mass of people congregating behind the camera. "This joint's busier than a bus terminal."

The shrill squawking of a telephone cut through the hubbub of onlookers, but nobody was picking up.

"Today's the day Miriam's character pushes her luck too far, and Bette's character retaliates by shaking her like she's a dead chicken."

"That's today?" Tristan's hand flew to his pale cheek. "Miriam's scared to death Bette will sabotage the first fifty takes."

The telephone stopped ringing.

"All these rubberneckers want to witness it."

A bespectacled guy in his forties emerged from the spectators. "There's a call for you," he told Nell. "The phone next to the exit."

"Are we close to doing the next take?"

He rolled his eyes. "Miriam doesn't like her hair and Bette hates her hat. Take as much time as you need."

Nell shouldered her way through the tourists. Nobody had ever called her on a set before. Was this leading to extraordinarily good news, or horrendously bad? "This is Nell Davenport."

"This is Miss Pierce from Mr. Wallis's office. He wants to see you."

"Are you sure you've got the right person?"

"A break has opened up in his schedule, so you need to get here immediately."

"We're shooting *Old Acquaintance*." Nell felt dampness collect against the bra strap stretched across her back. "I don't think I can—"

"I shall expect you in five minutes." The woman hung up before Nell drew breath.

*\*\*\**

Nell half-walked-half-ran to the administration building where Wallis had his office. The secretary said he would see her when he was done with his telephone call. Nell took a seat in an armchair.

"Enough with the bullcrap runaround, Irving," Wallis yelled into his phone. "For crying out loud, quit futzing with the goddamned screenplay. Your time is better spent thinking about how you'll perform the 'Hate to Get Up in the Morning' number because, let's face it, George M. Cohan you ain't. You may have written "Puttin' on the Ritz" and "God Bless America," but if you insist on being in *This Is the Army*, find an acting coach."

Nell gripped the armrests of her stiff-backed chair. If this was how Wallis talked to Irving Berlin, how was he going to treat her?

He ended the conversation by slamming the telephone receiver into its cradle and shouted at his secretary, "That put the fear of God into him. What's next?"

"Miss Davenport, sir."

"Who?"

"The young lady you asked to see without delay." Miss Pierce motioned for Nell to go in with what appeared to be *proceed-at-your-own-risk* impatience. Or was it her imagination?

Wallis's wood-paneled office wasn't as big as Warner's—of course it wasn't; nobody's could be—but it was large enough to accommodate a desk, a sofa, a long bookcase, and a four-chair meeting table. His wide-open Midwestern face masked an ambitious man with refined taste, a knack for casting, a nose for a satisfying story, and enough good old-fashioned horse sense to keep the broad view in mind when petty egos clashed over trivial details. He had visited the *Casablanca* set more often than he'd stopped by *Maltese Falcon*, but he'd never cast so much as a fleeting eyeball in Nell's direction.

He gestured for her to take any of the three guests chairs lined up along his desk. Nell lowered herself into the middle one and waited for him to speak.

"I'll cut to the chase. It's growing more and more difficult to find quality staff. Most men are in the service, and most women are chasing bigger paychecks at the war factories, but it's short-term thinking. What happens when the war ends and they all close down?"

He regarded her with a skeptical glint. Was this a trick rhetorical question? She felt like she had to respond. "Those women can sock all that money away for a little nest egg. But when the boys come home again, they'll have babies and bake cakes and knit sweaters."

"Is that your plan, Miss Davenport?"

Was it Nell's imagination, or did he lean on the word 'Miss' a little? "I can't say that turning out a perfect pineapple upside-down cake holds tremendous appeal, Mr. Wallis."

He considered her response while maintaining a rigid poker face. Had he appreciated her pluck, or taken her answer as insolent? If she kept talking, would she be digging herself into a deeper hole?

Wallis crossed one leg over the other, "Give me some ideas about what you would emphasize in a PR campaign for *Casablanca*."

In the outer office, Miss Pierce's typewriter stopped clacking; a few seconds later, Nell heard the sputter of her cigarette lighter. The buzz around the studio insisted *Casablanca* was shaping up to be a major release. Taplinger and his PR team would have dreamed up all kinds of nifty ways to put it across. Why would the picture's producer care about the opinions of the girl who was just a script continuity—

Bette Davis's words came roaring back to her: *Don't say you're 'just' anything.* She was here because Bette must have had a quiet word in Wallis's ear. Or Taplinger's. Or somebody's.

This might be my one shot. Don't blow it. She crossed her legs, mimicking his pose. "First, zero in on Bogart's transformation from tough guy to romantic hero. Encourage moviegoers to reassess how they think about Bogart."

She paused to give him a chance to respond, but he held his poker-face veneer in place, so she plowed ahead.

"Second, talk up the chemistry between Mr. Bogart and Miss Bergman. Those two weren't close, but they're talented actors who know what needs to be done. If the dailies I saw are anything to go by, the on-screen results are spectacular."

If Wallis had planned on responding, she didn't give him a chance.

"And third, we should capitalize on news of the North African campaign. Who's to say some decisive battle won't happen near Casablanca? It's on the western coast and has an airport. We should prepare publicity materials to exploit it, just in case."

She had purposefully used "we" to show she already saw herself as a member of the department. Assuming that was why he had subpoenaed her. She studied his inert face for signs of life. After all, this was a job interview . . . wasn't it?

He picked up a gold-nibbed fountain pen and jotted down some words. A furtive glance rewarded her with the words "African campaign," "battle in city," and "prepare materials for potential outcomes."

He replaced the cap with a sharp snap and returned his unblinking gaze to her. "You're currently working on *Old Acquaintance?*"

"Yes, sir."

"It's one of Henry Blanke's?"

Wallis's question was superfluous, and he knew it. Producers were acutely aware of each other's film slate, often because they had fought to nab especially hot properties. Nell buried both hands in her lap and said nothing.

"I'll work things out with Henry so that you're free to join PR first thing in the new year. I'll also notify Taplinger that you're to work on my films: *Casablanca*, which opens in January, *This Is the Army*, which starts filming in February, and *Thank Your Lucky Stars*."

She frowned. "But *Lucky Stars* isn't one of yours."

"No, but it's Mark Hellinger's first picture back here. Between you and me, his heart isn't doing so great, so I'm worried that all those star cameos will be too much for him to handle. He'll need help, and tons of it. You're also friendly with Bogart. Is that right?"

Oh, crumbs. What was the best response? 'I'm friendly with everyone, sir'? Or 'He and I are like *that*'? Or 'Only to nod hello'? Was there a wrong answer that could cost her this job? She decided on a diplomatically noncommittal response with a splash of humor to throw Wallis off his guard. "Enough to allow me to see him without his toupée. Does that count?"

She released her breath when he flashed her a *touché*.

"I'll recommend to Taplinger that he assign you to all of Bogart's pictures as well. His marriage is a mine field. Right then, until the new year?" He half-rose and extended his hand for her to shake.

Thrilled as she was over this turn of events, half the reason she had pursued this opportunity was for a raise. Her two-thousand-dollar debt for her wedding-that-never-happened wasn't going to magically disappear. And this new job he was dangling in front of her brought with it more responsibility than scribbling notes on a script.

"How much does it pay?" It didn't sound like her voice. A jolt ran through Nell that she hoped Wallis hadn't noticed. "Or should I take that up with Mr. Taplinger?"

His face darkened. "What's your current salary?"

"This job comes with more responsibility and consequence, so it bears no resemblance to what I'm currently doing." There was that foreign voice again. She liked how it sounded: crisp and confident. "My roommate used to work in Bullocks' shoe department for twenty-two dollars a week. She now attaches propellers to B-17s at the Lockheed plant in Burbank for seventy." In fact, she earned fifty-five, but Nell gambled that someone like Wallis wouldn't know that.

"I see." He tapped his chin with his right index finger. That unblinking stare had returned. "I like to work with bright and astute people."

"We have that in common." Nell crossed the fingers on her left hand.

"How does sixty sound?" He extended his hand again and left it in mid-air.

Nell had doubled her salary. She stood up and grasped his powerful hand as hard as she could. "It sounds both fine and dandy."

# 8

A couple of weeks after her interview with Wallis, Nell and Tristan braked their bicycles outside 1705 Rancho Avenue. "It's rather odd, isn't it?" she said.

Tristan slipped off his Schwinn and loosened the seat of his pants. "If our greatest sacrifice is to bike everywhere because of gas rationing, then we've gotten off lightly." He lifted his leg. "My thighs are firming up. Have you noticed the new chef in the commissary? He was giving me the eye—"

"I'm not talking about your thighs, you big goose." She ran her finger along a lacquered-wood sign mounted on the fence, with the name *RIVERBOTTOM* burned into it. "Hollywood's biggest female star doesn't live in Beverly Hills. This is Glendale. Nobody of her stature lives over here."

"Buying a house ten minutes from the studio sounds practical after a long day melodrama-ing. Remember: Miss Davis is from hardy Yankee stock."

"Knowing that she and her husband bought a place for sensible reasons and not for the fancy-schmancy address makes me like her more."

Tristan looked at her, puzzled. "You didn't like her before?"

"She *is* a force of nature. But when she confessed to being anxious about her song, she seemed like a regular person."

Maybe it was because she'd seen Bette in her scanties while Tristan fixed her busted zipper. She was no longer Queen Elizabeth, or that Julie Marsden jezebel, or scheming Regina Gibbons. She was just a woman who had been nervous about singing in front of the entire world.

***

Bette answered the door wearing a mint-and-cherry-striped romper with wooden buttons the size of quarters, and her hair tied back with a matching ribbon. "No offense," she announced, "but I was rather hoping you weren't going to show up today."

"You can't avoid us forever," Nell told her.

"We don't film the number for another month, yet I'm practically breaking out in hives already."

Dark brown octagonal tiles sheathed her foyer and ran up the staircase. Double French doors on the left opened into a long, sunken living room. Late-morning sun streamed in through broad picture windows and filtered through the branches of a Christmas tree decorated with orange velvet bows. Past it sat a black Steinway piano.

"Can I go first?" Tristan asked. "I have more training to complete at the Red Cross later this afternoon."

Bette untied the ankle straps of her espadrilles and kicked them into a corner, where a pair of carved wooden reindeers stood nose to nose. As he laid out the basic steps she'd need to master, Nell wandered to a window. It looked out over a copse of miniature dogwood trees, their pimento-red leaves flaring in the sunlight. Past them, the recently concreted Los Angeles River curved to the left and out of sight.

Eighteen girls were now living at the boardinghouse, four of them hot-bedding it. The inconvenience was nothing compared to what the men were enduring on the North African deserts and on far-flung South Sea islands. Nevertheless, once, just once, she'd love to shave her legs in peace.

Tristan repeated, "Rock step, side, side, quick, quick, slow, slow," as Bette gasped and groaned.

What a delight it must be to come home to a place like this. Quiet. Sunlight. Elbow room. Maybe one day, when Luke was home, and life could go back to the way it was. She didn't need a two-story house and a backyard big enough for a swimming pool. A little cottage somewhere would be fine. Maybe she'd even try her hand at baking a pineapple upside-down cake. And then she and Luke could laugh at her woeful attempt as she tossed the disaster into the trash can.

"I doubt Ginger Rogers and Eleanor Powell have anything to worry about."

Nell turned to see a man standing in the doorway. She knew little about Bette's husband, Arthur Farnsworth, other than he'd been a New Hampshire hotel manager when Bette had met him a couple of years back. Six feet tall and barrel-chested, he exuded a take-charge air without the usual tetchiness that Nell had found accompanied men married to Hollywood's prima donnas. He held up four sheets of music. "She asked me to give you this."

The lyrics were all about how the men on the home front were too gray or too grassy green, too bald or too bold, too fast or too fast asleep. Nell was no expert in reading music, but she could recognize a simple melody when she saw one. "I think Tristan and I can allay her fears."

"If you could obliterate them altogether, it'd sure make my life easier."

"Any tips?"

"Be firm." A smile dawned on his face as though he'd uncovered life's meaning. "She likes that. Or respects it, at least."

"Now you're cooking!" Tristan exclaimed.

To Bette's credit, she was keeping up without counting out

loud. Nor was she spitting out "Damn!" or "Shit!" on every other beat.

Nell took a seat on a tufted sofa upholstered in tea-rose-patterned chintz and began leafing through the score.

A few minutes later, Bette joined Nell on the sofa, fanning herself with *Good Housekeeping*. "Honest to God! I don't know how Judy does it. Between the singing and the dancing and the acting, how does she not sweat like a lumberjack?"

"Nobody's asking you to sing 'Musetta's Waltz.'" Nell rattled the music in her hand. "It's a cute comedy number with a straightforward melody. Audiences won't expect you to sound like Ella Fitzgerald."

As Bette pursed her lips, Nell spied a glimmer of respect and—was it possible?—acquiescence. "You're telling me to make the best of it."

Good heavens, Farnsworth's advice worked! Nell placed the music in Bette's lap. "We can start with memorizing the lyrics or I can plunk out the melody on your piano. Your choice."

Bette tossed the music and the *Good Housekeeping* onto the glass-topped coffee table. "I choose tea and the molasses cookies I baked yesterday." She rocked to her feet and headed out of the room.

Nell collected up her purse and followed Bette into the kitchen. She waited until Bette had filled the shiny chrome kettle and lit a gas jet on the stove before pulling out a small gift-wrapped box and placing it on Bette's counter.

"What's that?"

"A gift," Nell told her.

Bette widened her eyes with confusion. "If anybody should be handing out gifts, it's me." When she tugged at the pink ribbon, the light blue wrapping paper fell away, revealing a black velvet box. Bette snapped it open and gave out a little yelp. "Why, these are darling!"

They were silver earrings fashioned to resemble buttercups, each with a tiny yellow tourmaline gem in the center. They weren't expensive, but they were the best Nell could afford. "They're a thank-you."

Bette looked up from the velvet box. "Whatever for?"

"I got the job!"

"You did? Congrats." The kettle's whistle pierced the air. Bette reached over to shut off the gas. "What job are we talking about?"

"Remember when Tristan mended your zipper? And I said that I'd love a job in PR and you said you were getting along fine with Robert Taplinger and it was best to strike while the iron was hot?"

A long moment crawled by as Nell came to see that Bette hadn't approached Taplinger, or Hal Wallis, or Jack Warner—or anyone.

Bette laid the earrings on the table. "I had every intention of speaking to one of those mucky-mucks on your behalf, but between the obligations of the Canteen, and the dread of performing this song, and dealing with Miriam, I simply hadn't found the time."

Nell felt the color seep from her face. "When Hal Wallis called in me into his office—"

"Hal offered it to you?"

"It was the day you wrung Miriam's neck—"

"You didn't need anybody's help!" Bette pressed Nell's hands between her own. "You won the job you wanted *by yourself*. This needs to be celebrated. Tea and cookies will not cut it." She marched to the icebox. "Vincent Sherman gave me this on that same day we filmed the scene where I strangle Miriam. I think it was his way of saying 'Thanks for not finishing the job.'" She produced a bottle of Pol Roger champagne. "Voilà!"

Nell stood rooted to the gray-and-white speckled linoleum as Bette found some crystal coupes and decided that Camembert and crackers would go very well indeed. Nell was still reeling from this unexpected turn, but one thing was clear: She had not bagged that job on her own. Hal Wallis sat at the top of the totem pole. Men like him didn't order script girls to his office and offer them jobs at double their salary. Not without a suggestion, an insistence, or—gulp—a threat.

Bette popped the cork and filled the coupes. She lifted them into the air and handed one to Nell. "Onward and upward!"

The bubbles tickled Nell's tongue as she sipped her first French champagne. Oh my, it slithered down smoothly, didn't it? Nell didn't mind being beholden to the unknown someone who had whispered in Wallis's ear. In fact, she was really quite grateful to them, whoever they were.

9

Nell had stood at the threshold of the Warner Bros. publicity department tons of times, but the building had always been empty. The only sounds she'd heard were from the squawking crows and scrub jays in the sycamore outside the windows. And the only light had been from the single electric bulb near the stairwell.

She felt the thrum of dozens of people, each of them straining at the bit to help the moviegoing public to realize how much brighter and happier their lives would be if they saw Warners' latest release.

The door swung open, pulling Nell forward into a cannonade of clattering typewriters and blaring telephones, exactly how Nell had always pictured it.

"Sorry!" A girl with thick chestnut hair caught Nell by the elbow before she tumbled to the floor. "You in the right place, hon?"

If only she knew what this moment meant. "I'm Nell Davenport, and—"

"The new girl! It'll sure be good to have another female face around here. I'm Ginny. Let me take you to your desk."

Nell followed her into the long room. *My* desk! *My* telephone! *My* trash can! Why did the thought of a trash can tingle the nerve endings along her arms? Was it because the sight of a trash can full of crumpled paper had always struck her as a sign that some busy bee had sweated over a pithy, crisp logline that convinced moviegoers to buy a ticket at the local box office?

Oh, how this room *teemed* with people. Men in shirtsleeves with their neckties pushed askew, and whose cigarettes threatened to burn their lips. Aftershave mingled with tobacco smoke and the bitter aroma of black coffee—this place smelled nothing like it did at midnight!

Ginny stopped at a desk halfway along the room, next to a window that looked out over the alleyway between the duplication building and projection rooms. "We thought we'd welcome you to the gang with these." She waved her hand over a glass vase of white camellias.

Nell breathed in their sweet perfume. "That's very thoughtful of you all."

Ginny snorted. "Don't thank any of those blockheads. These are from me and Paisley." She indicated a dark-haired woman in a smart navy-blue suit and ruffled blouse. "She's Taplinger's secretary. I'm needed at the art department, but go introduce yourself as soon as you're settled."

Robert Taplinger looked nothing like the typical screen version of a movie publicity chief: a cigar-chomping, whiskey-swilling, fast-talking bamboozler. He was, instead, a self-possessed middle-aged gent in a gray flannel three-piece suit with neat stacks of advertising copy and newspaper clippings spread over the surface of his broad desk. He was sipping his coffee from a matching cup and saucer when she knocked on the doorjamb.

He looked her up and down. *So this is the girl they've forced on me.* He motioned for her to take a seat as he barked into the mouthpiece. "Okay, so your poster for *In Our Time*. Wrong typeface. Needs more color. That pink is too wishy-washy. Use a stronger red for the title and the background for the two faces. And make their names the same size. She's the bigger star, but he's got *Now, Voyager* and *Casablanca* under his belt." The receiver dropped onto its cradle with a loud clatter. "Where were we?"

Paisley came up behind Nell and marched past her through the door. "You wanted to see the production stills on *The Desert Song*. The OWI is still objecting to how we're treating the French in this movie." She slapped a handful of vivid photographs in front of him—Arabs in flowing robes, extras in bright red fezzes, and exotic women in sapphire turbans—and scurried out to answer her telephone.

Taplinger flipped through the images, examining each one for a second or so. "I'll give you the morning to settle in, but this afternoon, be outside Stage Seven at one p.m. Get there at a quarter of in case she's early."

"In case who's early?"

"Louella Parsons. She's visiting the set of *Thank Your Lucky Stars*."

"Louella Par—" Nell's voice had jumped an octave. "What am I supposed to do when she arrives?"

Taplinger looked up from the *Desert Song* photos. "I was led to believe you've worked here for several years."

"Yes, I—"

"Please don't tell me you're still star-struck."

"Not at all."

"Glad to hear it."

"This being my first day and all, I'm just wondering if it's wise to put someone like Louella Parsons in the hands of—"

"Are you telling me you're not up to the task I've assigned you?"

Nell stared at her new boss. *This is like that time Father took me out on my first driving lesson. Not in some deserted parking lot, but on the rough country roads out of town. Throw her into the deep end and see if she drowns.* "I certainly am, sir."

"You should be through by mid-afternoon, and then you can start redrafting the press kit for *Casablanca*. Mr. Wallis dreamed up some new ideas. Meanwhile, treat Louella like the queen she is. Say all the right things, regardless of the truth. Remember, Miss Davenport: You're in publicity now. Truth is an elastic concept."

The telephone at his left elbow jangled. "Portrait studio," Paisley called from her desk. "They're calling about those shots of de Havilland for *Princess O'Roarke* you want done over."

"Good luck," he said, "and report back to me after you've waved Louella goodbye."

* * *

Nell loitered in the shade of a tall truck parked outside Stage Seven's elephant door.

"How did this all happen so fast?" she muttered to herself. "First day on the job and he hands me Louella Parsons. Good gravy, would it have killed him to give me a list of Do's and Don'ts?"

"They've already got you talking to yourself, I see."

Bogie was in a dark, pinstriped and double-breasted suit with a white pocket square. A four-day growth shaded his chin. She was pleased to see him clear-eyed and alert—had he and Mayo avoided quarreling throughout the holiday season?

"Taplinger sent me to escort Louella onto the *Thank Your Lucky Stars* set. Can you believe it?"

Bogie cocked his head to one side. "He's testing you."

"Of course he is." Nell's guts tightened. "He wants to be able to say, 'See? She's no good to me. Throw her back where you found her.'"

Bogie slung an avuncular arm around her shoulders. "It's easier to pass when you know you're being tested." A blue Buick

Roadmaster turned onto C Avenue. "Louella will do what she wants, but try your best to steer her clear of me. Going over my lines with you helped a lot, but I rarely get to play comedy, so this scene with Cuddles has got me rattled. It's times like this I wish Leslie Howard was still around instead of back in Europe, banging the drum for Britain. He helped me get over my opening-night jitters in *Petrified Forest*."

"You're filming your cameo *today*?" This was no coincidence.

"If you can run interference, I'll owe you one." He bolted inside.

The chrome stripes on the Buick caught the noon sun as Parsons' chauffeur pulled up. She stepped out wearing a misshapen tweed ensemble that hadn't been the height of fashion since 1927.

Nell wiped her right hand down the back of her plaid skirt and offered it for the woman to shake. "Welcome to Warner Bros., Miss Parsons. My name is Nell Davenport—"

"I know who you are."

Hedda Hopper might have suffused those words with a pinch of snark, but Nell detected no trace of sly artfulness. "They don't send the script girl out here to greet me, so I assume you've been promoted to the publicity department." She gave an approving nod. "We, the sisterhood of working women, need to support each other because heaven knows the menfolk won't. That's at least one opinion Hedda and I share."

Hedda's version of this conversation had been all about how good she was at reading people and strategizing their next vault up the ladder. The contrast between the two women left Nell lightheaded.

Careful what you say. This *is* Louella Parsons. You *are* being tested.

"If the two of you can find common ground, there's hope for the world, Miss Parsons."

She smiled benignly. "Please call me Louella. Now that you

work in publicity, our paths will cross from time to time."

It was a point Nell hadn't considered, leaving her unsure what to say. Not that it mattered—Louella decided that had been the end of their conversation. She strode onto the soundstage bellowing, "HELLO EVERYBODY!"

The crew cleaved a path to the chairs Nell had arrayed near the set built for Bogie's cameo. As Louella settled her generous rump onto the one closest to the camera, the *Thank Your Lucky Stars* director bounded toward her, his arms outstretched.

Louella hissed to Nell out of the side of her mouth, "Who's this?"

"David Butler. Directed a bunch of Temple pictures at Fox, and the latest *Road to* at Paramount."

"Mr. Butler," Louella purred, with a smile sweeter than cotton candy, "How thoroughly I enjoyed *Road to Morocco*! I bet you had your hands full with Crosby and Hope."

As Butler told her that his job had been to tell the cameraman when to start and let his stars do what they did best, Nell observed Bogie pacing in the far-right corner of the set, script in hand, using Cuddles Sakall's generous girth as a shield to hide behind. Louella tuned in again as Butler took his leave.

"Was that Humphrey Bogart I spied over yonder? Is he in this picture?" Louella had tried to make her questions sound airy, but her dark eyes, hard as slate, betrayed her.

"He's one of fifteen star cameos in *Thank Your Lucky Stars*." From her jacket pocket, Nell fished a folded list she had drawn up during her lunch break and held it out. "In case you want to refer to it as you draft your article." Louella perused it so fleetingly that Nell doubted it registered. "Each star is donating their appearance salary to the Hollywood Canteen. It was Bette's idea because, of course, she poisoned the tomato soup in the commissary and now half of the Warners staff are dead."

Nell threw in that last part to see if the old bag was listening.

Louella drummed her fingernails against her armrests. "Tell

me, dear, how often does Humphrey bring his wife to the set?"

"Hardly ever." Nell refolded the list, which still rested between her fingertips. "He prefers to avoid distractions."

"Have you met Mayo?"

"Once or twice, in passing."

"I was in Ciro's once and they were seated close to the dance floor, in full view of everybody. Who knows what they were quarreling over? Politics, probably. The moment he turned his back to chat with Howard Hawks, she took her cigarette lighter and set fire to his sleeve." Louella tsked like Beulah Bondi. "Whoever performed on stage that night, they can't have been half as entertaining as the Battling Bogarts."

So Parsons was on a fishing expedition. And she was doing it by employing what Nell assumed was a tried-and-true method: Insist on addressing each other on a first-name basis, then adopting a just-between-us-chums congeniality.

"Speaking of entertaining," Nell indicated the backstage set, "the whole scene between Bogart and Cuddles Sakall is a squabble filled with verbal ping-pong. They'll be—"

"I often wonder if Bogie and Mayo fight at home the way they do in public."

Nell thought of the time Luke had told her about the supply of spare back doors the Bogarts stored in their garden shed and how he'd replaced two in less than six months.

"I really wouldn't know. But I will say this." Nell paused to give Louella a chance to lean in. "I've never worked with anyone more professional or more dedicated to his craft than Humphrey Bogart." Louella reeled backward as though Nell had puked on her two-toned oxfords. "I know! I know!" Nell laid a gentle hand on Louella's forearm. If she wanted just-between-us-chums congeniality, then she was going to get it. "It doesn't make for sensational stories for your column. But he's very punctual, very prepared, with his eye always on the ball. Does that sound like someone who spends his evenings plotting revenge?"

Louella's lips puckered as she struggled to formulate a response, then turned as a plump woman with a pinched frown arrived.

"Vere is my hussbund? Ach! I am zo late! My poor Cuddles must be starvink!"

Sakall's wife, Anna, carried the same picnic basket she'd brought to the *Casablanca* set. As much as her husband adored the United States, he pined for the food of his native Hungary, so Anna brought his lunch with her to the set, filling Rick's Café Américain with the aroma of goulash, stuffed cabbage, and meat stew.

"This'll make for a perfect squib." Nell waved at Cuddles' wife. "Anna! Oh, Anna! Over here!" The woman patted down the long, gray braid that wreathed her head like a tiara. Nell turned to Louella. "You must meet S.Z. Sakall's wife. Anna, this is Louella Parsons. Show her what you've got tucked away in your basket today."

She guided Anna to her chair and then melted into the crowd that always gathered around in the hope that today's dessert was *dobosorta*, a chocolate buttercream-layered sponge cake.

Nell hurried to the corner where Bogie had been going over his lines.

Bogie looked up, annoyed. "What?"

"Did Mayo set you on fire at Ciro's?"

He winced. "Louella was there that night?"

"Didn't you read about it in her column?"

"You think I waste my time reading her badly spelled tripe?"

An assistant approached them. "They're ready for you, Mr. Bogart."

Bogie nodded at him, then turned back to Nell. "What do you think's going on?"

Jack Warner had forbidden Nell to tell Bogie what he and Hedda Hopper had discussed; however, he'd said nothing about Louella Parsons. Okay, so maybe it was a loophole that might not hold up in the Court of Warner, but she was willing to take a chance. "Everybody smells blood in the water."

"Whose blood are they sniffing?"

Nell paused a moment to choose her words. "Your marriage is on shakier ground than the San Andreas Fault."

Bogie scowled. "When I signed a contract with this studio, it was to act in their pictures. There was no clause about my private life being fodder for public consumption."

"WHERE IS MR. BOGART?" Someone had found a bullhorn for David Butler.

Bogie grasped Nell's elbow and dragged her toward the set. "I'm a last-century guy. I take my marriage vows seriously. I'm not one of these walk-away types. I play for keeps."

Nell could have remarked that Mayo was Bogie's third wife, but it would have been an unfair point to bring up minutes before he had to step in front of the camera. "If she mentions it again, I'll tell her what you said."

Bogie stuffed the loose script pages into his back pocket and stepped onto the X taped to the floor. "What'd I say?"

"About being a last-century guy. That's a great quote."

"CLEAR THE SET!"

As Nell approached Louella, she caught the columnist's knowing smile: *I'm about to get what I drove all the way over here for.*

Realization slapped Nell across the face. Louella knew very well that Bogie was not the type to talk about his personal life, especially not if his marriage was crumbling like yesterday's sandcastle.

She came to see *me*. She thinks I'm raw enough and dumb enough to blab everything. Nell bent her mouth into a generic smile as she slipped into the empty chair next to Louella. "Did Anna Sakall let you try her Hungarian deliciousness?"

"He's avoiding me." Louella had locked her attention on Bogie once more.

"He's not used to playing comedy, so he feels as though he's swimming into uncharted waters."

"His *Maltese Falcon* was a big hit. And now, with the buzz surrounding *Casablanca*, I want to interview him. But if he's shunning me—"

"Not just you; it's everyone."

"I noticed you and he had a fine old chat. But no matter. I don't like to interrupt an actor preparing for a scene." Louella turned in her chair. "I could tell that you enjoy his confidence and it gave me an idea."

Louella's about-face left Nell with conversational whiplash. Oh, God. What now?

"I write four articles a year for *Motion Picture* magazine on whatever topic takes my fancy. What about 'A Day in the Life of a Hollywood Studio Publicity Agent'? You'd make a terrific subject."

Nell's head swiveled to the left so fast that she almost gave herself actual whiplash. "I'm awfully flattered, but this is my first day on the job."

"You're starting out, which makes you very relatable."

"I see," Nell said, though she wasn't sure she did at all.

"The publicity department must be gearing up for *Casablanca*'s release, so it ties in nicely, doesn't it?" She shifted as though getting to her feet. "Well, they're about to start and I feel like I'm in the way, so I'll be going."

"So soon?" Nell was out of her chair before Louella was.

"I promised Claudette Colbert that I'd have sherry with her in her dressing room over at Paramount. She's filming that picture about Army nurses and—"

"Let me walk you to your car."

It had taken Nell a moment to get her bearings, but now she was up to speed. Louella had concocted a snow job about a *Motion Picture* article, but it was clear she wanted the same story Hedda wanted, and was using Nell as her patsy.

The hell she will, Nell told herself as she waved Parsons goodbye. The goddamn hell she will.

## 10

*P*rojection room number three smelled of Cuban cigars and—Nell sniffed the air a second time—Wrigley's spearmint gum. Someone had been mighty nervous about their movie.

She knew the feeling. Not that she was anxious about *Casablanca*. It belonged in the lightning-in-a-bottle, everything-works, once-in-a-career category. Pretty much everybody who had seen it agreed—except the star of the picture.

She waited until they had settled in the center of the middle row. "I know you were miserable making this one," she said, trying her best to finesse businesslike determination with diplomatic tact. "And that you didn't warm to Ingrid."

"She did a fine job . . ." He thought for a moment. " . . . considering I gave her nothing but the bare minimum to work with."

"And yet you both put in career-changing performances."

He let loose with a cynical "Ha!" that Rick Blaine himself would have approved of, and pulled a pack of Chesterfields from inside his jacket. The flame from his cigarette lighter illuminated his sneer. "If you don't tell the projectionist to roll it soon, you'll be watching this movie alone."

"For heaven's sake, Bogie, why are you resisting this so much?"

He took a quick drag and blew the smoke in her face. It was ill-mannered and out of character. Was it a test? If she breathed in his smoke without moaning like a crybaby, would that mean she passed?

He set his elbow on the armrest between them. "I had to play-act in a romantic melodrama when my own melodrama was dragging me through the mud. One failed marriage is bad enough. Two is insufferable. But three? I don't know how to fix it, or if it can be fixed. When we were filming *Casablanca*, Mayo stabbed me. And now that's what I think about when I think of that movie."

"Perfectly understandable." She laid a tentative hand on his forearm. He didn't shake it off, so she kept it there. "However—"

"Everybody has a 'however' shoved up their sleeve."

"The Casablanca Conference is happening as we speak."

"I do read the papers, you know."

"The name is on everybody's lips, which makes it the most magnificent publicity opportunity since DeMille arrived to make *The Squaw Man*."

"Oh, brother," he said from behind a cloud of smoke. "You really have landed in the right department."

She pulled her hand off his forearm and went to spit out a retort when she realized that his comment held no malice or spite. It was a statement of fact. A compliment. Did it mean she was softening his steely opposition?

"Roosevelt and Churchill are planning how the rest of the war will unfold as *Casablanca* opens next week. It's bound to come up in interviews, and when it does, what are you going to say? That you've not even seen your own movie?"

He crushed his cigarette butt into the ashtray embedded in the armrest as though it were a cockroach. "After Jack Warner refused to pay me for my time and expenses going to the New York premiere, I thought, 'Screw it. The hell with the lot of them.' But it hadn't occurred to me I might have to lie through my teeth during interviews. Some stars have a knack for that, but not me."

"Good," Nell said, waving to the projectionist, "because Louella wants to interview you about your recent stellar rise in fame."

"I guess I can't avoid her forever, huh?"

"So you'll do it?"

"Do I have a choice?"

"You could choose the location. Now that you have a proper brick-and-mortar dressing room, you could host her on your own turf."

The lights dimmed and the Warner Bros. shield logo appeared on the screen.

"Romanoff's."

"I can call her and set it up?"

"You're a good man, sister."

She started at this non sequitur line from *The Maltese Falcon*. "I am?"

"The thing nobody tells you about getting to the top is that the number of people who give you the straight dope dwindles to a handful. Peter Lorre is one. So was Luke. And I've just realized that you are, too."

"Thank you, Bogie."

He pressed a finger to his lips. "Shush. Don't you know that a career-changing performance is about to begin?"

\* \* \*

Nell had never worn this shade of green—a dark crème de menthe hue she doubted would suit her—but when she had put on the dress earlier that evening, she found it complimented her brown hair and hazel eyes.

Okay, so perhaps there were advantages to having fifteen roommates. The dress was Elsie's, the handbag was Sylvia's, and the shoes were Adelaide's. Apart from her step-ins, the only garment of her own Nell wore were her nylons. They were her third-to-last pair, and with stockings so hard to get nowadays, she had saved them for a special occasion—such as a business dinner with Humphrey Bogart and Louella Parsons.

She caught sight of herself in the mirror of Romanoff's foyer and ran a hand down the sleeve. Was she the only girl in the world who hadn't known how warm and comfortable velvet was?

"Waiting for someone, ma'am?" The central-casting maître d', silver-haired, cultured, restrained, held himself like a ballet dancer.

"She's with me," said Bogie.

Nell had told Louella that they would meet at eight, but suggested to Bogie that he get there at a quarter of, so that they could present a united front.

She breathed a silent sigh of relief. Bogie was no fan of gossip columnists, nor the publications they wrote for, but he was a man of his word. "Where's the missus?"

He eyed her with a weary scowl. "You want the excuse I'm telling Louella or the truth?"

In other words, Mayo was too drunk to put on a good show. "It's probably just as well. This is a boring work dinner."

"Miss Parsons arrived a few minutes ago," the maître d' said. "We've already seated her at your table, Mr. Bogart."

Doggone it. Nell had wanted to show Bogie what was in her purse. Not that he could do anything about the news in the crisp, expensive envelope, but as Grandma Davenport would have said, a problem shared is a problem halved. It was why Nell had never worn velvet before tonight. It was all Grandma Davenport ever dressed in. All those stuffy Victorian dresses. So old-fashioned. So stuck-in-the-past.

"Thanks, Barnabas," Bogie said with a sigh. "We'll see our own way."

. . .

"Aren't we early birds?" Louella offered Bogie her cheek for him to kiss. "The virtue of punctuality says so much about breeding, don't you think? After all, Humphrey, you were brought up on the Upper West Side."

A tall waiter with suspiciously black hair arrived with menus in hand. Bogie ordered a martini. Nell followed his lead; Louella told him to make hers a Gibson.

"I hoped Mayo would join us. It feels like forever since I've seen her. Is she well?"

He flipped open his gold cigarette case with a large 'B' engraved at the center. "My wife believes the working day is for work and the evenings are for everything else." He lit up and took a deep drag. "She sends her best, though."

He might have sounded more convincing if he had injected sincerity into the line instead of slapping it on the table like a comatose catfish.

"Docky agrees with her." A sullen glower passed across Bogie's face. Louella missed it, but Nell could read it: *Of course her husband would agree with Mayo. He's a world-class lush, too.* "The problem is, this industry never stops."

Nell needed to take control of this conversation. "Speaking of stopping, did you hear that Roosevelt and Churchill have decided that the only path to postwar peace is a policy of unconditional surrender?" She felt a coating of sweat along her hair line. Now she knew another reason why she'd avoided velvet. It was also too damn hot.

"Unconditional surrender, huh?" The cynicism in Bogie's voice had soured his smile into a lopsided smirk.

"Surrender must be absolute," Louella said, picking up her menu and surveying it, "otherwise we'll never be rid of those dreadful people." She laid it down again. "But isn't it the most remarkable coincidence? They've held their conference in the exact place where your new movie is set."

"Yuh-huh." Bogie's cigarette lighter matched his case. He flipped it between his fingertips.

"We had planned to open *Casablanca* on twelve screens," Nell put in, "but now Mr. Warner has upped it to two hundred. The duplication department is working around the clock."

Bogie looked up from the lighter and shot Nell an eyeful, bright as a neon sign: *That's four times more than any of my previous pictures.*

She volleyed back at him: *Now do you see why I dragged you into that projection room?* After the lights had come up, he'd said, "At least it's a halfway decent romantic melodrama." She had been happy to accept his begrudging admission now that the tendrils of comprehension were taking root—that this picture was going to be a huge deal.

"Honestly, Humphrey," Louella said, "I believe it's some of your finest work."

*She's buttering you up! Don't drop your defenses now!* Nell cleared her throat. "I have a favorite scene, but I'm wondering what yours is."

Louella kept her eyes trained on Bogie. "It's when you're sitting alone with your hand strangling a liquor bottle. We can see the torment, the regret, and all the heartache in your face as you make that speech about all the gin joints Ingrid could have walked into." She clapped her hands together, causing several more heads to turn. "My heart wept buckets for you!"

Bogie sat back in his chair, staring across the packed restaurant. His eyes took on a faraway look. Nell hoped this eleventh-hour enthusiasm wouldn't blindside him to the real reason Louella had pushed for this dinner.

The waiter appeared with their drinks and asked if they needed more time or were ready to order their meal.

"This is your favorite restaurant." Louella tapped Bogie's wrist as though he were the favorite nephew and she the doddering aunt. "How about you order for us?"

Bogie rattled off the order—Foie Gras de Strasbourg, Shrimps à la Russe, Cherrystone Crabs, and Chateaubriand for three—as Louella eyeballed the surrounding crowd, sizing up who was here, who they were with, and whether stopping by their table was worth her time.

It had been a week since Louella had alluded to her idea for a 'Day in the Life . . .' article. *Casablanca* was going into theaters very soon, so wasn't time running out? Not that Nell had believed Louella had any intention of writing an article about her. The proposal was only her way of getting to Bogie. But she now found the heft of disappointment pressing against her chest. An article like that would have given her proof she could send home. See? I'm not wasting my life—or whatever it is you disapprove of. No less than Louella Parsons thinks I'm interesting enough to write about. Doesn't that count for something?

Not that *Motion Picture* magazine was likely to turn the tide in her favor. Not for people who hadn't seen a movie since Mary Pickford was the be-all and end-all. But still. Miracles did happen. Even ones that took place outside of Matthew 14:13–21.

Getting her parents off her back would be easier if Luke were around. No, I can't go home. I'm dating someone now and it's serious.

She stared at her purse and thought about the letter inside it. It was from Boris Osterhaus's New York lawyers, responding to her request to extend Luke's deadline on account of him fighting for the future of democracy.

Nell nearly choked on her martini when she checked back into the conversation. Bogie was talking about how he and Mayo were thinking of mounting a USO tour.

"Is she the dancer in the family?" Louella asked.

"We have a running gag that I've got two left feet—and she's got the two right ones."

Louella canted her head to one side and squinted. "The two of you have worked up an act?"

He motioned to the waiter for another round of drinks. "We're noodling some ideas."

It was time to steer this conversation away from Mrs. Bogart. "You want to do more for the war effort than your weekend forays for the Coast Guard."

Louella deliberated with an unhurried sip of her Gibson. "You have a fun name for your boat, don't you, Humphrey?"

Nell chewed on her olive. Oh, you're a sly one, Louella. I'll give you that. You know very well Bogie's boat is called *Sluggy*, which is the nickname he gave to Mayo after her penchant for slugging him.

A tremor of fervent murmuring rippled around the restaurant. Nell and Louella rotated in their chairs to get a better view of a tall man, slightly stooped, and dressed in an impeccable suit of dark gray he'd teamed with a brick-red necktie. He had an angular face, bisected by a pencil mustache. A blonde, probably half his age, hung on his arm. Pretty, but not spectacular. Men like him accessorized with Lana Turner or Hedy Lamarr look-alikes—or sometimes the genuine article.

"Who's that?" Nell asked.

"My dear," Louella's tone took on a scolding timbre, "if you're going to work in publicity, you'll need to recognize Billy Wilkerson from *The Hollywood Reporter*."

Bogie kept his gaze fixed on his drink. "Is he with Kathryn Massey?"

"It's someone new." Louella watched the pair thread their way through the tables to a booth on the south wall. "Please excuse me." She slid out of her chair. "Won't be long."

Bogie waited until she was out of earshot. "What's on your mind?"

"She's here to dig dirt on your marriage; all the rest is window dressing. We must avoid the subject of Mayo altogether."

"That's why I mentioned the USO tour. A couple who's on the

skids doesn't talk about spending ten weeks traipsing around sand dunes laced with land mines, playing to shell-shocked GIs."

"You were on the up-and-up?"

He lit his fifth cigarette. "I really do want to contribute more."

"But you can't sing or dance."

"Or do comedy pratfalls, play an instrument, or even goddamn juggle. Maybe inspiration will hit us the next time Mayo stabs me—hey!" He snapped his finger. "A knife-throwing act! Like in the circus!"

How could Bogie joke about Mayo's predilection for sharp objects? The situation must have been worse than Nell imagined if he was contemplating traveling to an honest-to-goodness war zone.

"Only if you're the one throwing the knives. Otherwise, you'd be safer in Guadalcanal."

He chuckled, though it sounded a little on the grim side. "Heard from Luke yet?"

"No." She fished out the letter she'd received that morning. "But I heard from the executor of Grandpa's will. I explained to them that Luke's away at war and hard to contact, and was there a way to extend the deadline. Extenuating circumstances, et cetera, et cetera."

"Did the et cetera, et cetera work?"

"War or no war, failure to claim his inheritance means he forfeits everything. Thank God I have nearly two years to track him down."

A couple of booths from where Louella was grilling Wilkerson, Ida Lupino was dining with her husband, Louis Hayward. She was due to film a cameo in *Thank Your Lucky Stars* soon. She raised her highball to Bogie, and then mouthed, "Best of luck!" He mouthed, "Thanks" before turning back to Nell.

"I know two years sounds like a lot, but the wheels of the military are clogged with red tape, subcommittees, and everything in triplicate. I've spoken with Army brass about this USO tour idea. Jesus! The paperwork alone."

"You know Army brass?" Nell asked. "Could any of them help track Luke down?"

"He's in the Navy."

"They must know their counterparts."

Bogie barked a laugh. "The Army and the Navy are united only in their hatred for the Axis. We'll have to think of an alternative."

"That *was* my alternative." Nell's stack of letters to Luke had grown so thick she had relocated it to her bureau drawer, where it still barely fit.

Louella moved on to Ida.

Bogie said, "What you need is someone with a connection to the Navy. How about Hedda Hopper?"

"Anyone but her." A wave of hostility surged from Nell's chest, up her neck, and splashed onto her face. This velvet dress had been a terrible choice.

"Hear me out." He pulled at his collar. "Hedda's in big with the Navy. Her son, William, is serving in the Office of Strategic Services. God knows I hate that bitch's guts with every fiber of my existence, but I'll call her if it means tracking Luke down."

"Thanks, but Hedda's due on *Lucky Stars* on Thursday. That's the day Bette films her number, and I'm pretty sure Hedda plans on playing Madame Defarge. The last thing I want to do is ask that heartless old biddy for help—"

"Attention on deck!" Bogie cut her off. "She's back."

Louella plonked herself into her chair. "I seem constitutionally incapable of quick hellos." She picked her up Gibson. "Who were we talking about?"

# 11

Nell sat her derriere on the low brick fence out front of Preston Sturges' restaurant, The Players, and pulled off her right shoe.

"What were you thinking?" Tristan asked. "Wearing brand-new shoes, knowing we'd have to walk for blocks and blocks."

"It's not every day you get invited to Mocambo."

"In case I haven't said it enough: thank you, thank you, thank you!"

Tristan had repeated his gratitude more than enough times on the walk from Laurel Canyon, where the streetcar had dropped them off. Not that she minded. His excitement matched hers.

"It's like going to Wonderland," she said, rubbing her heel. "You hope and pray that one day you'll get to see it for yourself—"

"But then you hear the prices and think, 'Four-fifty for Beef Stroganoff?'"

The cool January air felt good against the burning soles of her feet. "So you go to Schwab's and order the Number Five Club Sandwich and root beer for ninety-five cents."

Tristan parked himself next to Nell. "Tonight is his treat, right?

I've got three seventy-eight on me, which means I can afford the onion soup and split a Sanka for dessert."

She slipped her shoe back on and pushed herself off the fence. Jiminy Christmas, what kind of idiot wears new shoes to a night out at one of the fanciest joints in town? They continued their death march west along the Strip. "Bogie's starring in the biggest picture in the country. There's even chatter of Academy Award nomination. A guy like that doesn't go Dutch when the check arrives."

"No offense, but of all the people that Mister Popular could have asked to join him and the missus, why'd he pick you?"

An icy winter wind blew down Sunset Boulevard; Nell pulled him closer to her for warmth. "Luke once told me how Bogie admitted that he and Mayo got along better when Luke was with them."

"So we're cushions?"

"With Bogie hitting the big time, it's important they don't break out the Battling Bogarts act. So when he suggested bringing a date, I thought 'Who can I invite that's good with people, has a quick wit, knows his way around a lively conversation, and will whisk Mayo to the dance floor until tempers simmer down?'"

The Mocambo sign with its two large Os came into view. Tristan stopped. "Awww," he whimpered, "and you thought of me."

"I thought of Ronald Colman, but he was busy, so—"

"Witch!" He pushed her away. "When Mayo starts hurling whiskey-bottle hand grenades, I'm using you as a shield."


Inside the foyer, a sofa in dark blue damask sat against a wall painted in dusty crimson. The walls curved up to an ornate crystal chandelier. Samba music blasted from the room behind the maître d's podium. In place of the standard tuxedo, the maître d' wore a bolero jacket of vibrant orange and yellow vertical stripes with matching pants. When Nell told him, "Humphrey Bogart is expecting us," he collected up some menus and instructed them to follow him.

The main room hit Nell like a lemon meringue pie to the face. The place was a riot of bold colors. A pair of papier-mâché giraffes painted butterscotch yellow hung suspended from the ceiling with rough twine. One had a tangerine-colored monkey hanging from its jaw; the other wore a straw hat topped with a gold pompom the size of a bowling ball. An eight-foot figure of a dark-skinned dancer in a gaily embroidered skirt dominated the center of the room. She held her arms out, dangling a copper hurricane lamp from one elbow and holding a candelabra in her other hand.

Bogie and Mayo sat near the dance floor, where two dozen couples gyrated to a Carmen Miranda tune. As Bogie made the perfunctory introductions and ordered a round of Old Fashioneds, Mayo took a long draw on the Parliament jammed into her Bakelite holder and looked Nell up and down. "Nice dress."

Having learned the lesson that velvet was not a good idea in crowded restaurants, Nell had splurged on a calf-length cocktail dress in purple silk at Mullen and Bluett on Hollywood Boulevard. After all, a girl didn't get to dine at Mocambo every day.

"Thank you," she said. "You know how you try a dress on and as soon as you zip it up, you find it falls where it's supposed to?"

Mayo's cream rayon blouse strained across the bust. Evidently, it had been a while since she had experienced the satisfaction of trying on a comfortable outfit.

"That happened to me once," Tristan announced. "Naturally I bought it."

Mayo's elbow slipped off the table's edge. "You what?"

"Before he started at Warners, Tristan was a female impersonator," Bogie explained. "What was your stage name?"

"Trixie Bagatelle."

Mayo narrowed her bleary eyes. "You have a bland face that a good makeup artist can do wonders with."

"Thanks." Tristan glanced at Nell, then at Bogie, then back at Mayo. "I think."

"Before you two arrived, we were talking about Hump's new project at Columbia. It's one of those all-men war movies, where he gets to run all over, pretending to shoot Nazis." Bogie's face looked like a balloon suffering from a slow leak. "They'll be shooting in Brawley, south of the Salton Sea," Mayo continued. "In other words, the middle of no damn place. And *that* means there'll be sweet Fanny Adams to do all night. A million miles from LA and nobody to screw. Lucky for me, there are no women in the picture."

"Come on, honey. Let's not." The tremor in Bogie's voice told Nell that he was trying his best to thwart her attempt to start yet another public tussle.

"True, though." Mayo thumped her empty tumbler onto the table.

An unwieldy silence flattened the group until Tristan said, "The other day, I was doing a fitting with Eleanor Parker. We got to chatting about John Garfield and I asked her, 'How do you keep your hands to yourself when you're working opposite someone who puts the hub in hubba-hubba?' She laughed in my face and said, 'Between remembering your lines, hitting your mark, keeping mindful of the camera, your director's instructions, your costume, your props, your makeup and hair, who the heck's got the energy to make it with your co-star?' And then she said, 'It doesn't happen nearly as often as people think—unless you're Errol Flynn.'"

The waiter appeared with their Old Fashioneds and asked if they were ready to order. Mayo told him, "Another round of drinks. Doubles." She turned to Bogie. "You made a picture with her a coupla years back. What was it called again? Oh, yeah. *The Big Shot*. Look at you now, Mister Big Shot."

The percussionist finished the band's number with a thunderclap of cymbals. As the audience showered them with appreciative applause, Nell observed a couple of familiar faces three tables away.

After Louella had reproached Nell for not knowing who Billy Wilkerson was, she had pawed through the publicity department's archived copies of the *Reporter*. As she had leafed through the years, she'd found one column that made her stop. It had featured a photograph of Kathryn Massey outside the El Capitan Theatre at the *Citizen Kane* premiere, a smile straining her face.

And now Nell was staring at the same face from twenty paces, only this time, she had stopped to table-hop with Sheilah Graham. The two columnists were snatching glances at the Bogart table. What were they waiting for? Flying champagne coupes? Slapped faces? A litany of unprintable cussing?

Yep, Nell wanted to tell Tristan, we're cushions.

"Don't fret, Hump, my boy." Mayo yanked the cigarette butt from her holder and dropped it, still burning, in the ashtray. "Even podunk Brawley is bound to have a couple of tramps."

Nell searched the room for a diversion. A tall man with prematurely gray hair and a grimly determined expression filling his gaunt face wended his way around the tables. A woman in a bold-checked jacket trailed in his wake.

"Do you know Howard Hawks?"

"We've met a few times," Bogie replied. "Why?"

"He's torpedoing in this direction like you're a U-boat."

By the time Bogie had looked up, Hawks was already looming over the table.

"Mind if we join you?" Without waiting for a response, he borrowed two spare chairs from a neighboring table and inserted himself between Bogie and Mayo, leaving his companion to fend for herself. "Such a fortunate coincidence."

Bogie pulled back. "It is?"

"Not an hour ago, I was saying to my wife—" he gestured to

the woman "—this is Nancy, but everybody calls her Slim." She nodded with a bemused smile that told Nell she was used to being the oasis of composure around which this long-legged tornado twisted. "I was saying how I need to track Bogie down."

"And why is that?"

"I'm tits deep in negotiations with Howard Hughes to buy the rights for *To Have and Have Not*."

Bogie straightened in his chair. "The Hemingway novel?"

"I want you to play the fishing boat captain in Key West. The way you adore the open ocean, I can't picture anyone else."

"How's about casting me as the romantic lead?" Mayo cut in. Had she not already downed quite so many drinks, she might have been able to deliver her appeal with a festive lightheartedness. But she was past that now. It landed with a heavy-handed thud.

"Sounds like there's room for two girls," Tristan piped up. "One that Harry Morgan can have and one he can have not."

"That's good." Hawks smiled, albeit fleetingly. "I want to cast an unknown as Marie. I know, I know, it's a lot of trouble to start from scratch, but I've got my eye on a striking young model who Slim unearthed on the cover of *Harper's Bazaar*. Do you have it with you, honey?"

"He makes me carry it everywhere," Slim deadpanned. She pulled a folded magazine from her handbag and handed it over to Bogie.

Mayo cast a jaded, jealous eye over the image. "She's striking *because* she's young. That's all you old geezers need to get your peckers twitching. I bet you twenty bucks this kid ain't even over the age of consent."

Their waiter arrived with the drinks Mayo had ordered. He placed a full tumbler in front of Bogie, who swiped it off the table.

*Oh my God, he's not thinking of throwing it in her face, is he?* Nell snuck another peek. Massey was now seated at Graham's table. They were staring back, no longer bothering with the pretense of propriety.

The band launched themselves into a South American-tinged arrangement of "Ac-Cent-Tchu-Ate the Positive." Nell shot to her feet. "Bogie! You promised me a dance." She commandeered him onto the dance floor, where he wrapped his arm around her waist.

"I've been drinking pretty steady all evening, so I can't guarantee any slick maneuvers."

"You were about to throw that drink at Mayo, weren't you?"

"A guy can only stand so much."

"Did you see Kathryn Massey and Sheilah Graham?"

"Where?"

"Watching your every move." They danced in silence for a few bars. "May I give you some unsolicited advice?"

Bogie's eyes had lost their focus. "Sure."

"Everyone in the PR department says the same thing: Bogie's batting in the big leagues now. He knows it's a slog to the top of the Hollywood mountain, but does he realize how easy it is to fall off?"

He sighed. "We've turned into Punch and Judy."

To say anything further felt like grinding salt into the wound, so Nell kept mum.

"Kathryn and I were neighbors when I lived at the Garden of Allah," he said. "But Sheilah's not above writing a bitchy item." Bogie squeezed Nell's hand. "You've saved me from a catty headline. I owe you one."

"Now that I've been in the publicity department for a whole month," she said, drenching her voice in self-mockery, "I'm quite the expert."

"How's it going?"

"It's . . . a lot." Everybody juggled multiple projects while on the phone to art departments, newspaper editors, and talent managers. Nell had been overwhelmed at first. That is, until she realized Hal Wallis had adopted all three of her suggestions on how to market *Casablanca*. Nobody had acknowledged her contribution, but that was okay. It had proved that she had a knack for this new job.

Bogie belched. "I want to sneak out the back door."

"What about Howard Hawks? *Sergeant York*, *His Girl Friday*, *Ball of Fire*—they've all been whopping big hits. And besides, sneaking out the back door is not A-list behavior."

"Jesus, Davenport, when did you get so bossy?"

"Twirl me like you haven't a care in the world before you go back and tell Hawks you're in."

Before she had taken her seat again, Nell had already started to compose the letter to Luke that she planned to write later that night.

*Dear Luke, you wouldn't believe the evening I had at Mocambo tonight.*

12

Three layers of costume racks towered over Nell on both sides. Blue-and-white Venetian gondolier outfits were bundled next to Wild West cowgirl costumes. French Foreign Legion uniforms hung against Arabian belly dancer ensembles. "Where are you?"

Tristan sing-songed his falsetto reply. "Fourth roo-oow."

She dashed past Canadian Mountie hats and diamanté tiaras and rounded the far end. He was holding two tutus. One was made of stiffened tulle that shot out ninety degrees; the other had layers of gauzy muslin wafting in the air.

"*Mission to Moscow* left the Bolshoi Ballet sequence until the final week. But their lead dancer twisted her ankle this morning, so they've found a replacement. She's quite striking, but two inches taller. Which one says 'Russian prima ballerina' to you?"

"The stiffened tulle.' Nell pulled an envelope from her handbag and waved it in the musty air. "I got a letter!"

"After four months? Finally!" Tristan headed for the exit. "You'll have to walk with me. The understudy is waiting in her dressing room and you know how patient Curtiz is. Gosh, honey, you must have peed your pants."

She had worked late into the previous evening. *This Is the Army* was about to start shooting and Hal Wallis had asked her to ghost-write an article for *Motion Picture*. She'd been dragging herself to the boardinghouse staircase when she'd noticed the square tan envelope marked "War & Navy Departments V-mail Service." The grind of a fourteen-hour day melted away.

Outside the costume department, she held up Luke's letter.

Tristan frowned as they headed down C Avenue. "They censored more words than they allowed. Read it out loud to me—or is there some spicy stuff intended for your eyes only? In which case, read it twice."

*Dearest Nell,*
    *It's been an eon since you heard from me but* ■■■■■■■ *life is* ■■■■■■■. *My training in* ■■■■■■ *and* ■■■■■■ *nearly made* ■■■■■■. *But I got through it—mostly thanks* ■■■■■■ ■■■■■■. *Looking at it every morning and evening helped me* ■■■■■■.
    *But now I've settled into the swing of things. I get up* ■■■■■■ *and my first duty is* ■■■■■■ *then* ■■■■■■. *When I've finished that I* ■■■■■■ *so that* ■■■■■■ ■■■■■■ ■■■■■■ ■■■■■■ *where I sit, usually* ■■■■■■ ■■■■■■ *until* ■■■■■■.
    *I wish I'd packed a camera because* ■■■■■■ *is everything* ■■■■■■.
    *I'll write again soon but don't hold your breath because* ■■■■■■ ■■■■■■ ■■■■■■.
*With all my love,*
*Luke xxx*
    *P.S. The* ■■■■■■ ■■■■■■ *was the first one built in* ■■■■■■ ■■■■■■. *I never knew that!*

They walked through Stage Eight's elephant door to a theatre set with a proscenium arch and a curved line of footlights. Dancers in ballet toe shoes and long wispy dresses lounged in chairs clumped into pairs and trios. Tristan raised the tutu above his head as though it were a gift to the gods. Michael Curtiz jabbed a thumb upstage left. Nell followed Tristan up a short flight of steps that led to the wings and headed for a door with a crude star painted on it. "Did he enclose a return address?"

Nell tapped the *From* section in the V-mail's top right-hand corner, where a Navy censor had blotted out all three lines.

"How unfortunate, but a first letter means there'll be a second one." He knocked on the door. "See you for lunch at the commissary?"

"I've got Hedda on my agenda today. Escorting her to *Thank Your Lucky Stars*."

"Yeesh."

"Even she can't bring me down. I can't speak for Bette, though. Today's the day she films her song."

"In front of Hedda? Double yeesh. That woman could chop a four-star general off at the knees with a single side-glance." He disappeared inside the dressing room, exclaiming, "Look what I found!"

\* \* \*

Nell rapped on Bette's dressing room door. "It's Nell Davenport. You decent?" When Bette told her to come in, Nell found her standing at her vanity. Milo Anderson had designed an olive-green, two-piece suit for her. He'd studded the jacket with light-catching mirror fragments sewn into a wavy pattern, but the skirt draped all the way to the floor. Had nobody told him that Bette would be jitterbugging in this number?

"Don't you look a treat!" Nell picked up the pair of baby-pink silk gloves dangling on a chair. "And these are just the ticket to complete the ensemble."

Bette snatched them out of Nell's hands. "To conceal my

sweaty palms. I don't want that galoot out there to lose his grip at the crucial moment. How thoughtful of you to check up on me."

"I wanted to be sure you're aware Hedda'll be on the set today."

"She *knew* I'd be twitchy with nerves." Bette looked up, her eyes flaring. "Promise me Hedda won't be in my sightlines. That bitch knows every distracting trick in the book."

"I promise." Nell stroked a bottle of Hudnut Deauville perfume sitting next to the oval mirror. "I hear this is lovely."

Bette hitched the gloves to her elbows. "Give yourself a liberal spray and think of it as a secret defense weapon."

"You mean like how we sprinkled peppermint oil to repel skunks back home?"

"Yes, but Hollywood skunks are harder to fend off, so make it two squirts."

\* \* \*

Hedda's hat looked like the misbegotten offspring of an anemic zebra crossed with a derby, then decorated by a blind milliner who thought orange blossoms could fix anything.

She raised her eyebrows when she saw Nell approach. "We meet again."

"Hello, Miss Hopper."

"I distinctly recall telling you to call me Hedda."

Nell stuck her hand out, hoping Hedda would take the hint that although they might be on a first-name basis, they weren't at the cheek-press stage yet. And they never would be.

Hedda hooked her alligator-skin handbag over her left elbow and shook Nell's offered hand. Hers was a firm handshake. Professional. Neutral.

Halfway to the chairs near the camera, Hedda said, "You're not carrying around a script." She stopped at the prop taxicab Bette would get out of at the top of her number. "I'm glad your interview with Hal Wallis had the desired result."

She continued, but her comment had rooted Nell to the spot. "How did you know about that?"

"I told him to hire you."

Nell wasn't certain what was worse: that Hedda Hopper could interfere with studio hiring and firing, or that Wallis had made his offer under threat from someone who had the power to sink every picture he made between now and retirement. "You told Hal Wallis to give me this job?"

Hedda waved at the *Lucky Stars* director, David Butler. "Hal is free to make his own decisions. I informed him that the publicity on his recent pictures has become stale."

"They've hardly been flops," Nell pointed out.

"Nevertheless, I persisted until he said what I wanted him to say, which was 'And I suppose you know just the person?'"

"You gave him my name?"

"You have to play the game smarter than that. No, no, I gave him three names. But neither of the other two borderline morons works at Warners. I knew you would have impressed him—" Hedda let off a wicked snicker "—but it doesn't hurt to improve the odds."

Butler announced they were ready for a take and asked Bette to step inside the taxi. Nell had rearranged their chairs so that they would not be in Bette's path as she made her way from her dressing room.

Hedda had weighted the scales in Nell's favor, seeing to it that her only competition had been morons. And now Nell was earning twice her old salary, which meant she could pay down her debt without being reduced to woeful penury. All of this was a good thing, but Nell still wanted to slug Hedda with her own alligator-skin handbag.

Bette's stand-in stepped aside as the set of a nightclub entrance flooded with light. The opening bars of 'They're Either Too Young or Too Old' played over the loudspeaker.

But now, a nagging voice deep in Nell's gut insisted, *You're indebted to Hedda Hopper. As one of the few women with power in Hollywood, her life can't be a downy bed of rose petals. She knows how hard it is to get ahead, and what a boost a word in the right ear can be. Is it too much to expect her to have at least one altruistic bone in her body?*

"HEDDA!" Bette's voice javelined across the set. "WHAT A SURPRISE TO SEE YOU!"

Bette shot Nell a glare that could have felled a woolly mammoth as Hedda made to bolt toward her.

Nell pulled at Hedda's elbow. "I was thinking you two could catch up once filming is over."

"Oh, but Bette and I are old chums."

"Miss Grable thinks nothing of miming to her own voice." Bette's teeth weren't clenched, but her tone was. "But this is a first for me."

"Of course." Hedda let Nell draw her back to her chair, where she pulled a notebook from her purse. "It's rather heartening to see there are some things that intimidate the highest-paid woman in America." She took her time jotting down some notes. "Now, what were we talking about?"

Nell forced back the bile rising in her throat. "I believe I owe you a great big thank-you."

13

Nell patted the letter in the pocket of her green-and-blue plaid skirt, mildly surprised that it hadn't burned a hole clean through the wool. She wasn't sure why she'd kept it on her all morning. Or why she hadn't set a match to it, for that matter. She would have preferred another letter from Luke; it had been two months since she'd heard from him.

Set dressers were piling up mounds of fake snow around Dijon Square for a new adventure yarn, *Northern Pursuit*. Errol Flynn as a Canadian Mountie wasn't such a stretch, but this picture featured a massive avalanche, which wouldn't be much fun for anyone.

Avalanched—that's how Mother had made her feel. And by a two-page letter in which Mother had stated her position:

Five years was more than enough time to "get all that silly Hollywood tomfoolery out of her system" and now she must come "back to South Bend where she belonged." Especially now that the Studebaker factory had been requisitioned as a war factory to assemble M29 Weasels. And did Nell know they paid top rates? "Between fifty and sixty dollars a week. How's them apples?"

But that's what I'm earning, Nell wanted to tell her, so them apples weren't so tempting as you might think.

All four of her sisters were working at Studebaker now. Ruth's husband was in Africa—"although by the time you get this letter, he could be in Italy." And Vesta was getting married in May before her beau shipped out to the Pacific. Why not come home for the wedding? South Bend wasn't the sleepy burg Nell had deserted. "Although the town is empty of eligible bachelors, three war factories keep things 'hopping,' as the kids say."

Mother had gone on to let Nell know Father was "still apoplectic about your entire situation. It's only because of gas rations that he hasn't driven to California and hauled you home. He did it when your Uncle Blake went to work on a Mississippi riverboat and fell in with gamblers, so it's no empty threat."

But the real painful clincher that had gouged her squirming entrails was Mother's final line:

*Come home, Nell. It's time.*

She passed out of New York Street and headed down First to Costuming. Bogie was scheduled for wardrobe fittings for his next picture, now that he was back from filming *Sahara* for Columbia.

Dressing room three was at the end of a corridor. She knocked on the door. "It's Nell. Can I come in?" Bogie told her sure, and she opened the door and stepped in. He was standing in front of a three-part mirror wearing a trench coat.

"Look what they've put me into," he said. "It's the final scene from *Casablanca* all over again."

The wardrobe assistant shifted her weight from one foot to the other. "It's what Milo pulled from the racks."

"It suits you. By God, it does." Sydney Greenstreet waved at Nell. "What do you think?"

This one wasn't quite so careworn as his *Casablanca* coat. "This picture is set in New England, so at least it makes sense."

Bogie plucked a fedora from the assistant's hands and fixed it into position. "If I wear a trench coat too often, the audience is going to expect to see me in one every time."

"Do you have one in a different color?" Nell asked the woman. "Darker, perhaps?"

A deep, male voice roared along the corridor. "WHERE THE HELL IS BOGART?"

Sydney jumped. "Who the dickens is that?"

"Hawks." Bogie opened the fitting room door and yelled, "Pipe down, you ill-bred palooka."

Howard Hawks rushed headlong inside and flung a scruffy Panama aside as though it were a grenade. "You know that *Harper's Bazaar* model I told you about?"

"The one you want to audition for *To Have and Have Not?*"

"I managed to get her a seat on the Super Chief. She's only nineteen, for Chrissakes. I can't have her wandering about Union Station like a lost soul. She's arriving in—" he checked his watch "—an hour. I have to be at Legal in twenty minutes to sign the option with Hemingway's lawyers."

"Can't you send your partner, Charlie?"

"He's meeting with William Faulkner. I want him to write the screenplay."

"Your secretary?"

"Someone needs to look after the office."

"What about your wife? Slim is great at meeting, greeting, and fleeting."

"She's in Palm Springs. Can *you* go?"

"Play Mister Welcome Wagon?" Bogie pulled off his trench coat. "She's going to assume they've already cast her. Don't do that to the poor thing."

Nell shot her hand into the air. "I'll go."

Anything to clear her head. If she stayed at the studio, she'd sit around and mope about the damn letter in her pocket and torment herself over how on earth she'd reply. Or *if* she would.

Hawks produced a ring of car keys. "Black Cadillac."

"Does this fresh-faced ingenue have a name?"

"Betty Joan Perske, which is god-awful, so it'll be the first thing we change. We've rented an apartment in Beverly Hills. Two seventy-five South Reeves. Help her settle in, then drive her to our office. You know where it is?"

Nell had sent a ton of correspondence to Hawks-Feldman Productions. "On Wilshire."

Hawks nodded. "Charlie will take her to the Derby, where I'll meet them for lunch. Now, go. GO!"

\* \* \*

The redcaps started pushing their carts as the Super Chief rolled to a halt. Nell had seen this girl's photo on the cover of Slim's *Harper's Bazaar* but only briefly. She remembered a brunette with wide-set eyes, but that was about it. She might have to wait until all the other passengers had departed, leaving a solitary young woman with dreams of instant stardom glittering in her imagination.

Nell positioned herself halfway along the platform so that she could scan the weary travelers disembarking from the railcars with their hand luggage, matching trunks, hat boxes, and pint-sized dogs.

Oh, God. What if she was one of those precious mademoiselles who traveled around with a tiny dog the size of a stunted raccoon? What if the darned creature peed in Hawks' Cadillac? Or worse?

A platoon of GIs loitered next to a mountain of precision-stacked boxes marked "Camp Ross, San Pedro, California." A couple of cars past them stood a tall teenager in a tailored light blue suit that had the freshly ironed look of a recent purchase. She held a matching mushroom hat in her hands; a small brown suitcase sat at her feet.

From what Nell could recall, the *Harper's Bazaar* girl was no prettier than a thousand other photogenic girls. She wasn't sure what Slim had seen in this particular one to give her a screen test clear across the country.

But in person? Oh my! She was a whole other game of cribbage. Two of the cockier GIs were nudging each other, drumming up the courage to make a pass. She ignored them, cool and unruffled, as though they barely registered as background noise. There was a sultry allure to the way she held herself, ramrod-straight like a ballet dancer, but with a poise and elegance Nell could never hope to emulate.

Nell stepped around the girl's luggage. "Miss Perske?"

"The telegram said that someone would meet me." Her voice had a low growl to it. "But didn't say where or who."

"I'm here to take you to the Beverly Hills apartment Mr. Hawks has rented for you. My name is—"

"Pinch me." The girl pulled back the sleeve of her jacket. "I'd consider it a favor." When Nell obliged, she let out a shrill "OH!" that obliterated the sensual huskiness. "Betty Joan from Brooklyn living in Beverly Hills. Well, now, if that don't beat all."

Ah-ha! So she was only a femme-fatale-in-the-making on the outside. On the inside, she was still coming to grips with the breathtaking reality that she'd scored a one-in-a-million opportunity.

"You're from Brooklyn?"

Perske's green eyes lit up. "You too?"

"My boyfriend is."

"Which part?"

"Bensonhurst."

"Practically neighbors! We're on Ocean Parkway."

"Ever heard of Valenti Construction?"

"Who hasn't? Wait, your boyfriend is a Valenti?" Perske scrutinized her with a renewed once-over.

Nell picked up the suitcase; it was heavier than she had expected, and she belched out an involuntary grunt.

"I don't expect you to carry my luggage." Perske wrestled it from Nell's grip. "Mama Natalie didn't raise no namby-pamby jellyfish."

That's a relief, Nell thought. If this greenhorn with her Klein's two-piece was going to survive the wilds of Hollywood, she was going to have to fend for herself. "This way," she said, pointing past the GIs. "We're parked out front."

"You have a car?"

They sidestepped the soldiers who were now gawping at them—at Miss Perske, anyway. "God, no. But picking you up on my bicycle seemed inauspicious."

Perske let fly with another high-pitched cackle. "I can see we're going to get along fine."

"Mr. Hawks lent me his Cadillac—"

"He must trust you."

Until about an hour ago, Howard Hawks wouldn't have known Nell Davenport from a box of turnips. "Let's just say he was real thankful when I told him I'd be happy to welcome you."

"Oh, I get it." Perske hefted her suitcase to her other hand as they entered the cavernous waiting hall with the cathedral ceiling. "You drew the short straw because nobody wanted to come pick up the hick."

"I'm from Indiana," Nell said. "If anyone's a hick, it's me."

"A hick who drives a Cadillac."

"A Cadillac that doesn't belong to me."

"Say, I cut you off before you told me your name."

"Nell Davenport."

"Pleased to meet you, Nell Davenport."

"Likewise, Betty Perske." Hawks was right; that name would have to go.

"Can we take the long way to Beverly Hills? I may never be back here."

Don't worry, thought Nell. You're not going anywhere, except maybe onto the big screen. "How about we drive down Hollywood Boulevard?"

"A dream come true!"

They walked through Union Station's front entrance and into the golden light of early summer. Nell wiggled her fingers toward the line of palm trees waving in the morning breeze. "Welcome to California!"

* * *

Betty gazed out the window. "Everything is so clean. People here have the space to breathe."

"It's not like this in Brooklyn?" On their last night together, Luke and Nell had splurged with a dinner at Chasen's. Over the famous chili, he had told her how he'd marveled at "the luxury of Californian elbow room."

"We're all piled on top of each other. But you don't give it much thought." Betty craned her neck as they passed Sardi's Hollywood. On the north side of the boulevard, the large sign on top of Pickwick Books crept into view.

"Did they tell you which role your screen test will be for?" Nell asked.

Betty shrugged. "If Mr. Hawks has one in mind, he hasn't told me."

Nell swung the car onto McCadden Place. "We're going shopping."

Pickwick Books was two stories tall, packed floor to ceiling, and open until ten every evening, making it everybody's *de rigeur* destination for reading material. Nell breathed in its unique aroma of paper, dust, and literary ambition.

"Getting a screen test happens to only one in ten thousand girls," Nell told her. "Mr. Hawks is a highly educated, erudite man.

The best way to impress him is show you're no ditz who reads the funnies and calls it a day." A large display of four religious novels stood near the entrance: *The Song of Bernadette*, *The Nazarene*, *The Keys of the Kingdom*, and *The Robe*. "*Bernadette* for you; *Robe* for me. Now, let's see, what else?"

Betty drifted to the New Releases table. "Back home, everybody's talking about that one." *A Tree Grows in Brooklyn* featured a drawing of a tree sprouting from the sidewalk of a deserted street leading to the bridge. Nell picked it up and weighed its significant heft. "How did your folks feel about you traveling across the country to immoral, lecherous Hollywood all on your own?"

"Dad's not in the picture, but my mom saw me off at Grand Central. It was the whole megillah."

"The whole what?"

"That's Yiddish for the whole nine yards: waving handkerchief, tears, hugs so tight I could barely breathe and for so long I almost missed my train." A wistful smile curled Betty's lips. "Did she *want* me to go? Probably not. What was she going to do, lock me in the hall closet?"

It's what mine would have done, Nell thought, which is why I snuck out. "Ever read *To Have and Have Not*?" Betty shook her head. "Hawks is a real Hemingway kind of guy." They roamed the shelves until they found the Hs. Nell pulled the last copy from the shelf and added it to the pile. "Tackle this one first."

A hesitant look filled Betty's soft green eyes. "Can I ask you a question?"

At first glance—and second, and third, even—this girl came across like a new Katharine Hepburn, or Rosalind Russell. Nell was almost relieved to see a glimmer of apprehension denting her self-confidence. "Anything."

"Mr. Hawks . . . Is he married?"

"If you saw his wife, you wouldn't need to ask."

Betty ran a finger down the spine of *To Have and Have Not*. "Tell me about her."

"Her name is Nancy, but everyone calls her Slim. She's the epitome of style and sophistication. Tall, svelte, and has the best taste in clothes of anyone you'll ever meet in your life. And sporty, too. Tennis, swimming, golf—plays everything with great confidence. Oh, and Bogie told me—"

Betty's head shot up. "Humphrey Bogart? You know him?"

"I've worked on most of his recent movies."

"What do you do?"

"I'm in the publicity department at Warners." A balloon of pride swelled her chest. How good it felt to say those words.

"What did Humphrey Bogart tell you about Mrs. Hawks?"

"He mentioned Slim was once on the cover of *Harper's Bazaar* —hey! Just like you . . ." That last word trickled off into a whisper when Nell pieced together the motivation behind the girl's line of questioning.

Tall.

Svelte.

Confident.

Classy.

*Harper's Bazaar.*

"If you're thinking what I think you're thinking, it's not what you're thinking."

A jaundiced uncertainty had replaced the optimistic glow. "You can't blame me for wondering."

No, Nell had to admit, she couldn't. In Hollywood, men changed wives almost as often as they changed their BVDs. "It was Slim who came across your cover and showed Mr. Hawks."

"I didn't know that," Betty said quietly.

"She told him he'd be a fool if he didn't bring you out here." Nell wasn't sure about the last part, but her argument must have been convincing because here they were. "Slim is sharper than a pitchfork. I doubt her husband has ever tried to put anything over on her that she doesn't see coming from a hundred miles away."

Betty took in a deep breath and let it out in a throaty sigh. "I've been tormenting myself over that since Albuquerque."

Nell tidied the five books into a stack and heaved them off the table. "Let's get going. You're having lunch at the Brown Derby."

"First Beverly Hills and now the Brown Derby? This day gets better and better."

*Oh, Miss Perske, I suspect it's only just beginning for you.*

14

*N*ell stepped up to the Technicolor camera. She hadn't worked on any of Warner Bros.' previous color releases, so she hadn't seen one up close. The cameramen on *This Is the Army* had explained how the three-strip process worked, but it'd all gone over Nell's head. Something about three strips of black-and-white film and beam splitters and filters and reflectors? She had no desire to know the technical ins-and-outs, but it wasn't altogether impossible that an inquisitive journalist from *Ladies' Home Journal* or *Screenland* might ask.

"You're Nell, aren't you?"

She had only met Slim Hawks that one time four months ago at Romanoff's. "How nice of you to remember."

Slim toyed with a dark orange silk scarf roped around her neck and pinned to her blouse with an anchor-shaped brooch lacquered in black. "Betty's mentioned you several times these past few weeks, saying how welcome you made her feel."

"You were right on the money about her. What a knockout."

"Yes, but she needs lessons in deportment, speech, posture: the usual movie-star stuff. And, of course, a new name."

"What have they settled on?"

"Her mother's maiden name was Bacal, so we've added an extra L on the end, otherwise people might think it rhymes with 'jackal.' There are already too many Bettys, so Howard chose Lauren."

"Lauren Bacall." Nell repeated the name to herself several times. "Fits her nicely."

"I agree. Listen, there's a favor we'd like to ask of you."

A commotion erupted on the far side of the set. Irving Berlin was here to film "Oh! How I Hate to Get Up in the Morning," a fun tune he'd written for *This Is the Army*. He had let it be known that he wanted to be treated as one of the boys. "Don't introduce yourself," Nell's boss had told her. "Just be close in case any problem arises."

A predictable knot of admirers had huddled around him and his co-stars, George Murphy and Charles Butterworth, but they parted as Louella Parsons, in a dark brown jacket and matching halo hat, approached them.

"You look surprised to see her," Slim commented.

Nell had to consciously unclench her teeth. "She's supposed to clear on-set visits with Mr. Taplinger."

"You've got Irving Berlin appearing in Warner Brothers' first Technicolor musical, directed by the wizard who helmed *Yankee Doodle Dandy* and *Casablanca*. I'd be shocked if she wasn't here."

Taplinger wouldn't bar Louella from any production. But the director and his company were here to do a tough job while battling a ticking clock; it was polite and professional to let a studio know ahead of time. Why, then, had she chosen to show up unannounced?

"As I was saying," Slim said, recapturing Nell's attention, "the favor?"

Nell hated to take her eyes off Louella, but Slim Hawks was not easily ignored. "I'm happy to help however I can."

"Being from New York, Betty doesn't know how to drive; we were hoping you could teach her."

Whatever Nell had been expecting this favor to be, it wasn't that. "I've never given driving lessons before."

"You can drive, can't you?"

"Sure. I drove your husband's Cadillac when I went to collect Betty at Union Station."

"Did you crash it?"

"No, but I was having kittens every time a car came too close."

"If you can drive it, you can teach it. And it'll give the two of you some time to get to know each other."

"I'm happy to help out any way I can, but all I've got is a bicycle."

"Charlie Feldman is lending her nine hundred dollars to buy a 1940 gray Plymouth he passed en route to lunch at the Ambassador."

Nell found herself smiling at the idea of seeing Betty again. The girl exuded sardonic shrewdness mixed with guileless candor. She had been savvy enough to ask about the boss's wife, but had gaped like a goldfish at the prospect of eating at the Brown Derby.

"If you supply the car, I'll supply the lessons."

A momentary frown passed across Slim's face. "I don't suppose you know if Betty is single?"

"Not that she mentioned."

"Clark Gable wired us he'll be on furlough this coming July Fourth, so I'm throwing a dinner party and feel Betty might make a suitable date for him. The poor guy's still cut up over Carole's death, of course, but Betty's such a striking girl. At the very least, she could offer Clark some pleasant diversion."

"Name me one woman in America who'd say no to that." Nell went to excuse herself—she ought to investigate Louella's impromptu appearance that she suspected wasn't impromptu at all—when Slim caught her by the elbow.

"And one last thing." Nell saw Louella clasp Berlin's hands as she threw her head back in a repellently hammy move. "Howard is worried about how her voice squeaks."

Nell looked at Slim. "When she gets excited?"

"You noticed?"

"Hard to miss."

"The only roles she'll get are screeching viragos. Howard wants her to take a book, the heftier the better, find some deserted spot and read it out loud at the top of her lungs. But read it like a man. Tell her to pretend she's Victor Mature. When you give Betty her driving lesson, park the car where nobody'll hear her and have her recite out loud until her voice goes kaput. It'll take a few sessions, but it could end up making her career."

"*The Robe* is long and filled with big words."

"Perfect!"

"Leave it to me." Nell jacked a thumb toward Louella and Irving's hangers-on. "I need to see what's going on over there."

"When Betty gets her phone connected, I'll cable you the number."

As she ambled to the center of the soundstage, Nell reflected how handy it must be to have a telephone of one's own. To call or be called any time of the day or night. What luxury! Someone like Louella probably had several. Was it too hard to pick up one of them?

"Nell! NELL!"

Oh, crap. What now?

Perc Westmore, the head of Warners' Hair and Makeup, was dashing headlong to her with a woman in her forties trailing behind.

"Now, look," he said, "I don't mean to sound like an alarmist, but things are pretty dire." He raked his fingers through his hair. "Between guys getting enlisted and girls joining the WACS and the WAVES, Helene and I are running out of people!"

"What are we going to do when *Hollywood Canteen* goes into production?" the woman asked. "Can you get ahold of the movie's schedule of which cameo will film on what date? We need to plan ahead."

Nell wasn't sure how Bette Davis had convinced Jack Warner to make a movie set at the Canteen, but woe betide the fool who underestimated that force of nature in heels. It wasn't one of Nell's projects, but she had seen a list of at least thirty stars who had been wrangled into making an appearance.

"We're reaching crisis point," Perc insisted.

Nell had nodded appreciatively through this exchange, but she really, *really* had to see what Louella was up to. "I'll get back to you," she said, pulling away from them. "I promise!"

Louella tucked her chin into her folds of skin down her neck and peered up at Nell with her best Betty Boop impression. "You're terrifically mad at me, I expect. No advance phone call to you, or your boss, or Mr. Curtiz."

Nell took the vacant seat next to Louella and forced a smile. "You're welcome here anytime, Louella."

"I learned only last night that Jack Warner has decided some of the profits for this picture will go to the Army Emergency Relief Fund. What a remarkable gesture!"

For all his contradictory flaws and annoying idiosyncrasies, nobody could deny Warner's commitment to the war effort. He was the first studio head to pull his movies from the European market in the face of escalating Nazi atrocities. And the first to devote significant resources to produce pro-Allies films.

"Did you know Warners will donate forty percent of the profits to the real Canteen?"

"It's an expensive, seven-day-a-week operation. They need all the help they can get to keep the doors open." She closed her notebook with a well-practiced flick of the wrist. "I understand you have a boyfriend in the Navy."

Nell stiffened at the ninety-degree angle this conversation had taken. "I do. But how—"

"And that you have no way of contacting him."

Nell had told only a handful of people about Luke's letter: Bogie, Tristan, and her landlady. Bogie would do anything to avoid talking with Louella. Tristan was a low rung in Costuming. Mrs. Carp was an Eastern European refugee from the Great War who rarely left her boardinghouse. Nell could think of only one other suspect: Betty Bacall.

Luke's name had come up when Nell had been helping her unpack at the apartment. She kept his letter in her handbag all the time now, and it had spilled out when Betty had asked her for a tissue to blot her freshened lipstick.

"Is that right?" Louella demanded.

Nell blinked away the dots she had connected. "I'm sorry, what?"

"That you're unable to contact your sweetheart."

"Well, yes, but—"

"I got to thinking." She tapped a finger at her temple like a woodpecker. "Who do I know high up the Navy chain of command?"

"Really, Louella, it's okay. Luke will—"

"My daughter, Harriet, is at RKO now. She coordinated with the Navy for one of her films. And not with just any old pencil pusher, but an admiral. So how about it?"

Nell blinked again. This exchange was unfolding too briskly for her to grasp. "How about what?"

"I'm sure I can get information about your beau. As long as . . ." Louella let her words peter out. Nell knew she didn't need to ask, 'As long as what?' She could see the answer coming a mile away. *Wait for it, wait for it.* "You tell me the moment Humphrey Bogart leaves his wife."

*And bingo.*

"Why does everybody think Bogie and Mayo are splitting up?"

"Oh, my dear, happily married couples don't treat each other like that behind closed doors, let alone with half of Hollywood watching."

"Bogie told you at Romanoff's that they're planning a USO tour."

Louella raised a dismissive shoulder. "Can you imagine those two slogging up some North African sand dune?"

Nell couldn't even picture Mayo getting dirt under her fingernails without unleashing a rope of cuss words. On the other hand, Bogie, who had thrived filming the crashing North Atlantic swells and the baking heat of the Sahara Desert, would relish the opportunity to rough it under a raggedy tent, making do with a jury-rigged latrine and a can of cold beans for dinner. But Louella's lips had curled downwards into a sullen pout that told Nell there was nothing she could say to convince her otherwise.

"I've seen no evidence of the end of the Bogart marriage." It was true. Bogie had never mentioned it to her. Not in so many words.

Louella shifted her gaze to Irving Berlin, who was taking his place on the Army camp set. "I want to hear about it the moment he starts an affair with Michele Morgan."

"What makes you think he's going to?"

"She'll be co-starring with him in *Passage to Marseille*."

"You've got Bogie all wrong. He's not the philandering type—"

"He's a movie star, isn't he? She's beautiful, isn't she?"

"So is Ingrid Bergman, but—"

"You're with the PR department now." Louella swung back to face Nell, her eyes hard as basalt. "Your loyalties are to columnists: me, Hedda, Sheilah, Kathryn, all the others. Without us, you have nowhere to plant your stories, your hints and gossip. Stars need publicity and we provide it. Every person in every studio PR department knows that, and it's about time you learned it, too."

Michael Curtiz called for quiet on the set.

Louella turned back to watch Berlin prepare for his first take. Overhead, the banks of blinding lights needed to film in Technicolor flooded the set. Nell closed her eyes. What sort of hole had she dug for herself?

## 15

*B*etty giggled as she steered her Plymouth around a hairpin turn in the serpentine road that meandered along the spine of the Hollywood Hills. "I'm a New York girl. All subway tokens, crowded sidewalks, and looking for a cab when it's raining and you're loaded up with packages from Gimbels."

Nell reached over and adjusted the steering wheel before they nosedived down the embankment on the other side of the manzanita bushes. "Now that you've signed a contract with Mr. Hawks, you're all outdoor tennis games in January, year-round tans, and saying no to coconut cream pie for dessert because the camera adds ten pounds."

Betty braked as another sharp turn came into view. "Why are we up here? I thought we'd ride around some empty parking lot for my first lesson."

"My dad's from the 'Throw Her into the Deep End' driving school. He took me out to the dirt roads past South Bend airport. It wasn't until later that I realized if I could tackle them, regular city streets would be a cakewalk."

"What's this road called?"

"Mulholland Drive."

Betty slowed the car to a crawl and pointed to a cluster of lights down in the valley to their left. "What's that?"

"Universal Pictures."

"When you grow up in Brooklyn, the stars, the studios—they're all so far away."

There was that startling rise in pitch. It was even more jolting in a closed space.

Nell had forgotten how saucer-eyed she herself had been on her first visit to Schwab's. How she had sat at the counter, trembling at the thought that some burly security guard might tap her on the shoulder and tell her that those seats were reserved for people who belonged there. It was nice to see her nineteen-year-old self reflected at her in this girl's shiny eyes.

"Not everybody gets offered a contract in their first month here."

Betty hit the gas and they lunged forward. "I'm very appreciative, really, I am. And a hundred bucks a week! I barely know what to spend it on."

"Even with rationing, it's easy to burn through money here. Promise me you'll put some aside every week."

"Yes, ma'am."

Nell wriggled her fingers to a point farther down the winding road. "When we get to the next hairpin, pull into the turnout."

"To do what?"

"Just get us there without plummeting down the slope. It's a long way down."


Gravel and dirt crunched under the tires as Betty pulled off the road. "What's here?"

Nell reached into the back seat where her copy of *The Robe* sat next to her handbag. She swayed the book in her hand and swung her car door open. "Out we get."

Traces of early-summer warmth blew across their faces. A pair of doves flew past them to a clump of eucalyptus trees. A nest of baby birds squawked, and in the distance, the klaxon of an old Tin Lizzie cussed the air.

Nell groped for the least offensive way to explain what needed to be done. This girl was still walking around with her rose-colored glasses jammed on her nose. A thousand different futures lay ahead, each one filled with possibilities more breathtaking than the last. But not if she hung onto that habit of launching into a piercing shriek every time she opened her mouth.

Here goes nothing. "A few days ago, Slim Hawks and I got to talking about the way your voice rises in pitch—"

"I can't help it." Betty kicked a large pebble over the bluff. "Whenever I get excited or nervous, it goes so high only dogs can hear me."

"When you get onto a movie set, you'll be excited and nervous —and a whole bunch of other emotions besides. It's normal and human, but until you can control it, you won't be any good to Mr. Hawks."

Betty paused to absorb the news. "What's with the book?"

"Slim suggested reading from it out loud."

"How loud?"

"Top of your lungs loud. If you do it at home, you'll frighten the neighbors. So I've brought you up here where—"

Betty pushed herself off the hood of the car. "My mother raised me to be a nice girl. 'Only scruffy street urchins scream, and Brooklyn has enough of them,' she always tells me. 'You're better than that.'"

Nell twirled in a circle. "Nobody'll hear you." Betty stared at her, unconvinced. "I used to do it all the time back home. Jump on my bike, pedal into the open woods out past Notre Dame and let loose."

"Which book would you read from?"

Nell's arms hit her sides with a dull slap. "In my family, secular music is a big no-no, so I'd sing my heart out—"

Those last four words caught in her throat. She hadn't told anyone about her singing. Not even Luke. She'd meant to. Wanted to. But it had to be the right time, and the perfect opportunity had never presented itself. And then Beatrice's boyfriend had got him into the Navy, and suddenly he was gone.

"You have to go first," Betty said. "And if nobody calls the cops on us for disturbing the peace, then I'll read out loud from—" She picked up the book. "Oh brother, that's bound to have some tongue-twisters."

Nell approached the escarpment. She had only ever sung to the backwoods chipmunks and cardinals. Except for that time her family came home from church early and caught her singing "Summertime."

"Not as easy as it looks, huh?" Betty called out.

"I'm deciding which song to sing."

"How about 'Alexander's Ragtime Band'?"

Nell turned her back on the ravine. "Why that one?"

"I saw Irving Berlin on the Warner lot the other day. Do you know it?"

Nell swung around and stared out across the horizon. She fixed the Hollywoodland sign in her sights, and drew in a deep breath.

"Come on along, come on along, let me take you by the hand,

"Up to the man, up to the man who's the leader of the band,

"And if you care to hear the Swanee River played in ragtime,

"Come on and hear, come on and hear Alexander's Ragtime Baaaaaaaaand!"

Oh my. That did feel good. She felt the pounding tom-tom of her heart. It's not panic that's causing my heart to race. It's—it's—

Exhilaration.

Two firm hands spun her around. Betty's mile-wide grin threatened to crack her face in two. "I thought you meant you were good enough for the back row of the church choir!" There was that screech again. "Where did all *that* come from?"

Nell shrugged. "It's what falls out when I open my mouth."

"'*Falls* out'? No. That *shot* out. No. It *escaped*."

Outside of Bette and Tristan, it was Nell's very first compliment on her singing, and it felt like a slug of expensive brandy on a winter night. She gave Betty a quick smile and then, blushing, forced herself to refocus. Overhead, a dusky sun was bleeding into the afternoon sky. Nell figured they had an hour and a half before she could no longer see the words printed on the page. That ought to be enough time to lower her voice by at least half an octave.

"Your turn."

Betty picked *The Robe* up off the roof of the Plymouth. "You're a tough act to follow." She cleared her throat. "'Chapter One. Because she was only fifteen, and busy with her growing up—'"

"LOUDER!"

"'—Lucia's periods of reflection were brief and infrequent.'"

"DEEPER!"

"Make up your mind," Betty said. "Louder or deeper?"

"Both." Nell pointed to the Hollywoodland sign. "Pretend that each of those thirteen letters is hanging on your every word. But they're far, *far* away, so you have to—" she cupped her hands around her mouth "—PROJECT!"

"'But this morning she felt weighted with responsibility. Last night, her mother, who rarely talked to her about anything more perplexing than the advantages of clean hands and a pure heart . . .'"

\* \* \*

"""I wonder if you will ever see him again," Mother had said; and, in answer to her question, Marcipor appeared in the doorway. "A young Corinthian has arrived, Master," said Marcipor.""" Betty closed *The Robe* with a sharp slap. "I sound like Eugene Pallette with a head cold."

"Let's call it a day."

"Thank heavens. I'm in no rush to repeat that experience."

"You're not done until you've read the whole book out loud."

"All five hundred pages?!"

Nell snatched the novel out of her hands before Betty thumped her with it. "Or until you've erased the dog-whistle end of your vocal range."

Betty flinched. "Bad as all that?"

"It doesn't jibe with how you're likely to come across on screen."

"Which is what?"

"Sultry seductress."

She threw out a gravely "Ha! That'll be the day."

"Your job is to be whatever the script calls for."

As the sun slipped behind the crest of the canyon to the west and the sky bled into a murky gloaming, a bank of twelve parallel searchlights shot straight up from the bottom of the valley in front of them. A second bank of lights joined it. They slowly raked the deepening night sky in orchestrated unison.

"What's going on there?"

"Combing for Japanese aircraft," Nell said.

"Oh." Betty's voice trembled.

"You're in California now." She angled her head toward the Pacific. "Pearl Harbor is a hop, skip, and a jump thataway."

Betty approached the edge of the gravel and craned her neck. "Where are those lights coming from?"

"The Bowl."

"I'm *this* close to the Hollywood Bowl?"

"Want to go?"

"Right now?"

"As long as you do the driving."

Betty hesitated. "At night?"

"This is the 'Deep End' traffic school, remember?"

* * *

Nell led Betty through the gate and waited for the "Wow!" she knew was coming. She'd said it herself the time she'd first walked through this gate. She spent seventy-five cents she couldn't spare for a cheap ticket to see Benny Goodman and his clarinet not long after she had arrived in Los Angeles.

To their right, a gentle, creamy light illuminated the nine concentric half-circles that made up the Bowl. In front of the stage, two banks of twelve spotlights faced each other and scraped the night, back and forth, meeting in the middle to create a white X reaching several stories high. Spectators filled a scattering of seats here and there.

Nell and Betty sat in the third row and watched the lights sweep from east to west and back again. After a few minutes, Nell noticed a discarded *Saturday Evening Post* in the row in front of them. She picked it up and studied the Norman Rockwell painting on the cover. It was a of a red-headed woman in blue overalls. One hand held a ham sandwich; the other lay on top of a lunch pail with "ROSIE" written in white letters. A grimy jackhammer rested across her lap. It looked heavy, and loud—and exactly what Nell might operate if she were working to crank out Weasels in the Studebaker factory. She held up the *Post* for Betty to see.

"That gal looks like a friend of mine from high school," Betty said. "Her brother died in North Africa, so now she works at the Brooklyn Navy Yard. Practically runs the place."

A trio of women stood on the stage, two of them in their twenties and a much older one carrying the air of a maiden aunt. They stood shoulder to shoulder and swayed to a silent rhythm like they were the Andrews Sisters.

"Anyone can go up there?" Betty said.

Nell cast the *Post* to one side. "Yup. Including us." Rounding the searchlights, they raced up the steps. Giggling breathlessly, they clung onto each other as they approached the center of the stage.

The rows of seats stretched as far as the horizon. "Just imagine it," Betty said. "All those people sitting there looking up at you, waiting."

The thought of getting up on the Hollywood Bowl stage—or any stage, for that matter—was too intimidating to contemplate. Nell's singing to date—well, except for that little incident on top of the hill just now—had only resulted in calamity. "There's a difference between singing and performing. I may be an amateur singer, but you're a professional performer."

"We'll see about that." Her half-smile disappeared as quickly as it had bloomed. "Perske is too Jewish, isn't it?" Nell hadn't seen this girl look so solemn before. "They've changed my name. I'm Lauren Bacall now."

"I think it's rather nice."

"It is—even though it feels like someone else." Betty turned away from the empty seats. "Tell me straight: Is it naive of me to think they've signed me because they think I've got a special quality to offer?"

"It's *why* Mr. Hawks has signed you."

"But the first thing he did was change my name. And now he wants me to change my voice. What's next? Dye my hair? Arch my eyebrows? Paint Joan Crawford's mouth on me and make me walk like Mae West?"

Nell looped her arm through her friend's and hugged it to her side. "Practically every actress changes her name when she gets here. It's no big deal. I agree with them about your voice, though. You have a striking, unique look, and they're right to want your voice to match it. But if they tell you to dye your hair, or change your eyebrows, or paint someone else's mouth on you, tell them, 'Go to hell.'"

Betty burst out laughing. "Tell Howard Hawks to go to hell? I don't think so!"

"Maybe Betty Joan Perske couldn't, but I bet Lauren Bacall can." Nell watched the light in Betty's eyes shift as the searchlights swiped across her face. "Do you know who invented hot fudge sundaes?"

"No, but I'd like to shake his hand."

Nell led her back to the steps leading off the stage. "C.C. Brown's on Hollywood Boulevard."

"Is that where we're going next?"

"Prepare to die and go to heaven."

# 16

Nell plunked her handbag onto her desk. Jiminy Christmas, where to start?

*Destination Tokyo* was due to commence production in a couple of weeks, which gave her time to prepare advance magazine copy for *Modern Screen*, *Boxoffice*, and *Screenland*. Cary Grant had previously been on the lot for *Arsenic and Old Lace*, but had clashed with Frank Capra. Maybe Jerry Wald had poured on the blarney to convince him that Delmer Daves wouldn't browbeat him into a performance he wasn't comfortable giving.

Meanwhile, as Louella had so bluntly pointed out, it was her job to plant cute stories with the columnists. She ran through the list of names in her head. That guy at the *Hollywood Citizen-News*, Don Somebody-or-other. He'd seemed nice when he visited the *This Is the Army* set on the last day of shooting.

She dug around in her desk drawer for his card without much luck. Or much enthusiasm. All she wanted to do was read the V-mail in her purse. She had read it twenty times since she'd arrived home the previous night. Then twice more over breakfast this morning.

No, she told herself. Keep your head in the game. For now, you track down Don Somebody-or-other.

Paisley, Taplinger's secretary, dropped a telegram in front of her. "Delivered late last night. This one's a doozie."

She slid out the cable and read the name of the sender: Drew Kipling.

Oh, God. Him again? Why didn't anyone warn her that actors who got a teeny, tiny spotlight were more trouble than all the Bette Davises and Errol Flynns combined? The guy had a minor role in *Three Cheers for the Irish*, a slightly larger one in *The Great Mr. Nobody*, and a featured part with screen credit in *The Big Shot*. Three parts in three years and now he thought he was entitled to bigger parts, and cabled Nell every other week to remind her.

BIG SHOT SHOT DOWN IN FLAMES STOP
SHOOT JACK CARSON IN MY BED INSTEAD STOP
REPLACE SMITH WITH JONES STOP
CALL ME YESTERDAY STOP
DREW KILPING

The Western Union clerk shouldn't have accepted Kipling's money if he'd been drunk enough to send a telegram like that. She dropped it into the trash can, then fished Luke's V-mail out of her purse.

I'll read it once more and then put it away until lunchtime.

*Dearest Nell,*
*You'll get this V-mail hopefully because I'm not sure* ■■■■■■■ ■■■■■■■! *You, I assume, have now got lot of paper. Please note all that'll happen around about Warners. I must know every detail! Especially on*

*stage five with Irving Berlin's clever words. Meanwhile my US Navy life keeps me very busy at near idyllic beaches of* ▪▪▪▪▪▪▪ *Montauk. I had forgotten how intense the weather is here! Big storms make everyday things difficult and a lot more complex than* ▪▪▪▪▪▪▪ ▪▪▪▪▪▪▪!

*Won't you please tell Bogie stay happy and that I long to hear from him? Probably not likely! Is he going to star in Hemingway's "To Have"? He'll have to school himself the art of learning Hem's dialogue.* ▪▪▪▪▪▪▪ ▪▪▪▪▪▪▪ *easier than Japanese.*

*My brother, Tony, is in the Wadsworth Hospital over in Sawtelle. I don't have any specifics. Could you maybe visit with him?*

*I was told they censored the address I gave you, so I had to go over the head of my C.O. and appeal to* ▪▪▪▪▪▪▪ *to get one you can write to. With any luck,* ▪▪▪▪▪▪▪ *won't hold a grudge forever. I'm willing to put up with* ▪▪▪▪▪▪▪ *if it means hearing from you.*

*Please write to me at the above address. It's the best I can do under the circumstances.*

*With all my love,*
*Luke*


The address read: U.S. Maritime Service, Radio School, Huntington, Long Island, N.Y. Nell planned on spending her lunch break poring over the large atlas in the props department to see where Huntington was.

"Oh, that Hedda Hopper!"

She turned to see Leo Grayson, a battle-weary journalist who'd been with Warner Bros. PR since before *The Jazz Singer* turned the movie world inside out. He smoked his first Cuban stogie each morning at nine and ate double whiskeys for lunch. "She's got more nerve than Patton."

"What has she said now?" Nell asked.

Grayson folded his *L.A. Times*. "Some two-bit, nobody actress is filing a paternity suit against Chaplin. Claims they've been having an affair for two years and he's knocked her up."

"Didn't he recently marry Oona O'Neill?" Paisley mused. "That's going to be one hell of an awkward dinner table tonight."

"Hedda throws knives at him every chance she gets," Taplinger said from his office. "And that dame's got more cleavers than the chef at Perino's."

"Plus, she's in cahoots with the FBI," Grayson added.

"You can't know that for sure," Nell said.

"Hoover hates Chaplin's British guts, which means the Bureau has it out for him. Hoover and Hopper march further right than Himmler. Her column is nothing but a coordinated smear campaign. The Terror of the *L.A. Times* has found the ideal patsy to bring Chaplin to his knees with—" Leo checked Hedda's column "—Joan Barry, who she claims waltzed into her office in tears. Jeez. She's outdone herself." Grayson lobbed the paper at the wall behind him. It hit a faded *No, No, Nanette* poster and fell to the floor. He raised a bushy eyebrow at Nell. "You had to deal with her yet?"

"A little."

"She'll turn on you faster than Paisley can sprint on the day Cary Grant drives back onto the lot." He paused as Paisley acknowledged him with a giggle. "If Hedda's willing to take Chaplin down, she'll do the same with anybody."

*  *  *

When Nell gave Tony's name at Wadsworth, the nurse on duty breathed in sharply. "If anyone needs a visitor, it's him."

"He's in a bad way, then?"

"He lost most of his right leg at Guadalcanal."

Nell's hands flew to her chest. "Heavens!"

"Most of our patients have trouble accepting what's happened. We give them time and space to come to grips with it all, and in due course, they adjust to their new situation. Nearly all of them do it with gallows humor." She smiled weakly. "You hear a lot of grim jokes flying around. Nicknames like Armless Andy, or calling their stump Long John Silver."

"I've heard that laughter is like medicine."

"Sometimes it is." The nurse nodded gravely. "But some of them can't move past their injuries. They sit by themselves, and they brood, and mope, and stew. They never get to the turn in the road that shows them hope lays ahead."

"Has anybody visited him?"

"Not a soul."

The nurse took her out to a lush, emerald lawn. "You'll find him in that thicket of willow trees."

"Should I ignore his wound or bring it up?"

"Pretending it's not there is the least helpful action you can take."

The man in the shadows of the waving willow tree bore little resemblance to the brash character she had met the day Luke had toured him around the studio. But all that piss-and-vinegar pep had drained out of this hollowed-out husk.

"Hello, Tony," She saw now that he was in a wheelchair parked next to a wooden bench. "Remember me?"

He continued to stare at her, unblinking, until she had sat down. "Luke's girlfriend," he murmured.

"That's right. My name is Nell."

The corners of his eyes puckered as some sort of unfathomable conflict played out behind that torpid gaze of his. "I lost my leg, not my brain."

He had folded his pant leg into a neat crease a couple of inches above where his right knee used to be. "Given a choice, I'd much rather lose that than . . . my brain." She tried to say it with a gay sparkle, but lost confidence halfway through and stumbled over the last two words.

"Who am I, the Scarecrow?" The question sounded like one of Drew Kipling's drunk telegrams. "Or the Tin Man? Which one didn't have brains?"

"You don't strike me as the type to go see *The Wizard of Oz*."

"My wife, Audrey. She insisted." He ran a fingernail along the folds of his pant leg.

"Luke asked me to come see you."

A spark of life flared in his eyes. "Luke knows where I am? I haven't even told Audrey yet."

"Your wife doesn't—"

"I didn't want some faceless Navy bureaucrat blabbing my news. Told them I'd write to her myself. Come to find out, a letter like that ain't so easy."

"How long have you been trying?"

"What's today?"

"June third."

He stared into his lap, remaining mute.

Nell caught sight of a brawny orderly in crisply laundered whites walking toward them. "We're getting company."

"Stormin' Norman," Tony muttered under his breath. "Here for my death march."

"Bad as all that?"

"I hate my crutches."

"He's not carrying any."

"I hid them under that bench."

"What if I offer to accompany you instead?" Tony's silence was stony. "And then afterwards I can help you draft a letter to Audrey. From a womanly perspective."

Norman stepped in front of the two of them now and looked at Tony expectantly. Tony took his time meeting Norman's eye. "This here's my sister-in-law," he said at last. "Nell will take me for my afternoon constitutional."

Nell could picture Norman moseying down Western Street on the Warners backlot, a Colt six-shooter in each hand, a wad of chewing tobacco jammed inside his cheek.

"Why didn't you tell us you've got family in LA?" Norman asked him, giving Nell a once-over.

"I've been working in a war factory up in Stockton these past couple of months." Nell pulled out the crutches from under the bench. "I can take Tony around, can't I?"

"One hour." Norman held up his index finger. "One *full* hour."

They waited until the orderly was halfway back to the main building. "What were we talking about?" Tony asked. "Oh yeah—writing to Audrey. It'd be swell if you could—what are you doing?"

Nell lifted his crutches. "I promised Norman I'd take you on your walk."

"That was just to get rid of him."

She lowered one until it was level with his right knee. "If don't you stand up in the next five seconds, I'll poke you right in your stump."

Tony's jaw dropped open. "Who the Sam Hill do you think—"

"What's happened to you is beyond awful. No question. But isn't it high time you got on with it?"

Tony balled his fists. "You don't know the first thing about how this feels."

"I know that you're lucky that you weren't killed outright. That Audrey's lucky she's not a widow. And that your little girl won't grow up without a father. It's a lot to be thankful for right there, I'd say."

Nell wasn't sure where she'd summoned up the nerve to lay it on the line to an appallingly damaged man she had met only once. But if it was Luke who had been hurt and was convalescing in a home somewhere and hadn't contacted her to say he was alive, she was pretty darn sure she'd be all riled up like this; maybe more.

Mute as a graveyard, Tony pushed himself into a standing position and nodded. She handed over the crutches one at a time. "Where does this gravel path go?"

"Around the perimeter."

The crutches wobbled as he swung his left leg forward, then

the crutches, then the leg again. Nell drew alongside him as they ambled along the winding path.

"How come Luke ain't here?" Tony asked her, concentrating fiercely.

"He's an ensign now."

Tony broke into a hint of a smile. "Gosh, that's swell." He swayed his crutches in front and propelled himself forward. "That day at the movie studio was my last decent memory. We battled rough seas the whole way to the Solomons. Next thing I know, I'm slogging through the Guadalcanal jungles toward Henderson Field, shrapnel flying in all directions until—" he jerked his chin toward his stump "—this."

"You're better on these crutches than I expected."

"They fitted me with a wooden leg last week."

"How did that go?"

"Terrible. Stormin' Norman told me they got the measurements wrong. Hopefully, the next one'll be more comfortable."

The path curved to the right and ran parallel to San Vicente Boulevard, which lay nearly empty. With gas rationing now in place, it was shocking to see so little traffic on the roads these days.

"What does the family know about your situation?" Nell asked.

"The Navy told them I was injured. I was supposed to fill them in with the rest."

"But you haven't."

"Hand to heart: I'm afraid."

"Of . . . ?"

It was a while before he replied. "Everyone'll see me as less than a man."

"You're making all sorts of assumptions."

"And anyway, what the hell am I gonna to do? I was a roofer, and a damn good one. But that's all gone now."

An idea struck Nell. She wasn't sure if Tony would go for it, but it was worth a shot.

"Roofing isn't your only skill, is it?"

He sucked on his lower lip for a moment. "Does drinking beer count?"

"I'm talking about hairdressing."

Tony planted his crutches into a wide stance. "What a rat."

"Luke was very touched that you confided in him."

"Yeah, well . . ." He dug the tip of his left crutch into the gravel.

"What if I could get you a job doing hair?"

He drew in a jagged breath. "How? Where?"

"Warner Brothers."

"You could do that?"

"No promises, you understand." She'd said too much already. As soon as she had learned that Tony was recuperating in Wadsworth, she should have anticipated that he might not be the cocky hothead she'd once met. But oh, look at that hope shining in his eyes. So desperate. Such longing. "Next Monday, *Hollywood Canteen* goes into production with dozens of cameos. But Hair and Makeup are woefully understaffed, so I was thinking—"

His ragged breathing deteriorated into a string of turbulent gasps. "I only ever did my wife's hair. I don't—I just—it's been so long. Maybe I can't do it anymore." He stared at the tips of his crutches for a moment, and then looked back up at her. "Hey, could I practice on you? Show you what I can do before you talk to them studio people?"

She pulled at her dead-straight locks. "You'd need concrete to do anything with this. However, I have a friend who's going to a fancy-schmancy party. She'll want to look super-great because her date will be Gable."

"*Clark* Gable?"

"Think of it as a test drive, and we'll take it from there."

\* \* \*

Nell had felt pretty darned good about herself when she had stepped on the bus back to Hollywood. The Tony Valenti she had found moping in his wheelchair was not the same Tony Valenti who had seen her to the gate, a sliver of hope glinting his eyes. She had no idea what Perc Westmore would say, but with manpower shortages everywhere, she suspected he'd even take a one-legged gunnery sergeant with no beauty school training.

The glow of her visit faded to ashes, however, when she read the shocking headline on a discarded *L.A. Times*. She grabbed it and read the article, her heart in her mouth. From then until her bus reached Sunset Boulevard, she thought only of Bogie. His house was only three blocks away from the bus stop, so she took a chance and walked straight there.

She tucked the paper behind her back and knocked on the door.

A gruff "Coming!" rang out from deep inside the house. It took a while before the door opened and Bogie stood staring at her through bleary, bloodshot eyes. "What's up?"

She stepped into the vestibule. "Is Mayo here?"

He pulled at the lapels of his frayed smoking jacket. "Last night's bender was momentous, even by our standards. I fell into bed around three. I rolled out of bed ten minutes ago, so I've got no idea where she is."

That meant he still hadn't heard the bad news.

She deposited her handbag on the narrow mahogany table standing against the foyer wall. "You need to prepare yourself." She brought the *L.A. Times* out from behind her and unfolded it so that he could read the headline:

*LESLIE HOWARD ON THE PLANE SHOT DOWN BY FOE*

. . .

"But he's on a lecture tour. Talking up the British cause in Portugal."

"He was." That word—*was*—tasted bitter in her mouth.

"Portugal's neutral. It's how all those Europeans fled the Continent. By getting to Lisbon—the entire plot of *Casablanca* hinges on it."

"But then he caught a flight to Bristol. It flew too near to Bordeaux, which the Germans consider a sensitive war zone."

"So they shot it down." Bogie's voice wasn't much more than a rasp, laced with hostility and agony. He lurched sideways and grasped the doorframe. "He gave me my first break . . . He brought me to Hollywood for *Petrified Forest* . . . Without him, I wouldn't have this career . . . "

"I know, Bogie," Nell whispered. "I know."

A guttural moan broke from his chest. His forehead landed on her shoulder. "Those goddamn kraut bastards killed my friend."

"They did." She stroked his temple. "I'm so sorry you've lost him."

## 17

*N*ell stirred her martini with the skewered olive. It was a bit too vermouthy, but this was Betty's first attempt, so she kept mum and peeked around the apartment Howard Hawks had rented for her. Light-filled, airy, quiet, and roomy, it was everything Nell's boardinghouse wasn't.

"Aren't you dressed yet? Tony'll be here soon."

"I want to do Tristan's dress justice," Betty called from her bedroom.

He looked up from his *L.A. Times*. "Knowing that you're wearing it on a date with Clark Gable is all the justice I need, honeybuns."

Betty emerged in the open doorway. "What do you think?"

Tristan had dreamed up a cocktail dress that was the right combination of knock-Gable's-socks-off va-va-voom and "I'm a nice girl so, no monkey business, mister." The bateau neckline cut across her shoulders then sloped into a deep V in the back. Cinched at the waist to show off her camera-ready figure, it ballooned into a full skirt that ended mid-shin. It swooshed as she swanned into the living room. "Should I even ask where you found the silk to make this?"

"I broke into Orry-Kelly's secret stash."

"But silk is rationed!"

"Miss de Havilland and Miss Davis will have to do with repurposed outfits." Tristan thrust his newspaper aside with a dramatic flourish. "Twirl for us. Make that skirt fly!"

It splayed out as Betty followed Tristan's direction.

Nell broke into applause. "What I wouldn't give to watch Gable's face when he gets a load of you."

Betty lifted a nonchalant shoulder, and crossed to the bar, where she poured herself a generous helping of martini. "We'll see."

After a month of regular visits to the uninhabited stretches of Mulholland Drive, Betty's voice was starting to match her alluring woman-of-mystery exterior.

"You seem awfully composed," Nell said. "I'd be a stuttering shambles who changed her outfit four hundred times an hour."

"For starters, I don't have four hundred outfits. I only have this." Betty pinched the silk. "Which is perfect. Plus, he must be more than twice my age, so nothing's going to happen, romance-wise. And anyway, I'm only there to fill an empty seat and even the numbers." She took a second, thirstier sip. When she put down her glass, the inscrutable woman of mystery had vanished. "Look, guys, I'm trying hard to keep myself from behaving like some blushing thirteen-year-old with a crush the size of the *USS Iowa*." She released an exaggerated growl that, several months ago, would have been shrill. "You're not making it easy!"

"But it's Clark Gable!" Tristan stage-whispered.

"Hush up, you." Betty read the clock above the living room mantel. "Should we have picked up Tony? I got a new book of gas rations—"

"He insisted on getting here under his own steam, so I—"

A heavy clump-clump, clump-clump sound seeped through an open window.

Nell stole a quick peek, just long enough to spot Tony halfway up the ten steps, where he had stopped to rest. She zipped over and opened Betty's front door. "Need a hand?"

He shook his head. "I'm still learning to get up and down stairs with this new leg. Fits a whole lot better than the first one. Still a bit tricky, though."

Betty had set up the professional hairdressing tools she'd bought for tonight on the bar and had placed a stool in the middle of the room.

"You must be the girl of the hour," Tony said, his breathing labored from the effort. He told her to take a seat, then examined her hair, felt its texture, and scrutinized the way it fell to each side of the part. "Yes, yes," he murmured, "I know what to do here."

As he settled into his task, Nell chanced a surreptitious peek. A rosy flush in his cheeks had replaced the drawn, pained look he'd had at the convalescent hospital. His eyes were a little clearer and his hands had lost their slight tremble. Even if this hair-styling job ended up being a one-off, maybe it was all the life buoy he needed to pull himself from his pit of despair.

Tristan returned to the sofa and opened the *Times* again. "I was just reading Hedda Hopper."

Nell read all the Hollywood gossip columnists, but this morning, work had begun on digging her boardinghouse's victory garden and Mrs. Carp had mandated the attendance of all sixteen residents. "Who is she impaling today?"

"The Battling Bogarts, naturally."

Nell hadn't seen Bogie since that ghastly day he had bawled in her arms. Blotting at his tears, he had told her how thankful he was that the news had come from her, but now he needed to get blind drunk and would she please excuse him. In her last sighting of him, he had both hands grappling the neck of a bottle of Canada Dry bourbon.

Tristan cleared his throat theatrically. "'The Battling Bogarts were at it again last night. This time, at Mike Lyman's Hollywood Grill. The poor unfortunates who got caught in the crossfire were

Bogie's frequent co-star, Alan Hale and his wife, Gretchen. Their brouhaha was about General MacArthur, of all people. According to my eyewitness, Bogie's against him, though I can't guess why. Within minutes Bogie was hitting Mayo over the head with a highball glass and she was biting and scratching him.'"

"Should I be scared?" Betty asked.

"Of what?"

"Mr. Hawks has mentioned this movie he's putting together, *To Have and Have Not*. It'll star Humphrey Bogart and there might be a part in it for me. Gosh, Nell. Thank heavens you told me to pick up a copy of it that day we were at Pickwick Books."

Tristan shot Nell a *You sly fox, you* look. "She then says, 'After the July Fourth holiday, Bogie will start work on *Conflict*, which is awfully apt seeing as how that's all Bogie and Mayo seem to do. The couple will celebrate their fifth wedding anniversary next month, so how's this for irony? Bogart's character decides to kill his wife not long after their fifth anniversary. Isn't it about time someone rings the death knell on this marriage and tells us what's really going on? Otherwise, heads may have to roll around the Warners lot.'"

Tony looked up from the back of Betty's head, hairbrush in one hand, scissors in the other. "Whoever that dame is, she ain't too subtle."

"Oh, Nell," Tristan said in a sing-songy, come-hither voice, "there's something I need to show you."

He waited until she'd settled in beside him before he drew a finger along a sentence in Hedda's final paragraph: *Isn't it about time someone rings the death knell on this marriage*, except that she had written "death knell" as "death Nell."

Tristan scrunched his eyes at the corners. "I don't suppose that's an innocent typo."

"Nothing about that conniving witch is innocent." She looked at the page again: *death Nell*. "It's a warning shot across the bow."

"Warning against what?" Betty asked.

"A few months ago, I learned the conniving witch got me my job in PR."

Tristan drew back. "She actually did someone a favor?"

"Her style of favor involves mutual back-scratching."

Tony stepped away from Betty. "What do we think?"

He had swept her cascading locks into an updo, piling those curls into a soft nest atop her head, adding five years and a halo of sophistication.

"Oh, Betty!" Nell exclaimed. "If Gable can bear to pull his eyes off you for even so much as a second, the man has obviously lost his wits."

* * *

Nell found Bogie on the set of Sydney Greenstreet's office, next to a wide window with venetian blinds cutting the light in long slashes. Dressed in a dark suit and conservative tie, he was studying his lines with one hand holding his script, the other jammed into his trouser pocket. He looked like last week's cream of wheat: pale and lumpy and gone sour two days earlier. It didn't help that his toupée wasn't in place yet. He frowned as the hesitation on her face registered. "What's up?"

"The *Modern Screen* interview—it's scheduled for tomorrow."

"The usual fluff?"

"I was on the phone with the journalist they're sending." It hadn't been a pleasant conversation. The woman was new to motion-picture reporting and was far from happy to toe the studio line. "She's less 'fluff' and more 'gruff.'"

"I like her already."

"No, you won't."

Bogie dumped his script on the office desk next to them. "And why's that?"

"She's going to bring up Hedda's Saturday column. I begged her not to, but she insists on asking you about it."

He crossed his arms. "What'd Hedda say this time?"

"You don't read her?"

"Why would I? She always writes about me like I'm covered in horseshit."

"She reported on the tussle you got into at Lyman's, and how you hit Mayo with a highball glass. Please tell me that's not what happened." His lopsided grin answered for him. "For Pete's sake, Bogie, how long is this marital free-for-all going to last?"

"Until someone calls the undertaker."

"She also drew parallels between the plot and title of *Conflict* and the state of your marriage."

"I battled with Jack Warner for weeks to get out of making this melodramatic claptrap. I told him the parallels hit too close to home. But Jack said nobody would notice. Leave it up to Hedda."

"If Nora Finlayson from *Modern Screen* brings it up—and she will—it might be prudent to have a ready answer."

"Or I could terminate the interview."

"You need to know what's being said about you, and what people suspect might be true, so that when it comes up—"

He cut her off with a harsh sigh. "You got her column with you?"

She did, but only because her boss had told her to get through to him that these puerile antics harmed him, harmed Warner Brothers, and harmed Hollywood. If he noticed the veiled "death knell/death Nell" threat, he might ask her about it. And if he did, she would have to go into more detail than she wanted. She pulled the article from her purse. "I'll read the relevant part."

He snatched it from her with a mocking smirk.

Over his shoulder, sitting on a bookshelf, sat a familiar statue. She went over and stroked its head. Why on earth would the set decorator place the Maltese falcon in a scene between Humphrey Bogart and Sydney Greenstreet? Still, she was happy to see it there. Her mind began to wander. July must be the best time to be in Montauk. The Atlantic Ocean lapping at all those sandy beaches. She'd been tempted to send Luke all her letters in one big box, but decided it would be safer to mail them in four bundles. If one got lost, three others might get through.

"Thanks for the warning." Bogie handed the article back to her. "It's time I put my rug on. Follow me."

A toupée lay on a mannequin head on his dressing room makeup table. "I don't suppose you know how to put these things on?"

"Where's Verita?"

"In Arizona with her ailing grandmother."

"Can't Perc get you someone?"

"Probably—if I hadn't bawled out Perc Westmore and his staff for presuming they had access to my toupées. Which they don't. So now I'm persona non grata. I've watched Verita do it hundreds of times." He sucked on his teeth. "It's harder than it looks."

"Maybe next time you shouldn't run off at the mouth."

He slid the toupée off its stand and held it out. "Shut your wisecracker trap and do your best."

"ME?"

He waved the limp hairpiece back and forth. "Pinch the rear edge and slide it from the top of my forehead over my crown. I'll know when it's in place."

It took three attempts before they agreed the fourth was good enough. With some careful combing, and a word to the lighting guy, he could get away with it.

He stood in front of his vanity and tightened the knot in his tie. "Why is Hedda Hopper threatening you?"

"What do you mean?"

"How else would you interpret 'death Nell'?" He articulated each syllable with weighted deliberation.

Heat blossomed upward from her neck and reached her cheeks before she had the presence of mind to turn away.

Bogie stepped around her until they were face to face again. "Does it have anything to do with her getting you into PR?"

"You know about that?"

"I was in a meeting with Hal Wallis. It was one of our more pleasant conversations, meaning we didn't end up lobbing ashtrays at each other. He asked me, 'What can you tell me about Nell Davenport?' He said that Hedda Hopper had been on the blower telling him to send you to Publicity. I told him you were a great kid, loaded with potential, and that you'd be terrific."

So Hateful Hedda wasn't *solely* responsible for her promotion, after all? "Oh, Bogie! You don't know how much that means to me."

"I wouldn't have said it if I didn't mean it. But what was that 'death Nell' jab?"

"I suspect it was a warning shot. She wants reimbursement for getting me the job."

"Like what?"

"The scoop that the Bogarts are kaput."

He slapped the vanity table in frustration. "Why is everybody so obsessed with my marriage?"

She slapped it too, to arrest his attention. "Because everywhere you and Mayo go, you make spectacles of yourselves. Screaming arguments. Smashing glasses. Gallivanting around like nobody knows who you are."

He rolled his jaw around as though she'd socked it with a bulldozer of a right hook. "I see."

"I hope so," she told him, "because the future of your career might ride on it. Mine, too. Jack Warner threatened to blackball me from the whole industry if I told you what Hedda was after. And if that happens, I'll probably have to go home to South Bend. And that's a fate worse than death, as far as I'm concerned."

Bogie rubbed his fingers across his freshly shaved cheek. "I wish someone had thought to tell me that I have been *gallivanting* from one end of LA to the other. But I guess I've been too preoccupied with screaming arguments and smashing glasses." He mugged an *OH MY!* of wide-eyed campiness that would have made Eric Blore sulk with jealousy.

"Please, Bogie," she begged, "you need to take this seriously."

He took her hands in his. "If I'm going to be in Hedda Hopper's crosshairs, there's nobody I'd rather be in there with than you."

# 18

"Let me get this straight," Betty's mother, Natalie, said. "This picture is about Don Ameche arguing with the devil because he knows he *belongs* in hell?"

"Which is why it's called *Heaven Can Wait*," Betty said. "He feels he's lived such a dissolute life that hell is all he deserves."

They found four seats together about two-thirds back from the screen of the Fox Wilshire.

Betty's mother had jumped on the first train she could find as soon as she'd heard about her daughter's date with Gable. Betty had summed up the evening with an indifferent two-word review: "No spark," so Nell wasn't sure why Mama Natalie had assumed Betty was carousing in nightclubs and crawling home as the sun was chasing away the final wisps of the night.

"Gene Tierney is all I care about," Natalie said, settling into her seat. "I go see everything with her."

"I often see her handing out cookies at the Canteen," Tristan said. "Meanwhile, they've got me scrubbing pots and pans."

"I keep meaning to sign up as a volunteer," Betty said.

"You should," Nell told her. "Some of those fellas have apprehension dripping off them like sweat. It's not the toughest job in the world to give them a warm memory of dancing with a charming girl."

The lights dimmed and the burgundy velvet curtains parted as a fanfare trumped through the loudspeakers announced the beginning of a *Fox Movietone* newsreel. Like every newsreel, it was a zippy mosaic of life: The Allies' invasion of Sicily, Betty Grable's handprint ceremony at Grauman's, the fire that had gutted Ciro's. By the time they were talking about the Criollo horse of the Argentine pampas, Nell's thoughts had wandered.

She closed her eyes to soothe away her pangs of guilt over the Canteen. She had regularly volunteered there when she'd been a script girl. But this PR job required more of her time, often requiring her to come in early to work up some copy when news had broken overnight, or to stay late when a newsworthy incident had happened and she knew reporters would be asking her about it the next day. *If Bette Davis can find the energy to be there practically every night, I have no excuse.*

She opened her eyes to a travelogue of Boulder, Colorado. The commentator extolled its peerless topography in the Rocky Mountain foothills, its vibrant fall foliage, and the prestige of its university.

The scene cut to a brick building, three stories high, with a curved roof. Panning right, the camera stopped at glass double doors before pulling back to catch a student in a blue Navy uniform.

Nell jackknifed forward. Wait! What? How?

The camera followed the guy as he walked onto a patch of lawn and sat under a spruce tree. He drew his knees toward his chest and wrapped his arms around them.

Nell had seen Luke do that a million times.

Tristan's hand grasped hers as THE END filled the screen.

"I wasn't seeing things, was I?" Tristan whispered.

Nell mouth had gone dry. She couldn't talk. Even if she wanted to.

Tristan hoisted her to her feet and threw a brisk "We'll be right back" at Betty and her mom. He hustled her into the deserted foyer. A water fountain stood next to the auditorium. Nell slurped from it as she freed herself from the cobwebs of confusion.

"Luke's in Colorado?" she blurted out.

"And why would the Navy have a base in Boulder?"

"Studying at the university, maybe?"

"Didn't Captain Stamina want him *because* he speaks German?"

Nell leaned against the water fountain. "I'm feeling woozy."

"I'd be in shock too if I discovered my boyfriend was in Boulder. Of course, I'd first have to have a boyfriend—"

"Know anybody at Fox?"

"One of René Hubert's assistants—assuming he has hasn't been drafted. These days, you never know."

"Can you ask him who at Fox Movietone News I need to speak to?"

"Sure, but then what? Are you planning on going to Colorado? Have you tried to get on a Greyhound lately? Good luck with that dream, honey."

"Luke still doesn't know about his inheritance. If I can talk to whoever put that newsreel together, maybe I can reach him that way."

"Of course." He stroked her arms to calm the panic rising in her eyes. "First thing tomorrow. But for now, let's go back inside and see if Don Ameche ends up in hell."

\* \* \*

When Nell walked through the gates at 20th Century-Fox, she felt as though she'd parachuted behind enemy lines.

Admitting that she worked at a rival studio might have jeopardized her chances of seeing Luke's newsreel again if Tristan's friend had asked. He didn't, so she kept her piehole shut and let him assume whatever he wanted to assume. And now she was sitting in a Fox screening room.

She pressed the intercom button and told the projectionist, "When we get to the part I need to see, can you play it at one-quarter speed, then freeze frame it when I yell 'Stop!'?"

"Sure."

She pulled her handkerchief from her purse. Twisting it around her fingers helped allay the nerves uncoiling inside her. The lights went down; the newsreel started up. The Allies in Sicily . . . Grable at Grauman's . . . Ciro's fire . . . Argentine horses . . .

A picturesque shot of Boulder nestled against the Rocky Mountains appeared. She instructed the projectionist to cut the speed and bent forward as the Movietone camera panned across gold and yellow leaves drifting onto sparkling creeks and carpets of wildflowers. She twisted her handkerchief tighter when the brick building with the curved roof appeared and the camera zoomed in on its glass double doors.

This time, however, Nell glimpsed a hand-lettered sign she hadn't previously noticed: *US NAVY SCHOOL*.

The camera pulled back. Nell laid her finger over the intercom button. A door swung open and the guy in the sailor uniform walked through it. His face was in profile and in shadow. It *looked* like Luke, but now she wasn't so sure.

*Don't tell me this is just some wild goose chase.*

The camera followed him to the grass and stopped as he dropped onto his butt under the tree. "Look up," she whispered. "Look at the camera!" He tilted his chin toward the sun.

She hammered the intercom button. "FREEZE!"

\* \* \*

Nell poked her head inside Stage Three and listened for the usual moviemaking sounds: a director barking out instructions, the sharp snap of a clapperboard. Hearing nothing, she dodged a wide scrim hanging from the ceiling and stepped onto a makeshift set someone had thrown together in ten minutes. A rattan peacock chair with a fan back stood in the center. On one side, a tall brass vase held a dozen orange-dyed ostrich feathers; on the other sat a standard lamp taller than Nell, with a shade of flocked velvet in deep cardinal red.

In front of it stood a big-chested woman cinched into a garish corset that gave her the hour-glass figure of a Wild West bordello madam.

"Looking for Reggie?" the woman asked.

Screen tests were usually given to apple-cheeked neophytes like Betty Perske, not well-seasoned broads who, Nell guessed, had to be in her mid-forties at the very least.

The woman mugged an exaggerated smile. "I may or may not get cast in *The Dolly Sisters*, but when they offer you a screen test, you don't say no. Am I right?" She extended her hand. "My name's Violet Beaudine."

Her handshake was firm and confident. "Nell Davenport."

"Reggie ducked out to fetch me a fan." She ran a hand down her corset. "I'd forgotten how these contraptions hurt like blazes."

"I hope they don't expect you to dance in that torture chamber."

"They do. And sing!"

A man about Violet's age appeared with a large wicker fan in his hand. Tall and gangly, he sported a halo of tumultuous hair that all the Vitalis hair tonic in California couldn't tame. "A projectionist told me you were on your way."

"I didn't realize you were filming a screen test," Nell said. "I'm happy to wait until—"

"No, sweetie, you go right ahead." Violet took the fan from Reggie. "I could do with an extra twenty minutes' rehearsal."

He led Nell to a long sofa with an ornate back carved in walnut. "What can I do for you?"

"The Movietone newsreel currently in theaters—I understand you shot the Boulder segment."

She withdrew a photograph from her purse.

The projectionist had obliged Nell's request for an eight-by-ten print from the frame of film that showed Luke most clearly. It had caught Luke mid-smile, the sun drenching his face. It had taken her more than a few minutes to recover from the longing that rose from seeing his face again.

The affability in Reggie's face dropped away. "You know Valenti?"

"He's my boyfriend."

"You're Nell?"

"I am!"

"He talked about you. Quite a lot."

Suddenly, it felt like Luke was sitting next to this Reggie guy. Almost close enough to touch. "How'd he come to be in your newsreel?"

"Because he saved our hides. Our flight was two hours late. All the decent U-drives had been rented, so we ended up in some trashy old jalopy. It was dark. We took nineteen wrong turns and ended up on the lonely side of some reservoir miles past no-damn-where. And *then* we blew a tire. Eventually, this Navy jeep appeared."

"Luke?"

"He wasn't going to stop because he'd signed the jeep out until six p.m. and it was almost that time. But he took pity on us and towed us into town. Our hotel was right near the university, where he was living in one of the empty dorm rooms. We were so grateful that we treated him to dinner. I guess Navy grub ain't so hot because he gobbled it down like it was cordon bleu."

"Luke's studying in Boulder?"

"Ah . . ." Wariness crept across Reggie's face.

"It's hard to overlook your boyfriend when he's twelve feet tall."

"Um... sorry. I'm not being cagey on purpose."

"I saw the US NAVY SCHOOL sign on the door, and you said he's staying in the dorms. Does two plus two not equal four here?"

"He was very chatty with us until I asked him what he was studying."

"What did he say?"

"He changed the subject. When he showed us his dorm room, his desk was stacked with what looked like textbooks. We got together for dinner on the second night and I asked him again, but even after three shots of Wild Turkey, his lips were tighter than a nun's—at any rate, it was all hush-hush, so I didn't push it."

All this time she'd been picturing Luke sitting inside a Quonset hut on some wind-swept Montauk beach hunched over—well, she really didn't know. A radio? Probably shortwave? Listening in to German transmissions?

"I'm supposed to be directing a screen test," Reggie said, "so if there's nothing else...?"

"Did Luke tell you what he was doing in the middle of nowhere?"

"Tons of wildlife live around the reservoir, so he used to go sketching there."

"'Used to'? Meaning he doesn't anymore?"

"His marching orders came through when we were there."

"Do you know where they were sending him?"

He shook his head. "Neither did he."

"Can you tell me anything? I'm trying to contact him. Please, any clue at all?"

"Don't you have a Navy address?"

"He gave me the U.S. Maritime Service radio school's address, but now I find out he's been in Boulder."

Reggie fixed her with a quizzical stare. "That address acts as a central clearinghouse. I must get back to work." He stood up. "Sorry I haven't been much help."

"Yes, you have. I'm very appreciative."

Reggie turned to go, then hesitated. "Those textbooks in Luke's dorm room. The thickest one had squiggly little lines on it." He cocked his head to one side. "Have you ever seen shorthand?"

"No."

"It's looks like a three-year-old's meaningless scribbles."

"The Navy sent him to Colorado to learn shorthand?"

"It doesn't make sense, but then wartime never does." He turned away again.

"How was he?" The question erupted out of her. What a terrible person she was for not asking this first. "Did he look healthy? Did he seem happy?"

"Oh, yes. He was on top of the world."

19

Nell pushed aside advertising mockups for *Destination Tokyo*, set her handbag on her desk and peered inside it. The card was still there in its baby-blue envelope of expensive parchment. She didn't take it out, or look through the photographs of her sister's wedding her mother had enclosed.

She had no desire to look at photos of Vesta in Nell's own wedding dress. The one she was supposed to be wearing the day she'd skipped out on poor, unsuspecting Hank. She had skipped out on poor unsuspecting *everyone*, but Hank was the one she'd left at the altar. He deserved an apology letter, but she hadn't found the guts to write it. She'd tried. A whole bunch of times. But every sentence had tumbled onto the page in clunky phrases that failed to say what she wanted to say, no matter how many times she rewrote it. And then four years had flown by. Even the most perfectly worded missive was all too little, all too late. Hank Elliott deserved better than the hand he'd been dealt.

And anyway, Vesta looked prettier in the dress than she had— even though she hated wearing hand-me-downs. But was it a hand-me-down if Nell had never worn it?

No, no, no. She didn't need to subject herself to all that. And she wasn't sure why she had thrown the card into her purse this morning. But she had, and now it sat there, nestled between her compact and her latch key.

Nell jumped at the sound of her name through the layer of cigarette smoke that hung below the PR department's ceiling. Her boss was looking directly at her. "In here. Now."

When she walked into Taplinger's office, Howard Hawks offered her a curt nod from one of the guest chairs.

Nell took the other chair. "What can I do for you gentlemen?"

"It's like this," Hawks said, cracking his knuckles. "I'm probably going to cast Betty opposite Bogart in *To Have and Have Not*."

*Heavens!* "I see."

"But first I need to know if there's chemistry. She's a nothing little nobody meeting a famous movie star; she's bound to be nervous. I figure she'll feel more at home with you around."

"You want me to take her to Bogie's set?"

"Make like you're dropping in," Taplinger said. "Real casual."

"Encourage conversation between them," Hawks said. "Act like nothing special's going on, but listen and pay close heed."

"Look for any sign that they'll get along. I want this meeting to be as spontaneous and offhand as possible."

"Got it." Nell wondered if she had the self-control to stop herself from blabbing to Betty that she was *this* close to being cast in a major picture opposite an A-list star at a major movie studio right off the bat.

"Encourage chitchat, but take a step back and see how they are together." Hawks permitted himself a droll smile. "Oh, and good job lowering her voice. That annoying squeak of hers has disappeared."

"Anything else?"

"Nope. That'll do it. She's waiting in reception."

"She's here?"

"With filming on *Destination Tokyo* now done, I thought you'd—"

"Yes, yes, that's fine." But how am I going to stop myself from screeching *You've beaten the one-in-a-hundred-thousand odds!?*

Betty wore a smart suit of deep yellow that brought out the green in her eyes. She leapt to her feet. "Don't tell me it's *you* taking me to meet Bogart? Does this mean I've got the role? Does it depend on what Bogart says? Does he have—what's the term?"

"Cast approval. I don't know about that." They took a right at the commissary and headed down First Street. "But everybody's life is easier if the star of the picture likes his leading lady."

"I'm going to be Humphrey Bogart's leading lady?" A couple of months ago, those words would have flown out of Betty like a fire truck siren, but that was before *The Robe*.

Nell ached to grab her by the shoulders and jump up and down, screaming YES! YOU! ARE! "Not yet, you're not. Nothing is cast in stone until the cameras roll on Day One. I've even seen performers replaced after a week's filming."

"Right. Yes. I see." Betty kept her focus glued to the alleyway. "What should I do?"

"Nothing."

"I'm about to meet a huge movie star and you want me to stand there like a blob?"

"Just be yourself."

"Is that enough?"

"It was enough for Hawks to bring you out here, put you up in a comfortable apartment, give you a screen test." They were at Bogie's soundstage now. Nell pulled her into a shaded nook. "He's about to meet you, too. Chemistry is a door that swings both ways."

Confusion flickered across Betty's face. "Chemistry, huh?" She adjusted her straw beach basket hat, which had slipped to one side. "So I should act natural?"

Nell had said too much. She shepherded Betty out of the

alcove. "No. Not *act* natural. *Be* natural. And let the rest take care of itself."

They found Bogie leaning against the window of a printing shop set, its name, *LE VERITÉ FRANÇAISE*, painted across the top in block letters.

"Bogie," Nell called out, "I have someone I want you to meet."

He pushed himself off the glass as they approached. "You're Betty Bacall, aren't you?"

Betty's eyelids fluttered. It wasn't hard for Nell to read her mind: *Humphrey Bogart recognized ME!* "It's Lauren now."

Bogie shook her hand. "An elegant name. It suits you."

"Every time I hear it, I assume they're talking about someone else."

Bogie presented her with his trademark wry smile. "If it's any comfort, I've been at this game a long time and I still think that."

"But isn't Humphrey Bogart your real name?"

His eyelids fluttered the same way hers had. *Someone's done their homework.* "I read in Hedda's column that—"

"You've started reading Hedda again?" Nell butted in.

Bogie kept his eyes on Betty but tipped his head toward Nell. "The boss here ordered me to keep up with what the Hollywood witches' coven says about me."

"Not 'ordered.'" She landed a soft punch to his chest. "Suggested."

"No less than Elsa Maxwell threw you a birthday lunch, huh?"

"She did, if you can believe that."

"If Whedda Whopper said it, of course I can."

Betty surveyed Bogie with narrowed eyes, then Nell, then back to Bogie. "I'm guessing you have history with her?"

"Everybody in this burg does—right down to the shoeshine boy outside the Biltmore."

Betty crossed her arms. "She gave me my first mention in an important column, so I'm grateful to her for that."

Taplinger had said to keep things casual, but they were veering into a potential pit of quicksand. "That luncheon," Nell said, "it was at the home of Evalyn Walsh McLean, wasn't it?"

"Her house! I thought, Wow, this sure ain't Brooklyn."

The Bogart eyebrows shot up. "You're a New York girl?"

Betty unfolded her arms. "Born and raised."

"Okay, so, Rumplemayer's. Bavarian Strawberry Pudding or the Patisserie Française?"

Betty didn't miss a beat. "I'm more of a Riz a la Crème girl."

The Bogart eyebrows climbed one notch higher. "I see. And did Mrs. McLean show you the Hope Diamond?"

"She let me wear it!" Betty slapped her fingers against her cheeks. "I nearly passed out from euphoria."

"Is it heavy?" Nell asked.

"Of the thousands of diamond necklaces I've worn, I can definitely say it's the heaviest."

"An extraordinarily deep blue, from what I hear."

"It's what I imagine the Pacific looks like a hundred feet down. I'm an emeralds girl, so I wasn't terribly impressed." She brushed a lock of hair out of her face with an exaggerated flick of the wrist as though she were Barbara Hutton and a three hundred-thousand-dollar jewel might have been made of flint glass for all she cared.

But there had been a flair to the way she'd carried it off. A cheeky mix of guilelessness and I'm-in-on-the-joke knowing that made Bogie laugh out loud.

"I think you and I will have some fun making this picture." He turned to Nell as Betty's jaw dropped open. "You know that USO tour I told you about?"

"You're doing it?"

"Thirty-five thousand miles through western and northern Africa, then on to Italy."

"How long will you be gone?"

"Ten weeks starting next month. We're going to need someone to look after the house and our two Scottie dogs. Would you like a break from your overcrowded boardinghouse?"

No waiting for the bathroom? No snoring roommate? No making do with leftovers if you don't make the seven o'clock dinner? And it means I could now reply to Mother, *Sorry I can't come home because I'm looking after Humphrey Bogart's house for two and a half months.*

"All I need is twenty-four hours' notice." She paused. "Who am I kidding? It'll take less than an hour to pack."

"I'll let you know when our USO contact gives us a definite go-ahead. Now, if you ladies will excuse me?" He picked his script off the window ledge and jiggled it in the air.

As the two women stepped out of the soundstage, Nell waited for Betty to speak first.

"He's just a regular person, isn't he?"

"Says the girl whose first Hollywood date was with Clark Gable."

Betty wrinkled her nose. "But that guy . . ." She threw her thumb toward Stage Four, "He could've been some Ocean Parkway neighbor."

"Is that a good thing?"

"I won't be quite so nervous shooting a scene with him. Assuming I get the role."

"Oh, Miss Betty Joan Lauren Perske Bacall." Nell hooked their arms together, "I'm pretty sure you've been cast."

\* \* \*

Emmeline checked her volunteer list. "I've put you at the coffee station," she told Nell. "Your partner isn't here yet, but Mary Astor's holding the fort by herself. Would you mind helping her out?"

When Nell arrived at the table, Mary looked at her as though she were the cavalry. "These boys are thirstier than the French Foreign Legion. I can't pour fast enough."

They soon had a well-oiled operation going. As Mary handed out the cups, Nell transferred the dirty ones to the back table. "We've met, haven't we?" she said between welcoming smiles to the servicemen crowding their table.

"*Maltese Falcon*. I was the script girl."

"Of course! Nell, isn't it? How lovely to see you."

It was all the conversation they could manage amid an endless stream of servicemen. Ten, maybe twenty minutes had passed—it was hard to keep track of time in the rowdy pandemonium with Jimmy and Tommy Dorsey performing a double act—when Nell felt a tap on her shoulder. She found Beatrice behind her, a wide smile splitting her face.

"Howdy, coffee partner!" She turned to Mary. "Sorry I'm late. My ride never showed up, so I ended up hoofing it all the way from Highland."

Mary headed for the exit as Carmen Miranda, bedecked in one of her lavish fruit salad getups, took to the stage with Bob Hope, leaving Nell and Beatrice without a customer.

"It feels like ages since I saw you," Nell said, stacking used cups. "How've you been?"

"A bit on the lonely side, to be honest. I'd be happy if Keaton wrote me once in a blue moon."

"You and me both. I've heard from Luke just twice in more than a year. And even then, half his V-mails have been censored."

"All this waiting and not knowing—gosh, it grinds away at a girl, doesn't it? On the positive side, I'm now a floor supervisor at Kress."

"Congrats!"

"Came with a hefty raise, too."

"Double congrats."

"Factory jobs pay much better, so they have to. They don't

need to know that I don't want to drill nuts and bolts into aircraft engines. I'm no Rosie the Riveter."

Nell poured them each a cup of coffee from the fresh pot that Cesar Romero had dropped off. "I got a promotion, too." She handed a cup to Beatrice. "Here's to us."

They clinked cups as Tristan approached their table wearing a crimson suit with matching sequins down the lapels. "I need some java bad before I hit the stage."

"That explains the sparkles." Nell ran a finger down his chest. "Will it feel strange to be up there dressed as a man?"

Nell hadn't seen a female impersonator before Tristan had stepped onto a makeshift stage at Romanoff's the night of a European Film Fund charity event. Tristan's metamorphosis into Trixie Bagatelle had left her speechless.

"This time I'm working with a pro." He gulped down his coffee. "We're filling in when Bob and Carmen take a break. We've only had one rehearsal, but she's ex-vaudeville, so she's a real trouper." He deposited his cup on the table and melted into the sea of military uniforms—as much as a tall, thin dandy dressed head-to-toe in bright red could melt anywhere.

Minutes later, Hope and Miranda exited stage left as the Dorsey orchestra's brass section saturated the Canteen with the 20th Century-Fox fanfare. The spotlight swung to stage right, where Tristan and a woman in a full skirt the same color as his suit twirled toward the microphones in a tight clinch.

He released her into a brisk spin. She landed with her feet spread apart, her hands planted on her hips, and her enormous bosom sitting so high it looked like she was serving it up on a tray.

"HELLO, BOYS!" she called out. "WHAT'S COOKIN'?" The cheer that erupted from her appreciative audience could have drowned out a broadside from the *USS New Jersey.*

Nell blinked. "I met her on the Fox lot; she was filming a screen test. I can't recall her name, though."

"Perhaps it'll come back to you when our five hundred bloodhounds have cooled off—although with sweater stretchers like those, it won't be any time soon."

Their number, part song-and-dance, part comedy routine, part improvised audience participation, was about an Army private protesting latrine duty as his girlfriend tried to convince the drill sergeant to give him a twenty-four-hour pass.

After they finished, Miranda and Hope returned to stage. This time, however, Miranda was in a tux and Hope was all gussied up in an over-the-top concoction of ruffles and papier-mâché pineapples. They threw themselves into "The Lady in the Tutti Frutti Hat" as Tristan led his buxom partner around the perimeter of the room to Nell and Beatrice's table.

"When I told Violet about my pre-show coffee, she asked if it was real."

The singer did a double take at Nell. "Aren't you the gal who came looking for Reggie?"

Nell handed the woman a steaming cup. "I'm Nell and this is Beatrice."

"Pleased to meet you. I'm Violet Beaudine." She swallowed half the coffee in a single mouthful. "That Postum stuff is okay in a pinch, but nothing beats the real thing."

"How did your screen test go?"

"Reggie said I came across like gangbusters, but he's hardly an objective party. We'll see." She winced. "Is there any place we can sit down? I borrowed these pumps from Jane Russell and they're a half-size too small."

Tallulah Bankhead and Deanna Durbin—a mismatched pair if there ever there was one—appeared behind them. "Our commander-in-chief informs us it's time for your break," Tallulah shouted over Hope's "Ay! Ay! Ay!"

Nell led them to the sanctuary of the volunteer lounge, an L-shaped space crammed with second-hand sofas and dented office chairs. Tristan waited until Violet had extracted her feet from Jane's shoes before he exclaimed, "You girls won't believe this—I can barely credit it myself—but Violet here was one of The Four Blooms!"

The name rang a bell with Nell, but only in the vaguest way. "Remind me who they were."

"They worked the vaudeville circuit in the twenties. The quartet that Luke's Aunt Wilda chaperoned. I had an enormous collection of their memorabilia but lost it in the boardinghouse fire."

"What?" Violet turned to Tristan. "You knew Wilda Doyle?"

"Not personally, but we know someone who was very close to her."

"This Luke guy you mentioned?"

Tristan held Violet's hand like it was delicate as a butterfly. "I would have told you all this sooner, but I only put it all together right before the show."

"Sweet Jesus!" Violet drummed on her right knee with the fingers of her free hand. "Put what together?"

"Nell has a boyfriend. His name is Luke Valenti, and he is the son of—" Tristan paused for dramatic effect— "Lily Osterhaus."

"My darling Lily?" Violet's eyes misted over. "She lit up every room she waltzed into. Without her, The Four Blooms wouldn't have gotten half as far as we—hold on. Lily had the baby?"

"A little boy named Luke," Nell said. "But she died in childbirth."

"Wilda told us the Spanish Flu got her."

"Probably because Lily's father forced her to."

"Boris? Ugh! I couldn't stand that son of a bitch."

"When Lily died in childbirth, he took the baby to its father and said, 'Here, this kid is yours. You raise it.'"

"If that don't beat all." Violet shook her head. "How old is he now?"

"Twenty-four. He's an ensign in the Navy."

"Gosh, I'd love to meet him one day."

"So you can imagine my surprise when he popped up in a Movietone newsreel that Reggie shot in Boulder. I was at Fox to see if he could help me track down Luke. I have some news he needs to know—"

"That kid in the newsreel? On the university campus? *That* was Lily's boy?" Violet tried to blink away her tears. "Gosh darn it. Look at me with no handkerchief to mop up the waterworks." She dabbed at the corners of her eyes until Beatrice fished one from her purse. "Was Reggie able to help you?"

Squiggly little lines on the cover of college textbooks weren't exactly the lead Nell had been looking for. "It was a long shot."

"Isn't everything nowadays?" Violet fell back onto the sofa. "Oh, brother, do I ever need a whiskey right now. Is there not a drop of hooch permitted in this place?"

"Doesn't Bette keep a bottle stashed in one of her drawers?"

"We are *not* breaking into her desk," Nell said.

"We don't have to." Tristan pulled out a silver flask from the inside pocket of his red jacket.

"Bette'll kill you if she catches you with that!"

"Yeah, well, Miss Davis didn't have to follow Bob Hope and Miss Chica Chica Boom on stage tonight, did she?" He took a swig, then smiled as though he were Salomé holding the head of John the Baptist. "Anybody else?"

## 20

Nell lifted the gold five-point star out of a May Co. Home Décor box. "Natalie, would you like to do the honors?"

Betty's mother shook her head. "I might slip the ladder, knocking it all over the everything."

Nell found the woman's Romanian accent hard to penetrate sometimes, but her look of horror got the message across clear enough.

"Oh, Ma. What are you, ninety-three? It's a step stool."

Natalie tipped Bogie's Scottish terrier off her lap and rose from the sofa. She took the golden star from Nell and mounted the stool one step at a time.

Nell liked Betty's gentle-souled mother, but could tell she was overwhelmed at the path her daughter had embarked on. She suspected that Natalie hoped Hawks wouldn't cast her little girl in his next movie, and that Betty would accompany her on the train home to New York, where she could find work as a secretary, the way Natalie had. Businessmen always needed competent secretaries.

They stepped back to admire their handiwork trimming the fir tree they'd bought from a W.C. Fields-lookalike selling Christmas trees in an empty lot on Holloway Drive. "Is beautiful," Natalie said. "Now time for drink."

Minutes later, the three women were sitting on the Bogart sofa clinking Old Fashioneds.

"How long will they be gone?" Betty asked.

"Ten weeks in all, another six to go. The slower the better."

What a heavenly month it had been. An entire house, all to herself—not including the two Scottish terriers whose names she had trouble sorting out. Sleeping in the master bedroom didn't feel right, so Nell had settled into the nautical-themed guest room where Luke had lived after the boardinghouse fire.

Oh, the joy of spreading her makeup all over a bathroom. And a kitchen where she could eat what she wanted to eat—within the limits of ration coupons, of course. Plus, a dining room! A formal parlor! A library! Okay, so the chintz upholstery with the bold floral pattern wouldn't have been Nell's first choice. And the Nikolay Dubovskoy seascape was a little too bland. But who cared, when she could indulge in the unmitigated luxuriousness of it all?

What a shame her boardinghouse landlady couldn't hold her bed open for her. No, not even if she paid the room in advance for the entire time the Bogarts would be on their ragtag tour. "I got ten factory workers waiting for every bed in my house," Mrs. Carp had told her. Moving out had been a risk she might come to regret, but Nell intended to make the most of the next month and a half.

"You nervous?" she asked Betty.

"About what?"

"Howard may have decided which actress he's casting as Marie in *To Have and Have Not*. What better place to announce it than the Cocoanut Grove on Christmas Eve with your mom sitting next to you?"

"Ooooooooooh." Betty stretched the word over six syllables.

"Thaaaaaaaaat." Mischief ricocheted around her deadpan face. "I hadn't given it any thought."

Natalie swatted her daughter's knee. "Such a liar my daughter is. It is one month and one-half since you make the introduction to Mr. Bogart."

"Isn't it time we brushed our hair and checked our lipstick?" Betty leapt to her feet. "It'd be rude to keep the Hawks waiting."

\* \* \*

The monkeys sitting amid the fronds of the papier-mâché palm trees were stuffed toys. The stars in the night sky were tiny light bulbs screwed into a stucco ceiling painted midnight blue. This was where The Anointed were presented with their Academy Awards. Four-grand-a-week heavy-hitters ordered fifteen-dollar bottles of wine as though they were nickel bottles of Pepsi-Cola. Pretty girls flashed their perfect smiles at cigar-chomping studio bigwigs endowed with the power to elevate them from a sea of hopefuls.

The Hawkses weren't at their table, but that was okay because Tristan was. "Merry Christmas, you two good-time gals, and fare-thee-well, Mama Natalie." He greeted her with Continental flair—a kiss to each cheek—then pulled out a chair for her. "You'll never guess who's playing tonight."

"Those letters spelling out 'The Andrews Sisters' in the poster out front were hard to miss."

"Remember that evening at the Canteen when Violet and I slayed the GIs with our hilarious comedy number? One of them is the brother of the guy in charge of entertainment here. A week later they made Violet an offer of a four-week run."

"That's how Hollywood works most of the time," Nell told Betty. "Somebody spots somebody and thinks—"

But Betty wasn't listening. She had trained her eyes on the Cocoanut Grove's front doors.

Nell whispered, "Staring at the entrance won't make their car go any faster."

"What if he gives Marie to Ella Raines instead? Will he drop my contract? Do I start pounding the pavement? Or write off this experience as a gay lark and go home?"

"Darling," Tristan said, "it's seventy degrees outside in December and you're not buried up to your armpits in snow. That's a lot to be thankful for."

"You're right." Betty stroked her black cashmere evening wrap. "Worrying won't get me anywhere."

"You don't have to worry about getting cast tonight," said Slim, dropping her clutch onto the table. "Howard Hawks is AWOL. It's just me." She was dressed in a tight-fitting sheath of indigo blue shimmering with translucent bugle beads. "Victor Fleming called to invite us to an impromptu dinner party. Howard wanted to go because Johnny and Ginger Mercer are going to be there, as well as Hoagy and Ruth Carmichael and the Gary Coopers. I said we already had plans." She pulled a pack of Viceroy cigarettes from her purse, extracted one, and held it out for Tristan to light. "We got into a knock-down-drag-out fight, which ended with Howard storming out in the biggest huff since Napoleon lost at Waterloo." She blew a plume of smoke above their heads. "Whatever we're drinking tonight, order me a large one."

Nell watched the final embers of hope die out in Betty's eyes. "On our very first date," she told the group, "Luke ordered us champagne cocktails. I don't remember what's in them, but they sure were delicious."

The Paul Whiteman Orchestra filled the room with the opening bars of "You're the Top." Slim wriggled her fingers so that the sparkle in her enormous sapphire ring caught the attention of a passing waiter. "Please, sir, we're a desperate bunch."

* * *

They were halfway through their first round when Slim asked Nell if she had heard from Bogie. "Or have he and Mayo stabbed each other in some mud-soaked tent in Algiers?"

"I've had several V-mails," Nell told her. "Despite the crude conditions, the two of them are getting on famously—or so he says."

"It's remarkable how severe adversity can help bring a couple closer."

Was she referring to her own marriage? Howard had struck Nell as the taciturn type, a man who concentrated on his current film to the exclusion of everything—and everyone—else. "Do you think the Bogart marriage is salvageable?"

"God, no. It's liable to burst into flames, but not while they're roaming around the hell holes of northern Africa gnawing on K-rations and drinking whiskey distilled in a rusty bathtub by Mohammed from Tunisia." Slim turned to Betty. "I saw your screen test and have to say that you were absolutely marvelous in it."

Betty took one of the Viceroys Slim offered her. "I've never been so nervous in my life."

"It's all about how you come across on camera. Howard will tell you where to put your hands when the time comes."

"Are you saying she's got the role?" Nell prodded.

"If my husband weren't such a self-centered prig, he'd be here to field that question. But he thinks nothing of accepting subsequent invitations. And so, to quote Ralph Waldo Emerson—" she patted Betty's wrist as though she were a visiting aunt encouraging a favorite niece "—'Patience and fortitude conquer all things.'"

Betty let out a hoarse yip.

Tristan clapped his hands. "This calls for celebration with another round of these oh-so-delicious libations."

Over Tristan's shoulder, Nell spied a familiar silhouette at the bar. She excused herself and approached him.

She hadn't seen Gus O'Farrell around the studio much lately, which was unusual, as he always seemed to be everywhere. Tonight, though, he was slumped over a butterscotch-yellow cocktail in a martini glass.

"Hello stranger."

A moment or two passed before recognition sparked in his eyes. What a heck of a change from the self-assured braggart he used to be. She took the bar stool next to him as the orchestra started playing the *Thank Your Lucky Stars* theme song that had reached the top of the *Your Hit Parade* radio show. "It's Christmas Eve, but you don't look so merry."

"I had to get out of the house. Pop's condition, it—he—" Gus seized the glass like it was a lit firecracker and swilled a mouthful. Not all of it reached his mouth. "We hadda stick him in some booby hatch up north, near the Castaic prison farm." He stewed in his memories for a moment. "It's kinda pretty up there, not that he knows it."

"When did all this happen?"

"Yesterday."

She laid her hand on his. He didn't flinch as she expected he might. "No wonder you're down in the dumps."

"That man was always criticizing, never praising, always yelling, never encouraging. He was a monstrous father, and yet, when Mom and I drove away, I felt like my heart was getting pulled out of my chest."

"And your mom?"

"When we got home, she took a bottle of Hennessy into her bedroom and closed the door. I couldn't stand the thought of spending another minute in that house."

The bartender delivered a second yellow cocktail. Nell held it aloft. "Let's make a toast."

"To what?"

She pushed the half-empty coupe into his hand. "To a better 1944." She sipped the Sidecar. Back at her table, Tristan was holding court with popped eyes and puffed cheeks, and his arms twirling like aircraft propellers. As she swung back to Gus, a familiar face caught her eye.

It shouldn't have come as a surprise that Hedda Hopper was here. The Grove was one of her favorite haunts. And Nell might have pretended she hadn't seen her, but there was no ignoring the smirk plastered across the woman's face.

It said *I know something you don't know, but I know that you'll want to know it and I'm going to make you work for it.*

Slim whooped as Tristan reached the climax of his story. Nell watched Hedda, who glanced at the table, but only for a split second before returning to Nell.

Had Hedda learned who Hawks had cast? Surely he would tell Slim first. Or would he?

"How about you join us?" she asked Gus.

"I'm not fit for company right now. I'd spoil the festive mood. Thank you, though." He swiveled around to face the bar.

Message received loud and clear.

Nell downed the rest of the Sidecar and set off for Hedda's table, where she sat with three women, none of them familiar. Hedda got to her feet and intercepted Nell under a palm tree. "Follow me." She marched through the club's etched glass doors and into the Ambassador Hotel lobby, where she turned right past the check-in desk and the Colonial Room and went into the deserted Embassy Ballroom.

She closed the doors behind them. "I know where your boyfriend is."

The domed ballroom suddenly felt bigger than the Grand Canyon. Nell crossed her fingers behind her back. "Where?"

"In Colorado. Specifically, in—"

"Boulder."

"How could you—"

"More to the point, how do *you*?" Annoyance quivered across Hedda's pinched face as the elation of her scoop dissipated into the room's stuffy air. "It's not that I don't appreciate your efforts." *Even though I mistrust your motives.* "But how did you come by this information?"

Hedda lifted her chin. "I asked Edgar to do me a favor."

"Is this Edgar guy in the military?"

"My dear, I'm talking about J. Edgar Hoover. We're very close."

Nell staggered backward a half-step and then collected herself. "Isn't the location of military personnel a matter of national security?"

"I was thrilled when my boy, Bill, signed up. But then I learned he'd volunteered to join the Office of Strategic Services. Well! You can imagine how my maternal instincts kicked in."

As far as Nell could see, Hedda Hopper had all the maternal instincts of a bucket of donkey droppings.

"So I virtually begged Edgar to make enquiries. And then I thought of you and your beau, and how relieved you'd be to discover he's been studying at the naval school in Boulder. But you know all about that. If you ever get sick of studio PR, you'd make a great columnist."

Hedda wasn't the type to hand out compliments like penny candy. If only she knew that Nell's source had been a newsreel available to anyone with a quarter to spend on a ticket to the movies.

"Did Mr. Hoover tell you what he's been studying?" Nell asked.

"Aviation Communications, mostly." So the squiggly lines on the textbooks Reggie saw were—what? A modern version of Morse Code? "I was about to ask for more information, but then his telephone rang and he bustled me out of his hotel room."

"I guess I wasn't quite so well informed as I imagined."

"And yet far better than *I* imagined, so it all evens out." Hedda's usual tone, a spiky blend of snark and scorn, had made a swift comeback. "Ever heard of a lanternfish?"

Nell repeated the word in her mind, but came up blank. "No. Why?"

"Before Edgar tossed me out like a bag of food scraps, I read the memorandum concerning your boyfriend. When you do what I do for a living, you become adept at reading upside down. I couldn't see the whole thing, but that word leapt out because it was in capital letters. If I'd asked him, he'd have figured out I'd been reading documents marked 'For the eyes of Mr. Hoover only.'" She tapped her chin. "Lanternfish. A curious word, isn't it?"

Wisps of a Strauss waltz from the string quartet in the neighboring Colonial Room wafted in as the conversation between the two women died. After a few moments, Hedda said, "We should get back to our tables."

"Why did you go to the trouble of asking Hoover about Luke?" Nell didn't imagine that Hedda and Louella had much in common, but it came as no surprise that Hedda agreed with Louella's proclamation that PR department loyalties were to the columnists, not the studios. Nothing had come of Louella's 'A Day in the Life of a Hollywood Studio Publicity Agent' article, but Nell had to wonder if Hedda was playing a longer game. "I mean, why did you do that for *me*?"

"It's so heart-wrenching to have a loved one in the service, and I thought, 'He's already getting some lackey to make inquiries about Bill, so while he was at it . . .'" She scattered the rest of her explanation with a flittering hand.

*In other words, you're not going to tell me.* "I appreciate the gesture," Nell said. "Thank you. I really must get back out there. My table's probably organizing a search party."

"Mine, too."

The two women walked back into the Cocoanut Grove in silence.

## 21

*B*etty turned into the Wadsworth parking lot. "I hope Tony'll see you. It'd be a shame to waste your precious gas rations."

"I need to be able to tell Luke that I tried." Nell hated hearing the hesitation in her voice.

"It doesn't sound like he's received any of your letters."

Luke hadn't mentioned them in the V-mail that had arrived a few days ago. It was the least censored, but also oddly worded, as though he'd written it half-sauced. For all Nell knew, maybe he had.

*My dearest darling,*

*Forgive your sailor. He studies his uncertainties too closely in the night. Bigger than Colorado skies, they are, and now I wonder if we're finished. Have you at last transferred your tender, undying love to someone else?* ▪▪▪▪▪▪▪ ▪▪▪▪▪▪▪▪ ▪▪▪▪▪▪▪. *If you've reassigned your fond affectionate heart to someone else, I* ▪▪▪▪▪▪▪. ▪▪▪▪▪▪▪ *or deeper than a submarine and brighter than a lantern* ▪▪▪▪▪▪▪ ▪▪▪▪▪▪▪ *or* ▪▪▪▪▪▪▪ ▪▪▪▪▪▪▪ *with the fish.*

*Is it that I'm going crazy? I doubt, but toward it? I am nearly midway to feeling like an island. Many guys do too because their girlfriends don't write. I would really love right now to listen to you speak, even to briefly hear the feeling behind the language. Out of sight, out of mind? Is the distance between us our enemy?*

*Sorry for all the questions, but it's hard to know what's going on when I never hear from you.*

*Luke*

The way he'd signed off had cleaved Nell in two. Not "Love, Luke." Not "With all my undying love until I see you again." Just "Luke."

But she'd have to worry about that another time. For now, she had to focus on his brother. The manager at the Chapman Park Hotel had told Nell over the phone that they'd found nineteen bottles of Mount Gay rum lined up along the windowsill and Tony so catatonic that a bucket of ice water hadn't brought him around.

Nell and Betty headed up a wide flagstone path edged with lavender-and-white crocuses that led to the main building.

"Ah, yes. Valenti." The gaunt nurse on the front desk pinched her lips into a thin line.

"He was fine last time we saw him," Nell said. "They had fitted him with a new wooden leg—"

"We prefer the term 'prosthetic.'"

"He was very pleased with how well he could get around."

"Most of them leave here, never to be seen again."

"But the others?"

"A new prosthetic gives them increased mobility, but the reality of the rest of their lives comes crashing in on them. It took us a week to dry him out."

"Since then?"

The nurse see-sawed her hands. "You'll find him working in our victory garden with Gunnery Sergeant Muir."

"Does Gunnery Sergeant Muir have a first name?"

"Hollis, but don't expect much in the way of conversation." The nurse's lips relapsed into that grim line again. "He took a ton of shrapnel to the stomach on Guadalcanal. The corpsman who attended to him in the field did a first-rate job patching him up, and he was recovering quite nicely. At first, that is."

"And now?"

"Time doesn't always heal all wounds."

Tony was leaning on a pitchfork, its prongs embedded deep in the earth. Even with his thick jacket keeping out the winter chill, his concave torso looked like a hollowed-out tree trunk.

Nell cupped her hands to her mouth. "Ahoy there, sailor!" She waved, hoping the 'ahoy' greeting hadn't sounded too corny. He straightened up but didn't wave back.

His face had taken on a lean pallor. The eyes, once so like Luke's, now shone with a sharp austerity. They belonged on a self-flagellating monk, not a Brooklyn roofer who loved the New York Yankees more than he loved his beer.

"Hello, Tony," Betty said.

His forced smile came out a little on the wishy-washy side, but he was making an effort. "Did Gable fall madly in love with you?"

"Barely looked sideways at me," Betty said, with an I-don't-care shrug. "It was more fun writing to my family about it. I'm not sure they believed me, because meeting Clark Gable is pure fantasy when you're a brat from Brooklyn."

A spark of curiosity glistened in Tony's eyes. "Brooklyn, huh? I don't think I knew that."

"Ocean Parkway. You're Bensonhurst, right?"

This girl has no idea how much charm she oozes from every pore, Nell thought. Magnetism can't be conjured up out of nothing. Either you've got it or you don't. And whether this so-called brat from Brooklyn knows it or not, it radiates out of her like heat from a bakery."

Tony's eyes dimmed. "Sixty-seventh and Sixteenth."

Nell gestured toward the five-foot corn stalks swaying in the sea breezes off Santa Monica. "This looks very healthy—unlike the victory garden at my boardinghouse. All us girls working on that woeful patch of doom, and not one of us knows what we're doing."

Tony frowned. "Hollis's handiwork. I'm just helping out. Keeps me busy."

Nell ventured a step closer. "I got a call from your doctor."

"I wondered why you were here."

"He told me about the Chapman Park incident."

Tony pulled the pitchfork toward himself. The prongs dislodged a mound of dank earth. "Last time you saw me, I was at the top of the roller coaster. My new leg fitted me real good; I was proud of Betty's hair; felt like I was on my way. But I forgot that when you get to the peak of the Coney Island Cyclone, down, down, down you go. Then you go up again. Some days I'm go-get-'em-cowboy. But other days I'm so damn glum, it's all I can do to get out of bed. Then there are the days I can't be trusted with a razor blade."

He said nothing for a few strained moments as his knuckles blanched around the handle of the pitchfork. When he looked up, it was at Betty. "That afternoon at your swell apartment, doing your hair, and your pal was reading from the *L.A. Times*—it was one of the best days of my life."

Betty stepped closer, ignoring the freshly turned dirt muddying her white shoes. "We were just goofing around. I needed the distraction; otherwise, my nerves might have gotten the better of me. It wasn't at that party ten seconds before I realized that Slim Hawks invited me so that Howard could see how I handled myself in the major leagues."

Tony's mouth opened and closed like a goldfish's.

"Was it doing hair that made you feel good?" Nell prompted.

"From the moment I picked up those scissors. Twenty years of roofing and I never felt the way I did that day."

"What if you could do it all the time?"

"What are you saying?"

Should she even be suggesting this? It seemed cruel to get his hopes up when Bogie or Perc Westmore or any of the front-office bigwigs could nix her idea. But this man needed a reason to stay away from his razor blade. Shoveling dirt and weeding corn stalks weren't going to do it.

Nell chose her words with care. "Humphrey Bogart wears a toupée. His regular person has returned to Arizona. He needs someone new."

"Don't movie studios have people for that?"

"He doesn't want to rely on them. Bogie's on a USO tour, but he'll need a replacement when he gets back."

"Doing Betty's hair for a date is one thing, but a toupée? I've never touched one." He tugged at his thick, Italian locks. "Cue balls don't exactly run in the family."

"I'm minding the Bogarts' house while they're away. He keeps all four of his rugs in his bathroom. What if you came over to study them? See what they look like. How you apply them. Style them. When Bogie gets home, he'll have one less worry."

He jammed his hands into his pockets. "I'm on board with it if Mr. Bogart is."

"I can't recommend you if there's any chance you'll disappear on a bender. Waking up in a hotel room with nineteen bottles of Mount Gay is a foolproof way to get yourself fired."

"I get it."

"It also means Bogie won't trust *me* ever again." Okay, so that last one might not have been true, but Nell wouldn't blame Bogie if he didn't.

"A job like this would give me hope."

Finally, a smile. Not just any smile, but the shy, almost bashful sort that Nell had last seen on Luke the day he went to war and asked if she would write to him.

She fished into her purse for the small notepad she kept with her in case she overheard a witty comeback she could use in advertising copy. She wrote down Bogie's address and telephone number. "Tuesday night," she said, tearing off the page. "Seven o'clock?"

"Come hell or high water." He tucked the slip into the pocket of his grimy dungarees. "Speaking of high water, what's the latest from our favorite ensign?"

"The Navy has sent him back to school."

"Studying what?"

"Do you know what Aviation Communications means?"

Tony ran a hand over his two-day stubble. "Could be anything from radio operator to cryptanalyst."

"What's that?"

"Codebreaker."

Nell gasped softly. When Captain Vance had been talking to Luke about getting his 4-F overturned, he'd mentioned how cracking the German–Japanese codes could be a turning point.

"Those Japs are cunning little sonsabitches. I hate their guts even more than I hate Red Sox fans, but they're real smart, so we had to be smarter. We used codewords for everything."

"Was 'lanternfish' one of them?"

Tony rubbed his stubble again. "Not so's I recall. Why?"

Nell thought quickly. Hoover had broken military confidentiality by sharing information with Hedda. A situation like that could get out of hand if too many people knew about it. "Luke was mentioned in a Navy report that also included the word 'lanternfish' in capital letters."

"Like it was a name?"

Nell looked at Betty, who was already staring at her. *That possibility didn't occur to us.* "A ship?"

"Close, but no cigar."

This unfamiliar voice was raspy and grating, as though this person had read *The Robe* out loud seventeen times over. The corn stalks parted, revealing a man in dungarees even filthier than Tony's. Half the buttons were missing from his sun-faded shirt. He'd torn off the sleeves, exposing both arms to the chilled air. His skin was beetroot red and pitted with deep pockmarks. A long, angry welt snaked around his left elbow. Another one started at his chin and slashed a wide path across his cheek before disappearing around the top of his left ear.

"This is my pal, Hollis Muir," Tony said. "Hollis, this is my brother's girlfriend, Nell. And this here's Betty."

Nell stuck out her hand. "Pleased to meet you." Muir looked at it, but didn't shake it. His left eye had almost completely clouded over. "The nurse at the front desk told us that you were a gunnery sergeant at Guadalcanal like Tony. Is that where you met?"

"You might say," Muir replied, his voice low and hoarse.

Nell wasn't sure how they'd veered onto a touchy subject. "So you were saying about lanternfish?"

Muir nodded. "The Navy's built an improved model of submarine. Goes faster, stays underwater longer. Torpedoes shoot further with greater accuracy. My pal was on the design team in Groton, Connecticut. Says they'll change the course of the war."

"How close are they to launching them?" Nell asked.

"All six of them plunged into Elliott Bay off the Seattle coast a couple of weeks ago."

"And how do lanternfish fit into all this?"

"It's a type of critter that only lives in the deepest parts of the pond. Could be your boyfriend is someplace under in the Pacific Ocean on the USS *Lanternfish*."

Nell thought of Luke's recent letter. *Deeper than a submarine and brighter than a lantern.* Was that what he meant?

## 22

Nell checked the Bogarts' kitchen clock. Just gone ten a.m. The Super Chief was due into Union Station at nine. Assuming the usual gang of reporters greeted them, plus the drive to West Hollywood, she figured Bogie and Mayo wouldn't be pulling into the driveway until at least ten-thirty, which gave her enough time to read Hedda's column.

Most of the eleven columnists she tracked each day toed the party line by regurgitating the press releases that people like Nell drafted to ensure the status quo: Everything's dandy! The picture is pure delight! Actor X and Actress Y are a marvelous screen pairing!

And then there was The Mighty Quartet: Sheilah Graham, Kathryn Massey, Louella Parsons, and Hedda Hopper. They had enough power to write whatever they damn well pleased. Generally speaking, Sheilah and Kathryn wrote columns that didn't make Nell want to set fire to her eyeballs. But Louella and Hedda were a whole other matter, which is why Nell left them to last.

She pushed the *Examiner* along the breakfast nook with the other newspapers and opened the *Times* to Hedda's "Looking at Hollywood" column.

. . .

*Arriving home from battle-scarred Italy today are the Battle-Scarred Bogarts. Here in L.A., Bogie and Mayo slugging it out on the dance floor at Ciro's is pretty much an everyday sight, but those poor New Yorkers never knew what hit 'em. And hit 'em and hit 'em and hit 'em. What a shame all that terrific goodwill they accrued on their USO tour gurgled down the drain as soon as they planted their feet on Manhattan asphalt. I hope the Gotham Hotel whacked them with a huge bill to cover the damages. Next time, he'll think twice about wrecking someone else's property.*

Cripes, Bogie. You and Mayo held the truce through torrential downpours, muddy bivouacs, primitive latrines, canned-meat dinners, and toilet paper shortages.

This was not the ideal press for an actor who was about to start an important movie based on a Hemingway novel and directed by the man who'd scored three hits in a row. Nell wanted to take Bogie by the shoulders and beg him to not throw away everything he'd worked so hard for.

The crunch of tires on the driveway gravel seeped through the open kitchen window. Nell ran to the foyer and yanked open the front door. "WELCOME HOME!"

Mayo's surly mood pulled the edges of her thin lips toward her sagging chin. "Deal with the bags yourself, you stinkin' pile of beaver shit." She marched past Nell without so much as a cursory once-over.

A half-smoked cigarette dangling from his mouth, Bogie emitted a weary grunt as the taxi driver popped the trunk. Tucked inside were a dark blue traveling trunk, two mismatched, medium-sized suitcases, and four pieces of hand luggage.

"You didn't cart all this around the Sahara, did you?"

Another grunt. "Just the suitcases. Madam accumulated the rest on the mother of all New York shopping sprees."

Nell waited until the taxi had backed away. "So the rumors are true, then?"

Bogie spat what was left of his cigarette onto the gravel. "Depends on what they say."

"The tour was a success, but then you guys got to New York and things grew—" *Choose your words carefully, Davenport.* "—combative."

"We spent two and a half months in appalling conditions you wouldn't wish on Himmler, and yet our troops endure them every day. Hundreds and hundreds of them. I tell you, Nell, they're the greatest bunch of lads you'll ever meet. Performing our crummy little third-rate act under tents and lean-tos was the finest experience of my life." His eyes shifted toward the house. "Even Madam would agree."

"So what changed?" Nell asked.

"Our taxi driver from the dock in New York told us the big news story about how they need alcohol to make ordnance, so nobody has distilled hard liquor since November. America's got only two hundred million gallons of whiskey to last us till the end of the war."

"So you went out and drank all the whiskey you could."

He treated her to a one-shoulder shrug and self-deprecating smile. "Seemed a good idea at the time." A white rock the size of an underfed golf ball had found its way onto the driveway. Bogie kicked it. It flew in a low arc, hit the curb, and shot across Horn Avenue. "I need a new car, and I want to get it before production starts on the new picture."

Nell narrowed her eyes. "I thought only doctors, police officers, essential war workers, and traveling salesmen were allowed to buy new cars."

"You must know by now there's always a way to get around anything."

It must be nice to swim around the top of the Hollywood food chain. "But you start filming on Monday."

"Today's Saturday and I'm not sure the Cadillac lot is open on Sundays."

"You want to go shopping *today?*"

"Madam usually comes along for her two cents' worth, but right now, I want to throttle the life out of her." Bogie flinched when he pulled his hands from his pockets. The knuckles on his right hand were raw and scraped. The fingernail of his pinkie was the color of overripe plums and would fall off before long.

Nell picked up one of the suitcases. "We should at least bring your luggage in first."

\* \* \*

Bogie told Nell to turn left onto Wilshire. "Cadillac is about ten blocks down. Now that we're back, I guess you'll be moving back into your boardinghouse?"

The whole time the Bogarts had been away, Nell had searched for another place to live. It seemed like every day LA's housing shortage grew worse. The words she'd heard over and over were "No Vacancies." As the end of her luxurious stay at Casa Bogart grew closer, her only prospect was to move into Luke's berth on the *Arabella*. It had only been two days ago that Nell had called her landlady and asked for a bed—well, begged, really, for any bed. She didn't care where. Mrs. Carp eventually agreed to shove a camp bed in the corner of the attic—where four other cots were already accommodating six other girls in a rotating hotbed arrangement. It was better than nothing—but barely.

"Yep." This wasn't subject she wanted to dwell on. "I've solved your toupée problem."

"I wasn't aware I had one."

"Unless Verita is back in Los Angeles."

Bogie ran his thumb along the crease of his trousers. His hands and feet had been in continuous motion from the second he'd climbed into the car. "You've found someone?"

"Luke's brother."

"The gunnery sergeant does hair?"

"Slim Howard invited your fresh-faced co-star to a dinner party and Tony fixed her hair. Betty was so pleased she didn't care much that Clark Gable scarcely looked at her."

"Gable, huh? Little Betty Brooklyn isn't wasting any time."

"I'm warning you now, Mr. B., it would be a mistake to think she's just another empty-headed tenderfoot." A huge blue-and-white neon sign—*WILSHIRE CADILLAC*—towered over the sidewalk. Nell pulled into the lot. "Tony lost a leg at Guadalcanal and has had trouble adjusting. He needs a decent break."

"You should clear it with Perc Westmore. I don't want his nose out of joint."

She had already won Perc over. Maintaining Humphrey Bogart's toupées wouldn't be a full-time job, so Tony would be free to help out wherever he was needed. "I'll tell him to be at the studio at seven."

They got out of the Packard and surveyed the sparse scattering of Cadillacs. Now that car manufacturers were churning out aircraft and tanks, no new American automobiles had been manufactured in three years.

Bogie gravitated toward a four-door sedan. "Any word from Luke?"

Nell decided to lead with the least worrying news. "He turns twenty-five today."

"If I'd known, I'd have sent a gift to Montauk."

"You—uh . . . he's not—" Nell hadn't expected tears to spring to her eyes. She dug around her purse for a handkerchief.

"Luke's okay, isn't he?"

She found a scrap of lace, more like a doily, and about as helpful for mopping up these tears she wished she could stop. "I might be wrong. The evidence is circumstantial at best, cobbled together from several sources. None of which I can trust." *Damn these tears. Why are they coming now, when I'm standing in the middle of a car lot?*

"And what does this untrustworthy, circumstantial evidence point to?"

"A submarine," Nell replied. "In the Pacific."

"Holy cow."

"I assumed he was tucked away in some makeshift lean-to eavesdropping on the Germans. What if it's like *Destination Tokyo?*"

He laid his hands on her shoulders. "Shush . . . shush," he murmured. "The Pacific is a mighty big place."

"But the Japs control most of it, and—"

"Are you forgetting Midway and the Solomons?"

"The nearer we close in, the harder they'll fight."

She dumped her useless doily into her purse and dabbed at her eyes with a pinkie finger. She spotted a guy in a cheap suit of dark blue serge, no tie, no hat, ostensibly perusing the vehicles. "Tony's got a pal at Wadsworth. Hollis is a gunnery sergeant who got shot up at Guadalcanal, too. He knows a guy who helped design the Navy's new-and-improved model, so . . ."

There wasn't any end to her sentence, so she let it dissipate in the afternoon air. The hatless guy had looked in their direction a half-dozen times. He was browsing, but not for a Cadillac.

Bogie said, "How about I start at the western end and work my way east? You go east and work west, and we'll compare notes in the middle."

He took off toward the far end of the lot. Nell pretended to look inside the nearest Cadillac. Mister Hatless Blue Serge was now two vehicles away. He lacked the slack-jawed, eager-beaver halo of a typical Bogie admirer. There was a cautious skulking to the way he crept from one car to the next, almost sideways, like a crab hungry for dead shrimp. He slunk to a burgundy convertible, his eyes still trained on Bogie, when a salesman approached him to ask if he needed any assistance.

*Oh my gosh!*

Nell wasn't sure. Not a hundred percent. But she was more than fairly sure.

She waited for the salesman to retreat to his office before she stepped out, blocking his path. "You're Jaik Rosenstein, aren't you?"

"I might be."

"I saw you with your boss at the *Casablanca* opening. And again when the Hollywood Canteen's one-millionth guest walked in."

He appraised her with the usual once-over. "You have me at a disadvantage."

"We've spoken a few times. I'm Nell Davenport, from Warners."

Now that she had caught him out, Hedda's right-hand man smiled. "That night at the Canteen sure was memorable." He casually crossed his arms. "That lucky bastard got himself smooched by Grable, Dietrich, Turner, *and* Durbin."

The atmosphere had crackled with excitement in the hour-long lead-up to Emmeline counting each uniform through the door. When Sergeant Bell arrived, a roar had ignited that Nell guessed could have been heard in a three-block radius.

"Why are you here?" she asked.

"Shopping for a car."

"Hogwash. You're here to spy on Bogie. For Hedda."

"You're free to think whatever you like. As am I."

"What's that supposed to mean?"

"From where I was standing, it looked like Humphrey Bogart was hopped up on pep pills. Benzedrine, I assume. It sure explains trashing their hotel room."

Even though Rosenstein had jumped chasms of conclusions, Nell couldn't blame him for wondering why Bogie had been a touch on the jittery side. Whoever heard of shopping for a car the day you returned home after being away for three months? Nell suspected that the past week with Mayo had been far worse than Bogie had let on, but she wasn't about to admit that to Hedda's legman.

"You'd be antsy, too, if you'd spent ten weeks roughing it around a war zone, overdid it once you got back to the States, and then spent four days cooped up in a train compartment. And besides, Benzedrine isn't Bogie's thing. Everybody in Hollywood knows he's a whiskey man."

"Yeah, you're right. That bennie crack was a cheap shot."

Despite the mute up-and-down appraisal Rosenstein gave her, Nell liked this guy. His suit cried out for a professional pressing, his shoes needed a skilled bootblack, and his face had the crumpled furrows of a flunky who'd witnessed more of the seedy side of life than he'd ever planned on. But for all that, he lacked his boss's brittle grandstanding and knee-jerk judgments. In fact, he had a certain charm about him. Disheveled and a little careworn around the edges, perhaps. But not without appeal.

She softened her tone. "How come you're stalking Bogie like he's the lead suspect in a murder case?"

He took a moment to weigh his options, but from the way his mouth relaxed into a knowing grin, Nell knew she could probably believe whatever was about to come out of him.

"Have you read Hedda's coverage of the Motion Picture Alliance for the Preservation of American Ideals?"

Who hadn't? Over the past couple of weeks, Hedda had ensured her readers had heard about a new organization of self-proclaimed patriots who'd decided that commies and fascists were infiltrating Hollywood. They had decided it was high time someone showed the world that Hollywood wasn't an unrestrained hotbed of liberals, libertines, leftists, and lotharios.

"Of course I have."

"Do you think Bogie will join them?"

"You knew the answer to that question before you asked."

His aw-shucks expression fell away. "Do you remember the Dies Committee hearings?"

"Not really."

"It was a government committee looking at the infiltration of Bolsheviks and communists—real, imagined, alleged, and/or rumored—into the American way of life. Hedda was obsessed with it, and when Bogart was named a suspected commie, she kicked up a ruckus like you wouldn't believe until he got subpoenaed as their star witness."

"When was this?"

"He had to take time away from shooting *High Sierra* up in the Sierra Nevadas, so that must have been in 1940. When he took the stand, Bogie was three miles past furious. To his credit—and I gotta say, I admired him for it—he delivered such a blistering testimony that Dies' case collapsed, forcing the bastard to declare that there was no evidence connecting either Bogart or any of the others to the Communist Party."

"I bet Hedda took that real well."

"Fit to be tied. Soon after that, Bogart gave up his policy of staying neutral when it came to politics and joined the campaign to reelect FDR—"

"—whom Hedda hates, loathes, and detests."

"She's never forgiven him for it."

"All this because of a grudge?"

"Of monumental proportions."

She watched as Bogie stepped into the sales office. If she got rid of Rosenstein while he was signing the papers, Bogie could drive home in an improved mood with which to face whatever potpourri of ugly temper and caustic putdowns Mayo had in store for him.

"I can't go back to Boss Lady empty-handed," Rosenstein said. "If you're going to block my access to him, you need to give me a something I can take back to the office."

"He starts shooting his next picture on Monday."

"Hemingway's *To Have and Have Not*, directed by Howard Hawks. It ain't news."

"What do you know about his leading lady?"

"Newcomer, right?"

"Oh boy, what a firecracker."

He pulled out a notepad and pen. "I'm listening."

"Lauren Bacall is fresh, but world-weary. Excited, but plays it cool. And she's got a voice on her like nobody else."

"You've seen her screen tests?"

"I have."

"How does she come across?"

Most performers were easy to describe. Betty Grable was the new Alice Faye. Carole Lombard was the new Mabel Normand. But every now and then, an original came along, quite unlike anyone who had come before her. Nell hunted around for the right way to describe her until she landed on the perfect snippet: "Lauren Bacall is the female Humphrey Bogart."

* * *

Hedda must have thought Nell's snippet was quotable because she'd used it the next day in her squib about Humphrey Bogart shopping for a Cadillac. But it was a heck of a heavy yoke to hang around the neck of a nineteen-year-old neophyte.

Nell headed for the line of temporary dressing rooms set up along Stage Twenty-Eight's western wall. They weren't much more than tents with wooden doors set into a makeshift frame, but they offered Betty a tiny oasis of tranquility where she could pull herself together. She paced back and forth like a lioness in a circus cage.

"Nervous?" Nell asked.

Betty pulled at the sleeves of the striped robe "What's three notches above 'nervous'?"

For her very first scene, Hawks had cunningly chosen to film the one he had selected for Betty's screen test so that she would be familiar with the material and could focus on hitting her mark and staying in her key light.

"You've already played this scene. It's a terrific one. Lots of zippy banter."

"That was with some anonymous guy in Howard's office. But on a set? In front of a huge camera and dozens of crewmembers? Playing opposite Humphrey Bogart?" She caught the grin on Nell's face. "What's so funny?"

Nell slung her arm around the girl's shoulders. "You're the ultimate Miss Cool Cucumber."

"It's an act!" Betty insisted. "On the inside, I'm pure Jell-O."

"It's *all* an act. That's why they call it 'acting.'"

Betty's reply caught in her throat. She managed only a croaky squawk. "Howard towers over me. And that monotone way he speaks. It's so measured, so controlled. I never know what he's thinking."

Nell thought of Michael Curtiz's on-set theatrics: the yelling, throwing his script across the set, the Tuesday afternoon girls. "There are worse directors you could be making your film debut with. A lot worse."

"When I get out there, I'll be shaking worse than a leaf in a squall. I couldn't get my head to stop quaking during the screen test."

"Not once did I see your face bouncing like a basketball."

"I found that if I lowered my chin toward my throat, I could control it a little."

"Do that, then."

"And look at Bogart through the tops of my eyes?"

"It'll make you look sultry."

"I'm about as sultry as last month's gefilte fish."

"Maybe you're not, but Marie is."

Betty froze, her mouth closing as she digested Nell's observation.

"I'm going to check on Bogie now," Nell said. "I'll be out there if you need me, but I don't think you will."

A sign saying *BOGART* hung outside a dressing room two doors down. Inside it, Bogie sat at his makeup vanity. Tony stood behind him, comb in one hand, hairbrush in the other.

"My, oh my! It's seamless." Nell hadn't told Bogie how Tony had already practiced a dozen times in the Horn Avenue bathroom. She threw a soft punch at Tony's shoulder. "You professional hairdresser, you."

Bogie stood up and reached for the dark jacket on a hanger suspended from a coat rack. He winked as he checked his reflection in the mirror. "See you guys out there."

Nell was pleased to see that Tony's face had recovered from the ghastly pallor it had taken on the last time she'd seen him.

"You've saved my life," he said quietly.

"Hey! Leave the hyperbole to the PR people."

"I was in a bad way when you came to see me." The chords in his neck bulged as he strained to stop his lower jaw from trembling. "But look at where I am now."

"Your God-given talent got you here; all I did was goad things along. Come on. It's time you witnessed your first movie take."

She hooked her arm through his, but he resisted. "I was hoping for a favor—or rather, for my cornfield buddy."

"Hollis?"

"I don't suppose you know Mary Astor?"

"We've worked on a couple of pictures together."

"He's had a crush on her since they went to high school in Quincy, Illinois. It would perk him up if you could arrange for her to visit. The poor bastard's going through a real rough patch."

"Would he come to the Hollywood Canteen? I've seen her there several times."

"Gosh, I dunno." Tony rubbed the back of his neck. "He's not too sociable these days."

"Mary's a darling; I'm sure we can come up with an idea that'll work." Nell hooked his arm again. "Let's go. Betty needs moral support."

Hoagy Carmichael was passing Bogie's dressing room as they stepped outside. Hawks had cast him in *To Have and Have Not* as Cricket, the pianist in the hotel where much of the action played out. Lanky and laid-back, with an easy smile and an affable laugh, his casting had been newsworthy, and Nell had met with him a couple of times to help shape press releases and magazine copy.

Nell introduced the two men as they made their way to the set of Bogie's character's hotel room. They settled into a line of chairs as Hawks prepared for the first take.

Betty took her position and looked at Nell, her eyes wild with dread. With slow deliberation, Nell touched her index finger to the tip of her chin and guided it toward her throat. Betty took a deep breath and copied Nell's movement.

When Hawks called "Action," Betty launched into her speech about how Steve wasn't so hard to figure, and how sometimes she knew what he was going to say. By the time she had delivered a line about Bogie being a stinker, she had lowered herself into his lap. As she planted a kiss on his lips, a lock of her hair fell between them and the camera. The kiss lingered longer than Nell expected —and Bogie too, if his expression, part startled, part pleased, was anything to go by.

They had some banter about whether Betty's Marie had enjoyed kissing Bogie's Steve, and how she needed to go in for a second opinion. This time, the kiss lasted even longer. Bogie responded by clamping his arms around her. But only for a moment before she pulled back, got to her feet, and walked away from the camera, turning around only when she reached Steve's hotel room door. More banter. More innuendo. More heat. She opened the door with her chin tucked downward. The next line was Betty's. It was the best line of the scene, and if she could pull it off, Nell knew the rest of the movie was going to be a breeze. Well, not a breeze, perhaps, but not an overwhelming ordeal.

She held her breath as Betty leered at her co-star and delivered the line about knowing how to whistle.

"And cut!"

Nell turned to Hoagy. "Did you see what I just saw?"

## 23

The lobster-red counter at the Seven Seas bar opposite Grauman's matched its stools. Nell chose the last three. "You ever been to one of these Polynesian places?"

Betty took in the rattan mats and hand-painted vistas of palm trees and tropical lagoons, the tiki masks and colored glass buoys suspended from the ceiling by fishing nets of knotted twine. "Chang's Chop Suey House is about as exotic as Brooklyn gets." The bartender slung a couple of menus toward them. She ran down the list of choices. "Samoan Delight? Shark's Tooth? What are these, witch doctor voodoo spells?" She tapped the second one down. "I've always wondered what a daiquiri is."

Nell ordered two frozen daiquiris, then stroked Betty's lapel. "This looks new."

"I got embarrassed showing up to the set in the same three outfits. And then I realized I'm earning a hundred bucks a week. I don't know about you, but to me, that's a fortune. So when Tristan suggested shopping at I. Magnin's, I went on a mini spree."

Nell's sixty a week was a fortune to her, too. After sending a sizable chunk of it to South Bend, she had never felt like she was rolling in clover, though. "This jacket should last you for years."

A ukulele's gentle strumming filtered through the loudspeakers as a deep male voice sang about the surf on Waikiki Beach and pining for a life beyond the reef. At least he didn't have to deal with co-workers talking all day about Hedda Hopper's announcement that she'd be at Pearl Harbor to commemorate the attack's third anniversary. There seemed to be no getting away from the woman.

The bartender presented them with their cocktails and eyed the empty stool beside Betty.

When Nell had asked Avery Osterhaus to join them, he'd sounded distracted. He didn't strike her as the fickle type, but between the mercurial war news in Europe and the Pacific, food rationing, fuel shortages, blackouts, brownouts, and every other person working round-the-clock shifts, life hadn't been predictable in a very long time. She clinked her glass to Betty's.

They sipped their daiquiris. "Lime and . . ." Betty sipped again. "Oranges?"

"Curaçao." Nell deposited her cocktail on the bright red counter and prepared herself to pose the question she'd been wanting to ask for a week. "So," she said mildly, "are you still pulling your chin down to keep the nerves at bay?"

Betty ran a fingertip around the rim of her glass. "Howard thinks holding my face at that angle creates a mysterious look, so now he gets me to slant it that way in most of my scenes. Some days I have such a crick in my neck. Still, if it looks good . . ."

"You haven't seen any dailies?"

Betty shook her head. "Howard says he doesn't want me to feel inhibited. Why? Have you?"

"I might've snuck into one or two."

"And?"

Nell did her best to whistle like a lecherous sailor on shore leave. "Your scenes crackle and pop—and then some."

Betty's eyes shone in the sunset-tinged mood lighting.

"And Bogie?" Nell asked. "How's he treating you?"

"Such a doll. Keeping me relaxed, clowning around. He loves it when I dish it right back at him." Betty broke eye contact and tried another sip of her drink. "He's taken me under his wing."

"And how is it, snuggled under there?"

Betty let out a girlish giggle, despite her newly earned raspy voice. "Is it that obvious?"

"I watched your first take, remember?"

"When he kissed me, he really *kissed* me! So when Marie goes in for a second smooch, I—" She bugged out her eyes.

"You smooched him back."

"I couldn't help myself!"

"You helped yourself to a great, big slice of Humphrey Bogart pie."

"It's a crush." Betty grabbed her daiquiri with two hands as though it might fly away. "And anyway, he's so much older. *And* married."

"But what if Bogie makes a move on you?"

Her head shot up. "Do you think he would?"

Nell lifted a nonchalant shoulder as if she'd never wondered what might grow out of their palpable chemistry. "You're gorgeous; he's human."

"I'dbepowerlesstosayno!" Betty blurted out her response in a single-word confession.

Bogie's trouble, Nell knew, was that he thought of himself as "a last-century guy" who took his vows seriously, but was trapped in a marriage that was anything but mutually adoring. The Battling Bogarts were poison to each other and, she feared, were heading straight for the final scene from *Romeo and Juliet*.

Nell studied fresh-faced Betty, with her mix of guileless naivete and candid temptress, and wondered how long Bogie could hold back.

Rumors of the stars of Warner Bros.' upcoming *To Have and Have Not* setting the screen on fire were usually the product of a

PR department's fervent imagination. But this time it was real. Anybody with functioning eyeballs could tell that.

Including Hedda Hopper, who had a finely tuned antenna for hanky-panky. She hadn't yet called in her favor for securing Nell's PR job, but it was only a matter of time. If Hedda ever found out that Nell knew of a Bogart–Bacall affair and hadn't told her about it, there would be hell to pay. And her hell exacted an exorbitant price.

"Good evening, ladies."

Nell hadn't seen Avery since the night of Luke's wild dash to Union Station. He was squarer in the jaw than she remembered. And the gray flecking at his temples lent him a distinguished air he hadn't possessed before. But how could she have forgotten that he had Luke's eyes? That exact same shade of hazel brown. And Luke's Roman nose. His lips were shaped like Luke's, too. She swallowed a wave of longing to hear Luke's voice as she introduced him to Betty and waited until he'd ordered a Rob Roy.

"How are things with you these days?"

He settled onto his bar stool. "I've rented my house on Norton to eight women who work various shifts at Northrup, sewing parachutes and bolting propellers into place. They're earning tons of dough and pay me a small fortune."

"Sounds like the plot for a racy farce starring Eddie Bracken and a bunch of Goldwyn Girls," Betty said.

"I wish!"

He contrived the semblance of a smile that fooled no one. If Nell couldn't be around Luke, this guy was a more-than-decent substitute. "But what did you do with all those—" she hadn't told Betty about Avery's forgery skills "—tools of your trade?"

"I've gone legit." He lifted his Rob Roy. "I even pay my taxes fair and square."

"Welcome to society." Nell clinked his cocktail glass. "Who reformed you?"

"I got a too-good-to-turn-down job offer at Universal. A pal of mine is fighting in France, so I sublet his apartment in Toluca Lake and spend my days painting posters and backdrops. Right now, I'm working on *Sherlock Holmes in Washington*. Evidently, we're ignoring how Basil Rathbone was a Victorian Londoner."

"That's ludicrous," Betty exclaimed, "but anything for the war effort."

"Speaking of," Avery said, "did my handiwork have the desired outcome for Luke?"

"It did," Nell said. "He's in the Navy now."

"I'm happy for him," Avery said. "He was keen to do his bit."

"I have some other news."

"Oh, yeah?"

"It's about your father. Did you know he passed away?"

Avery's face froze. He didn't even blink. The plinkety-plink music changed into a slide guitar–backed torch song about how 'aloha' means 'welcome and goodbye.'

"Luke told me that you and your dad hadn't spoken in years, so I wondered if anybody had—"

"How did you find out?"

"His lawyer sent Luke a letter care of Warner Bros. The mailroom guy gave it to me. It looked important, so I opened it."

This awkwardness now enveloping them was why Nell hadn't rushed to track down Avery and tell him of Boris's passing. But Violet Beaudine had contacted Nell, asking to meet with Lily's brother and wondering if she could bring him to the Seven Seas, where she was now the featured singer in their floor show.

"The old bastard stuck it to me until the very end." Avery drained the last of his Rob Roy, then joggled his glass at the bartender. "Tell me, is Violet the one I keep hearing on the radio?"

A talent scout from Decca Records had seen her perform at the Cocoanut Grove, and shortly after, had booked her to record a song called "When My Boy Helps to Liberate Gay Paree." It was an audition piece, but it had turned out so well, Decca had released it. And now every radio station along the West Coast had picked it up.

Nell exhaled a silent breath of relief that they'd skimmed over a pit of potential emotional quicksand. "Yep, that's her." A fast-moving blur of wafting mauve georgette caught Nell's eye. "And here she is."

Violet folded Avery into her arms and crushed him to her substantial bosom. "Don't make me cry!" Avery's muffled response came from somewhere deep in her cleavage. She clutched his shoulders and thrust him to arm's length. "I'd have known you were her brother from clear across Hollywood Boulevard. All I can see is my precious Lily. You'll have to excuse me." She dabbed at her watery eyes. "Just the sight of you floods me with memories. Wasn't she just the dreamiest on stage?"

"I cleared out before their vaudeville act happened, so I never got to see her sing."

"What a shame. She was born for the spotlight and had the talent to back it up. You missed out there, my boy."

Nell smiled. My boy? Violet and Avery had to have been the same age, give or take a few years. But Violet had a maternal quality about her, as though she knew instinctively how to nurture anyone, regardless of their age. Or maybe it was those big bazoombas.

"I've been hearing you on the radio," Nell said.

"Crazy, ain't it?" Violet released Avery from her grasp. "Waiting until I'm forty-six before things start to happen. I was shocked when the offer from this place came in. Let's face it, I'm nobody's idea of Princess Leilani. But the guy who runs this joint said, 'As long as you include "Aloha Oe" in your set, sing whatever you like.'" She winked conspiratorially. "With any luck, someone from Ciro's might come in. They pay the *really* big bucks." She turned to Avery, who was, by now, halfway through his second

Rob Roy. "I have nine hundred thousand stories about your sister."

As she threw herself into a tale about the night when The Four Blooms played the Orpheum in Wichita on a bill that featured Vernon and Irene Castle, Nell noticed a distracted look on Betty's face. Her eyes kept bouncing to a spot across the nightclub. Nell nudged her knee and jacked up her eyebrows.

Betty jabbed her lit cigarette past Nell. "Isn't that Peter Lorre?"

A quick scan of a table nestled in a nook to the left of the stage was all Nell needed. "And his wife. I wish I could recall her name."

"Celia," Betty stated, then backed up a little. "Bogie often mentions them."

When Nell looked at Lorre again, he waved. But it wasn't a cheery how've-you-been-doing. She excused herself and made her way to Lorre's table. After he introduced her to his Viennese actress wife, Celia Lovsky, a knowing leer unfolded across his face. "Is that her?"

"Uh-huh. And she sounds even better than she does in that song of hers—"

"I'm talking about the glamour girl. Bogie's mentioned her once or twice."

"Every chance he gets," Celia put in.

Nell looked back at the group. Reggie had joined them now. Were he and Violet an item? How interesting. She asked Lorre, "Is Bogie smitten?"

"Utterly. Thoroughly. Completely." He raised his Sloe Gin Rickey in Betty's direction. "He tells me the two of you have gotten to be pals."

"She's terrific."

"Does she return the affection?"

Holy cow. What should I say to that? Had Betty's admission been in for-your-ears-only confidence? Should I encourage this fledgling romance?

The success of *To Have and Have Not* would hinge on the combustible alchemy between the two leads. The picture had three marquee names going for it: Ernest Hemingway, Howard Hawks, Humphrey Bogart. It was a lot to risk for what might be just another short-lived love affair that petered out when the cameras stopped rolling.

But what if this were the real thing? Didn't Bogie deserve his shot at happiness?

Lorre was still waiting for her answer.

"I need to talk to Bogie about all this."

"What did I tell you?" Lorre triumphantly raised his cocktail.

Nell poked him in the chest. "Don't you go putting words in my mouth."

"You didn't say no."

Violet was hugging Avery again. It was coming up to eight o'clock, and Nell knew she needed to go and prepare for her show. "I have to get back," she told Lorre. "Please don't say anything."

"Bogie's one of my closest friends. I only want what's best for him. And Mayo isn't it."

Nell was still sorting through the ramifications of Peter Lorre's revelation that it took her a moment to realize Reggie was thoroughly sauced.

"I've never seen Peter Lorre look so intense." He slurred his words together so that it was hard to make out where one word ended and the next began.

"He'll be back on the Warner lot to film his *Hollywood Canteen* cameo. You know how actors can be sometimes." Nell waved her hand dismissively. "They want to control every fifth word of dialogue *and* their PR hoopla."

"HA!" Reggie's reaction was so loud it turned heads.

"Goodness gracious, Reggie!" Nell tapped his double bourbon. "Shouldn't this one be your last until after Violet's finished her—"

"I knew you were sharp enough to cotton on to Luke's code. I just *knew* it."

Nell stared at him. Luke had been tight-lipped about why Captain Vance had recruited him, but if she had accurately interpreted the few hints he'd dropped, Vance had wanted him at Montauk in some sort of code-breaking role. But now Luke was thousands of miles away—in one direction or another. So how could he have a code? All she'd received were his often strangely worded V-mails—OH!

Nell presented Reggie with her best coquettish smile. "You know about his code?"

"He taught it to me in Boulder. When Movietone sends me on a last-minute filming assignment, it's to beat out *March of Time*, *Metrotone*, or *News of the Day* for a big scoop. I hate disappearing on Violet like that, so I send her a Western Union. She knows to read every fifth word to figure out where I am. Clever, huh?" Reggie tapped his temple, but he was so far gone that he almost poked himself in the eye. "That Luke of yours is one wily kiddo."

The lights dimmed to half-power and a tinkling chime rang through the loudspeaker. "Good evening, hula girls and tiki gods. The Seven Seas proudly presents the inimitable Miss Violet Beaudine!" A five-man band played in the intro to "When the Swallows Come Back to Capistrano." The packed house broke into an appreciative round of applause, but Nell barely heard it.

Luke's V-mails were in code? She should have been reading every fifth word? Like 'submarine,' 'lantern,' and 'fish'?

Violet hit the stage in a baby-pink spotlight as Nell snatched up her handbag and whispered to Betty, "I have to go."

"Did Peter Lorre upset you?"

*Has Luke been telling me where he is all this time? Or where he's going? Or how to contact him?* "I'll explain later."

The cold February night air smacked her across the face. So

had this revelation about a code. How did Luke expect her to know she was supposed to read every fifth word?

She needed to get home as fast as she could. And of course, there was no streetcar in sight. There never was one when you needed it. A block east, she spotted a taxicab parked outside the Hollywood Hotel. She bolted toward it, screaming like a lunatic.

## 24

Orry-Kelly had concocted Bette Davis's Edwardian dress out of rayon and lace reclaimed from some other costume he'd made for some other actress, and then dyed it pale blue.

Bette stood at a full-length mirror, picking at her strawberry-blonde wig. "These curls," she told the photographer. "I'm sure they were piled higher." She spotted Nell lurking inside the portrait studio doorway. "Come see if you can fluff it up a bit. I'm expected at the Canteen soon." Bette adjusted the décolletage of her dress so that it sat across her chest more flatteringly. "Glenn Miller and his orchestra are playing for the first time, so *of course* Warner and Taplinger decide they're not happy with the *Mr. Skeffington* publicity stills and need replacements immediately, if not sooner."

Nell's dead-straight hair had never responded to curlers or permanent waves. The teasing comb might as well have been blacksmith tongs, but who was she to tell Bette Davis no? She tinkered with the wig as best she could.

"Taplinger sent me down to apologize for the short notice," she said. He had done no such thing, of course. When Nell had heard about the situation, she figured someone ought to go and thank Bette. Plus, it gave her a chance to escape the din of the office and report to Bogie what she had discovered in Luke's letters. "Speaking of the Canteen, I'm hoping you might do me a favor. And it'd be good publicity. A two-birds-one-stone scenario."

"State your case and make it quick. Ann Sheridan's due here at noon."

"My boyfriend, Luke, has a brother."

"The gunnery sergeant I met when Luke brought him here? How's he doing?"

"Tony lost a leg at Guadalcanal."

Bette twisted around. "No!"

"He's in Wadsworth, where he helps out in their victory garden with a chap named Hollis, who's had a tough go of it since they pulled a whole mess of shrapnel out of his stomach, his arm, his neck, and his face."

Bette returned to the mirror. "And they wonder what drives me to run the Canteen."

"Might it be possible to open it early one evening? Hollis's favorite star is Mary Astor and nothing would thrill him more than to have a dance with her."

"He can do that during regular hours."

"It's hard for him to be social. Especially getting jostled around by over-excited servicemen. Tony said it would buck up his spirits terrifically well."

"I'm not sure I should play favorites."

"Ten minutes before opening. They could have a long dance on an empty floor."

"Hmmm."

Did Bette's *hmmm* mean she was considering the idea? Or that Nell's listless efforts with the teasing comb were having the desired result? "And what great publicity. A human-interest story narrowed down to one serviceman, the way Ernie Pyle does so that his readers can relate."

Bette snapped her fingers. "Let's do it. But we ought to get a high-profile columnist involved."

And now they had arrived at the point where Nell's suggestion might go awry. "I was thinking of Hedda."

"Ugh." Bette picked up a light brown feather lying on a nearby vanity and twirled it around her fingertips. "Why her?"

"She did me a big favor and expects to be paid back." And it might detract her from the juicy gossip Hedda would kill her first-born for: the brewing affair between Humphrey Bogart and Lauren Bacall.

"Of course she does."

"Hedda's become so astringent in her columns. FDR can do nothing right, and the Motion Picture Alliance for the Preservation of American Ideals—"

"Don't get me started on that bunch of conservative, backward-looking, fusty old sticks."

"I thought I'd pitch her along the lines of 'This is a story that'll appeal to everybody.'"

Bette inserted the feather into the knot at the rear of her wig and faced Nell. "You really have taken to this PR job, haven't you? I'm so impressed."

"So it's a yes?"

"Is Nell Davenport in here?" a voice chirped from the hallway.

Before the war, the studio messengers had been boys, but now they were all girls, freshly minted from high school, and equally fast on their bicycles. With her mop of curly red hair bouncing in the LA sun, this one was hard to miss as she darted around the lot.

"You're wanted on Stage Twenty-Eight."

That was where *To Have and Have Not* was filming. "Is there a problem?"

"They told me to tell you on the double."

\* \* \*

She found Betty pacing back and forth behind the hotel foyer set. "What's happened? Are you okay? You didn't —?" *Confess your crush to your co-star, who blew a fuse and refuses to look you in the eye anymore?*

Betty knitted her fingers together until her knuckles turned pale. "They want me to sing!"

All things considered, that didn't seem so bad. "Since when is Marie a saloon singer?"

"They've rewritten the script and now I'm supposed to get up in front of that camera and warble some Hoagy Carmichael tune like I'm Dinah Shore." Betty drooped into a nearby loveseat. "I could feel the blood drain from my face, so I mumbled some hogwash about needing to attend to an urgent matter in my dressing room. That's when I asked the redhead to go find you."

"They add last-minute dialogue all the time, but a last-minute song?" Nell whistled. "That's a tall order." She joined Betty on the tufted love seat. "Bette Davis felt the same way singing in *Thank Your Lucky Stars*, and I helped coach her through it."

"You did?"

Nell nodded. "When are you shooting this number?"

"After lunch."

"Today?!"

"Now do you see why I ran away?"

Betty pointed to sheet music lying on a side table. Nell read the title out loud. "'How Little We Know.'" It was in the key of A-flat major, which Nell suspected Hoagy had done on purpose to suit Betty's voice. "The melody isn't too complicated."

"Says you, who can sing like Jo Stafford."

The clock above the soundstage exit read ten forty-five. Nell pulled Betty to her feet. "Let's go find Hoagy and we can walk you through it."

Betty yanked herself from Nell's grasp. "I need to calm down first. Tell me some news to distract me."

"Brace yourself." Nell retrieved a slip of paper from out of her jacket. "Last night at the Seven Seas, in his thoroughly pickled state, Reggie let slip a little secret that he thought I already knew."

"What kind of secret?"

"Luke's been sending me coded messages in his V-mails."

"No!"

"If you read every fifth word, he's telling me where he is and what he's doing. Not in his first V-mail. That made no sense. But in his second one, and his third? Whole different story." She waved the paper in the air like it was a football pennant. "The one from May last year says, 'Hopefully you got note about every five words.'" Nell looked up. "Which I didn't. Then he says, 'Life at Montauk intense. Job big difficult complex. Won't stay long. Probably boulder school learning Japanese.'"

Betty's eyes darted around the room. "The squiggly lines on his textbook weren't shorthand."

"Not even close. And from late last year," Nell returned to her slip of paper, "'My studies in Colorado now finished. Transferred to—' The next word was blacked out, but it must have read 'Seattle.' And then he says, 'Reassigned to submarine lantern fish. Going toward midway island because I now speak the language of the enemy.'"

"Midway Island?!" Betty tightened her grip on Nell's forearm. "But that's—"

"Halfway to Japan."

"Neither option makes a girl want to break out her tap shoes and dance her troubles away."

Nell folded the slip of paper. "Has it worked? Are you sufficiently distracted to tackle this song of yours?"

Betty jammed her hands onto her hips. "You made up this whole story?"

"Nope. It's all too real." Nell gathered the sheet music. "You ready to warble, Miss Shore?"

\* \* \*

The cast and crew were filming one of Bogie's close-ups when Betty and Nell crossed to Hoagy, who was seated at his character's piano. He nodded at the music in her hand. "If we work through lunch, we'll have three hours to get this number into shape. Johnny and I made sure there was nothing you'd stumble over. Your starting note is middle C." He struck a key on the piano.

"Just sing that note," Nell told her as the crew around them set up the next shot.

Betty sang a note, but it wasn't anything close to middle C.

"It'll help if you push your tongue to the back of your lower teeth. Let me show you." Nell asked Hoagy to play it again and sang it herself, holding it until her lungs ran out of air. "Now you do it."

Betty followed Nell's instructions; the note came out perfectly. "See? You *can* do it!"

Betty's eyes shone with surprise. "I did, didn't I?"

"The first phrase is seven notes, one for each syllable. 'May-be it hap-pens this way.' See?" Betty nodded. "It's a matter of building the song one phrase at a time."

"You're gonna knock the socks off every guy in the audience!"

Tristan approached them, holding a two-piece gown of shiny black sateen with squared-off shoulders and a large black ring coupling the top section to the bottom. Even on a wooden hanger, the outfit was slinky and seductive, and draped to the floor in sensuous folds. Nell rubbed it between her fingertips. So smooth it almost felt wet.

"No offense, honey," Tristan said, "but ain't nobody going to be listening to your voice."

Betty dissolved into anxious giggles before rolling her shoulders like an Olympian sprinter approaching the starting blocks. "Let's conquer this beast."

Dressed in a black jacket, white open-necked shirt, and peaked sea captain's hat, Bogie hunkered down in a shadowy alcove. He didn't budge the whole time Nell and Hoagy helped Betty master the material, note by note, line by line. When Hoagy declared that Betty was ready for a run-through, Nell retreated to Bogie's hideaway.

"If you think you're being discreet, you're not."

Bogie kept his gaze fixed on Betty. "It's not just her face and her figure. It's everything. The way she moves, her sense of humor. By the end of our first day of shooting, we were insulting each other with wisecracks and put-downs. Cracking each other up over the silliest things. That twenty-year-old gives every bit as good as she gets, and I can't stop thinking about her."

"You planning on making a move?"

"When I start working up my nerve, reality pops me one, bang in the kisser. Reminds me that she's half my age, she's knockout gorgeous, got everything going for her, so why would she respond to a middle-aged, old coot like me who's already married?"

"You're right." Nell unleashed an exaggerated sigh. "Why the hell would she?"

"We have this blazing chemistry. All natural. No effort. But if I make a pass and she turns me down, it could all fizzle out. This picture is shaping up to be one of my best. Do I want to risk sabotaging—" He broke away from talking about Betty. "You were being sarcastic, weren't you?"

Nell batted her eyes like a soubrette. She made a slow, deliberate sweep of the hotel set, her gaze finally landing on Betty. Then back to Bogie. Then back to Betty.

"Are you saying that I should try my luck?"

"I haven't said a thing."

"Please, Nell, I need you to be a pal right now. Has Betty showed that she—she would . . . You think I should make a move?"

A desperate longing had filled his face. It was cruel to keep the truth from him. "You'd be a fool not to."

He looked down at his battered brogues. "Howard's not going to like it. He sees that girl as his personal property."

"She's not a used Cadillac. You deserve somebody to share all your success with. Someone other than Mayo. I got my shot at happiness and Luke might not come back. I say grab yours wherever and whenever you find it."

He returned his yearning gaze to Betty. "You think she's my shot at happiness?"

"Go find out."

Bogie's body shook as he swung back to face Nell again. "Why do you think Luke might not make it back?"

Nell pulled the decoded messages from her pocket. "It's a good thing you're sitting down."

## 25

Betty set her corded rayon shoulder bag on Nell's desk and tugged off her matching gloves. "This is where you work, huh?"

Nell deposited Taplinger's Philco next to Betty's bag with a grunt. He'd told her that his radio was portable but had neglected to add, "if you're six foot one and two hundred pounds." She plugged in the set and switched it on.

Betty looked around the deserted office and let out the same sound Bogie had trilled at the end of their whistle scene. "It must be a hive of activity around here during the day."

Nell twirled the tuning knob until it found KFWB. Static spluttered as the set warmed up. "Zingers fly around this room like Robin Hood's arrows. The same way they do in Stage Twenty-Eight."

An involuntary smile surfaced on Betty's face.

Everyone had been talking about the flirty atmosphere on *To Have and Have Not*. And how the sizzling chemistry between the two leads had made the air crackle. And how every time Mayo had called, she was told that Bogie was with the cast. In this case, "the cast" referred to Betty.

The presenter reported that the broadcast of the sixteenth Academy Awards ceremony from Grauman's Chinese was due to begin in nineteen minutes.

A blush flared across Betty's cheeks. "What do you give *Casablanca*'s chances tonight?"

"We've got *Princess O'Rourke*, *Sahara*, *Air Force*, and *Destination Tokyo* also in the running, but *Casablanca* should pick up at least a few awards, even though it has only eight nominations to *Song of Bernadette*'s twelve."

"And if it does, what then?"

Nell turned to the ads she had mocked up on the neighboring desk. "I paste strips on these so that they're ready for the *Times*, the *Examiner* and the *Hollywood Citizen-News* by four tomorrow morning."

Betty ran a fingertip along the BEST ACTOR AWARD WINNER! flag across a *Casablanca* ad. "Wouldn't it be thrilling if Bogie won?" Her voice had taken on a distracted quality.

Oh, yes, Nell thought. The "cast" is in it up to her love-struck eyeballs. "How's it all going?"

"It's hard to tell when you're in the eye of the hurricane."

"And Howard? Is he treating you okay?"

"I wish he wasn't so standoffish."

*That's because he had designs on you, but Bogie's muscled in on what he presumed was his exclusive turf.*

The ceremony's opening fanfare blasted out of Taplinger's Philco, followed by Jack Benny's welcome monologue. With the US fighting two war fronts, the Academy had foregone the usual splashy gala in favor of a streamlined ceremony. Handing out twenty-four awards in thirty minutes sounded like a tall order, but it suited Nell. If Warners proved to be a big winner tonight, she might not have to work until all hours.

"You're lucky Michael Curtiz isn't at the helm," she told Betty. "He wouldn't hesitate to chew you up and spit you out."

"I've been lucky in so many ways." Her moony tone had disappeared; Betty now sounded downcast.

The first category was Best Documentary Feature; Warners had no horses in that race. "I hear Mayo's been calling the set."

"At least once a day. Bogie hates it. Says it ruins his concentration. She always leaves the same message: 'Call me immediately.'"

Nell would have bet twenty bucks that Bogie had taken Betty to see his pride and joy at the Newport Yacht Club.

Jack Benny announced the next category: Best Supporting Actor. *Casablanca*'s Claude Rains had been nominated, so Nell held off a moment. When Charles Coburn was declared the winner for *The More the Merrier*, she said, "Luke went out on the *Sluggy* a few times."

Nell had fallen a little deeper in love with Luke when he'd described the horror he'd felt looking into the bottomless blue of the Pacific, and how a suffocating panic had overtaken him when Bogie had flung him into the drink. Bogie had maintained that it was the best way to cure Luke's fear of deep water. Nell wasn't sure that Bogie's impetuous remedy had done the trick, but hoped like hell it had if Luke was now steaming fifty feet underwater toward Midway.

"I was expecting a flashy cruiser," Betty said. "I should've known that's not his style. It's comfortable. Real cozy."

Ray Heindorf was announced as the winner of Best Scoring of a Musical Picture for *This is the Army*—hooray for Warner Bros.! And when *Casablanca* snapped up Best Screenplay for Howard Koch and the Epstein boys, Nell couldn't help but smile. It had been the most chaotic, most rewritten, and most fly-by-the-seat-of-everyone's-pants production she'd ever been a part of. And yet, through some sort of elusive alchemy, a lush, romantic masterpiece had emerged, proving that a movie was far more than the sum of its parts.

It was one reason why Nell loved working in the movies. Nobody ever knew if the picture they were toiling so hard on was destined to be the next *Gone with the Wind*, which everyone had called 'Selznick's Folly' until it had started minting money at the box office. Or the next *Wizard of Oz*, which Hollywood had assumed would be a gigantic hit, but had lost MGM more than a million bucks.

Between her new job, Luke's V-mails, and the budding Bogart–Bacall romance, Nell had been able to keep from brooding over what she called 'the South Bend situation.' But then a postcard from her sister, Vesta, had arrived warning that if it weren't for rationing on gas and rubber, Mother and Father would have driven to Los Angeles and brought her home to start living "your real life." The reason Nell had given—house-sitting the Bogarts' place—had long expired.

Max Steiner was up for his *Casablanca* score for a dramatic picture, but Jack Benny announced Alfred Newman's name for *Song of Bernadette*.

"Cozy enough for two?" Nell prompted.

Betty was now studying the display ad that would go into tomorrow's *Hollywood Citizen-News* if Bogie or Curtiz won in their categories, or if *Casablanca* nabbed Outstanding Motion Picture. "Especially after the tourists and weekend skippers have gone home."

Nell was all for this May–September romance, but Miss May needed to know the current Mrs. September was hardly the slip-quietly-into-the-night type. "Did Bogie tell you where the name of his boat comes from?"

George Murphy ran through the nominees for Best Actor. Betty squeezed Nell's hand extra tight. "He'll get it. I just *know* he will."

"And the winner is Paul Lukas for *Watch on the Rhine*."

"NO!" Betty let go of Nell's hand. "I was so sure," she said, her eyes awash with tears. "He told me he didn't care if he lost or won." She accepted Nell's handkerchief. "I can read him like a kid's picture book, though. I accused him of lying to himself and said that deep down he was hoping to win."

"What did he say to that?"

"He admitted I was right, and that he feels a bit of a fraud. Isn't that the craziest idea you ever heard?"

"He told me once, 'People always say I'm pretending to be tough. The truth is I'm defensive.'"

Coming from out of the blue on the set of *The Maltese Falcon*, Bogie's comment had stuck with her. Perhaps because that was the moment she'd realized everybody was pretending to be one thing or another. "Winning an Oscar would mean his peers considered him a serious actor," Nell said. "We all need to feel as though our efforts amount to something." She dropped the BEST ACTOR AWARD WINNER! advertisement in the trash can and pictured Bogie propping up his face with a valiant smile, wondering how long he'd have to hold out before he could get a drink.

Betty dabbed at her bleary eyes. "You get him, too."

"Yes, but I'm not the one in love with him."

Betty's mouth popped open; she inhaled a quiet gasp. "I had no idea this—" Her eyes darted back and forth while she groped for the word she didn't want to acknowledge out loud. They fell still when she realized it was the only fitting word. "—this affair would become so intense. It's quite overwhelming."

"So the two of you are having an—"

"That word—affair. It sounds tawdry and fleeting." Betty paced back and forth in front of Nell's desk. "I know all the reasons why I should restrain myself. I tried. He did, too. But in the end, we crumbled."

"You're only human."

"I've seen a million love stories on the screen, and listened to a million love songs on the radio, but I never dreamed it would feel like this."

"Goes to the depths of your soul, doesn't it?"

"It does!"

"And you can't remember what it was like to not have this

person in your life."

"You really can't!"

"And if you lost him, you're scared that you'd curl up and die."

"Is that how it is with Luke?"

"We went with Bogie and Ingrid to a fundraiser at Romanoff's. Tristan was still dressing up as Trixie Bagatelle back then, and he hauled Luke up on stage to perform a memory trick. I could tell Luke wanted to be anywhere but in the spotlight. But he put on a brave face and played along, anyway. That was pretty much it for me."

"When that moment hits you, and you know that you know? It's pretty wonderful, isn't it? I count the minutes till we see each other again. I crave his kisses. His smile. The sweet nothings he whispers in my ear. The time between takes feels like an eternity. I can't wait until Howard calls 'Action!' because then I have a valid reason to feel his body pressing against mine."

The two of them fell silent as Mark Sandrich announced that Michael Curtiz had won Best Director for *Casablanca*. Nell rearranged some advertising mockups, adjusting a banner that said *ACADEMY AWARD WINNER!* above the heads of Bogart and Bergman in a clinch.

As happy as she was for Betty, Nell felt she wasn't a good friend unless she force-fed the girl a dose of reality.

"I've seen on-set romances like this before. Jack Warner won't be happy, Howard won't be happy, and Mayo *definitely* won't be happy."

"Add my whole family to that list."

"Let's not forget Hedda."

Betty drew back. "But she likes me. Said so herself. She gave me my first mention in the press."

"You were a fresh, exciting face. But now she could cast you as the scarlet jezebel breaking up a movie-star marriage."

"Everyone knows they've been teetering on the edge for years."

"Hedda will slant it any way it suits her. And it suits her to paint Bogie as a Commie-loving reprobate—"

Betty stared at her. "Bogie? A Commie?"

"You'd be surprised what Mr. and Mrs. Middle America will believe if they see it in a paper."

The sound of Sidney Franklin clearing his throat percolated through the Philco's speakers. "And now, the award for Outstanding Motion Picture."

As he recapped the names of the ten nominated films, Nell was tempted to buoy Betty's spirits with an everything-will-turn-out-fine speech. But this wasn't a schmaltzy Hollywood movie where the brave couple overcame an obstacle course of plot complications before the screen faded to black. If it were, she wouldn't be nearly so apprehensive about Luke. But this was real life, and Betty needed to plunge forward with her eyes open, so Nell said nothing as Franklin announced that the picture of the year was *Casablanca*.

* * *

Nell checked her calendar—March 5th, 1944—then ran down the list of movies now under her purview.

The September 1st release of *Arsenic and Old Lace* was six months away, so she didn't need to worry about that for now. *The Adventures of Mark Twain* was opening on May 6th, so it got bumped to top priority. *The Mask of Dimitrios* was scheduled to go into theaters in July. Even though it starred Sydney Greenstreet and Peter Lorre, it was a low-rent *Maltese Falcon* retread and wasn't likely to set the box office on fire. Bogie's *Passage to Marseille* was coming out in a week's time, which left *Hollywood Canteen*, due to start in June, and *To Have and Have Not*, which would be shooting for a couple more months and open in October. As well as the refreshed advertising campaign for *Casablanca* now that it had won three Oscars.

And to think she had once assumed PR people only worked

one motion picture at a time. *What blissful ignorance you lived in, you foolish, naive girl.*

The number of cameos planned for the *Hollywood Canteen* movie stood at twenty-six. Or twenty-seven, including Roy Rogers' horse, Trigger. It was bound to be a hellaciously busy set. She shoved a pencil into the sharpener and ground the handle around, wondering how filming was going over at *To Have and Have Not*. She had dropped by a couple of times. Stage Twenty-Eight vibrated with sexual tension from what Nell could only assume was now a physical relationship.

*If* passions didn't get out of hand, and *if* they stayed inconspicuous, and *if* Mayo didn't catch wind of what was going on until production had finished, then the studio bigwigs would be fools to not play up the romantic angle. But that was a lot of ifs. Could those two lovebirds keep their extracurricular activity on the q.t.? She didn't blame Bogie for falling hard for Betty, but he had worked so long and so hard to reach the top. Had he thought through the consequences?

Her intercom buzzed. Taplinger's voice asked, "You got a minute?" which meant 'Come here.'

He was hanging up as she walked into his office. "Did you invite Hedda Hopper onto the lot?"

"Not unless it's absolutely necessary."

"She just arrived—with a guest." He studied his telephone as though it might bite him. "Mrs. Bogart."

A frisson jolted Nell. That night at the Mocambo, when Hawks had told Bogie about his plan to film *To Have and Have Not*, his disdain for everything Mayo said had spread across his face like a syphilitic rash. "Mayo has recruited Hedda as a bodyguard."

Taplinger raised a worried eyebrow. "Wherever Mayo goes, trouble follows."

"Especially with Hedda in tow." Nell started backing away. "I'd better run down there and reconnoiter." She was out the door before he could question her any further.

\* \* \*

When Nell arrived, Hawks was blocking a scene in which Betty talked her way into Bogie's room, using the context of needing a cigarette, making breakfast, and drawing a hot bath in order to prolong her seduction and make him think it was his idea.

Hawks placed his two leads face to face. Bogie stared, unblinking, into Betty's eyes with an almost euphoric rapture. Nell hated to be the Cassandra of Warner Bros., presaging news nobody wanted to hear. She hadn't seen Mayo or Hedda on her mad dash to the set. Perhaps she ought to take a lap around the building in case she could head them off at the pass. Where was Trigger when she needed him?

Nell hadn't taken five steps into the sunshine when she heard Hedda's piercing laughter. "Oh, Mayo!" Hedda squealed. "You're a caution!"

"Not only that," Mayo shot back, "but he ain't got the faintest idea I burn them on purpose. He just thinks I'm a terrible cook!"

Hedda shrieked again. "Men! What's a girl to do?"

They approached the entrance into Stage Twenty-Eight, arms linked like they were bestest girlfriends out for a stroll in between Art History classes.

"Ladies," Nell exclaimed, "this is a lovely surprise."

"Don't you work the publicity game now?" Mayo asked mildly.

"I do. Part of my job is to check on filming. You never know what's going to happen on a set that'll make for a terrific promotion angle." She turned to Hedda. "I'm so glad to have bumped into you."

Hedda pressed her lips into a tart moue. "I'd have called ahead, but I ran into Mayo shopping at the Broadway Hollywood—and suddenly here we are."

Sure. Yeah. And the Japanese attacked Pearl Harbor 'suddenly,' too.

Nell peeked at the red light above the door and prayed it

would start blinking. A flashing light meant that opening a door would ruin an expensive take. "I've drawn up a list of cameos in our *Hollywood Canteen* movie. Perhaps we can pop into the PR department, where we could go through the list and you could tell me which ones you'd like to watch filming their bit."

"We're here to visit the *To Have and Have Not* set."

"I wouldn't bother. Everybody's waiting for the gaffer to fix an uncooperative bulb."

"They're standing around twiddling their thumbs?" Hedda replied. "Perfect timing!"

When would that damned red light start up?

"It's quite a list," Nell improvised. "Andrews Sisters. Eddie Cantor. Barbara Stanwyck. We've even got Trigger. Although I refuse to be the one with the broom, if you know what I mean."

Hedda narrowed her eyes. "I have my list too. It pays to keep track of who has failed to follow through on their promises."

Mayo laughed an empty laugh. "I wouldn't want to end up on any list this gal draws up."

Neither would Nell, except that she was already on it. "I wonder if our lists overlap. We'd all prefer to avoid awkwardness on the set."

"There's none if everybody does their job."

"I haven't sent the *Hollywood Canteen* list to Louella yet. I thought I'd give you first look-see."

"I appreciate that," Hedda said airily. "Meanwhile, Mayo and I are going inside—"

A harsh bell cut her off. The red light flashed on and began to rotate.

Nell donned her sweetest smile. "Now that we have a few minutes, I've got an idea I want to run past you." She ignored the you're-pushing-your-luck-girlie glower Hedda threw at her. "It'll make for a heartrending human-interest story."

"Hedda's hardly the sob-sister type."

Mayo was right, but the wariness in Hedda's eyes dissipated.

"I met a gunnery sergeant at Wadsworth Hospital. Took a ton of shrapnel at Guadalcanal."

Hedda tsked. "How is he now?"

"Some good days, but many dark ones, too. He mentioned how he went to high school with Mary Astor and admitted he had a big crush on her back then. I suspect he still does, so I asked Bette Davis if she would open the Canteen ten minutes early so that Hollis could have a dance with Mary. It'd mean the world to him."

"What did Bette say?"

"She could see what an inspirational article it would make."

Hedda's gaze drifted away. "It could at that."

"And with you traveling to Pearl Harbor for the third anniversary, I thought it could make a worthwhile piece. It's got everything: one sailor's path to overcoming terrible tragedy, patriotism, the Navy, the war effort, a movie star, the real-life Hollywood Canteen."

"Oh, Hedda," Mayo said, "you could get a lot of mileage out of that."

"When does this romantic pas-de-deux take place?" Hedda asked.

"Mary's shooting that St. Louis musical with Judy Garland at MGM right now. She's only got another week, then her schedule clears."

The red light stopped flashing.

Hedda grasped the chrome handle on the door. "When you've got a definite date, let me know." She pulled the door open and told Mayo to follow her.

\* \* \*

Nell bit into her chicken salad sandwich and wondered what the heck she was going to do with *The Mask of Dimitrios*. The convoluted plot opened with the corpse of a Turkish fig-picker-turned-murderer washing up on an Istanbul beach and involved an unsuccessful assassination, stolen maps, and blackmail. If only there had been an actual mask, then she could ask the prop department for a photograph.

She took another bite of her lunch.

*Egad, what I wouldn't give for a thick slice of succulent ham. When, when, when will meat rationing end?* Not before the outcome of the war, certainly. But at least her landlady hadn't resorted to horsemeat. Or maybe she had? A girl at the boardinghouse had said that if you brined it with two tons of herbs for a week, nobody would assume it was anything but beef.

A wave of murmuring rustled across the office. The hazy air, heavy with cigarette smoke, sharpened as Humphrey Bogart strode up the aisle between desks like he was General Eisenhower storming the Western Sahara. He was still wearing his costume: navy-blue jacket with matching cravat knotted around his throat, white shirt, and peaked sailor cap.

A-listers summoned peons to their dressing rooms; they *never* chased down a lowly galley slave. Nell rose to her feet. "Is there a problem?"

Bogie's dark eyes ricocheted from side to side. "Walk with me." He kept mum until they were outside. "I can't thank you enough."

"For . . . ?"

"Hoagy was sneaking a cigarette as Betty and I rehearsed our kiss. He saw how you waylaid Hedda and Mayo till the red light started flashing. As soon as it stopped, Hoagy bolted inside and sent up a flare. If he hadn't, all hell would have broken loose."

"Why?"

"We were still kissing, even after Howard had yelled cut." He flapped his arms to his side. "I can't help myself when I'm around her."

"If you're alone, sure. Whoop it up all you like. But on a set? Jeez, Bogie, that's called skating on thin ice."

"I know! I know!"

"You've got a lot farther to fall than she does—and more to

lose. Don't forget, you took on your father's debt, as well as caring for your aging mother and your sister. That sanatorium she's in can't be cheap."

Bogie had only mentioned his manic-depressive sibling once or twice. Only when he was drunk, and always with a doleful mix of melancholy and upright Victorian duty.

"You're right," he said. "But Betty's everything I want. Everything I've been looking for." He stopped outside the portrait studio and lit up a cigarette. "It's hard for us to be alone, so every night after work, we leave at the same time. We drive over to Highland, then right onto Hollywood Boulevard, and another right onto Selma, where we park our cars. I leave mine and climb into hers."

"You neck right there in public?"

"There's a two-block stretch with no working streetlights. Nobody sees us."

Poor bastard. He looked so haunted, so conflicted, and yet so desperately in love. "How long do you spend together?"

"Twenty minutes, but of course, it feels like twenty seconds. Then we get back into our cars and drive up to Sunset." He sucked on his cigarette again, deep and hard, like it was pure oxygen. "But all that could have unraveled today if you hadn't hijacked Mayo and Hedda in the nick of time. So, thank you."

"I'm glad it worked."

"No, really, it means the world to me. Betty, too. We owe you one. But it's different now that you're in PR. You deal with the Hedda Hoppers and Louella Parsonses of this world. People like me look on those contemptible bitches as the enemy, but you need them to do your job, and I want you to know that I understand the tricky position you're in."

"Very thoughtful of you. I appreciate that." She waited until he'd disappeared inside before she slumped against the brick wall. If Bogie and Betty were the rock, and Hedda and Mayo were the hard place, where did that leave her?

## 26

*E*xactly two weeks after the Academy Awards ceremony, Tony and Hollis were waiting out front of Wadsworth when Nell pulled up in Betty's car. Their ill-fitting second-hand suits were pressed, their shoes shined, faces shaved, hair pomaded.

"I expected to see you both in uniform," she told them as they climbed in.

Tony settled into the passenger seat beside her and shook his head. "Wearing uniforms in public ninety days after discharge is a no-no. However," he fingered a plastic gold pin on his lapel, "we're wearing our Ruptured Ducks."

"We don't want to give anyone the wrong idea," Hollis said. "We want them to know that we've served and have been honorably discharged."

"I've never seen one of these things up close." Nell inspected Tony's pin of an eagle with its wings outspread, sitting inside a circle. "Very impressive." She turned to Hollis, who was gingerly settling himself into the back seat. The smell of talcum powder billowed around him. He looked even thinner than the last time Nell had seen him, but if he was suffering, he didn't let it show.

"Mary'll take one look at you—"

Hollis's forehead crinkled. "She will be there, right?"

"She proudly told me she's never missed a shift at the Canteen."

When Nell had tracked Mary down at her home, she had described Hollis as best she could, but Mary had no recollection of him. "Not to worry, I'll fudge it, especially after all he's been through."

"Mary knows to be gentle with me, doesn't she?" Hollis still looked worried. "My gut is bandaged up real tight, but sometimes it leaks at inconvenient times. Mostly if I overdo it, like in the victory garden. You know what? Forget I asked. Even if I do spill my guts out onto the floor, it'll be worth it."

Tony slid next to Nell. "I can't tell you what a morale booster it's been for us."

"What the devil are you talking about, Valenti?" Hollis piped up. "You work in a movie studio."

As Nell had hoped, Perc Westmore had conscripted Tony into the Hair and Makeup Department, where he coiffed anyone from A-list celebrities to anonymous chorines and dress extras.

"I'm excited because Glenn Miller is playing there this week."

"I can barely get it into my thick skull that in an hour's time, I'll be dancing *with* Mary Astor, *to* Glenn Miller, *at* the Hollywood Canteen." Hollis's voice had grown muddy from the effort of beating back his excitement. "Stupefied is what I am."

Nell mentally crossed her fingers that it would all work out. What if Bette Davis had forgotten to alert Emmeline they were opening early? Or if Mary had been recalled to MGM for reshoots? Nell had asked Violet to sing Hollis's favorite song as he danced with Mary, but what if she had booked another radio appearance? Or if the Army Air Force had ordered Captain Miller to report for an assignment? Or if Hedda had decided against covering the story?

You can't worry about any of that, she told herself. All those people are on their way to the Canteen right this very minute.

* * *

When Emmeline took in the two men trailing Nell, she greeted them with a rare smile. "Which one of you is Gunnery Sergeant Muir?" Hollis gingerly raised his hand. "An extra special welcome to you."

Hollis blinked as his emotions threatened to engulf him.

"Miller's orchestra is setting up," Emmeline told Nell. "The last time I saw Bette, she was at the big map talking with Hedda and her photographer. Mary's with them. Oh, and so is Claude Rains."

*Bette, you cunning minx! You know Hedda loves your* Mr. Skeffington *co-star. If anyone can mollycoddle Hedda Hopper into a good mood, it's him.*

Nell led Tony and Hollis into the main room. Oh my, how large the dance floor looked when it wasn't jam-packed with eager servicemen and pretty hostesses. A map of Europe filled half an entire wall near the servicemen's entrance. Blue thumb tacks charted the Allies' advances. As Nell approached it, Bette was pushing one into an Italian coastal city. If the Allies won the Battle of Anzio, they'd have a firm foothold and could then turn their efforts to Rome.

"Hello, all!" Nell said. "May I present our guest of honor?"

"Hollis Muir!" Mary took her cue and stepped forward. "We've come a long way from Quincy High, haven't we? Let me introduce you to Bette Davis and Hedda Hopper. And this gentleman is her photographer, Jaik Rosenstein."

It was the guy Nell had encountered on the Cadillac lot. He offered her nothing beyond a nice-to-see-you-again nod.

As Hedda quizzed Hollis on his war experience, Bette pulled Nell aside. "You need to speak with Glenn about the singer you lined up."

*Dammit! And we were so close!*

Nell discreetly left the group and approached the stage where Miller and his orchestra were tuning their instruments.

"Captain Miller," she said, "I'm Nell Davenport. You should have heard Gunnery Sergeant Muir when I told him you were playing today."

Miller looked up from his music. Six feet tall with wire-rimmed glasses, he had a long, serious face that softened when he smiled. "What's an extra ten minutes stacked up against what that man has endured?"

"Is there a problem with Violet?"

Miller jumped off the stage. "I got a call letting me know that Violet's come down with laryngitis."

"Laryngitis?!"

"Two shows a night at the Seven Seas, plus all those radio appearances. That girl needs to pace herself."

"But you're supposed to start in less than five minutes."

"We can still play."

"But 'Thank Your Lucky Stars' is his favorite song. The lyrics are all about being thankful and being lucky. He barely survived Guadalcanal. It won't be the same without Violet singing as he dances with Mary."

"I have a suggestion." Nell hadn't noticed Bette was now standing behind her.

"Please tell me Dinah Shore is rostered on tonight," Nell said.

"Why don't *you* sing it?"

Nell nearly dropped her handbag. "We can come up with a better solution than *me*!"

"Dinah's doing a USO tour with Abbott and Costello, God help her. That song's been playing on the radio nonstop since the movie came out, so you must know the lyrics by now."

"Well—yes—I suppose so . . ." Nell realized she was getting steamrolled, the Bette Davis way.

Bette clapped her hands. "Crisis averted!"

Hollis cracked a joke that made Mary giggle like a highschooler. He was grinning wider than Nell thought possible. She accepted Miller's offered hand to climb up onto the stage. "Can you give me the opener?"

He raised his slide trombone and played the first note. "To make it memorable, we're going to do the number twice, okay?" *Twice?* Nell nodded. "I'll count you in. Four, three—" *Oh sweet Jesus, I'm really doing this.* Nell faced the microphone. Hollis and Mary were already in position. *Here goes nothing.* "—two, one, and—"

Hearing her voice through the loudspeakers for the very first time made Nell stutter through the initial few lines. She recovered by the fourth line about "doin' fine" because she'd found that she was, in fact, doing just that. Was this how she'd sounded to Betty that night up on Mulholland Drive?

You're not too terrible. You're no Dinah Shore, and you wish Violet hadn't come down with laryngitis. God knows you wouldn't want to do this for a living, but you're not embarrassing yourself.

Nell got to the bridge about how everybody was getting along with less these days. That certainly was true. Thanks to a bunch of gardening tips Hollis had shared with Nell, the boardinghouse victory garden was making a slow but manifest recovery from the abuse it had suffered at inexperienced hands. And Bogie was living with more love in his life than he'd ever experienced. Especially right now, when he was on the *Sluggy* with Betty, knowing that Hedda was here and not snooping around the Newport Yacht Club. And as for Mayo, it was safe to assume that she was passed out on the sofa.

Perhaps it really was time everybody thanked their lucky stars.

As she neared the end, where she sang about how love was the only thing they wouldn't be rationing, she saw Olivia de Havilland walk in with Elsa Lanchester. Right behind them were Irene Dunne, Dick Powell, and Judy Garland. Of course, the Canteen's famous volunteers would start showing up before the opening time! Dick and Judy had proper voices. Compared to them, she felt like she was barking into the microphone like Rin Tin Tin with an acute case of distemper.

*Holy mackerel, and we're only halfway through.*

More people showed up: Marlene Dietrich! Orson Welles and Rita Hayworth! Joan Bennett!

Finally, a familiar face. Nell hadn't seen Ingrid Bergman since the *Casablanca* premiere. As Nell sang about keeping one's love life as sweet as candy bars, Ingrid did a double-take, popped her fists onto her hips, and mouthed the word "Wow!" Nell shifted her gaze to Hollis until she arrived at the final note, as Miller directed his percussionist to end with a crash of cymbals. By the time she had hopped off the stage, the first wave of servicemen had surged in and Nell had to shoulder her way through the swarm of uniforms.

"Nell!" Ingrid grabbed her hands. "You can sing!"

Nell hoped Ingrid couldn't feel how her fingers were quivering, or how the fine hairs along her arms were standing on end. "I was a last-minute replacement for—"

Nell glimpsed Violet through the swarming multitudes. Or was she? It was hard to think straight, especially with her heart still pounding against her rib cage.

"Thank you," she told Ingrid, "but I've just seen the person I least expected to encounter." She jostled around a clutch of airmen until she came face to face with Violet Beaudine. Laryngitis? Baloney! "What is this, April Fool's Day?"

"I bumped into Betty Bacall at the Jade Lounge, sitting by herself, waiting for someone. We got to chatting, and she told me about how wonderfully well you sing, but you don't realize how good you are. I didn't know either until I heard myself in an actual vaudeville house. I thought to myself 'I ain't too shabby!'" Nell's pounding chest and prickling skin subsided as the heady rush of exhilaration ebbed away. Violet clapped a heavy hand on Nell's shoulder. "You're good. Real good."

Little Nell, who had sung "Three Little Words" and "Happy Days Are Here Again" in the woods outside South Bend, would have given anything to hear praise like that. If she had, her life might have followed a different road.

Behind Violet, a man around Nell's age stepped away from Rita Hayworth's coffee station and turned toward the dance floor. He was in a first lieutenant's Army uniform with a garrison cap at a jaunty angle and his tie tucked into his khaki shirt. But it was his profile that sucked the air from her lungs.

It couldn't be.

Could it?

He's so far from home.

Then again, so am I.

And there *is* a war on, y'know.

"You'll have to excuse me," she told Violet. "I've just seen someone from South Bend."

She still had time to melt into the crowd. But no. That'd be wrong. Whether he would accept her apology was up to him. But this might be her only chance to ask for his forgiveness.

Nell arranged a welcoming smile on her face and stepped around a knot of sailors until she was almost next to the guy she had deserted at the altar.

Maybe he hadn't been standing inside St. Matthew when he had learned his fiancée had done a moonlight flit, but that was how she'd had always pictured him. Not that she had flitted by the light of the silvery moon. That Greyhound bus had left at eleven in the morning. Still and all, she had slunk out of town like a shamefaced wretch who knew it was only a matter of time before the villagers chased her with pitchforks and flaming torches.

"Ha-a-a-ank!" His name came out an almost-inaudible croak over the tumult of energetic dancers jitterbugging to Glenn Miller's boisterous music.

His blank smile dropped away like it was made of cement. He pawed at the knot of his khaki necktie. "Gosh, but it's good to see you."

*How could it be? I stood you up. At the altar.* She could only stare at him.

"I heard you singing up on stage," he said. He had to fill in the chasm of silence her stupor had opened up. "You sounded wonderful."

"Did you know I'd be here?"

"Before I left town, I called Vesta and asked for your address. Your landlady told me you weren't at home, but suggested I try here." His thick fingers dropped away from the tie. "You shoulda seen the expression on my face when I realized it was you coming through that speaker they've got set up out front. You're the headliner!"

"Me? Gosh, no." Where was her purse to occupy her shaking hands? "That was a one-off."

"You sure sounded like a real singer to me."

A gang of apprentice seamen elbowed past them.

She curled her finger for him to follow her, and wended through the throng to the western wall, then through a side door and into the empty lounge.

"The Canteen is for enlisted men only, but this way we can accommodate officers." She drew a circle in the air around his first lieutenant silver bar. "You qualify." That smile of his. Humble almost to the point of meek. *It's one of his most appealing features. How could I have forgotten it?* "So, the Army, huh?"

"I've been at Camp Campbell in Kentucky for the last year, but they sent me all the way here to take charge of a platoon. I've got a night's R-and-R before we head out at oh-six-hundred tomorrow."

Nell fought against a rising panic filling her chest, threatening to choke her. He had shown up for a reason, and she was pretty sure she knew what it was. She crossed to the bar and pulled out whatever bottle her hand found. Four Roses bourbon. It was the same brand Luke had developed a taste for thanks to hanging around with Bogie. She poured two shots, slid one across to Hank, and downed the other. It burned her throat and made her eyes water. "All right, then. Out with it."

Hank took the shot glass but didn't drink from it. "Out with what?"

"I slunk away like a spineless jellyfish without the decency to break our engagement to your face." Whoa! No wonder Bogie likes this Four Roses stuff. It delivers the goods faster than you can say 'I don't.' She poured herself another slug. "I waited until that very morning to climb out of my bedroom window and slink down back alleys like a—"

"Thief in the night?"

The jab was a knife to the ribs, but not unfair. "Yes, like some devious crook skipping town. Nobody deserves that, least of all you. You're a good guy, Hank. I didn't run away because you're a louse. But I did run away, and you have every right to yell at me. I've got it coming, so go on. Let me have it. Both guns blazing."

She threw back the shot of bourbon. It didn't scorch her throat like the first time, but filled her with enough Dutch courage to take her punishment. She clenched her stomach into a tight ball.

Hank deposited his shot onto the bar untouched. "I'm not here for that."

Hank wasn't screaming or cussing at her. Nor had he punched a hole in the wall like she'd been imagining all this time.

"Don't you hate me? Even a little?"

"Trust me, I did."

Okay, now we're getting somewhere. "I hated me, too."

"I had no idea humiliation could fester down that deep. It stopped me from leaving the house for days."

This conversation wasn't going the way Nell had always played out in her imagination. Not one little bit. She was tempted to swill a third drink, but decided she ought to keep her head clear. She moved to the window, where strands of "Tuxedo Junction" bled through the glass.

"That bad, huh?"

"I spent every waking moment stewing in enough self-pity to drown a hippo. Around about then I started drinking. Heavily."

This was not the budding pillar of the community and probable future South Bend city council member she had dumped in the most heartless way. "I can't even imagine that."

"It was shocking how quickly I took to it. And then one day I fell asleep in church."

"No!"

"I woke up sitting alone in the fourth pew."

"Hank!"

"I've never been so mortified. I asked Father Philip if he had a rock I could crawl under."

"What did he say?"

"He looked me in the eye, kinda cheeky-like, and said 'Steel yourself. I'm about to quote the Buddha at you.'" Hank smiled. It was a crooked little grin that lifted at one end, showing that snaggle tooth he always used to hide.

Why didn't he smile like that when we were dating? Why didn't he ever show me this side of him? "The Buddha, huh? Do you remember the quote?"

"I sure do: 'Holding onto anger is like drinking poison and expecting the other person to die.'"

Miller announced the band was taking a quick break. A hush settled over the officers' lounge.

"Father Philip always knew the right thing to say."

"I walked out of church a changed man. I marched straight over to your house and told your dad what he said. I was hoping it would get him to see a different perspective, too."

Judging by Vesta's letter warning her that Mom and Dad were running out of patience, Nell guessed that the Buddha's nugget of wisdom hadn't had the same effect. "I don't need to ask how that went over."

"Look, Nell, I didn't come here tonight to yell at you or make you feel guilty."

"I wouldn't blame you. I had it coming."

"It's all in the past now."

"That's big of you to say, Hank. Thank you."

"I came here because of your dad."

A tremor of dread shuddered through her. Dad had always been healthy as a racehorse. The joke in the Davenport household was that it'd take a runaway locomotive during a hurricane to bring him down. "He's not sick, is he?"

"Nah, he's fine. Well, physically, anyway."

"Did he tell you I'm paying off the wedding? Two grand at five dollars a week means I'll be free of that debt by 1951."

"Not if you come back to Indiana."

So that was it. Father had sent Hank to broker a surrender. It was a tremendous relief to know that Hank didn't hate her anymore, but to use the poor guy to act as a go-between? What a coward.

"You can tell dear ol' Dad that you've accomplished your mission. You've transmitted the message to the enemy, who acknowledges receipt and thanks you for your service."

"I came of my own accord." Hank's tone had thickened. She wished she hadn't sounded so high-handed. "Nell, I'm heading into war, most likely onto the front lines, where life is cheap. Your father is having a lot of trouble getting past what happened five years ago, so it's up to you to make it right."

"My moving back to South Bend might be right for him, but it's not right for me."

"So then show him what is."

"How do I do that?"

"I don't know, but figure it out." He checked his watch. "My pass expires at twenty-two hundred hours."

"Taxis wait on Cahuenga. Let me walk you out there." She turned to leave.

"I'd prefer we said goodbye here." He summoned a smile. "California suits you." She could only manage a nod in reply. "Do you have a special fella?" Nell wished she could do more than nod at him like a cheap kewpie doll, but words had deserted her. As he made for the door, she hoped he'd give her a backward glance to remember him by. He didn't, but instead closed it behind him with a firm click.

The band hurled itself into "Pennsylvania 6-5000." Nell leaned her forehead against the window. The opening chord shook the glass, sending a vibration over her scalp and down her neck.

"It's up to you to make it right, Nell," she told herself. "Figure it out."

## 27

Nell hadn't yet pulled the cover off her typewriter when Paisley came steaming toward her like a crazed dump trick. "Why didn't you tell me that you sing?" She slapped the *Examiner* onto Nell's desk.

Nell plucked off her gloves. A week had passed since that night at the Canteen, and not one of Hedda's columns had mentioned Mary dancing with her old school chum. Nell had given up hoping she would stick to her word.

*I was one lucky so-and-so at the Hollywood Canteen last week when I witnessed Mary Astor, so winsome in MGM's upcoming* Meet Me in St. Louis, *prove what an unflinching patriot she is by giving a plucky war veteran a memorable whirl around the dance floor to Glenn Miller's music. Gunnery Sergeant Muir took a beating at Guadalcanal, but his spirits soared in the arms of lovely Mary. But the most delightful surprise of the night came when a talented new singing sensation stepped up to the microphone. Her name is Nell Davenport and the big question on my lips is: Where has she been hiding all this time? Whenever and wherever she pops up next, I'll be there because this gal's really got it!*

. . .

Nell sighed. "I wish she hadn't done that."

"The boss agrees." Paisley tilted her head toward Taplinger's office. "I'm here to fetch you."

Nell thanked her for the forewarning and walked in, holding Paisley's newspaper. "You wanted to see me about this, I presume?"

He gestured at an empty guest chair. "The golden rule of the PR department is: Don't be the story."

"Violet Beaudine was supposed to sing that night, but at the last minute—"

"I don't care if you're Kate Smith. PR helps to make the story happen—"

"Yes, sir, but—"

"—so that the performers we have under contract get as much ballyhoo as we can drum up."

"Violet came down with laryngitis. We had three minutes to come up with a replacement. I'd rather not have done it at all, but Mary was there and the band was there—"

Taplinger bared his crooked teeth at her like a rabid dog. "I'm not happy, Miss Davenport."

"I can see that, sir. I know the spotlight is for—"

"I'm not happy—I'm delighted!" He burst out laughing.

Nell's vision clouded over. "You're not angry that—"

"We've got a little songbird in our midst! How marvelous! And not just because Orry-Kelly has tasked me with finding a singer for his send-off."

Nell wondered if Tristan knew about this yet. "Orry-Kelly is leaving the studio?"

"Keep it under your hat for now, but yes. He doesn't want a fuss, but Mr. Warner thinks it's a fantastic publicity opportunity, so he's insisting on a big bash, with everyone invited: stars and contract players, as well as every columnist, journalist, and press agent in town. There'll be entertainment; you'll be singing."

The hairs along her arms and up the back of her neck stood on end like they had at the Canteen. "Get Dick Powell to do it. Or Cagney. It'll remind him of his vaudeville days."

"No, I—"

"What about Martha Raye? She'll have 'em cheering from the rafters."

"No, I—"

"Frances Langford! Dennis Morgan! Any of the Lane sisters—better yet, all of them."

"Mr. Warner wants them circulating among the press. We need someone who can add atmosphere, not detract, and that makes you the perfect candidate."

Yikes. Getting up on the stage had been hard enough—and there'd only been a handful of people in the audience. The thought of appearing in front of everyone at Warner Bros. made Nell break out into a cold sweat. "When's this jamboree happening?"

"Not till June. You've got plenty of time to learn ten songs."

"*Ten?*" Double yikes.

"I've left it up to Leo Forbstein to pick them."

Forbstein was the genius head of Warners' music department, and every bit as talented as the composers who wrote film scores week after week. Learning ten songs in two months meant nearly a song a week. That didn't sound so bad. Not in theory. But there was nothing theoretical about getting up in front of God only knew how many hundreds of people and forgetting every word of every lyric of every song.

Make that triple yikes.


When Nell arrived on the *Have Not* set, Hawks was directing close-ups of Hoagy Carmichael, so she made her way over to

Bogie's dressing room. Tony stood at the vanity mirror combing Bogie's main toupée.

"Where is he?" she asked.

Tony looked up from his handiwork. "They've already released him and Betty."

"It's not even lunchtime."

"Today's been," he bugged out his eyes, "rough. Bogie kept blowing his lines over and over. The more he bungled, the more anxious he got. And that threw Betty off, so then she started blowing her lines, too. Which made Hawks fly off the handle."

Buttoned down and zipped up, Hawks was the most self-controlled person Nell had ever encountered. She didn't even think he possessed a handle to fly off from. "He let them go after half a day's work?"

"They were no use to him." Tony gave her a second, more considered survey. "What's up with you?"

She told him about Orry-Kelly's departure and how her boss had shanghaied her into performing, and how the whole idea was already giving her clammy hands and damp underarms.

"What about your makeup?"

"What about it?"

"You can't go on stage wearing nothing."

Nell was still getting used to the notion that Taplinger wanted her to sing at Orry-Kelly's party. What shade of lipstick she'd wear that night was hardly a top priority. "I'll figure it out."

He chewed on his lower lip for a moment, looking more like Luke than she had ever noticed. "I can do more than hair."

"Makeup too? Does Perc know about this?"

"Perhaps we could do a dry run. Find out what works best for you. If you like what you see, then I'll approach him."

"I'm not the makeup type."

"It'll give you confidence to waltz onto that stage and show 'em what you got."

"Mr. Warner wants a musical wallflower who doesn't detract."

"You still want to look good, don't you?"

Yes, of course, but there would be loads of time for that later. "I'm worried about Bogie. He's not the type to get rattled, no matter what's going on in his personal life. Do you think I should go see him?"

"Apparently there was an incident with a rifle."

"Oh, Jesus. Maybe I'll swing by his house on the way home from work."

He threw her a look that wasn't hard to interpret: *You should.*

Nell rang the doorbell. The long walk from the streetcar stop had given her time—too much, probably—to wonder if she was intruding where nobody had any business to intrude.

Mayo opened the door wearing a ratty housedress with faded stripes. "Oh, it's you." Three slurred syllables were enough to tell that she was blitzed to the gills. "Come lookin' for Bogie, I s'pose."

"I was passing by and—"

Mayo kicked the door to open more with the heel of her mule and tottered into the living room.

Sofa cushions were scattered all over. The tall porcelain vase with its bucolic English countryside scene lay in pieces at the foot of the grand piano; a puddle of water had seeped into the rug. One of the drapes had come loose from its hooks and now hung in dispirited folds. The place reeked of cigarettes and beer.

"Skuze the mess," Mayo said, waving the Parliament she had lit. "Bogie and I, we had ourselves a . . ." She curled her top lip as she ransacked her addled mind for a socially acceptable way to describe what had transpired. "Clash of opinions." She headed to the bar, where a half-empty tumbler of brandy awaited her.

"I thought I'd check on him after I heard he didn't have a great day on set."

Mayo whirled around to face Nell with bleary eyes, reddened

from too much booze, too much vicious fighting, and too much self-pity. "Who checks on *me?*"

A rifle lay on the sideboard underneath the window. Nell had been on the sets of enough war pictures to know a bolt-action .22 varmint rifle when she saw one.

*You were punch-drunk, wildly disorderly, and lucky you weren't arrested.* Nell eyed the rifle. "Were you carrying that?"

"I merely waved it around to show him I meant business."

"How'd he take it?"

Mayo's shoulders drooped as she slurped the dregs of her brandy. "He said that my stabbing him with a kitchen knife was one thing, but he drew the line at getting shot. That's when he packed a bag." She blinked very slowly. "He left me."

Oh, Lordy! It's happened! She pushed Bogie too far. "Do you know where he went?"

"My guess is the Garden of Allah. He stayed there when he came out here to make *The Petrified Forest.* If he ain't there, pfffft. Damned if I know. Damned if I care."

That last sentence wasn't true, but Bogie's state of mind concerned Nell more. She muttered her thanks and told Mayo she'd see herself out.

\* \* \*

Nell hadn't lived in Los Angeles too long before the Garden of Allah Hotel's louche reputation had wafted past her like an exotic perfume. Her boardinghouse landlady referred to it as "the House of Anything Goes." On the set of *The Roaring Twenties,* Nell had overheard Jerry Wald describe it as "the kind of joint you take your mistress because nobody cares how much noise you make."

She passed an explosion of vivid magenta bougainvillea and stepped inside the foyer. A little on the dark side, it looked like the scene of a Maria Montez picture set in Baghdad or Tangier. The bell under a pyramid-shaped Tiffany lamp conjured a friendly clerk in a white linen suit who told her that Bogie was in villa fifteen, and pointed her towards a door that led out to a pool.

On the pool's eastern edge, a gang of merrymakers had gathered around a table crowned with a striped umbrella. As Nat King Cole sang "Straighten Up and Fly Right" from out of an unseen radio, a woman screeched as she fell into the water. A gangly Gary Cooper cowboy type called out, "Who do you think are, Tallulah Bankhead?"

"No," the woman retorted, "I've still got my clothes *on*!"

Nell rapped on the door to Bogie's villa. He answered it with one-half of his shirt front worked loose from his beltless pants, no shoes, no toupée, and an almost-dead Chesterfield glued to the corner of his mouth. A filmy shadow dulled his eyes. "Sherlock Davenport, I presume?"

"May I?"

He lumbered backward. "Proceed at your own risk."

Inside, she sniffed at the air. It was stale and fusty. "On a scale of one to ten, how tanked are you?"

"The night is yet young." He tapped a full bottle of Wild Turkey; its neighbor was empty. He popped the cork, poured out a pair of double shots, and handed her one. "Here's to . . ." His glass remained aloft for ten interminable seconds before he flicked the cigarette in the general direction of an ashtray with an intricate 'Garden of Allah Hotel' logo stenciled on the bottom. She picked the butt off the floor before it burned a hole in the faded pink carpet and dropped it into the ashtray.

He flopped onto a couch upholstered in dark blue velvet and belched like a toad. "The infamous Battling Bogarts had just rounded the final turn into the straight when Madam pulled that knife on me. But they reached the finishing line yesterday when she swapped that knife for a gun."

"She told me she just waved it around."

"You've spoken to her?"

"I looked for you at the house."

"You're a braver man than I, Sherlock."

"The two of you really went at it, hammer and tongs."

"*And* tooth. *And* nail. Bataan had nothing on us. There's no bouncing back from getting shot at."

"She actually pulled the trigger?"

"I'm surprised our neighbors didn't call the cops."

"I'm surprised she didn't call Hedda Hopper."

Nell's comment induced a smile, tinged with gloom though it was. "Those two are welcome to each other."

Wild Turkey wasn't Nell's favorite tipple in the world, but it'd do in a pinch. And this was one hell of a pinch. She tossed it back. "You're all done with Mayo?"

He sprawled his loose limbs in four directions. "I've moved out, haven't I?"

"No chance you'll move back in?"

"None. Nada. Nil."

"In that case, if your marriage is over, you'll have to break the news via somebody. If you choose Hedda, it'd get her off my back. And possibly yours."

They sat in silence until Nell could no longer stand the stuffy, closed-in room. "Jeez, Bogie. Would it kill you to open a window?" She stepped over to the large one next to the front door and grasped the handle. It edged upward with a squeak. A velvety breeze blew in from outside, and with it the sounds of laughter and splashing water.

"What is it with you and Hedda, anyhow?" Nell joined Bogie on the sofa. "Jaik mentioned the Dies Committee."

"She snuck into a sneak preview of *Dark Victory*, then whipped off a review that raved over Bette's performance, and Edmund's direction, and Max's score, saving her one biting criticism for me. I was still ticked off ten days later when Mayo and I joined a studio press junket train to Kansas for the premiere of *Dodge City*. She was on board too, so one afternoon I bribed the porter twenty bucks to let me into her compartment."

"Oh God. What did you do?"

"Threw every ugly hat out the window."

"No!"

"And one shoe from each pair she'd packed. I bet there's some poor farmer outside La Junta, Colorado, still scratching his head."

"Did she know it was you?"

"I was the first person she accused. I denied it, naturally, and I planned to come clean before we arrived in Dodge City. But Jesus fucking Christ, she kicked up such a stink. Made life miserable for everyone on board. By the time our train pulled into town, we hated her guts even more than we already did. Every chance she got, she carped on at me about the stupidest shit. Criticized me for everything I'd ever said or done."

"The more she did it, the deeper you dug your heels in."

Bogie raised his glass to toast Nell's observation. "Not long after that, she out-scooped Louella for the first time. She caught wind that FDR's son was getting a divorce. We all thought, 'Finally, someone's giving Louella a run for her money.' What we didn't realize was that we had a bigger Frankenstein on our hands —one that hated FDR. Later, when I had to testify before the Dies Committee that I wasn't a Commie, I realized it was probably Hedda who'd been whispering in their ear. A whisper of a rumor was all it took. So when I was exonerated, I stumped for Roosevelt as often and as publicly as I could."

"Just to get her goat?"

"I think FDR is aces. Campaigning for him *and* infuriating Hedda Hopper was a productive use of my time."

"And now she wants to piss on the grave of your third failed marriage."

Bogie swirled a mouthful of bourbon around his mouth before forcing it down in a single gulp. "I need you to do me the biggest favor I could possibly ask of you."

An uneasy feeling of dread tightened around Nell's throat. "Okay."

"Go back to the house and convince Mayo it's time for Reno."

Nell thought of the rifle and was silently thankful she had missed a bullet now lodged in one of the walls. "The marriage is over, isn't it? Absolutely? Definitely? Positively?"

"You didn't hear what she said. It was bad, even for her. I can take that, but you wouldn't believe what she said about Betty."

"I got a taste."

He looked at her beseechingly. "Will you do it for me?"

"I have to give Hedda something. Now that the marriage is over, can I give her this?"

Bogie lurched forward into an upright position. "Not until Mayo spends six weeks in Reno."

"Mrs. Bogart disappearing from the social scene will raise eyebrows. Hedda's highest of all. If you tell me what to say, you get to influence what gets printed." Nell could tell she was getting through to him by the way he pulled out a fresh cigarette, but didn't light it. "You need to think of the delicate predicament Betty's in."

He lit the cigarette. "You're right. Tell her . . . tell her . . ."

"Where is Mayo from?"

"Chicago."

"I'll tell Hedda that Mayo's gone home to Chicago for an extended stay with family because she hasn't been back in so long."

"Right. Yes. Good." Bogie crossed his legs. His foot jiggled, but Nell doubted he was aware of it.

"How about 'It's a rocky marriage weathering life's storms just fine.'"

The jiggle halted. "Thanks for doing this."

"I haven't said I'll do it yet. Don't forget: Your wife has a rifle."

Nell seesawed half a dozen times in the thirty-seven minutes it took her to walk back to Horn Avenue. Was it really her place to talk Mayo into agreeing on a trip to Reno? Shouldn't it be some fat-cat, high-profile divorce lawyer's job? On the other hand, it might help to placate Hedda—at least for the time being.

She rang the doorbell and stood in the doorframe, ready to look Mayo in the eyes.

The muffled yapping of the Scottish terriers bled through the mail slot until Mayo slowly opened the door.

"Hello again," Nell said. "We need to talk."

## 28

Nell stared out of the window overlooking the path to the administration building.

Paisley joined her. "Expecting someone?"

"Kathryn Massey." It had taken six weeks to organize this visit, but the day had, at last, arrived. "I've invited her to the final day of shooting on *To Have and Have Not*. Ever met her?"

"She's a straight shooter. None of Louella's and Hedda's histrionics. Don't try to put one over on her, though. Be up front and she'll deal you a fair hand."

A woman in a cinnamon-brown suit and pale pink blouse marched along the path with purpose in her stride. It was exactly ten o'clock.

Nell walked into the reception area. Now that she could see the columnist up close, it was clear Massey had tailored her serge suit to show off her figure to its fullest advantage. It was quite unlike anything Nell had seen in the stores. "Hello, Miss Massey. I'm Nell Davenport."

Her handshake was firm as a man's. "Please, call me Kathryn."

"I should've met you out front."

"I could do with the exercise." Kathryn patted her stomach. "I had a big British dinner at the Cock 'n Bull last night, including their trifle pudding, which I should have said no to." They were out in the early-summer sun now, passing the commissary. "You ever been?"

"'Fraid not."

"It's excellent. Of course, that's easy for me to say because I live down the street."

"The Garden of Allah, right?"

Kathryn didn't bother to hide her double-take. "You've done your homework."

"Bogie mentioned it."

"I haven't seen much of him since he checked in. At the Garden, it usually means someone's on a bender."

This woman had a forthrightness to her that Nell had rarely encountered in Hollywood. What a refreshing change. She didn't strike Nell as being the fishing type, but that comment about being on a bender sure sounded like it.

"*To Have and Have Not* has been a delight for him," Nell said, "But it's also been a tough slog."

"A sixty-two-day shoot is enough to wear on anyone's nerves. Speaking of nerves, how about that Olivia de Havilland taking the studio to court? Who even knew we had anti-peonage laws? Talk about gutsy."

Nell breathed a little easier, knowing that Kathryn wasn't fishing for tawdry scuttlebutt. "Nobody believed she would win the right to walk away after finishing a seven-year contract."

"I'd imagine it'll change the way the studios do business with their players." Kathryn started to laugh, but cut herself off. "Oh, I'm sorry. If Jack Warner has instructed you all to toe the official line with the press, I'd understand."

They turned the corner of Stage One and headed down D Avenue.

"That depends on whether we're talking on the record yet."

"My three favorite words are 'off the record.' Let's assume nothing's official until we walk onto the set."

"In that case," Nell lowered her voice conspiratorially, "let's just say Mr. Warner screamed at his legal team for so long that he can't speak right now."

"Makes you wonder if there's a single vase left unbroken in the Warner manse."

They passed the elephant door of Stage Twelve, where the construction crew was building a replica of the Hollywood Canteen. A workman pushing a wheelbarrow full of raw wood planks stopped to mop his face with a raggedy kerchief. Nell took care to give his cargo a wide berth. The wood's splintery ends could all too easily rip a hole in her nylons.

Distracted by steering clear of the whole disaster zone, she paid no attention to the trio of broken café chairs stacked against the wall. A stray nail scraped Nell's left leg. She felt it split her stocking.

"Darn it!" She inspected the damage. "That was one of my last decent pairs. I should have saved them for the *To Have and Have Not* premiere."

"You should go see my friend Gwendolyn," Kathryn said. "She works in the perfume department at Bullocks Wilshire."

The gash was four inches long. It'd be impossible to repair. Nell straightened up. "Bullocks is out of my price range. And besides, perfume's not going to fix this."

Set painters in grimy overalls stepped out of the soundstage. Kathryn coaxed Nell forward and whispered, "She also sells nylons on the sly. Tell her I sent you."

Nell had expected to find a high-spirited company nearing the end of a long, tough shoot. She stopped when she sensed heavy air pervading the soundstage.

Extras filled the tables crammed onto the elaborate hotel café set, where a crewmember swung a smoke canister around like a Catholic priest with his thurible. It was the best way to add a smoky atmosphere when two hundred people smoking cigarettes represented too much of a fire danger. Off to the right, Betty, wearing the form-fitting two-piece with the bold black-and-white check pattern, leaned against Hoagy's piano. With Bogie nowhere in sight, Nell led Kathryn to her.

"Betty, I want you to meet Kathryn Massey from *The Hollywood Reporter*. Kathryn, this is Betty Bacall."

As the women shook hands, Betty said, "Officially, I'm Lauren, but I'll be damned if I can get used to it."

"Does it feel odd answering to some other name?" Kathryn asked.

Betty tucked her chin toward her throat. "Ask me again in three months after the movie comes out."

Betty's voice was tight; her words were rigid and stiff, the way they'd sounded on the first day of production. A large cloth bag hung from her wrist. She twisted its black velvet strap around her thumb, unwound it, then coiled it once more.

What the heck was happening? Nobody was talking, let alone laughing. Betty was taut as a tightrope. Bogie had disappeared. Hawks, too. The crewmembers were going about their work as though they'd taken a vow of silence.

"So," Kathryn said, "is it true that Howard beefed up your part when he saw how well you came across on camera?"

Betty shot Nell a sharp look. *Can I talk about that?* He had built up her role at Dolores Moran's expense because of the feverish chemistry between his star and his ingenue. Nell nodded and waited until Betty was deep into her explanation before she excused herself and picked her way through the extras to Bogie's dressing room.

She found Bogie at his makeup vanity, with one hand around a tumbler. A near-empty bottle of Wild Turkey stood at his elbow.

Tony stood behind him, a toupée hanging from his grip like a dead octopus.

"It's not even noon yet," she said.

"It is in London."

"Will someone please explain to me what's going on?"

Bogie made a you-tell-her gesture at Tony.

"Yesterday morning, Mayo returned home from Reno."

"But it's only been three weeks. That means she—"

"—hasn't qualified for a divorce." Bogie's voice was sour enough to curdle a bottle of milk.

"Is she back at the house?"

"Yep."

"Are you still at the Garden of Allah?"

"Nope."

Uh-oh. Nell hazarded a couple of steps closer. The funk of bourbon fouled the air. "She talked you into giving the marriage another go."

"I told you before: I'm a last-century guy who—"

"—marries till death do you part."

"Yes!"

"All three times."

A wounded look passed across Bogie's face. Nell wished she'd held off taking a cheap shot like that, especially when it was plain that his fidelity to marriage as an institution and his love for Betty were cleaving him in two.

She rested a hip on the edge of the makeup counter. "When you peer into the future, do you see yourself with Mayo?"

"Hell, no."

"And what do you see when you think about Betty?"

"A long and happy forever."

"Doesn't that solve your dilemma?" Bogie couldn't even manage a syllable or two in reply. "How has Betty taken this news?"

"I was expecting tears and shouting and flying paperweights."

"The girl I saw out there has battened down the hatches, but it'd be a mistake to assume she's taken it well."

"Should I check on her?"

"Not right now. Kathryn Massey is interviewing her. You're next."

"That's today?" Bogie hung his head. "Not that Kathryn would mind. God knows she's seen me more stinko than this."

"But that's private-life territory. This is professional time."

"I'm a selfish, miserable bastard son of a bitch, aren't I?"

"No, but you're acting like one." Nell pried the tumbler from his fingers. "Tony's going to slide that toupée onto your bean. And then you're going to practice your most charming movie-star smile. Not only for Kathryn. Or for Betty. But for everyone who's working so hard to make this movie great."

"You're right. They deserve better." He ran his hands over his thinning hair. "It'd help if you could scare up some coffee."

"Now you're talking." She left the dressing room before Bogie could ask for his bourbon back.

\* \* \*

Nell strode into the Bar of Music on Beverly Boulevard, hoping she had arrived ahead of Betty so that she could have a drink ready for her. But Betty was seated at a four-top with most of her Old Fashioned already guzzled.

Nell unpinned her hat and dropped it on the table. "Sorry I'm late. By the time Kathryn Massey and I said goodbye—"

Betty hoisted her empty glass until she caught the eye of the bartender. "I showed her my best 'Isn't It All So Wonderful?' face, but I'm not sure she bought it."

The nail polish on Betty's ring finger had a jagged chip out of it and her lipstick was crooked. "I swung by the soundstage at five o'clock, but you'd left."

"There didn't seem to be much point hanging around."

"Did you get through filming okay?"

"In my last shot, I say goodbye to Hoagy and then do a sexy hip-wiggle dance to his music as we make our exit. When Howard called 'Cut,' I kept walking to my dressing room, pulled off my costume, then drove off the lot and to the spot on Selma we used to meet at."

"For a little cry?"

"More like wailing like a wounded buffalo. I'm surprised nobody called the cops. 'There's a crazy woman driving a gray Plymouth. Send the guys with the straightjacket.'"

"I wish I could have been there for you."

The bartender arrived with fresh Old Fashioneds. They clinked glasses. Betty's sip was, Nell noticed, a lot longer than hers.

"I've nobody to blame but myself," Betty said. "I jumped in, feet first, eyes wide open. You hear about it all the time in movie rags. How two stars get carried away, extending their love scenes to the bedroom. I assumed it would burn itself out once filming was over. But now that it's—" Her voice faltered. She lit a cigarette, forgetting she already had one smoldering in the triangular ashtray. "Here I am, feeling like a chump."

"You're not a chump," Nell said. "Just a girl who fell in love."

"After he moved into the Garden of Allah, our bond grew deeper and deeper. We didn't have to keep one eye on the door, dreading that Mayo would come busting through with a pickax. That hotel is so low-key. Nobody cares what you're up to. I suspect it's because everyone else is doing the same thing. I even told Bogie how Howard called me to his house to tell me that I meant nothing to him—Bogie, I mean—and that he might sell my contract to Monogram."

This was news. Nell sat upright. "To Poverty Row?" For a girl like Betty, whose film debut was shaping up to be a turning point, this would be a fatal blow. "He was bluffing."

"That's what I thought. But not much later, Hedda warned me

about Mayo. She told me, 'You might have a lamp dropped on you.'"

That sounded like a typical Mayo comment.

"What was Bogie's reaction?"

"He said Hedda was full of baloney, but he drove straight to Howard's place. Slim told me later they had a shouting match on the tennis court that got so vicious she was tempted to turn the garden hose on them. He was still livid when he got back." She giggled. "I lured him into the bedroom and let him work out his anger on me." Her smile fell away as quickly as it had surfaced. "It backfired, though. We grew even closer. I never knew it could be like that. I mean, not like *that*."

Nell glanced quickly at the door, then back to Betty. Tristan and Tony would be here soon, so she had little time to say what she needed to say. The four of them were there to see Sabine Vogel, who had been the queen of Berlin cabaret before the war. Nell wasn't sure how Sabine had become a boardinghouse neighbor of Luke's, but she was glad to see Sabine was cranking up her singing career again.

"Is Bogart who you want?" she asked. "For sure and forever?" Betty nodded. "I still think that the Battling Bogarts are bound to implode sooner or later. You just have to be there when he needs someone to pick up the pieces."

Betty ran her fingertip back and forth across the chipped nail polish, hesitation splintering her face. "My mom doesn't approve of Bogie—to put it mildly. Now that filming is over, she's going home, so I was wondering if you'd like to move into the other bedroom."

Nell's heart stopped for a moment. "Move in?!"

"The rent'll cost you a lot more. You'll have to cook your own meals and I'm not terribly domesticated—"

"Yes! Yes!" Nell caught sight of a flurry of movement near the entrance. "The boys are here. We can work out the details later."

She squeezed Betty's hand as Tristan dropped himself into an empty chair. "Are those Old Fashioneds? I need one. Scrap that—I need a double. Who can we hump to make that happen?"

Tony put two fingers in his mouth and whistled loud enough to make every head in the place turn. "Another round," he called out to the bartender.

"Busy day at work?" Nell asked.

"Orry-Kelly's practically got one foot out the door, which is horrible timing. *Hollywood Canteen* is going into production, so it's fallen to me to organize all nine hundred thousand costumes. Meanwhile, the Hair and Makeup people are all but having a nervous breakdown. You know how short-handed they are." Tristan flapped his hand at Tony. "Go on. That's your cue."

Tony's hair had regained the luster it'd had that day he'd visited the studio before shipping off to Guadalcanal. His eyes, so similar to Luke's, were clearer now. The whites were whiter, and there was a sharpness to them that hadn't been there before. "Perc Westmore approached me yesterday. He said if I could do makeup too, he'd offer me a regular job at a salary I couldn't believe. Eighty a week."

"That's great!" Nell exclaimed.

"It is. But if I'm well enough to work on pictures, I'm well enough to go back to Brooklyn and face the music."

"There's music to be faced?" Betty asked.

Tony rocked side to side in his chair like he was trying to find his balance. "I didn't used to be the nicest guy. I'm a nasty drunk who gets into too many fights. I've tomcatted around and lied to my wife about it. I was getting sloppy on the job and didn't take Pop's criticism too well. When I left New York, everyone was relieved to see the back of me. I bet none of them have missed me."

Nell had wondered why he'd stayed so long in LA. Not to mention that the Navy must have a convalescent home on the East Coast, seeing as how the Brooklyn Navy Yard was practically in the neighborhood.

"I'm sure you weren't as bad as all that," she said.

"Seeing heavy action, losing a limb—it changes a guy. For most of us, it's a change for the worse, but it's been the making of yours truly."

"So you're going home?"

Tony broke out into a bashful smile. "When I told Perc no, he upped it twenty bucks. I thought, 'Is he screwing with me?' It was hard enough to turn down eighty, but a hundred? With this bum leg, where the hell could I make that kind of dough?"

"What did you tell Perc?"

"I wrote to my wife. Told Audrey all about what's happened to me, how I've changed, what I'm doing now, and how much they're offering me."

"Did you hear from her?"

"Straight away. She said that amount of money doesn't come along every day and suggested I take the job for at least as long as the *Hollywood Canteen* shoot."

"So you'll be around through the summer?" Betty asked. "Bogie's going to be relieved to hear that."

"So was Perc. *And* it gives me a chance to convince Audrey and our daughter to come out for a visit to see if they like it."

"Enough to move here?" Nell wondered how Luke would take this news. He'd never been Tony's biggest fan, but nor was this the brother he'd grown up with.

"We'll see."

As the bartender deposited the new round of drinks and cleared away the empties, Betty poked Nell's elbow. "Don't look now, but Hedda's here."

Nell rolled her eyes. "I've been looking forward to hearing Sabine all week, but now I'll sit and wonder when the old bat will start throwing daggers."

"She's racing over here like her ass is on fire," Tristan sing-songed.

Nell barely had time to gird her loins before she heard Hedda's piercing voice slicing through the air. "A word with you if I may, Miss Davenport."

*Demoted from 'Nell, dear' to 'Miss Davenport.' This can't be good.* "Sabine Vogel's about to go on. Can this wait until tomorrow?"

"Come with me." Hedda turned on her heel and beelined for the ladies' room.

"Excuse me, all," Nell said, slipping out of her seat. "I'm off to go ten rounds in the john."

Hedda walked past the cigarette vending machine outside the bathrooms and through a swinging door to the alley that ran along the back, then whirled to face Nell, her face swirling with outrage and contempt. "After everything I've done for you, you repay me by feeding me false information."

A whiff of decaying vegetables and moldy bread wafted over them. "About what?" Nell already knew the answer, but she was stalling for time until she could gauge what was going on.

"I devoted a full column to how solid the Bogart marriage is," Hedda snapped. "I told my readers, 'The rocky marriage is weathering all storms just fine, and any rumors to the contrary are only that.'" Nell tried to respond, but Hedda cut her off. "I stated in goddamn print how the Bogart marriage will endure long after others have crumbled. And I did that based on the information *you* gave me. You swore up and down that the marriage was fine."

"It was," Nell lied.

"You said she was going to Chicago when, in fact, she traveled to Reno, and Bogie moved out." Hedda crossed her arms. "I made a fool of myself in front of thirty-five million readers."

"I was as surprised as anyone to learn where Mayo was."

"I staked my reputation on your tip-off," Hedda screeched. "What's worse is that Louella's column tomorrow is all about how the Bogarts had separated, and how Mayo went to Reno but had a change of heart and the Bogarts have reconciled. Where does that leave me? The laughingstock of Hollywood, that's where."

Nell wanted to retort that her hats had already done that, but she could see gobs of spittle forming in the corners of the woman's thin lips. "Bogie and Mayo are allowed to reconcile," she said evenly. "And you are at liberty to write anything you wish. Continuing this argument is a waste of time. If you'll excuse me, Sabine is about to—"

"Don't think I didn't notice who you were sitting with," Hedda hissed. "Those two *are* having an affair. I once warned Betty Bacall to watch out for lamps dropped on her head. It's now plainly obvious that I was warning the wrong bitch."

## 29

"You know this is torture, don't you?" Nell asked.

Tony held up a gold tube. "I'm two seconds from painting your lips with Westmore's Hollywood Red, and *now* you talk?"

"There's no mirror! I can't see what you're doing."

"Where are we, the Spanish Inquisition?"

"Everybody who's anybody will be watching me, and I have no idea what they're looking at."

"You should have let me do a test run like I suggested."

"I've been busy."

"Shut up and let me do your lips."

My script girl job had been safe. I knew what I was doing. There was zero chance I'd be forced up on stage. Yes. Okay. Fine. I didn't make a fool of myself at the Canteen when Hollis danced with Mary. But this is different in almost every way.

"Your dress is a knockout," Tony said, brushing rouge onto her cheeks.

"Ann Sothern wore it in *Broadway Musketeers*. Tristan added these strips of black ribbon around the edges and the long fringe on the bottom." She shimmied her shoulders, sending the large gold spangles on her top into a frenzy. "My father would pitch a fit if he saw me."

"The sooner I finish, the sooner you can study yourself in the full-length mirror next to the stage." He produced a mascara wand and told her to close her eyes.

Shutting out the backstage madness, Nell took in a deep breath and let it out slowly. The specter of Hank's face shimmered into view. And his voice: *It's up to you to make it right.*

A month later and she still hadn't followed his advice. Four different times she had sat down to write her father a letter. On the third attempt, she had even started a second page. But it read like a seven-year-old explaining why she'd thrown mud pies at the Sutton boys down the street. The fourth attempt was even more stilted, so she'd stopped trying. Maybe next week, after she'd moved in with Betty, they could compose a more convincing argument. Two heads better than one, and all that.

"I'm done."

Tony's announcement jolted Nell back into the wings of the makeshift stage. She held her breath as she looked into the mirror.

"Oh!"

She'd never worn her hair in an updo before. How chic she looked! So grown up! And that little nest of curls—how had he done that? And her eyes! They were so big. So sparkling. The false eyelashes felt like a pair of baby caterpillars had fallen asleep on her eyelids. But who cared? They made her feel so elegant.

*It won't be Nell from Indiana getting up on that stage. It'll be this swanky glamour girl who nobody's ever heard of.*

She gripped Tony's forearm. "If I wasn't so worried about smudging your Hollywood Red, you'd be covered with grateful kisses right now. I can't believe you spent all this time sticking roofs on houses when all along you could . . ." She circled her outstretched hand in the air. "And my eyes! They look like beacons!"

"It's the white eyeliner. I first noticed it on Marlene Dietrich. Makes 'em pop open, don't it?"

"I feel like a proper, grown-up, adult *woman*."

"I wish Luke was here to get a load of you."

Nell caught Hollis's reflection in the mirror. "Well, hello there." Gone was the withdrawn fellow she'd met at the Wadsworth, or the shy one at the Canteen. This Hollis Muir looked Nell in the eye, beamed the best smile he could manage. The deep crevices etched around the corners of his mouth still pulled it down, but this was no meager attempt to fit in with social niceties. He stepped forward. "You look like a million bucks."

"Your pal here did all the work." She made a show of twisting around in her chair so that she could look directly into his eyes. "I appreciate the compliment, though."

"How much time do you have before you go on?" he asked.

"About fifteen minutes."

"Will exciting news boost your spirits, or will you find it distracting?"

"If it's about Luke, I want to hear it, right here, right now."

The three of them huddled together. "My submarine engineer buddy in Connecticut works for General Dynamics Electric Boat. They're the ones who built this new long-distance class."

"You mean the *Lanternfish*?"

"Yes, but his job ended the moment they hit the water. But he called in a few favors and put me in touch with a civilian who works at Naval Station Puget Sound, where they launched the subs from. He runs the officers' dining room, so he's around officers all day long. And he told me that during the weeks leading up to the launch, the phrase he heard over and over was 'the three-thousand barrier' and how they were all worried about it."

It was nine minutes to show time and Nell's stomach butterflies felt more like cantankerous crows. "Three thousand what?"

"It could refer to anything: weight, ammo, oxygen, food. But *I* think they were talking about distance. Three thousand miles in a submarine is pushing the upper limits, but the *Lanternfish* belongs to a new class designed to sail faster, dive deeper, go farther. So I found an atlas and did some measuring." Hollis shifted from one foot to the other, back and forth and back and forth like a prize-fighter about to jump into the ring. "Think of this as an educated guess. I believe those six subs are in a convoy to Midway."

For four long days over the summer following Pearl Harbor, Americans had held their breath as the US and Japan had bombarded each other to control a barren atoll in the middle of nowhere. It had cost the US plenty to secure Midway Island, but as the smoke cleared, they had emerged victorious.

"How far is it from Seattle?" Nell asked.

"Three thousand, two hundred miles."

Nell and Tony caught each other's eye. *Past the three-thousand barrier.*

"And from Midway to Tokyo?" Tony asked.

"Their next destination would be Wake Island, which is eleven hundred miles from Midway."

"But the Japs control Wake."

"If we wrestle it away from them, that puts Guam within reach. And if we can take back Guam—"

"Next stop, Tokyo." This conversation had been a welcome distraction, but Nell now wished they'd had it after she'd survived her ten-song set in front of every important person connected with Warner Bros.

Tonight's stage manager, Leo Forbstein's assistant, approached them. "This is your four-minute curtain call." He ran his gaze up and down her. "Golly," he said, then headed for Bette Davis, who'd been enlisted to introduce Nell.

"Now for the good news," Hollis said. "I know a radio operator on Midway. He was stationed there after recovering from his injuries at Coral Sea. I can get him to relay a message to Luke when he arrives—assuming I'm right about all this. But it has to be worded like official military business."

*Every fifth word.* Nell nodded. "We can do that. But for now, I need a moment to pull myself together." She turned back to the mirror as Tony and Hollis receded behind the musicians, who were collecting up their instruments.

She gave a small start when she looked at her reflection again. In South Bend, everybody considered the Davenport girls to be such charming debutantes—all except the family's ugly duckling. But look at her now, with her chic hairdo, her expert makeup, her movie-star gown. Way down deep, she knew it was awfully shallow to extract so much confidence from an artificial facade, but if this was what got her through the next hour, she'd take it. And if she lost her nerve, she'd remind herself that a chance of contacting Luke was within her grasp.

Bette's smiling face appeared in the reflection. "Don't you look a treat."

A tremor of excitement tingled down Nell's body. "I've never been all dolled up like this before."

"It's high time you were." Bette took Nell's hand in hers. "My speech will be short, sweet, and complimentary."

"Don't oversell me."

"All you have to do is knock 'em dead."

"If this is your idea of a pep talk—"

She laughed and prodded Nell toward the wings. "Just do it."

\* \* \*

As Nell sang the opening verse to "It Had to Be You," she worked up the courage to peer into the crowd of faces turning to see who was performing. Jaws dropped. Eyes widened. Wait a minute. Hold the phones. Is that Nell? The script girl who somehow wrangled a job in PR?

Conversations dried up. Movement across the soundstage halted. She caught Dennis Morgan mouthing, "Wow." Sydney

Greenstreet's eyebrows lifted halfway to his receding hairline. Ruby Keeler swayed to the music.

Applause started washing onto the stage before she finished the song, but Leo gave her no time to soak it up. "We'll save that for after the third number," he'd told her earlier. The band segued into "Just You, Just Me." As Nell crooned about finding a cozy spot to cuddle and coo, she detected Bogie and Mayo standing to the far right with Peter Lorre and his wife, Celia. Bogie raised his palm to waist height and made a discreet thumbs-up sign. Nell wondered if he'd seen Betty, who was looking especially lovely in a silk dress that flared from her waist.

*Oh my! Are Betty and Tristan surreptitiously edging their way right? Why, yes, they are. Past Eve Arden. Past Michael Curtiz. Past James Cagney. Past Max Steiner. Is Bogie aware of what's happening? Yes, oh yes, he is. He keeps looking left every time a passing drinks waiter distracts Mayo.*

Only Kay Francis, Vincent Sherman, and Alan Hale separated them now.

Now that she was a couple of numbers in, Nell wished time would slow down long enough for her to enjoy this moment. Inwardly, she did a double take. Goodness gracious! Was she enjoying herself?

*What I wouldn't give for Luke to see me now.*

As Leo's trumpeter blasted the opening chords for "That Old Black Magic," Nell spotted Jack Warner chatting with Hedda, who was all animated hands and overly vivacious smile. Nell wasn't sure who her performance was for, but Hedda was going all-out to ensure somebody noticed what gay company she could be.

Ann Warner stood at her husband's elbow. It was rare to catch Ann anywhere at all, let alone amid a gathering of what had to be five hundred people. *And look at that—she's smiling, too. Having a jolly old time, by the looks of it.* At Hedda's side stood her son. Would wonders never cease? It was common knowledge around town that Hedda

Hopper got along with Bill Hopper about as well as Jack Warner got along with Ann. He had made at least six pictures with Bogie, but Nell had rarely seen him smile on set, and yet here he was laughing it up.

Leo closed "That Old Black Magic" with a long, sweet note from the French horn that faded as applause broke out. Nell breathed lightly as it surged to a deafening pitch and enveloped her like a blanket. She glanced back at him. He raised his eyebrows: *See? I was right, wasn't I? Trust your Uncle Leo.* As the applause began to peter out, he raised his baton and propelled the band into "Why Don't You Do Right?"

By the time Nell had ordered some fella to get out and make some money, the most unexpected person in the place approached the giddy foursome. Bill Hopper extended his hand, squeezing Hollis's gently. At first glance Hollis looked like a regular guy, if perhaps somewhat on the thin side. How did Bill know to treat him so gingerly?

Hedda was presenting Hollis with a cheek for him to kiss. She had interviewed him at length the night of his dance with Mary, but a kiss to the cheek like she was his favorite madcap aunt? Nell thought of Hollis's detective work regarding Luke's whereabouts. It had taken weeks to put his theory together. And he hadn't done it alone. Was *he* the one playing the game? The guy had more guts than Nell had reckoned.

*  *  *

Nell held the final note of "Zing! Went the Strings of My Heart" until Leo closed her set with a rousing trombone blast. She sank into an awkward, all-elbows pose, then fled into the wings before anybody cottoned on to how she had executed the worst curtsy in history. Tony enveloped her in a hug. "Holy mackerel dipped in bacon fat!"

"That's good, right?"

"Tremendous!"

She wriggled free of his bear hug. "I saw Hollis from the stage. Could you go find him for me?"

She found Tristan in a three-sided alcove fixing a troublesome side zipper.

"My darling Davenport," he said, turning to her. "You were superb. Word-perfect. Note-perfect. Everything perfect." The zipper tag pinched between his fingers loosened. "Kelly told me he made this for Bette in *The Big Lie*. It gave him trouble back then, too. I think I've fixed it now."

Nell had chosen this outfit to wear while mingling with the crowd after the show. Made of light blue silk with gold thread embroidered through it, was less sparkly, less showy, and more her style.

She took the skirt from Tristan as she cast her mind back over the show. She could remember the first handful of songs, when every nerve ending prickled as every sound, every movement, every face deluged her senses. But somewhere around "Why Don't You Do Right?" the details blurred into a fuzzy jumble.

"You're not just telling me what I wish to hear, are you?"

"I only do that to people I dislike."

After Nell had changed, Tony reappeared with Hollis. She emerged from behind the screen. "Will you be spending Thanksgiving with the Hoppers?"

"I'm glad that's how it looked."

"What did I witness out there?"

"When Hedda was interviewing me about my dance with Mary, it came out that Bill and I have a mutual friend. Remember that submarine engineer buddy of mine who works for General Dynamics in Connecticut? He helped Bill get into the OSS."

"Small world, huh?" Tristan commented.

"Right after that night at the Canteen, we got on the phone. Bill was going through a tough time with his mom and needed an ear to bend. She ignores all his pleas to stop interfering, and he was mortified as she's ingratiated herself with the top brass to the point where she knows all their private phone numbers. Not only the OSS, but the Navy, the Army, and even the Coast Guard."

Nell lowered her voice. "When you were on the phone with Bill, did you also play detective?"

Hollis shot her a knowing grin. "Let's pretend you didn't ask."

"I'd be happy to, but you told me my message could get to Midway." The studio orchestra burst into "Opus One." She had to wait until the raucous introduction died down. "Is there any way that Hedda could stop it from getting through?"

"I seriously doubt it."

"She is well-connected to every branch of the military up and down the coast. That's a lot of fingers in a lot of pies. Not to mention how she's palsy-walsy with Hoover."

Hollis shook his head. "It'll be one of dozens of messages. Nobody has that many fingers."

"Okay!" Tristan clapped his hands together. "The commissary has only so many bottles of champagne they can open tonight. We don't want to miss out, do we?"

Nell checked her makeup. Good heavens, even after all that singing, Tony's lipstick was still flawless. "Gentlemen," she said, "let's mingle."

The wings were ten-foot burlap drapes. Tristan pulled one aside to let Nell step out into the soundstage. The first person to spot her was Jane Wyman, who was standing with Orry-Kelly's head seamstress. She cut herself off mid-sentence and clapped. Her enthusiasm spread to Lee Patrick, from *The Maltese Falcon*, then to Jack Carson, who'd been in the first movie Nell had worked on, *The Strawberry Blonde*. And then Geraldine Fitzgerald, who'd had a featured role in *The Gay Sisters*. One by one, they started to clap and call out Nell's name, followed by shouts of "Bravo!" and "Encore."

The ovation caught Nell by surprise. "What do I do?" she whispered to Tristan.

"Wave and smile like you're Eleanor Roosevelt," he whispered back. "You've earned it. Let it wash over you."

As they moved through the crowd of well-wishers, Nell felt their goodwill and—dare she even name it?—admiration drench her like summer rain.

## 30

"There they are." Nell pointed to the three black town cars gliding out of Gate Two.

Betty hit the gas and fell in behind the third car turning left onto Olive Avenue. Nell could see the outline of Slim's head in the back seat, nodding to whatever Howard was saying.

They had barely gone two hundred yards when Betty pulled to the curb. "I'm too distracted. You'll have to drive, otherwise we'll end up in a ditch."

She bounded out of the driver side, rounded the hood, and opened the passenger door. Nell scooted across, started the engine again, and hit the gas. The taillights glowed red as the convoy headed into the valley side of the Hollywood Hills. Nell hardly blamed Betty for losing her nerve. She should have seen it coming. Betty had been acting erratically around the apartment: burning biscuits in the oven, leaving the refrigerator door open, losing her house keys.

"It'll be quite a drive," Nell said. "What would you like to talk about?"

"Anything but movies, cameras, costumes, Hemingway, Howard, and Humphrey."

"Did you see the headline in this morning's *L.A. Times*? The biggest typeface since Pearl Harbor: INVASION—exclamation point."

"The report I heard said a hundred and fifty thousand Allied troops have landed on five French beaches. Can you imagine the organization that went into pulling off an operation like that?"

"And they still took the Germans by surprise."

Betty drummed on the dashboard with her manicured fingernails. "Our boys plunged into the water in full battle uniform. Must have weighed a ton. And they charged onto the shore, bullets firing in all directions. The sheer guts it took." The drumming halted. "And yet here am I getting all worked up over a stupid movie."

The convoy turned left onto Cahuenga Boulevard, toward downtown. "If Howard hadn't barred you from viewing the dailies, you wouldn't be tormented with dread to see how you come across on screen."

"Bogie didn't want me to see them, either. They wanted nothing to inhibit my performance."

They had landed on the one subject neither of them had talked about during the three weeks since Nell had moved in. She didn't want to intrude on Betty's heartbreak, figuring she'd bring it up sooner or later.

"It's been more than a month." Betty watched the wooden bungalows of Hollywood slip past. "I've turned into one of those halfwits who sits by her telephone waiting for a man to call. I jump out of my skin every time it rings, and then my heart plummets when I hear somebody else's voice. I'm a fool for holding a torch for a guy who's gone back to his wife."

Nell still thought that the Bogart marriage was built on rotted wood, but hell's bells, what was she supposed to say to that? Better to play the diplomat. "Do you miss him?"

"I thought what we had was true, deep love. I can't stop

wondering if it was nothing more than a temporary fling that was only meant to last until the end of production."

"You miss him a lot, don't you?"

"Yes, but no more than how you must miss Luke."

"Every hour of every day. It's worse now that I know he's on Midway. Just the thought of him being halfway to Japan gives me hives."

"How long has it been since you sent that message?"

"Seventeen days, but who's counting? They might not even be there yet. The Pacific is one hell of a stretch of endless ocean."

"I think you're awfully brave. If I were in your shoes and it was Bogie out there—" Betty turned away and looked out the window "—I don't think I'd ever sleep."

Who said anything about sleeping? Nell doubted she'd had a decent night's sleep since the day Luke shipped out. The perpetual tumult of boardinghouse life had been a helpful distraction. Somebody was always leaving for work, doing laundry, scratching together a two-a.m. snack. But now that she had settled into the luxury of her own room in a Beverly Hills apartment, she couldn't blame crappy sleep on her fifteen fellow boarders.

"What comforts me," she told Betty, "is that millions of girls all over the world toss and turn exactly like I do."

"Scant comfort, isn't it?"

The studio convoy turned east on Washington Boulevard. Taplinger's memo, which Nell had accidentally seen that morning, had said only that the sneak preview would take place in Huntington Park. The studio had its own theater down there. That's where they were headed!

"I'd sleep better knowing that my message got through," Nell said. "With D-Day happening, I bet a squillion messages are flying around military channels right now. If he gets it, what if he can't reply? Thank God for this secret preview. We need all the diversion we can get."

"Easy for you to say." Betty forced a throaty laugh. "You're not about to see a forty-foot version of your face projected onto a screen the size of a billboard."

"Think of it as your baptism of fire."

"Is that supposed to make me feel better?"

"Hey," Nell shot back with a laugh that sounded a little more contrived than she had intended, "you were all for me singing at Orry-Kelly's farewell. That was my baptism of fire; this is yours. Wouldn't you prefer to see yourself when nobody knows you're watching?"

Betty's silence filled the car until she found her voice. "Okay, Miss Smarty-Pants. You win."

*　*　*

The theater was five stories of Art Deco splendor with a twenty-foot blade sign spelling out "WARNER" in red neon.

The convoy entered the adjoining parking lot, but Nell drove around the block to give the big shots time to go inside. She pulled into an empty slot in the far corner. "Stay put and I'll recon the lay of the land."

She entered the foyer by the far-right door. In the *NOW SHOWING* display, a hand-lettered sign read *SPECIAL STUDIO SNEAK PREVIEW TONIGHT*. A scattering of military uniforms studded groups of moviegoers waiting for the doors to open. The studio brigade was nowhere in sight, which meant they were in the manager's office waiting for the lights to go down before they took their seats in the back row. She and Betty had plenty of time to slink in undetected.

Or not.

Damn! Of all people to spot her, did it have to be this guy?

Jaik Rosenstein stood near the *COMING SOON* display. He wasn't looking at the *Mask of Dimitrios* poster, but was, instead, staring at Nell, smiling like a bargain-basement Errol Flynn. Nell marched across the white-and-green mottled terrazzo, trying her best to match his knowing smile.

She had worked on a series of press releases talking up *To Have and Have Not*, and predicting that Lauren Bacall would soon become one of Warner Bros.' biggest attractions. If Rosenstein had caught wind of what tonight's preview was, did that mean Hedda had an eavesdropper in the PR department?

"Mr. Rosenstein," she said, approaching him with a professional hand outstretched.

He shook it warmly. "Miss Davenport. A genuine surprise."

She raised an eyebrow. "Is it?"

He blinked at her in what looked like sincere confusion. "This must have been a long ride on your trusty bicycle."

Between gas rationing and tire rationing, it had seemed pointless to buy a car when the studio was within biking distance of the boardinghouse. But now that Nell lived in Beverly Hills, it was a much farther jaunt. Pedaling like the devil over the Hollywood Hills wasn't a whole heap of fun, but it was healthy exercise, and felt as though it was part of her personal contribution to the war effort.

"I left my trusty Schwinn at home."

He nodded toward the preview sign. "You know what's being previewed?"

"We can play a few rounds of I Haven't a Clue, but I'd rather we skip it." She could see the rapid computations piling up behind his eyes.

"My mother lives in an old folks' home near the Hollywood Park racetrack. I visited her this afternoon but got shooed out when dinner was served. I remembered this place was on my way, so I took a chance on whatever was playing."

Nell crossed her arms. "Oh, come on, Jaik. You didn't know about this preview until you walked in?"

He bit down onto his lower lip; to his credit, though, he didn't look away. "I can't blame you, given—" He faltered, glancing down at his worn suede loafers. "Yes," he said, looking up again, "that *is* what happened."

Jiminy Christmas, this really was a coincidence? Either that or he'd picked up how to fake it from being around one of the best fakers in the biz.

"I think I believe you, Jaik. And," she added with a playful smirk, "that shocks last night's jellied chicken right out of me."

"I ain't such a heel—even if I do work for Hedda Hopper."

"All I can say is that I hope she pays you well."

"I don't have Beverly Hills–sized ambitions, so she pays me well enough." He jiggled his head from side to side. "Most of the time."

Nell wondered if she had witnessed a momentary chink in his armor of loyalty. "And the rest of the time?"

"Let's put it this way: Now and then she does the dirty on someone who doesn't deserve it." Hesitation flickered across his face. "Okay, look, I shouldn't be telling you this, but—" He blinked. "Is that Howard Hawks's wife?" Nell turned in time to see Slim enter the ladies' room. "This preview is for *To Have and Have Not!?*" He clapped his hands together like a gleeful five-year-old who'd heard the chimes of an ice cream truck. "Wait until I tell Hedda."

A uniformed usher opened the auditorium doors and announced the movie would commence in ten minutes.

"Lay low, for crying out loud," Nell told him, as he turned to gallop inside. "If Mr. Warner sees that Hedda's number one legman—"

"Warner's here?" Jaik's voice rose to a squeak. "He must think this picture is going to be a big deal. I should get in there before they see me." He disappeared inside.

When Nell returned to the Plymouth, she found Betty leaning against the hood, smoking a cigarette. Two dead butts lay at her open-toed shoes. "Coast clear?"

"It's now-or-never time."

Betty clung to Nell as though she were the last remaining lifeboat on the *Lusitania*. "I'm so goddamn nervous I don't know whether to faint or puke."

"I suggest deep breaths until the lights go out."

Nell guided her down the aisle to the fifth row. They shuffled past a pair of teenagers and found a pair of seats. "Deep breaths!" They sucked in lungfuls of popcorn-scented air until they couldn't keep it in any longer. Finally, a middle-aged man in a three-piece suit appeared at the edge of the stage.

"Welcome, everybody. You will, I'm sure, be glad to hear that tonight's sneak preview will be the new Humphrey Bogart picture, *To Have and Have Not*." He let an excited murmur ripple across the audience. "It's received a lot of talk because of the debut of a startling new star. And let me tell you, it's a debut that's going to make heads turn from coast to coast."

Nell leaned over and put her lips close to Betty's ear. "I wrote that part of our press release," she whispered, "calling you a 'startling new star' because you—" She cut herself off when she realized Betty was too rigid to respond.

The audience buzzed with anticipation as the house lights dimmed and the curtains parted. The opening chord of Franz Waxman's score filled the theater as the Warner Bros. shield appeared, followed by

HUMPHREY BOGART IN

Betty took in another deep breath and held it.

ERNEST HEMINGWAY'S
"TO HAVE AND HAVE NOT"

"Doing okay?" Nell whispered.

A<br>
HOWARD HAWKS<br>
PRODUCTION

Betty nodded but stayed silent, her eyes glued to the screen. "You're not going to pass out, are you?"

With<br>
WALTER BRENNAN<br>
LAUREN BACALL<br>
DOLORES MORAN<br>
HOAGY CARMICHAEL

Betty yelped quietly at the sight of her name.

The credits gave way to a map of the Caribbean island of Martinique.

The first glimpse of Betty came in a hotel corridor when Bogie's character, Steve, returned to his room. As he unlocked his door, she came out of her room.

Nell felt Betty's body jolt beside her. A couple of seconds later, the Bacall voice, made gravelly through those long sessions reading *The Robe* out loud, asked Steve if he had a match. The camera cut to Steve in the foreground and Bacall idling in the open doorway. Bogie threw her a box of matches; she caught it with one hand, cool as morning frost.

Cut to Bogie giving her a once-over.

Cut back to Bacall.

Her first close-up.

The light from the lit match flared, shadows crosshatching her face. Her hair tumbled to the shoulders of her checked suit. Her chin subtly tucked in, she tossed the match away with almost brazen insolence. "Thanks." Without breaking eye contact, she pitched the box back to him and made her exit.

Nell realized that, for once, her sales copy hadn't been overwrought hyperbole. Betty was unquestionably a startling new star. When this movie came out, her life would never be the same.

* * *

Nell had seen a handful of dailies. Snippets of scenes lasting thirty seconds. Raw footage not yet enhanced by the post-production magicians. But none of it had prepared her for the visceral reaction she had just experienced.

Yes, Hawks had directed Betty with an assured hand. Yes, the script had supplied seductive lines and witty banter. And yes, the lighting, the clothes, the makeup all helped. But stripping away the window dressing could not dilute her incandescence.

Her chemistry with Bogie was undeniable. Her unblinking self-possession. His jaded world-weariness. Her unalloyed chutzpah. His astute shrewdness. The two of them sparked like ten Roman candles strapped together and ignited with a blowtorch.

But more than that, Nell could only think of Luke. He wasn't anything like Bogie's Steve. Nor did Nell share a single quality with Betty's Marie. They hadn't met on Martinique. Luke didn't own a boat. Neither of them was helping someone escape from Devil's Island or fighting for the Resistance in Vichy-controlled Fort-de-France.

I miss our late-night tomato-and-cheese-sandwiches on the *Arabella*.

I miss the anticipation of sharing good news with him.

I miss waking up with him beside me.

I miss him kissing my earlobe.

I miss his fingertips gliding down my skin.

It wasn't until the lights came up that Nell finally put two and two together: Watching *To Have and Have Not* play out was watching Humphrey Bogart and Lauren Bacall fall in love.

I miss falling in love with Luke. We had only just gotten going when the Navy beckoned. And now I don't know when he'll be coming back. Or if.

Beside her, Betty sat motionless, her head hanging down, staring at her hands folded in her lap.

"Ready to leave?" Nell asked quietly.

"I need a moment to myself."

Nell told her to take her time and made her way into the foyer. Spotting Jaik lighting up a pipe in front of the *Mask of Dimitrios* poster reminded her of their unfinished conversation.

"Pretty good, huh?" she asked.

"The kid's a knockout."

"That'll be your opening line when you tell Hedda?" He nodded and sucked on his pipe. "You were about to say something before we went in."

"I was?" He tried to shrug it off as an innocent question but failed to camouflage the cagey light in his eyes.

"You said, 'I shouldn't be telling you this, but,' and then Slim Hawks distracted you."

"Right. Yeah. That." He took a long draw on his pipe. "Hedda knows you've sent a message to your boyfriend at Midway."

Nell had expected this revelation to be about Hedda cottoning on to how seriously involved Bogie and Betty had become. But not about this. Not about her.

"How could she possibly—?"

"She's going to Pearl Harbor for the third anniversary of the attack, so she's hunting around for a dozen sailors whose stories she can tell."

"What type of stories?"

"'Make the little guy a hero.' So she's been monitoring—"

"Who the hell does she think she is, disregarding national security and military safeguards?" Nell's voice echoed off the terrazzo flooring. Had Jack Warner and the Hawkses left the theater yet? This was the last place they should find her. She took a moment to calm the outrage pounding in her chest. "Whoever's helping her ought to be court-martialed."

"She's a woman with friends in high places."

"Hoover?"

"Don't go running down the warpath. She only needs enough information to whip up a story that sounds good on the radio. Names, ranks, vessels, sometimes naval bases. Typical Geneva Convention stuff."

"How did she find out about Midway?"

"All I know is she had to go digging elsewhere for that. Keep in mind that she might be justified in asking how *you* know where he is."

Nell resented the heat reddening her cheeks. "Is she out to get me?"

He shrugged. "Your name comes up fairly frequently around the office. So when she connected the dots between you and a name on her list, it sparked her interest."

"Did she intercept the message?"

"She's Hedda Hopper, not General Patton. Even she has limits."

Jaik's eyes followed someone's progress through the foyer. Nell turned to see Betty drifting toward the front door, almost in a daze.

"Why do you think your message was stopped?" he asked.

"I've had no response; it's been over two weeks." They both

watched as, outside the theater, Betty pensively lit up another cigarette. "Thanks for letting me know. I appreciate it."

Jaik slugged her with a sly grin. "You two snuck in here?"

"By the time we got to the end of the picture, she was quite overwhelmed."

"I'll keep your secret if you keep mine. Hedda'll murder me if she knows what I've told you."

The June afternoon had settled down into a surprisingly cool evening. The Plymouth was the only car left in the parking lot. Betty tossed her half-smoked cigarette onto the asphalt and crushed it under her heel. "If Howard had allowed me to see a glimpse—just one little scene—tonight mightn't have felt like such an avalanche. I'm wrung out. To see myself up there like that. Every flaw, every imperfection." She shuddered.

Nell unlocked the car doors, and they hopped in.

Poor kid, thought Nell as she started the car. She looked like a rag doll with the stuffing ripped out of her.

Nell had attended previews where actors had been aghast at seeing themselves on screen for the first time—not the least of whom had been Sydney Greenstreet in *The Maltese Falcon*—so Nell had known what Betty could expect. But how could she have foreseen her own visceral reaction as *To Have and Have Not* played out?

"Flaws, schmaws," she said, turning north onto Pacific Boulevard. "All I saw was Warners' newest screen sensation. When this picture comes out, that's when the real avalanche will sock you square in the jaw. If it makes you feel any better, you weren't the only one buried under the snow tonight."

"I suppose everyone rides the same rollercoaster their first time. I went from 'I look like *that*?' to 'Say, I'm pretty good there,' to 'I wish Howard had let me do another take,' to 'Tucking my chin almost makes me look like a real femme fatale.'"

"People will respond to you and to your movies in all sorts of ways. For instance, I had a different reaction. I thought about—"

"I thought I'd massacred Hoagy's wonderful ditty, but it wasn't a complete bloodbath, I guess. Not in that black dress with the loop in front."

Nell was only half-listening. All this time, she believed she had kept a lid on all the unknowns, all the unknowables. It wasn't so bad when she had assumed Luke was tucked away in Montauk. Of course he was safe. Of course he was out of harm's way. Of course he was coming back to her. Everything would be fine. Absolutely fine. But it had all been a fairytale. In reality, Luke had been learning Japanese so that he could jump on a submarine—him, with his fear of deep water—and sail into enemy territory. What if they attack the *Lanternfish*? What if it sinks? What if Luke never comes back? We'd only just met. How can he be snatched away from me so quickly?

"And the scene of our first kiss with my line about knowing how to whistle," Betty continued. "That robe they had me wearing. Ugh! What was Milo thinking?"

Nell heard a snap, a pinging in her ears, like a rubber band stretched beyond its limit. "For Pete's sake, Betty, you're not the only one who rode a rollercoaster tonight."

"What?"

"I've been trying—" As Pacific Boulevard curved to the left, the Plymouth shuddered and spewed out a harsh knocking sound. Nell reached the curb as they lurched to a stop outside a line of deserted stores. She looked at the gauge on the dashboard. "Out of gas. And here we are, a million miles from home."

"How was I supposed to know they'd drive so far?" Betty bit back. "I assumed they'd choose some place close, like, I don't know, the other side of Burbank?"

"There is no 'other side of Burbank.' It's just mountains!"

"Why are you yelling?"

"Because your tank is empty. It's eleven o'clock at night. The gas stations are closed. Even if they weren't, I haven't got gas ration coupons on me. Do you?"

"No, I—"

Nell flung open the door with a yowl that would have impressed King Kong and vaulted from the car.

Betty climbed out, too. "What's in God's name is going on?"

"I SPENT THAT WHOLE MOVIE—" This was supposed to have been a thrilling night for Betty. But now all these pent-up emotions were spilling out of Nell like lava. If she didn't say them out loud, she feared she might come apart at the seams. She drew in a fitful breath.

"I spent the whole movie thinking of Luke. Every time Bogie looked at you. Every time you kissed him. Every line of repartee. Even that damn song, 'How Little We Know.' I kept thinking how little I know about him because we'd only just fallen in love and the Navy snatched him away. I don't know what he's doing. How he's feeling. What'll happen to him and when will I hear about it? I miss him so damn much and there's *nothing* I can do about it." She tried to contain a sob as hot tears trickled down her cool cheeks. She swiped them away with her sleeve. "And as if that isn't hard enough, out in the foyer I bumped into Jaik Rosenstein, who informs me that Hedda knows about my sending a message to Luke."

"How—"

"Because she sticks her nose into everybody's business. He doesn't think that she blocked my message from getting out, but no blow is too low for that witch. Did Luke not get it because Hedda Hopper thinks she can play God?" Betty tried to respond, but the force of Nell's anger brooked no interruption. "I've got all this churning inside me, and all you can do is go on and on and on about yourself."

"This wasn't any old movie." Betty said tautly, pointing toward the theater. "Seeing yourself on the screen is staggering. It's you, but it's not you. It's somebody else, with somebody else's name, wearing somebody else's clothes, and behaving like somebody you've never met. It sucks the air out of your lungs. I *ached* every time I saw Bogie, reliving all those moments of filming." She faltered through those last few words, pushing them out like they were chunks of granite. "I've never missed him so much as I did tonight."

The last of Nell's strength gave way; a torrent of tears burst from her. "I miss Luke so much. I don't know if I'll ever see him again."

"And I don't know if I'll ever see Bogie again."

"If this movie hits big—and it's bound to—they're bound to pair you together again."

Betty made a harsh, grating sound. "Oh yeah, that'll be terrific. The man I'm in love with will be two feet away. Or worse, holding me in his arms, waiting for Howard to call 'Action,' and know that if we try anything, Madam'll come at us like Jack the Ripper. So instead, I sit by the phone, waiting for a call that won't ever come."

Nell's rage drained away. Nell flopped against the window of the shoe shop behind her.

"I've never seen you and Luke together," Betty said. "I guess I didn't realize how hard all this is for you."

Nell smiled sadly. "It's an ache you get used to. Sits there in the background, throbbing and throbbing. You tuck it away in some place safe. But then along comes that damn movie, and your radiant performance, and your real-life love affair unfolding before my eyes, drowning me with all the beautiful things I miss most."

Betty joined her at the window, leaning against the cold glass. "Here's me endlessly blathering about how I look, and how I sound, and how I move, and me, me, me, me, me. Meanwhile, sitting right next to me, my best friend is being dragged through hell and I'm completely oblivious."

Tears prickled the backs of Nell's eyes. "I'm your best friend?"

"Of course, you big birdbrain. Is that really so surprising?"

"It's just that I've never really had a best friend."

"Yeah, well, you're stuck with one now." Betty threaded her arm through Nell's and hugged it close to her side. "Even though she's maddeningly self-absorbed."

"Your first time away from home. Your first movie. Your first great love. That's a lot of plates for a girl to twirl at the same time."

"And thanks to you, Nell, I haven't had to twirl them alone. Together we got through *To Have and Have Not*." She smiled wryly. "It describes us perfectly, doesn't it? We have and have not."

A peaceful silence settled between them. After a few moments, Betty said, "The movie. It's good, isn't it?"

"Really, *really* good."

"I'd be braver facing everything that's coming if I had Bogie next to me."

Nell patted the back of her hand. "All of that is beyond your control. There's not much use worrying about it. But I'm here if you need me."

"Not when I've got a bigger problem to worry about."

"Like what?"

Betty looked balefully at her lifeless car. "How are we going to get home?"

"Walk."

"All the way to Beverly Hills? It must be ten miles! Maybe we'll come across an all-night diner where we can call a cab."

They were the only signs of life in all directions. Betty wiggled one of her shoes. "I might have to take these off at some point, which will kill me because I'm down to my last three decent pairs of nylons."

"Ruined nylons are the least of our problems." Nell snatched their purses out of the car. "Kathryn Massey knows someone at Bullocks Wilshire who sells them on the black market."

## 31

Three days after the *To Have and Have Not* preview, Nell's feet still hurt from the trek home. They hadn't come across an all-night diner to call a cab, so they had trudged the whole ten miles, then collapsed into their beds at a quarter of two in the morning.

She was prodding a blister on her right foot the size of a nickel and red as a lingonberry when the telephone on her desk rang. Taplinger told her to come see him when she had finished inspecting her foot.

"You've done a first-rate job on the press packet for *To Have and Have Not*," he said when she appeared. "Let's hope this Lauren Bacall girl lives up to your superlatives."

Nell doubted Taplinger would have disapproved of her sneaking into the preview, but she had definitely breached protocol. The blister throbbed. "I've been on the set a fair bit. She really is an exciting find."

"Evidently so, because Howard Hawks has rushed *The Big Sleep* into production."

"The Raymond Chandler novel?"

"He's beefing up the Vivian Rutledge role for her." Was Betty aware of this yet? Nell couldn't wait to get home and tell her. "I'll have you draft a press release about it later, but meanwhile, I have a special assignment. One that'll involve tact." Taplinger drummed the fingertips of both hands on his ink blotter like he was playing "Flight of the Bumblebee." He stopped as abruptly as he'd started. "One of the cameos in *Hollywood Canteen* films today. She's new to Warner Brothers, and will need the kid-gloves treatment."

"Sure. Who is it?"

"Joan Crawford." He said her name with a resigned sigh. "She's been on the payroll for almost a year and has knocked back every film we've offered her."

"That must be driving Mr. Warner nuts."

"He's had to bite his tongue so hard I'm surprised he hasn't gnawed it clean off. However, she has agreed to appear in *Hollywood Canteen*, which means today is her first day on a Warner picture."

"I'm happy to know you think I have the necessary diplomacy skills to play tour guide."

"You're a woman, which makes you the best man for the job."

Taplinger had been a decent boss, fair most of the time, not prone to yelling or screaming. But honestly, did these men ever listen to themselves?

"What time do I need to be where?"

"Security called me to say she drove through Gate Two a minute ago. With every soundstage in use, parking has become an issue. They had no choice but to direct her to the temporary lot set up between the *Arabella* and Philadelphia Street. If you run, you should be there by the time she pulls up."

Running anywhere was out of the question, but if Nell walked briskly on the heels of her saddle shoes, she might not keep Crawford waiting too long.

* * *

Crawford was getting out of her white Ford roadster as Nell reached the end of Sixth Street. "Miss Crawford! Hello!" Nell boosted her speed as much as her blister permitted. "I'm Nell Davenport. Mr. Taplinger, head of PR, asked me to escort you to the set and see that you have everything you need."

"Call me Joan." Crawford's handshake was firm but not pushy.

"This new hairdo of yours, the bangs and the darker color—it suits you."

"Why, thank you for noticing." Joan's left hand flew to the soft curls resting at the base of her neck. "Very kind of you to say."

They set off down Fifth Avenue to Stage Eight. It was tough going on Nell's blister—it was now howling in protest—but she had been around enough movie stars to notice most of them were comfortable when the spotlight remained on them. "You won't believe how accurately they've reproduced the Canteen."

"I have full confidence in Mr. Warner's set designers. And don't think for a moment that I haven't noticed you there, Nell."

"Even though that place is packed to the rafters?"

"Packed, yes, but with individuals. Each with their own story to tell."

Nell stopped. Partly because her blister was begging her to, and partly because this was not the high-maintenance, twenty-four-hours-a-day star she'd been expecting. "What a thoughtful way to look at it."

"I was at MGM for eighteen years. It was all so familiar, so second-nature. But now everything is new, and fresh, and I've learned it's beneficial to take note of the details. For instance, do you want to tell me why you're limping?"

Nell gazed down at her shoes and wondered if she could loosen the laces. "A few nights ago, my roommate and I ran out of gas. It was late. Nothing was open, so we had to walk ten miles home."

"Oh my!" Joan exclaimed. "A blister?"

"A real humdinger."

"Soak it in Epsom salts, then cover it in plain petroleum jelly. Back when I was starting out, I got noticed by competing in every Charleston contest in town. I went through a lot of jelly."

"Thank you. I'll try it," Nell said. "Let's get going. They're awaiting your arrival."

They started walking again, albeit at a slower pace. Joan, it appeared, was in no rush, which suited Nell's blister just fine.

"The director on this picture," Joan said. "Remind me of his name?"

"Delmer Daves."

"What's he like?"

"Started out as an actor, so he knows how it feels to be where you're standing."

"I've been told Michael Curtiz can be somewhat tyrannical. Is that true?"

*Where did that question come from?* "He's a decisive man who knows what he wants."

"You're being diplomatic, aren't you, Nell?"

*And you're fishing. Until I figure out what for, I'm staying neutral.* "Nothing good comes from bad-mouthing someone behind their back. I'm sure it was the same at MGM."

"It's the same at ball-bearing factories, department stores, and chicken dinner cafés."

*Oh! Now I get it!* Nell stopped again and rolled onto her heels. "They've offered the role to Bette Davis."

The gleam of recognition sparked in Joan's eyes. "Of course they have. She's number one around here and deserves first pick of the plum roles."

"The studio scuttlebutt says she won't take it, though."

"And if she doesn't?"

"In that case, Mildred Pierce will be up for grabs."

"I've been told Mr. Curtiz thinks I'm unsuitable, that I'm a has-been. In other words, he will need convincing."

"He's not a man who often changes his mind."

"What if I offer to do a screen test?"

Nell hid her shock by waving at some of the dress extras heading for the *Hollywood Canteen* soundstage. "But you're a major star. You shouldn't have to—"

"Stoop so low? Let me tell you, I know people look at me and all they see is big shoulder pads and a wide mouth and an oversized personality. And that's fine, I suppose, but it's not all of me. If I pull off a role they aren't expecting, make them sit bolt upright and say, 'I wouldn't have thought she was capable of *that*,' then I've got 'em where I want 'em. If my agreeing to a screen test makes Mr. Curtiz take me seriously, then that's what I need to do. The finished product is what I care about, and I'm prepared to do whatever's necessary to get there."

"You'll need to show him you're a hard worker, someone who comes to the set on time, knows her lines and hits her marks. And if you can do it all in one take, so much the better."

"In that case, he and I will get along fine." As they approached the soundstage, Joan started patting her hair into place. "If he gives me a chance."

"You need someone to go to bat for you," Nell said.

"Do you have anybody in mind?"

"Why not start at the top? Present your case, screen test and all, to Mr. Warner and let him do the heavy lifting."

"Thank you, Nell. I appreciate your astute advice." They were at Stage Sixteen's elephant door now. The assistant director, a capable man by the name of Arthur, was on his megaphone telling the uniformed extras that he needed them to line up along the right and the dance hostesses on the left. "And remember: Epsom salts and petroleum jelly."

\* \* \*

Nell found a chair tucked away in a corner and eased her throbbing feet out of her shoes. For Joan's scene with Dane Clark,

Milo Anderson had chosen a black dress with a white cat painted over her right shoulder. The darker hair made more sense now; it matched the outfit. That Joan, she sure was a canny one. Was she sincere about doing a screen test? She had come across like she'd meant it. Then again, Joan was an actress.

Nell might have saved herself—and Betty—some agony if she'd known about the Epsom salts three days ago. Did they sell them at Kress? Probably. She could hobble in there after work and say hello to Beatrice. It seemed like an age since they'd seen each other. But that was the war for you. Everybody was so busy working and volunteering and trying to get by on as little as possible.

Nell felt the air shift in the lively soundstage. The volume of chatter dropped off and most of the extras were now looking in the same direction. That meant somebody had arrived. Somebody special.

Nell stuffed her feet back into her shoes and picked her way through the extras until she came face to face with—

Oh.

God.

Her.

*Again.*

The hat was a wide-brimmed cartwheel of puce chiffon. Or at least how puce chiffon would look if it'd been left out in the rain, dragged through the mud, then washed with chimpanzee piss. The clump of five-pointed silk petunias stitched into the crown failed to lift the concoction's spirits, and instead hung limply, as though they'd been insulted by Groucho Marx.

"Why, Hedda!" Nell exclaimed. "This *is* a surprise."

"I don't see why," Hedda shot back. "I wouldn't miss Joan's first day of shooting on the Warners lot for all the cheddar in Wisconsin."

*Kill the bitch with kindness. She won't be expecting that. Maybe it'll even shake her off my tail.*

"You have your ear closer to the ground than Sheilah, Kathryn, and Louella combined." It was hard to miss the woman's why-are-you-being-so-friendly scowl. "Who'd have ever thought we'd see Joan Crawford at Warners? Talk about witnessing the dawn of a whole new era. When the chance presents itself, how about I ask her if a quick interview would be okay?"

Hedda tsked sourly. "Aren't you the cheery little miss today?"

"Let's be honest. Our jobs are about whipping up enthusiasm for films or performances that don't always deserve it. But can we talk about *To Have and Have Not*? This is strictly on the hush-hush, you understand, but goodness, if Lauren Bacall doesn't take your breath away, I'll eat that hat of yours."

"Oh, really?"

"From time to time, a raw beginner comes along and makes you go 'Wow!'"

Hedda carved a tight, smug smile on her lips. "My legman said as much."

"He did?"

"He lucked out by showing up at the right movie house on the right night when the studio had organized a secret preview. Came flying into the office the next day. Gushing praise for the girl."

On most of the ten-mile hike home that night, Nell had worried that Jaik's loyalties might have induced a morning-after seizure of repentance and caused him to blab everything to his boss. Evidently, all that fretting had been for nothing.

"It's no wonder," Nell continued, "that Hawks is plunging ahead with *The Big Sleep*."

Hedda's eyebrows shot northward. "He is?"

"That's what you get for being the early bird. A big, juicy worm."

"I can quote you on that?"

Nell nodded breezily. "And as if all that wasn't enough, I heard from my boyfriend from halfway across the Pacific. I don't know if you had any hand in that, but if you did, thank you!"

"Me?" This time, Hedda's shock wasn't feigned. "What makes you think—"

"Everybody's talking about your pilgrimage to Pearl Harbor for the third anniversary, and how you're collecting names of regular Joes to talk about each day on your broadcast."

"Yes, but where on earth—"

"I can't remember where I saw your list. Passed around the office, I expect. Imagine my surprise when I saw Luke's name. And right after that, I received a message from him, and I put two and two together. I can't thank you enough, Hedda. At any rate, when I saw the list of servicemen you plan on highlighting, I thought, 'She'll have half the country listening in to see if she mentions someone they love.' Talk about a genius idea."

Hedda's consternation melted into a self-serving preen. "I thought it was a pretty darned good one myself. But back to your boyfriend. Luke, isn't it?"

*You know damn well it is.* "Uh-huh."

"How did you learn what ship he's on?"

"He didn't go into any of that detail, more's the pity."

"I only need seven for the week I'm there, but I've got more just in case I need last-minute back-up."

"It's best to be prepared."

Hedda's smile pinched at the ends. "How many names were on that list?"

Oh, jeez. Hedda had cornered her with one simple question. "About a dozen."

"Horse hockey! It's twenty."

"I didn't stop to tally—"

"They're numbered!" Hedda hissed at Nell. "My list is not floating around anywhere."

Nell wanted to yank that ridiculous hat over Hedda's rabid face, but instead she blinked like an operetta ingenue. "You want maximum publicity for your Pearl Harbor junket. Who better to help you than a movie studio?"

"I put that list together by calling in favors. Mostly from the top brass."

"I hope you didn't strong-arm anyone into compromising national security."

"What's next? Telling me that loose lips sink ships?"

"Don't they?"

"My son serves with the OSS. The last thing *I* need is some Joanie-Come-Lately small potato lecturing *me* about military secrets."

"HEY!" Arthur's voice came blasting through the megaphone at them. "SOME OF US ARE TRYING TO MAKE A MOVIE. WHOEVER'S BACK THERE, TAKE YOUR ARGUMENT OUTSIDE."

Nell waited until they were clear of the elephant door. "Nobody will believe for one single second that you got those names from playing by the rules."

"Says you."

"Movements and locations of military personnel are confidential."

"How did you hear your precious boyfriend was going to Midway?"

"Wait. What? He's on Midway?"

"Enough with the playacting. You're terrible at it."

Hedda was right, but Nell could tell she wasn't one hundred percent convinced of it. "Midway, Pearl Harbor, the moon—the point is you shouldn't know."

"Neither should you."

"I didn't until you mentioned it just now."

"We both know that's crap. And so is this far-fetched story about my list being passed around."

"And yet I did know. So what's your explanation, Hedda? Did I bribe one of your secretaries into making a copy for me? That's the sort of stunt *you* would pull."

"My staff is devoted. They wouldn't betray me like that." She pushed back her hat and shoved her scornful puss close to Nell. "You broke into my office and snooped around."

"WHAT?"

"Again with the amateur theatrics."

Nell wanted to keep Hedda off balance by killing her with kindness, but now this bitch was throwing around accusations of committing a felony. That was too much.

"Breaking into your office like I'm some cat burglar out of a *Thin Man* movie? The whole idea is as ridiculous as your hat!"

"What people think of my hats doesn't faze me in the least. If it did, I wouldn't have lasted two seconds in this business. Whatever you're up to, if I catch wind of it, and if it's within my power, believe me when I tell you that I will block you. Especially if it means preventing you from hearing from your broken boyfriend."

A strangled gasp flew out of Nell before she could stop it. "My —what did you say?!"

The crows' feet around Hedda's eyes rumpled as an overweening sneer twisted her lips. "You. Heard. Me." She spat out each word with acerbic deliberation. "He can't even see colors. Which makes him 4-F. Which it should. We need able-bodied men to win this war. Not defects."

Nell's right hand flew up, her palm flattened and her fingers rigid for maximum effect.

"Do it!" Hedda hissed. "Slap me! With all your might.!" A prickling sensation spread across Nell's hand as she fought the urge to smack the sanctimonious disdain off this battle-ax's desiccated face. "I dare you."

It wasn't worth it. Not for five seconds of satisfaction. Not when the woman had a vindictive streak the size of the Rio Grande. Louella's words came back to Nell: *Your loyalties are to us columnists. We are the whole reason you exist.* She let her hand flop against her side.

"I knew you didn't have it in you." Hedda adjusted her hat so that it perched more squarely on her head. "I had high hopes for you when I got you that job."

"Goodbye, Hedda."

"You're no better than all those timid, lightweight girls who don't have the stomach to play in the big boys' sandbox."

Nell turned around and headed down Fifth Street. It was nowhere near her office, but she needed time to recover.

*  *  *

Nell had hobbled halfway back to the office before she realized her blister had burst open, soaking her socks. On any other day, she might have gone home, but Taplinger wanted the *Big Sleep* press release drafted before she left tonight.

It wasn't until she had plopped herself down at her desk, barefoot as a vagrant Okie, that she realized the entire department was unusually subdued. When Paisley approached her, she asked, "What's going on? Did someone die? By the way, do we have petroleum jelly in our first aid kit? Wait, do we *have* a first aid kit?"

"Mr. Taplinger wants to see you. Right now."

Nell followed her up the aisle of curiously quiet desks and tapped on her boss's doorjamb. "I can have the *Big Sleep* press release for you by—"

"Close the door and take a seat."

Taplinger had never been one for small talk, but this was terse, even for him.

She lowered herself into the guest chair. "What's going on?"

"What the *hell* were you thinking?"

"Believe me, the last thing I want to do is walk around barefoot—"

"I'm talking about Hedda Hopper!"

Of course Hedda had got to him first. Of course she'd made sure her version of events would set the pace. Damn this blister.

"Quite honestly, I think I showed more-than-reasonable restraint."

"Restraint?" Taplinger could barely get the word out. "I don't care if she called you the biggest whore since Madame du Barry. YOU DON'T HIT HEDDA HOPPER!"

Nell recoiled against the back of the chair. "Hit her?"

"You should have heard her just now. I'm surprised the telephone wires didn't melt."

"I don't know what she told you, but—"

"She said you were argumentative and abusive to the point where you slapped her so hard she fell against the wall, knocking off her hat, and scraped her knees on the asphalt."

"Not even close! Things got heated, yes. I went to slap her, but then thought the better of it. I walked away before it all got out of hand."

"Hedda is vitally important to this studio."

Nell dug her nails into her palms. "What are you saying?"

"You're very good at your job, and I like you personally, but—"

"You're *firing* me?"

"My hands are tied."

"But she—you can't let—"

"She threatened to call Mr. Warner if I didn't discharge you."

Nell could have asked since when did Hedda Hopper dictate hiring and firing, but there was no point in fighting back. Only the Warners and the Zanucks and the Mayers had the luxury of telling Hedda to go to hell. And even they would hesitate.

"I see." Nell stood up. She had to press her lips together to keep from crying out in pain as her feet hit the parquet floor.

"I'm very sorry to see the situation play out this way," Taplinger said. Nell nodded. If there was an appropriate response, she couldn't think of it. "I assume there's a reason you're barefoot. I could get a driver from the car pool to take you home."

Nell wanted to tell him, 'Screw you! If you're going to dump me like a sack of dead ducks on the say-so of a treacherous hypocrite like Hedda Hopper, then I want nothing from you but my final paycheck.' But it was a long walk to Beverly Hills.

"I'd appreciate that."

*　*　*

"Is it helping?" Betty asked.

"Where did you learn to make these so well?"

She shot Nell a 'Where do you think?' look. "He said you can make Old Fashioneds from whiskey, bourbon, or brandy, but do it right and use rye."

Nell drained her second cocktail inside an hour. "My feet are numb, if that's what you're asking."

"I wasn't talking about your blister."

"I'll take all the wins I can get."

The last glimmers of the sunset beamed into the living room through the window blinds, catching dust motes floating mid-air. This apartment was overdue for a thorough cleaning, and now she had the spare time to do it. "I've never been fired before. It's humiliating."

"I can't believe nobody said goodbye as you packed up your things."

"They were too busy finding chores to do in their desk drawers." Nell didn't blame them. They'd seen what happened when mere mortals incurred the wrath of Harridan Hopper. She lifted her empty tumbler. "A third, if you please?"

"Su-u-u-ure." Betty stretched out the word as though she weren't at all sure.

"I don't turn into a wailing mess until after my fourth."

"It's not that." Betty's eyes darted away.

"What is it, then?"

"You received a letter today."

Nell sat upright and plunked the glass on the table. "How come you didn't mention it?"

"Because you arrived home in such a state that I felt you needed to have a couple of stiff drinks inside you first." Betty pulled out a pale pink envelope from under a pile of *Look* magazines on the coffee table.

That copperplate handwriting—uniform, meticulous, careful—could only have belonged to Ivy Davenport. Nell stared at it until Betty slipped a knife in front of her and whispered, "Number three coming up."

Mother had addressed it to the boardinghouse, who had forwarded it. The folded stationery inside was the same hue as the envelope and made of the same expensive vellum.

*June 1$^{st}$, 1944*

*Dear Nell,*

*I don't believe in rambling letters and I shall not start now.*

*We have indulged your whim long enough. It's high time you came home and started living a normal life. Your father and I still don't understand why you left the way you did, but we can talk all that through when you return.*

*It can be well-nigh impossible to secure reservations, but your father will be pulling some strings to get you a seat on a Greyhound bus, probably by the July Fourth long weekend. He'll cable you the details when it's all set, but this ought to give you enough time to pack up your things.*

*There's no need to reply to this letter, but you must acknowledge your father's cable when it arrives. Trust me, you'll thank us in the long run.*

*With love,*
*Mother*

"BETTY!" Nell yelled out. "Make it a double."

## 32

Nell scattered Old Dutch along the length of the bathtub. "You fool." She thwacked the orange cleaning rag against the porcelain enamel. "Played right into her hands." Scrub, scrub, scrub, scrub. "Thought you were smarter than that." Scrub, scrub, scrub, scrub. "But you're strictly amateur hour."

She had blanketed the tub with more abrasive powder than she needed. But if she couldn't give Hedda's face a good going-over, it might as well be the bathroom.

Using both hands now, she zigzagged, huffing as she went. "I only stopped myself from clobbering that old prune because I thought I'd get fired. I should've slugged her when I had the chance."

She plunked her behind on the cool tiles. Maybe Mother was right. Hollywood has chewed me up and spat me out. Maybe it's time I returned home. If Luke wants to chase after a dummy like me, he'll have to get himself to South Bend.

"I should call Hedda and thank her." Betty appeared in the doorway. "We've got the cleanest bathroom this side of the Good Samaritan Hospital."

"I don't know who I'm madder at. Her for causing all this, or me for taking the bait."

"*Variety* and *Hollywood Reporter* are on the dining table."

"Why bother? It's not like I work in the movies anymore."

"There's also a—" Betty raised her angular eyebrows "—telegram."

So soon? Nell had been hoping she had at least another week before she heard from her father. However, Elias Davenport was nothing if not resourceful. She slapped the rag against the tub and clambered to her feet.

The Western Union envelope sat on top of the magazines. Nell tore along the edge and pulled out the telegram.

SECURED BOOKING ON GREYHOUND LEAVING LA ON 29TH STOP
DUE TO HIGH DEMAND YOU MUST CLAIM INSIDE 48 HOURS STOP
THIS IS FOR THE BEST STOP
HAVE MOVED HEAVEN AND EARTH TO GET YOU THIS SEAT STOP
FATHER

Nell slid the cable over to Betty and opened the *Daily Variety*. Out of habit, she flipped to Frank Scully's column. His headline read *'TO HAVE' TWOSOME ALREADY PAIRED IN FOLLOW-UP*. The studio's official announcement that they were teaming Humphrey Bogart and newcomer Lauren Bacall in Howard Hawks's *The Big Sleep* read like the press release Nell would have written had she not allowed herself to get caught in Hedda's crosshairs.

She stared at the blue-and-white gingham curtains Betty's

mother had put up. Outside the window, the leaves of a silver birch wavered in the breeze.

I should be fielding calls about *The Big Sleep*. I'd use the interest in this new film to beat the drum on *To Have and Have Not*. And I'd do it in between escorting stars to the *Hollywood Canteen* set where I could—oh, stop punishing yourself. You won't be on a movie set ever again.

"I expect you'll be hearing from Howard's office about interviews and whatnot."

Betty waved the telegram in Nell's face. "Are you going?"

Nell eyed it, but only fleetingly. "I don't have much choice."

"Another studio is bound to snap you up."

"I've got a scarlet letter. A great big H. I'm a leper. One of the untouchables."

"What about a job in a war factory?"

"Now that the Allies are on the Continent pushing back the Nazis, production is half of what it was this time last year. I'd only be putting off the inevitable."

"You're really leaving, then?"

"Looks like it."

Betty's shoulders slumped. "First I lose Bogie, and now I lose you. Who am I supposed to share the excitement of my debut with?"

"It doesn't come out for another six months. I'm sure you'll have tons of interesting new friends by then."

"Yeah, but none of them picked me up on my first day in LA and didn't hesitate when I told her to pinch my arm to make sure I wasn't dreaming." Betty tapped the telegram. "There's a Greyhound ticket office on Crescent. You want some company?"

"Thanks, but no. I need to do this by myself."

"When I drove past it the other day, the line was out the door."

"With the slowdown in factory work, I guess people are returning to their hometowns." Yeah, Nell thought. Like me.

\*\*\*

It was a deliciously warm mid-summer day with a refreshing hint of ocean breezes blowing off Santa Monica, but Nell felt like a death-row convict, taking a final walk to the electric chair.

The last place she wanted to be walking into was a bus depot to collect a ticket she didn't want to use. This was for the best, huh? The best for who? Not silly, deluded little Nell, who'd thought she could make a life in the movies. That was only for glamour girls.

Nell turned the corner onto Crescent Drive. The line snaked out of the Greyhound office and past the neighboring hardware store. She slowed her pace to a stroll. *If somebody joins the line before I get to it, it's a sign that I shouldn't leave LA, regardless of how much heaven and earth Father had to move.*

But she arrived at the end of the line with no one beating her to it.

*How will Luke find me? I could leave a letter with Bogie. What a shame this couldn't have happened after I'd told Luke about his inheritance.*

The line inched forward.

*If they close for lunch before I step inside, it means I'm not supposed to pick up that ticket. I had a job I loved. I had a great boyfriend in Luke. A terrific girlfriend in Betty. What went wrong?*

Preoccupied with her thoughts, she took no notice of the "Hey! HEY!" being shouted from a car crawling along the street.

*Hedda Hopper happened, that's what went wrong. Falling for her vicious manipulations like a greenhorn straight off the train from Hayseed, Arkansas.*

"NELL DAVENPORT! ARE YOU DEAF?"

Her head snapped back. *Tristan? Shouldn't he be at the studio fitting Alexis Smith for a dazzling gown?*

He hung out of the passenger window of Betty's car, which

was idling at the curb. "That's right, Nellie Numbskull, we're talking to you." He wiggled his thumb toward the back door. "Get in. Now."

"But I'm—"

"Not anymore, you're not."

Nell had barely closed the door behind her when Betty stomped on the gas and roared back into traffic.

"You should have stuck around to read Kathryn Massey's column," Tristan said to her over his shoulder. He rattled the *Hollywood Reporter* in his hand, making a big show of folding it over. "And I quote: 'The Warner Brothers lot is abuzz today—as is all of Hollywood—to learn that Hedda Hopper may have gotten her comeuppance at last. Miss Hopper dishes out criticism, spreads rumors, tosses around insults, scuttles careers, and flings accusations like she's part of a circus knife-throwing act. But what happens when she's on the receiving end? Two days ago, she pushed her luck a little too far with a member of the Warner publicity staff who slapped Hedda so hard her hat fell off and she ended up a crumpled, sprawling mess of puce and petunias.'"

"NO!" The word flew out of Nell like a flock of startled blackbirds.

"Hold on," Betty hollered. "There's more!"

Tristan returned to the *Reporter*. "'It's about time someone stood up to that self-important, bull-headed, opinionated windbag. Everybody in Hollywood—me included—has wanted to slap Hedda Hopper at one point or another but few of us have had the guts. Except Nell Davenport—'"

"She *named* me?"

"'—who should be applauded for it. But instead, she got fired. There's not a whole lot I can do to get her reinstated, nor is it my place. So here's my question: Who, within the walls of Warner Brothers, can?'" Tristan dumped the trade paper into Nell's lap. "You, my slaphappy darling, are a hero!"

"I can't imagine why Kathryn would stick her neck out for me."

"The studio is in an uproar. It's all anyone can talk about."

Betty added, "You're David in saddle shoes and pigtails, and you slapped Goliath!"

Nell picked up the paper, but the words printed on the page registered as meaningless doodles. "I didn't slap her. I wanted to, God knows, but I thought the better of it and walked away."

Tristan threw up his hands. "If Hedda wants to push the story that you slapped her, then this column here is exactly what she deserves. Only the two of you know what happened, and she will not retract her story. Her own lies will hang her. Meanwhile, you're the toast of the town."

## 33

Nell stopped outside the administration building and straightened the cuffs of her blouse. They didn't need straightening, but she wasn't quite ready to walk inside.

She had sent Kathryn Massey a card filled with effusive thanks for her stance. She had received no response, but that was okay; she just wanted Kathryn to know she appreciated the gesture. And maybe word had reached Taplinger, who had called her three days later to say the four words she thought she'd never hear: "We want you back."

And now it was the first day after the July Fourth holiday and here she was, jumpy as a squirrel on an electric fence.

Would she get a rousing cheer when she walked in there? Nah, that sounded like a scene from a Frank Capra movie. Deafening silence and resentful glares? Very Fritz Lang. Or maybe a cordial greeting from Taplinger: "Let's not mention what happened but instead move forward."

When Nell finally rallied her courage and stepped into the PR department, she encountered none of those scenarios. Everything seemed business-as-usual normal. Telephones ringing, typewriters clacking, someone wondering out loud where Burma was, and why was Flynn's new picture set there? A few people looked up from their work long enough to greet her with a brief "Good morning," but nobody registered surprise, relief, animosity, or gratitude.

But then she arrived at her desk.

It was bare of all its usual paraphernalia: typewriter, pencils, newspaper clippings, memos.

In their place lay a giant sheet of white cardboard, with large letters in barber-pole-red ink:

<br>

HEDDA HOPPER HATE CLUB
PRESIDENT: NELL DAVENPORT
ONE WRONG WORD AND SHE'LL SLAP YOU SILLY

<br>

Below that, an artist from the art department had drawn a cartoon of Nell swinging a right hook into the side of Hedda's face. A floppy hat the size of a car tire and covered in garish pink pompoms had flown a foot into the air.

Nell looked up from the gag to find everybody peering at her from the corners of their eyes.

"Bravo," she told them. "And thank you. I'll have it framed!"

Good-natured applause rolled down the length of the room before people returned to their work.

Nell pulled off her gloves as she examined the caricature. It was an admirable likeness—although Hedda might not be quite so pleased.

And more to the point, this was all well and good, but she couldn't pretend the last two weeks hadn't happened.

Taplinger was on the phone when she presented herself. To his credit, he told his caller that he'd have to call them back, and instructed Nell to take a seat as he opened a drawer. "I thought you might like to see this."

He handed her a stack of seven sheets of paper. Each page had two columns, and every line was filled in with a signature. Stars, screenwriters, costumers, secretaries, lighting guys, set construction workers, hair and makeup people. Page after page. She returned to the top one and read the heading: PETITION TO HAVE NELL DAVENPORT REINSTATED.

"Four hundred and twenty-two names in less than thirty-six hours," Taplinger said. "Mr. Warner decided it was my call, seeing as how I'm the one who deals directly with Hedda."

Nell fought against the tears stinging the backs of her eyes. "I'm overwhelmed."

"For what it's worth, I believed you, but . . ." Taplinger froze his shoulders into a shrug.

"You were stuck. I get it."

"This whole unfortunate situation put the entire studio at risk because it has prejudiced one of the most powerful columnists in Hollywood against us. And *that* makes our jobs more difficult. And so it's up to you to get back into Hedda's good graces."

Nell forced down a swallow. So keeping her job was going to come at a gargantuan price. "I understand."

"I do have some positive news, though. Louella was very pleased to learn you slapped her sworn enemy, so she's more predisposed to write favorable pieces about us. Consequently, *To Have and Have Not* and Bacall have received an avalanche of publicity and positive mentions."

How quickly the teeter-totter of power shifted. In letting everybody think she had smacked Hedda, she now owed Louella a favor.

Taplinger laid his palms flat on his desk. "Movie-star wrangling on the *Hollywood Canteen* set has become a nightmare since you left. What your absence taught me is that nobody around here wrangles stars better than you."

"You sound like a man with a problem child."

"I swear this isn't punishment, but I need you to take care of Trigger."

"Please tell me Roy Rogers will be there."

"Naturally. But even though he's the world's best-trained horse, Trigger will be surrounded by tons of extras who aren't used to being around livestock."

*And I am?* "You're probably right."

"But having him on set would make for a good story or two, which you can feed to your favorite columnist or whoever's the best fit."

*In other words, Kathryn Massey.* "Gotcha."

"They're due at nine o'clock, so you'd better get going."

Nell held up the petition. "May I keep this?"

"It's all yours. Now git."

\* \* \*

Nell ran through hundreds of names as she hurried over to the Stage Sixteen. It looked like the prop from a fantasy movie version of her life, a who's who of Warner Bros.' leading lights: Bergman, Bacall, Astor, Davis, Lupino, Cagney, Flynn, Henreid, Crawford. But now wasn't the time to pore over it. She'd save that for tonight when she and Betty could go through it at home.

She slid the petition into her purse as she walked into a soundstage teeming with skittish energy. Delmer was in conference with the picture's cinematographer, Bert, who departed as she approached.

"Anxious about Trigger?" she asked him.

"That horse is the most professional animal I've seen since Rin Tin Tin. If musicians and extras were as well-behaved as him, my job would be a piece of cake."

"What's with this jumpy atmosphere I'm feeling?"

"Roy's performing 'Don't Fence Me In' with his backing band, but someone forgot the instruments. You should've heard the yelling, the screaming, the accusations. If Louella or Hedda had walked in, I might've hit the ceiling." He drew closer. "In case you're not aware, a petition was doing the rounds."

"Taplinger showed it to me. I don't suppose you know whose idea it was."

Delmer thought for a moment. "No, but Greenstreet and Lorre brought it to me. You'll find them in the makeup galley." He pointed to his left. "We're shooting their scene with Patty Andrews this afternoon."

The galley was a line of five chairs along the south wall. Lorre and Greenstreet were seated, wearing protective smocks tied around their necks, but no makeup person was in sight.

"Miss Davenport," Sydney said, "I can't begin to tell you how satisfying it is to see your face around the studio once more."

Lorre giggled like one of his devious characters and pointed to his face. "I want you to show me where you socked Hedda right in the kisser."

Nell debated how much she had to gain or lose by clarifying that no such sock to Hedda's kisser had taken place, but the official story had already taken hold. Playing along would be the course of least resistance. She pulled the petition from her purse. "Can either of you tell me who started this?"

Without looking at each other, Lorre and Greenstreet chimed together in perfect unison, "Bogart."

Nell looked at the first page again and read the top-most name: *Humphrey Bogart*.

"He personally went from set to set, dressing room to dressing room, to get people to sign," Greenstreet said. "He told me not one person hesitated."

"I can't believe it!"

"Indeed?" Greenstreet lifted a skeptical eyebrow. "He thinks the world of you."

"It's just that I haven't heard from him."

"That's because he and Mayo are locked in a death battle."

Lorre snorted. "He admitted to me last week at the Finlandia Baths that he regretted it the moment he moved back in."

"That man won't find happiness until he cuts those apron strings," Greenstreet said. "She knows about Betty and monitors his every move."

"The only reason I could meet him there is that it's men only," Lorre added. "But you might be in luck. He's coming in today for costume fittings."

"For *The Big Sleep*? Already?"

"Jack Warner wants it rushed into production."

\*\*\*

Bogie was trying on a selection of misshapen hats that made him look somewhat on the fruity side.

"On the list of things I thought I'd never see." Nell gestured at his fedora with the front brim turned up.

"I get to play a bit of a swish in an amusing scene in this new one."

"Someone ought to tell Vivian Sternwood that. It'll save everybody a bunch of time." She pulled out the petition. "I'm told you instigated this."

Bogie yanked off the hat. "You took a stance that everyone in Hollywood has wanted to take at one point or another. I couldn't let you take it alone, so I did what I could. That's all."

"I wouldn't be here if you hadn't." She kissed his cheek. "Thank you."

He returned the fedora to the shelf behind him and selected a light gray version. It didn't suit him in the slightest, but he looked as he needed to keep himself distracted.

"I hear the situation at home is a battlefield."

"We put on nightly shows for the neighbors. Wednesdays and Saturdays we give them a matinee, too."

"Especially now that *The Big Sleep* has been announced?"

"Why do you think we started doing matinees?"

"Missing her much?" Nell asked quietly.

Bogie's reply came even more softly. "To the depths of my being. If I could talk to her. Hear her voice. We don't start filming until October. I'll go nuts if I have to wait three months."

"I could give her a message. "We're roommates now."

Bogie's head snapped up, his eyes brimming with hope.

"Since when?"

"Around about the time you moved out of the Garden of Allah. She was lonesome, and I was sick and tired of living at that boardinghouse."

His eyes started darting back and forth. "There's so much I want to say to her."

"She doesn't need a twenty-page saga. What's the most important thing you want her to know?"

"That I love her and that I'm desperate to talk to her. It's hard for me to call, but maybe when Mayo passes out on the couch because—"

"Hold your horses, Roy Rogers. How about I tell her you'll try to phone her tonight between, say, ten and midnight?"

Bogie shook his head mournfully and slotted the gray hat into its position on the shelf. "Madam and I are dining at The Players. Why don't you come with us? My treat. Bring Tony as your date."

The Players was a swanky club near the eastern tip of the Sunset Strip. Preston Sturges had opened it as a place to entertain his friends. But being an above-the-title director, his friends tended to be fellow A-listers, so Nell hadn't expected she'd be given the chance to see inside it.

"Are you sure Mayo won't mind us muscling in?"

"She's more likely to behave herself if there are other people. You'll be doing me a huge favor."

\* \* \*

Tony opened the heavy wood-paneled front door of The Players for Nell. "After you."

The foyer was done out in dark chocolate brown with cream trim. A large wooden chandelier resembling a stylized wagon wheel hung from the ceiling. The maître d' took them into a deep sky-blue dining room, where Bogie and Mayo sat at their table, stewing in tense silence. Their ashtray was already filled. Bogie got to his feet as he saw Nell and Tony approach, relief washing over his face.

"Glad you could join us," he said. "Mayo, you've met Nell Davenport, of course. And this is Tony Valenti, my new toupée maestro."

The poor sap was doing his best to be upbeat and let's-have-fun-tonight, but Nell watched him droop when Mayo said, "You're the one who lost a leg at Guadalcanal, right? God, that must have been awful."

"I've had better days, but things are looking up now."

"Someone I haven't seen for a while is here," Bogie said. "Order me an Old Forester. Make it a double." He headed for a table in the corner.

Well, that's just great. You want us here as a buffer against your fermented wife, and then you up and leave us high and dry. It almost makes me want to toss out the message I have from Betty in my pocketbook. Nell turned to Tony. "Tell Mayo about Audrey and Carol."

"Your wife and kid, are they, hon?" Mayo kept her eyes on Bogie as Bogie chatted with a pale, dark-haired guy, a little on the chubby side, but he didn't look familiar to Nell.

"Yes," Tony said. "They're coming out for a visit soon."

Now that Mayo was satisfied her husband hadn't gone skirt-chasing, she ripped the top off a fresh pack of Parliaments and looked at Tony.

"Life out here is a dream come true. One perfect fucking day after another."

She lit her cigarette, took a lengthy pull, held it in as long as she could, then let the smoke out in a slow, narrow plume. "Don't listen to me. I've been rather blue lately."

"You're speaking with someone who had a leg blown to shit in the jungles of Guadalcanal," Tony said. "So, lady, I'll match you blue for blue. But I'll warn you right now, my blues will out-blue your blues ten to one."

Mayo drew back in her chair, blinked at him, then laughed a low, raspy bark blighted from too many cigarettes. "A square shooter! I love it!"

"I've wasted too much time sitting in wheelchairs and on benches feeling sorry for myself. You can't help getting the cards life deals you, but you can help how you play them."

"You should tell Bogie that."

"Do you know who he's talking to?" Nell asked.

Mayo turned and squinted through the restaurant's dim lighting to where Bogie and the chubby guy were still talking. "Yeah." She swung around again. "Used to run the prop department. A real boating nut. The two of them went sailing together down at Newport."

"That's not Simon Kovner, is it?" Nell rose to her feet.

"Where are you going?"

Panic laced Tony's voice, but there was no time for that now: Bogie was talking to the guy who had made the hollow Maltese falcon that had brought Luke to Hollywood.

"Won't be long," she promised. "Why don't you . . ." She surveyed Mayo's bad home permanent. "Tell Mayo what you'd do with her hair." She took off before either of them could protest.

Kovner and Bogie were laughing over a lee shore joke. "Mind if I join you for a second?" Nell sat down. "You're Simon Kovner, aren't you?"

Seeing him up close now, she detected a vagueness in his eyes. Kovner nodded. "And who might you be, li'l darlin'?"

"This is Nell Davenport," Bogie said. "She works at Warners."

Kovner mouthed the studio's name a couple of times. "I used to work there. Before the war."

"In the props department," Nell prodded

"Yeah. Props."

Good grief. He's plastered, and then some. "Aren't you the guy who sent a copy of the Maltese falcon to your brother in Brooklyn?"

"My brother? Irving? I did?"

"It was hollow—"

"YEAH!" Kovner slapped the table hard enough to make his silver cutlery jump. "The hollow falcon. Sure. I remember that."

"But then you needed it back, so Irving sent a guy by the name of Luke Valenti."

The man's eyes gained a little focus. "Rings a bell, now that you mention it. Did he ever get it back?"

Bogie said, "Luke ended up working for me until he joined the Navy."

"He's a fellow gob? Ain't that a peach. Y'know, I was the very first Warners employee to sign up. O'course, if'n I'da known what was going to happen to me, I wouldn't have been in no hurry."

"Why? What happened to you?" Bogie asked.

"Ending up serving on the *Indiana*, didn't I?"

"Battle of the Philippine Sea?"

"Yeah . . . oh, yeah . . ." Kovner slumped over his beer as though Bogie had pricked him with a pin and now all the air inside him was leaking out.

"But wasn't the Philippine Sea a smashing success?" Nell asked. "You guys hamstrung the Japanese Navy, sinking two of their biggest aircraft carriers and downing hundreds of planes."

"Took firepower to do it." Kovner's voice was more like a sigh. "Tons of it."

"And noisy too," Bogie said. "Really, really noisy."

"But—" Kovner sat up straight in his chair "—at least I'm not part of that convoy that got themselves ambushed."

"Ambushed where?" Nell asked.

"Those poor bubblehead bastards. Where're they gonna run? From one side of the sub to the other?"

Nell's mouth ran dry. "Submarines?"

"The Japs, they were pissed—and I mean real pissed—that we clobbered them in the Philippines. So they went on the warpath. Revenge, y'know? Can't say I blame 'em. After getting hammered like that."

"They ambushed us?" Nell asked.

"I flew back stateside with a Navy flier. He was telling me about it."

"This isn't a conversation you should have in public." Bogie warned, though softening his voice with a casual and pally tone. "Loose lips, and all that."

Simon swiped the air dismissively. "We're among friends."

"Bogie!" Nell whispered. "I need to know." She turned back to Simon. "This Navy aviator, did he mention any names?"

"Might've. I dunno. My memory ain't what it used to be. There was a time when I had tabs on every damn prop on the lot. Especially when—"

"Were they named after fish?" Nell persisted.

"The subs?" Simon yawned. He looked like the air was seeping from him again.

"What about 'lanternfish'? Did that name come up?"

"Lanternfish, huh? They live in deep waters, don't they? If I was gonna name a submarine, I'd name it Lanternfish."

Nell tried to calm herself. Why get worked up over this guy? Did he even know what he was saying?

Kovner held his beer glass as though he'd forgotten it was there. "Six of our subs traveling on patrol somewheres in the Pacific. The Japs picked up their scent and hunted them down. They sank one, crippled another, and the rest of them sustained damage."

"Did they get away?" Nell asked.

Kovner shrugged. "My guess is they'd make for Pearl Harbor. That's where I'd go if I could still sail."

Bogie tapped Nell's wrist. "We've abandoned Tony long enough." He got to his feet. "Simon, ol' pal, it was great seeing you again."

"You still got the *Sluggy*? We should go out on it some time. Just like the old days."

"Sure thing."

Nell could tell he didn't mean it. She got to her feet as well. "It was nice to meet you."

A flash of bewilderment creased Simon's brow before he returned to his beer.

Halfway to the table, Bogie eyed Orson Welles and Rita Hayworth, who were taking their seats at a table near the stage. "Don't take Simon at his word."

"I know better than to depend on someone when he's drunk."

"He wasn't drunk. That poor bastard's suffering from battle fatigue."

It wasn't fair to stick Tony with Mayo longer than they already had, but Nell stepped in front of him. "You sure?"

Bogie nodded. "I got into the Navy at the tail end of the Great War. Spent most of my time working on the *Leviathan* ferrying troops back from Europe. The vagueness, the uncertainty. He's got it bad."

"You think any of that stuff about the convoy is true?"

"He probably got the basic facts right. But how many of our ships and subs are patrolling the Pacific right now? Hundreds. What I'm saying is, statistically speaking, don't go putting all your eggs in that basket case."

"But he said that six subs were on patrol in the Pacific."

"He did," Bogie replied evenly, "but right now, Mayo is probably eating Tony alive as an appetizer and we need to rescue him."

## 34

Betty pulled into Bullocks Wilshire's driveway and gazed at the colorful Art Deco mural that filled the portico's ceiling. "This place is super fancy, isn't it?"

"If the studio's footing the bill for your new wardrobe, why shop anywhere else?"

It was Nell who had realized Betty would soon start work on *The Big Sleep*, and right after that, the studio was sending her for a triumphant "Local Girl Makes Good" return to New York for the opening of *To Have and Have Not*. "If they want Miss Bacall to look her best," she'd told her boss, "someone needs to fork out some cabbage."

They froze at the sight of a two-story atrium of coral marble and frosted glass. A long, wide hall of sparkling counters filled with makeup and perfume lay in front of them. The air was thick with a potpourri of floral scents mixed with citrus and woodsy bouquets.

"First stop, fragrances," Nell said, stepping forward. "Kathryn Massey's friend works here, the one who sells nylons on the q.t. I can't quite recall her name, though."

"Will you know it if you see it?"

"Yes. No. Maybe."

As they browsed the counters, checking out perfumes and lipsticks far beyond their price range, Nell scrutinized the name tags on the salesclerks—Ruth, Eve, Jill—until they arrived at the Coty display, where a strawberry blonde in a figure-hugging sheath made of ivy-green rayon wore a tag that read "Gwendolyn."

Nell repeated it over and over to herself. She wasn't as sure as she wanted to be, but she was out of stockings. These were desperate times.

"Hello," Nell said. "Are you the Gwendolyn who is good friends with Kathryn Massey?"

A brief hesitation mixed with surprise suffused the woman's face. "I am."

"I showed her around the set of *To Have and Have Not*." Nell pulled Betty close. "And this is Lauren Bacall, who is starring in it."

"That's the new Bogart picture, isn't it?"

"Comes out in a few months."

"Congratulations." Gwendolyn smiled, emphasizing the subtle dimple pressed into her softly pointed chin. "Nice to see you again."

"Again?"

"I live at the Garden of Allah, close to the villa Bogie moved into during his recent separation. He dropped by now and then, needing an ear to bend. He was terribly torn up about everything. I happened to notice you come and go a few times." She threw Betty another tender smile before turning back to Nell. "You were saying about Kathryn?"

"While I was showing her around, I tore one of my last good stockings, which is when she suggested I come see—"

Gwendolyn cut her off with a hushed, "Ah," and raised a finger to her lips. "How many pairs, ladies?"

Nell thought they'd be lucky to buy one pair, but this girl was asking her to come up with a number? "Five each?"

Gwendolyn furtively looked around them, then tore off a sheet of notepaper from a nearby tablet and wrote down a number. "Total for ten." She slid it across to Nell and Betty's side of the counter.

It wasn't the outrageous sum Nell had been expecting. She looked at Betty, who nodded. "We'll take them." Nell fished in her pocketbook, where she had stashed the five hundred dollars Taplinger had given her.

"Not here," Gwendolyn murmured in almost a sing-song voice.

"Can we meet you some place?"

"You're practically Garden of Allah family. How about you come over tonight? Villa twelve. Shall we say nine o'clock?"

* * *

Betty slowed her pace as they passed villa fifteen. "That's where he was living."

"These midnight phone calls," Nell said. "Helping or hurting?"

"I live for them."

"Mayo's got him right where she wants him now, but that won't last."

A wicked giggle escaped Betty's lips. "You should hear the sweet nothings he tells me."

"I don't think I want to know!" Nell pulled at Betty's elbow. "Come on, it's past nine."

The garden outside villa fifteen had a bed of lettuces and carrots where petunias and chrysanthemums had probably once grown.

"I'm a little nervous," Nell confessed. "I've never bought off the black market."

"We can still walk away."

"Are you kidding?" She rapped on the door of villa twelve.

"Saddle shoes are comfortable, but a girl likes a flattering heel from time to time."

"I hope they're good quality," Betty said. "I've heard stories about girls paying ridiculous prices for what turns out to be shoddy merchandise."

The door swung open. "I can assure you, ladies," Gwendolyn said impishly, "my merchandise is first rate."

Her apartment had the same floral carpet as Bogie's, but her living room was slightly larger. In the far corner, a seamstress's dress form stood next to a sewing machine. That explained the gorgeous sheath she'd worn at Bullocks.

Ten pairs of stockings covered the square dining table. Nell picked up the first one. The material slid over her palm like it was barely there. "These'll do fine." She went to open her pocketbook to retrieve the cash when Gwendolyn's front door squeaked.

"I found it!" A guy in his mid-to-late thirties, moon-faced, wearing horn-rimmed glasses, strode into the living room, a large atlas in his hands. "Oh, I'm sorry. You should have told me you were expecting company."

"This is my neighbor, Marcus," Gwendolyn said. "Marcus, this is Nell and Lauren. Earlier this evening, we were talking about Hedda Hopper. You read her column, I assume?"

"I work in PR at Warners, so it's an occupational hazard, but I've been so busy working on the *Hollywood Canteen* movie, I didn't get around to it today."

Marcus slid the atlas onto one of Gwendolyn's dining chairs. "You're the Nell who slapped Hedda, aren't you?"

His handshake was soft and warm, and he didn't try to break the bones in Nell's hand to prove how virile he it was.

Gwendolyn said, "You know how once a week she features a message from a serviceman to someone on the home front, or vice versa?"

"They're often the only parts worth reading," Betty said.

"Today's mention was quite intriguing." She plucked up an *L.A. Times* from her coffee table and read out loud.

"'I feel remote like Johnston Atoll and wish I was now heading up your holiday table. East and west are memories and soon should be replaced. So please be in among the palmtrees of Pearl Harbor all prettily decked out for Christmas.'"

She dropped the paper onto the coffee table. "That message doesn't make a lot of sense, but it intrigued Marcus and me about where Johnston Atoll is."

Gwendolyn scooped up the stockings, and Marcus opened his atlas to a double-page spread of the Pacific. "Midway Atoll is around twelve hundred miles northwest of Pearl Harbor, Wake Island is twenty-three hundred miles west of Pearl Harbor, and—" he tapped a dot on the left-hand page "—Johnston Atoll is eight hundred southwest."

But Betty wasn't listening. She was, instead, rereading Hedda's column. She looked up from the paper, her eyes wide with astonishment. "This message is from Ensign Vee to Nellsie Dee. Isn't your boyfriend Luke an ensign whose last name starts with V?"

Nell snatched the paper out of Betty's hands. Nobody called her "Nellsie"—except for Luke. And even then, only in bed.

She locked eyes with Betty. "Does anyone have a pencil?" Gwendolyn took one from a pad near her telephone and handed it to her. But when Nell circled every fifth word, it was an indecipherable jumble.

Betty took the pencil from her. "What if you do this?" She underlined every fifth word and the adjoining one. "Read it aloud."

"Johnston Atoll now heading east and soon should be in Pearl Harbor for Christmas."

After months of silence and that ghastly encounter with Simon Kovner at The Players, this news was everything Nell could have hoped for. More than anything she'd dared hope. Luke was out there. He was safe. And he had reached her. Eight hundred miles from Hawaii. Via Hedda Hopper, no less.

The reality of what had happened hit her as though a wild buffalo had barreled through Gwendolyn's apartment, flattening Nell in its wake. She felt the color drain from her face as she sank to the sofa.

"Got any whiskey?" Betty asked.

"This is the Garden of Allah," Gwendolyn said. "We have everything."

# 35

Nell slipped into a table in a quiet corner of the commissary. These days, she couldn't walk ten paces without someone yelling "Hiya, Nell!" or "Put 'em up, Davenport!"

The limelight had been fun at first. It wasn't the worst thing in the world for everybody to go out of their way to be nice, to say 'yes' to every favor she asked, to let her have the last sugar-cured ham steak even though they might not see another one until after the war. Preferential treatment made a girl feel a little special. And for the first time, Nell understood how tough it would be to give up when a once-blazing career sputtered toward oblivion.

But all she cared about right now was her ham steak. She breathed in its sweet-smoky aroma. Meatloaf prepared with lentils and lima-bean burgers were all very well if you smothered them with enough ketchup, but nothing beat the flavor of genuine pork.

Where on earth had the commissary manager laid his hands on this? Off the questionable back of a nonexistent truck? All that mattered was how much she was going to enjoy every flavorful, succulent, slowly chewed mouthful.

"Is that real?"

Tristan loomed over her in shirtsleeves, his anchor-patterned tie askew, and desperation etched across his face.

"It ain't Porky Pig," she told him.

He dropped into the chair opposite her. "I haven't enjoyed ham in a thousand years. Can I have some? I'll pay you."

Nell inched the chunk of meat toward her lips until it was close enough to lick the tip. Oh! That flavor! She'd almost forgotten. "Not for all the chocolate in Hershey, Pennsylvania." She bit down, savoring the juice that set her taste buds tingling.

"Didn't your mother tell you that sharing is the Christian thing to do?"

"Are you referring to the mother who told me how thoroughly disappointed she is in me after I cabled them that I wouldn't be getting on that Greyhound? The one who told me that if I don't return to South Bend by the end of the year, they *will* drive all the way out here and *take* me home?"

Tristan's eyes were glued to Nell's ham steak. "Isn't that called kidnapping?"

She carved off a slice and handed it to him. "They regard it as 'rescuing.' From what, I'm not sure. What do they think I do all day? Lie about in some Chinatown opium den?"

Tristan's eyes rolled back in his head. "Oh, my godfather and his godfather before him. This ham. It's better than sex." He handed the fork to her, but refused to let it go. "You got nothing to worry about. How the hell will they get enough gas ration points to drive four thousand miles round-trip?"

She handed over her knife. "They've cast me as the wayward daughter. Everybody's going to look at me as the lost lamb who willfully led herself astray, but is ready to return to the narrow path of righteousness. I know what they'll say, the holier-than-thou tone they'll use, the Bible passages—"

"Bible?" Tristan swiped her napkin and dabbed at the drool leaking from his lower lip. "My poor, woebegone darling. There's a passage to justify any argument."

"And don't I know it. But hey, why did you come looking for me?"

"Oh, shit!" Tristan reared up from the table. "The sight of ham distracted me. Betty's getting outfitted for *The Big Sleep*. She took a look at the rack we've put together for Bogie and unraveled like a cheap sweater."

Late the previous Friday night, Nell had disappeared into her bedroom when the telephone had rung at ten-fifteen. An hour later, the call had ended, and Nell had peeked back out into the living room to find Betty drowning in inconsolable tears. Bogie had told her that, as much as he wanted to leave Mayo, he couldn't. His marriage vows had promised fidelity forever, and he felt morally bound to live up to the commitment he'd made.

"We'll be filming *The Big Sleep* for three months," Betty had wailed. "What am I supposed to do? 'Hello, Mr. Bogart. Let's do a love scene, Mr. Bogart.' And then go have chicken salad afterward?" Nell had poured her a brandy and had told the girl, yes, that's exactly what she would have to do.

Privately, though, her money was on Bogie taking one look at Betty during their first scene together and flinging all his matrimonial promises out the window.

But did Betty's resolve have to evaporate in the middle of Nell's first ham steak in forever?

"Is she still in Costuming?"

"She refused to move until you got there."

She cut off another slab of meat and handed it to Tristan. She then sliced another two, skewered them with her fork and stuffed the whole wad into her mouth. It wasn't piping hot now, but holy moly, it tasted divine.

---

Betty had sprawled herself over a deep purple damask loveseat. She was dabbing with a pink handkerchief at wet mascara streaking her cheeks as Nell rushed in.

"You'd have thought by now I'd have gotten it into my thick skull that he's not going to leave her."

Nell sat beside her. "None of us knows what's in our future." It was a vapid bromide, but it was as true for Betty's future with Bogie as it was for Nell's with Luke.

"Living with uncertainty isn't my forte," Betty said. "I don't suppose you know a good fortune teller?"

"No, but I have an idea."

"If it doesn't involve throwing rocks through the kitchen window of twelve-ten Horn Avenue, I'm not interested."

"I noticed in *Hollywood Citizen-News* that Billie Holiday is performing at Billy Berg's on Vine Street." Betty hoisted her head up, an encouraging sign. "How about you, me, Violet, and Beatrice go see her? We can commiserate about how much we miss our boys as Lady Day sings 'My Man,' then 'Lover Man,' then 'Lover Come Back to Me' and get sloshed on Sidecars."

"I'm in, but I have a question."

"Shoot."

"Have I completely lost my senses or does your breath smell like baked ham?"

\* \* \*

The four women stood inside the front door of the club and surveyed the remarkable scene fanned out in front of them.

"You girls seeing what I'm seeing?" Beatrice murmured.

Like most jazz joints, cigarette smoke choked the air, but it wasn't so thick that Nell couldn't see how white people sat at some tables, and Negroes sat at others. In front of the stage, three black men sat with two white women. At the same table. Together.

The bartender directed them to a four-top near the center of the room. Nell waved her thanks and ordered Sidecars. Seated at their table, they pulled off gloves, unclipped fascinators, and tried not to stare around them.

"You have to wonder," Nell said, "if this place is taking its cue from Bette Davis's decree that black servicemen are as welcome at the Canteen as white ones."

Whatever the reason, the unprecedented tableau made tonight all the more exciting. All day, Nell had been looking back at her teenaged self, madly pedaling her bicycle into those woods and singing her heart out. Often, they would be Billie Holiday songs: "What a Little Moonlight Can Do" or "I Cried for You." To a young girl pining for more, singing those songs had reached beyond the suffocating restraints that bound her to a smothering family that valued doing one's duty over individuality. If that little girl in the woods had known that, one day, she'd be sitting in a Hollywood nightclub hearing Lady Day sing, she might have passed out among the nannyberry, dogwood, and poison ivy.

The drinks arrived. Violet lifted hers. "Here's to seeing our menfolk sooner rather than later."

"At least yours isn't off at war like my captain," Beatrice said. "Where's Reggie these days?"

"Fox Movietone had nothing for him, so he took a one-shot job for Pathé News covering Frank Sinatra, every day, all day, and all night."

"That Sinatra's a dish and a half," Betty said.

"MGM plans to dangle a fat contract at him. Pathé wants Reggie to be there when Sinatra gets the call. I don't mind too much when he's so far away, but knowing he's in town just about drives me loco."

"I know what you mean." Betty swirled the twist of orange peel around her cocktail. "So frustratingly near and yet so abysmally far."

"I'd go batty if I learned Keaton was in LA and didn't—or couldn't—tell me. I'd rather he was thousands of miles away." She shook her head. "Good grief! Look at us. What a bunch of sad sacks." Beatrice drained the last of her glass and stared quizzically at Nell. "How come you're so down in the mouth?"

Betty came to her rescue. "Nell's under pressure to return home to Indiana."

Nell opened her purse to double-check she had remembered to bring pen and paper. She wasn't the autograph-hunter type, but this was Billie Holiday and she wanted to be prepared. "My folks can't understand why anybody would want to travel farther than the South Bend city limits. So when I turned into a runaway bride—"

"You *what?*" Violet shrieked so loudly that the lone jazz guitarist on the stage stopped strumming for a moment.

"Another story for another time." Where was that little pad? Had she left it back at the apartment? She piled the papers in her purse on the table one by one. "They've offered a no-penalty armistice if I move home. I've tried to tell them I'm not interested, but my dad's more of a won't-take-no-for-an-answer type, so—"

"What's this?" Beatrice picked up Bogie's petition. Nell felt silly lugging it around with her after so many weeks. But whenever her spirits flagged, reading all the signatures comforted her like a fuzzy blanket.

"Leaping lizards!" Beatrice cried out, looking down the list. "I thought your petition was a rumor to stick it to Hedda, but get a load of these names: Eve Arden, Joan Blondell, Dennis Morgan, Kay Francis, Paul Henreid." She turned the page. "Good God, even Al Jolson?"

"Charlie Butterfield's there, too," Nell said. "And he's from South Bend."

Betty lit up a Parliament. Nell wondered if she knew it was Mayo's favorite brand. Had she started smoking them so that Mayo wouldn't smell them on Bogie? "I think you ought to send this to your parents."

Nell found her pad and pen and stacked them onto the table. "What for?"

"This caliber of people stood up for you when you crossed swords with an odious old harpy," Beatrice replied. "They're bound to know you must be doing something right."

Their waiter arrived with a fresh round of drinks and let them know that Miss Holiday would be taking the stage in ten minutes.

Nell hated the idea of parting with the petition, but what if it helped Mom and Dad to understand she wasn't living some aimless, no-account life? One or two entertainers mightn't be sufficient to sway them, but four hundred and twenty-two might.

Was it enough on its own, though? What if she could send it along with a second enticement that made them open their eyes a tiny bit and think, *We weren't expecting that.*

The lights in the club dimmed to half. Anticipation stirred through the audience and fizzed in Nell's chest. She would think about the petition later. For now, though, she'd give Lady Day her devoted attention.

*\* \* \**

Nell stared at the microphone three inches from her face. She could see her lips reflected in the shiny chrome. It was distracting. She could close her eyes, but then she wouldn't be able to read the words on the stand in front of her.

STARDUST. *Lyrics by Mitchell Parish, Music by Hoagy Carmichael.*

"That's the one you should record," Hoagy had said. "Everybody loves it. There's nothing your family can take offense at. And I'll be happy to accompany you."

Halfway through Holiday's glorious, wrenching, sublime set, Nell had realized how she could convince her family that she already was where she belonged. The best way to plead her case wasn't to tell them, but to *show* them.

She would make a record.

But which song? The wrong choice would sink the whole

endeavor. The countless options had overwhelmed her until Betty had proposed seeking out Hoagy. She hadn't expected him to pick one of his own compositions, but when he'd suggested "Stardust," it seemed the right choice. *And* to have him accompany her on the piano? What could be more perfect than that?

Nothing . . . except . . . here she was, a week later, at a big microphone, the lyrics splayed out in case she forgot the words to a song she knew backward, forward, and inside-out. Hoagy sat at the keyboard, waiting for her hand signal—an "okay" sign to tell the engineer he could start recording, but her fingers wouldn't move and her arm refused to budge.

The feet on Hoagy's piano stool scraped across the linoleum as he stood up and sidled alongside her. "What's the problem? Melody? Words? The arrangement?"

"It's a gorgeous song that everybody knows with lyrics that won't offend."

"And yet?"

"What if they think I sound dreadful?" Nell blurted out. "Or worse: What if they don't even listen to it? What if they toss the whole package out?"

She felt a hand squeeze her right forearm. It was Betty.

"You helped me out when I was nervous as hell. Now it's my turn." Betty's self-possessed smile had a tranquility that Nell sorely needed, like diamantes need light to sparkle. "If this recording fails to impress your folks, they will cash in every gas ration coupon in a three-county radius and drive to California where, if necessary, they will tie you up like a prize hog and throw you in the trunk."

Pent-up nerves bubbled over into a fit of shrill cackling pitched so high it made Nell blush at the sound of her own voice. "If this is your idea of a pep talk—"

"Just sing the damn song as best you can," Betty cut in. "And if one day we hear your father's Studebaker pull up out front, I'll answer the door in my best Brooklyn Jewish Russian babushka accent. 'I no know what you speaking. Is nobody here. Only me. Please to go or I am telephone the polices.'"

Hoagy's laugh had an infectious jolliness about it. "There's an offer you can't refuse. How about we try a take?"

Betty raised her hand. "Hold on. I'm not done. Your ma and pa are against secular music, right? Maybe you should do 'Amazing Grace' instead."

"That's a good idea," Nell said. "They're more likely to listen to something like that."

"Personally, I think you can sing the hell out of 'Stardust,' so why not do both, then decide which one you think is best?"

"Or," Hoagy put in, "put 'Stardust' on one side and 'Amazing Grace' on the other."

"And let them decide," Nell finished for him.

She dropped her head onto her chest and breathed out. Then she pressed her index finger to her thumb and held up her hand for everyone to see.

## 36

Nell waved as Betty pulled into her parking space outside Stage Twenty. "Good morning!"

Betty removed her sunglasses as she got out of the Plymouth. "I thought we were going to drive in to work this morning."

"I had a bunch of things to do before filming got underway."

"Like what?"

"Tomorrow's New York premiere for *To Have and Have Not*."

Betty hung open her mouth in mock surprise. "I'd quite forgotten." She put her sunglasses back into place. "I barely slept a wink last night."

"It's out of your control, so why worry?"

"Because it ain't your mug up there for everybody to pick apart." Betty looked around. "Say, where are we going?"

"I have a surprise for you."

It was the real reason Nell had pedaled in the pre-dawn October chill all the way to Burbank. The day before, she had pointed out to Howard Hawks that tomorrow wouldn't just be the start of production on *The Big Sleep*; it was also the first day Bogie and Betty would have seen each other since he'd moved back into the Horn Avenue house. "You'll get a happier pair of leads if you give them some alone time," Nell had told Hawks. "And besides, doesn't Humphrey Bogart warrant a permanent dressing room instead of yet another makeshift tent?"

"I'm not sure I like surprises," Betty said as they began to walk.

"You'll like this one."

"Have you seen him this morning?"

"Who?" Nell asked airily. Anything to distract her from what was coming.

Betty didn't miss a beat. "Genghis Khan."

"Oh, yes. He and four thousand of his fiercest horsemen pulled up on Olive at around five-thirty."

They passed the makeup department. "I'll be mailing the record later today."

"What about the petition?"

"It's too precious to me. Mother and Father aren't impressed with movies; they'll throw it in the trash."

Betty slung her right arm across Nell's shoulders. "Let's hope it does the job."

"I doubt it. In any event, four copies of a record I made with Hoagy Carmichael isn't a bad consolation prize." Keeping one for himself, Hoagy had left her with five discs, which was remarkable, considering the war effort was gobbling up all the shellac. "Mind you, recording that song was easier than writing the letter to go with it. I stopped counting after draft thirteen."

"Your last-ditch effort needs to be perfect—wait." Betty took off her sunglasses again. "Aren't these the star dressing rooms?"

Nell, with Betty at her heels, mounted the stairs to the top floor, then walked to the far end of the building. She stopped at the second-to-last room and ran a finger along the name plate. "All yours, Miss Bacall." She swung the door open. "Genghis Khan awaits through the connecting door to your right." She tapped her wristwatch. "It's a quarter of seven now. Hair and makeup will be here at seven-thirty, and filming starts at eight."

Betty took Nell's hands and sandwiched them between hers.

"You set this up, didn't you?" She pulled Nell into a hug. "This means the world to me."

"And now you're down to forty-*four* minutes. I suggest you make the most of them."

* * *

When Nell walked onto the Sternwood mansion set, she found Avery talking to Slim Hawks. "What are you doing here?"

"Ta-da!" He stepped aside to reveal a full-length portrait of Betty as her character, Vivian, dressed in a shimmering sapphire ballgown with matching necklace. She looked every inch the society daughter of an obscenely wealthy man. "Warners made me an offer I couldn't refuse after *a certain someone* showed a couple of bigwigs the mural I painted in their home."

"We're converting one of the bedrooms into a nursery," Slim said. "I wanted an Alice-in-Wonderland theme. It turned out so superbly that I couldn't help but show it to everyone we know."

"Are you . . . ?" Nell made a circle in the air around Slim's stomach.

"We were supposed to start trying after *To Have and Have Not* wrapped, but then the big romance ignited. He assumed Betty would fall for him, so when she fell for Bogie instead, it threw a rather large wrench into his works. It took some effort to get back on track." Slim peered around them at the crewmembers going about their jobs until she was satisfied nobody was listening. "The poor bastard is always a nervous wreck at the start of filming. He throws up every day for a week until he finds his rhythm. This morning, he was completely off his hinges, so I insisted on driving him here. We had to stop twice so he could puke his guts up."

"Is it the double-whammy of *Big Sleep* starting today and *Have Not* opening in New York tomorrow?"

Slim crossed her arms. "I didn't even think of that. Poor lamb. You must excuse me. I ought to check on him."

Nell and Avery watched her hurry away.

"Any word from my nephew?" he asked her.

A trio of carpenters stationed themselves at the bottom step of the grand staircase to install a wooden figure of a woman with one arm stretched above her head. Nell led him outside and told him how Luke had used Hedda to transmit a message to her.

Avery chuckled. "Clever little son-of-a-gun. So his sub is crawling to Pearl Harbor for repairs?"

"I'm just glad he's alive."

He crossed his arms. "When did you say that inheritance deadline is?"

"December thirty-first."

The morning sun peeked its early rays over the mountain next to the studio, cloaking them in pale golden light.

"If Luke is one of Hedda's featured servicemen, and if he's going to be in Pearl Harbor, and if she'll be there for the third anniversary, how do you feel about asking Hedda to take a message with her to give to him?"

Nell's heart skipped a little. "You may have heard that Hedda's not my biggest fan."

"But she chose your boyfriend to feature in her column."

"Which she did *after* our famous slapping incident," Nell said. "Translation: 'Screw you, Davenport.'"

The two of them stood in contemplative silence as one of the mailroom girls hauled a metal cart piled with letters and packages toward the administration office. Behind her, Tony marched up to them holding a wig stand with a toupée pinned to it. "How long is this big reunion going on for?"

"I gave them until eight."

"This here's brand-new." He lifted the wig stand higher. It shook despite his white-knuckled grip. "I need extra time to make sure it fits. Bogie's got a pile of close-ups right off the bat. I don't want to let him down."

"Nothing happens until the star is ready. If he needs an

extra fifteen minutes, nobody's head will roll." Nell gently pushed the stand away. "Avery, this is Tony Valenti. He's Luke's brother. Tony, this is Avery Osterhaus, who is Luke's uncle."

The two men eyed each other.

"You work here too?" Tony asked.

"Art department. Is that a Brooklyn accent I hear?"

"So thick you need a butcher's cleaver to cut through it." Tony relaxed into a restrained smile. "Bensonhurst. Sixty-seventh and Sixteenth."

"I was Lexington and Fifty-sixth."

"Fancy address."

Avery made a scoffing sound. "So fancy that I hightailed it out of there the second I turned eighteen. You like it out here?"

"I do."

"He was supposed to go back East after *Hollywood Canteen* finished filming," Nell said. "But then Perc Westmore talked him into staying a little longer."

"Perc and Bogie whipped up a double act that was hard to say no to. Especially when Bogie offered to pay for my wife and kid to come out here."

"He did?" There was a time when Nell would have heard this news before most people, but Bogie had cut himself off since he'd moved back in with Mayo.

"The first reservations they could get on the Super Chief were early January."

"Quick visit?"

Tony seesawed his hand. "Audrey's a Brooklyn girl, through and through. Out here, it's so different. The way people live. The pace. The weather."

"You know what else is different?" Nell asked. "You." She had never seen him blush before. It almost made him look boyish. "I think Audrey will see a whole new husband."

As Tony's blush deepened, his resemblance to Luke strengthened. "Sorry about getting so hot-headed just now. This new rug of Bogie's is the first I've taken charge of from the get-go."

"Never apologize for being professional," Avery said.

Tony nodded, taking his time to reappraise his brother's uncle. "You guys looked like you were deep in conversation when I muscled in."

"We were talking about how Luke might be heading for Pearl Harbor, and if he is, how we might reach him. If we're right about the *Lanternfish* needing repairs, the crew won't be sleeping on board, will they?"

"Hell, no," Tony said. "The Navy's real good about giving bubbleheads lots of shore leave. Pack a guy inside a tin can for weeks on end and he'll crack up. When they get to Pearl Harbor, they'll move into the barracks right near the sub HQ. Each one even gets his own quarters."

"That sounds like luxury for the military."

"Guys cooped up in a sub sleep thirty-six to a compartment. They deserve some space. As far as military accommodation is concerned, it ain't bad at all, but the Navy blew its budget on building it. The walls are bare. They could do with some decoration."

Nell pictured Luke spending weeks cramped in that submarine and finally getting a room of his own, only to find blank walls painted military gray. How hard would it be to put up a painting? She turned to Avery. "What if *you* painted something?"

"Could you be more specific?"

"A portrait of Hedda Hopper. A very flattering one."

"Why would I do that?"

"Because she turns sixty next year, and that's a crucial birthday —especially in this town."

"Okay, so what if I do?"

"If I prevail on Kathryn Massey to bring up the barracks' bare walls, and tell her what a wonderful present it would be if they could ship a stack of paintings to Hawaii along with Hedda's show, then she could make a big deal of presenting them to the brass. An 'Anything for Our Boys' campaign with her at the center."

"Hedda Hopper, patron saint of the US Navy Submarine Force?" Tony asked.

"She'll eat it up!" Nell exclaimed.

"Yeah, but where does that get us?"

"You could ask her to carry a note to give to Luke telling him about the inheritance deadline."

"Why not contact the officer in charge of sub ops at Pearl Harbor?" Tony asked. "Or even better, the guy who runs the barracks? Get him to put a note in Luke's quarters."

"Because I'm not supposed to know where Luke is. He put me in the picture via a special code, which I'm guessing means he's sequestered away in some top-secret job."

"Okay," Avery said, "so I paint Hedda's portrait, and I tell her that I read the message she published in her column and that Ensign Vee is my brother, and I need to get an important message to him."

"That's right."

"The old bat's not stupid. She'll put two and two together as fast as you can say 'Double scotch, hold the rocks.' I'll need to make it clear that I don't know who Nellsie Dee is—"

"Or better yet, you do, but don't like me."

"*And* I'm trying to contact Luke without your knowledge."

Nell screeched. "She'll think you're going behind my back."

"But will it be enough?"

Nell turned to Tony. "Willing to help?"

"For Luke? Sure."

"You go with Avery and find a way to mention your wooden leg. She'll ask about it, and you tell her your story about serving at Guadalcanal. When she learns that Luke's brothers are ganging up on me," she clapped her hands together, "it's in the bag."

"Okay," Tony said, looking at his watch, "the two lovebirds

need to be done with their—" he cleared his throat theatrically "—reunion. I've got magic to perform. Let me know if you need me."

Avery turned to Nell. "I hate to poke a needle into your balloon, but this whole set-up with Hedda and her portrait and handing her a note—it's pretty far-fetched, isn't it?"

"It sure is."

"A ton of things could go wrong."

"Maybe even two tons."

When Nell had tipped off Betty that Bogie was on the other side of her dressing room door, Betty's entire face had changed. Color had flushed her cheeks with a rosy glow. Her green eyes had sparkled. A joyful grin had split her face. And an unrestrained cry had exploded from her, drenched with yearning and joy. Nell wanted that for herself, too. A tearful, passionate reunion with Luke. Sometime. Somehow. Somewhere. And she was prepared to do anything for it.

"Luke's deadline is less than three months away. I must get word to him at Pearl Harbor, and that vindictive bitch is the only person I know who'll be there between now and the end of the year. If you'd rather not tangle with Hedda, I'd understand."

"I don't want to see you disappointed, is all."

She had to get onto her tiptoes to kiss him on the cheek. "Think of it this way: crazy plans like this always work in the movies."

"Not without a hitch, though."

"A hitch or two along the way makes it more interesting. But in the final reel, the good guy always wins." A spontaneous chortle gurgled out of her. "Or good girl, as the case may be."

## 37

Nell hit the brakes of Betty's car and slowed to a stop under the portico of the Beverly Hills Hotel. "Thanks again for the loaner."

"I just hope there's enough gas left in the tank. If not, you'll have to go begging for ration coupons. But that won't be my problem—not for the next couple of days, at least."

Even in the depths of her misery over missing Bogie, Betty had smoldered on screen, exuding the magnetism that people born to be movie stars exuded. The studio-bought wardrobe helped. And so did Tony fixing her hair. But now that she had Bogie all to herself, she was so lustrously beautiful it was impossible not to stare.

Nell rapped a knuckle against the oxblood leather grip on Betty's lap. "Got everything?"

"We don't plan on leaving room 207, so there wasn't much to pack." She traced a fingernail around the initials L.B. embossed in gold near the handle. "And thanks for being smart."

"About what?"

"Without you telling me to be patient, I would have given up all hope."

"It's easier to call those shots when you're not the one sinking into quicksand. Now, get outta here before Bogie files a missing person report."

Betty pressed her cheek to Nell's. "You're such a good pal." She turned to face Tony in the back seat. "I'll be busting to hear how it all goes this afternoon." She lifted the blanket protecting Avery's portrait. "He's made her look like the glamorous aunt who everybody wants to sit next to at Thanksgiving."

Avery had put Hedda in a patriotic outfit of red, white, and navy blue, teamed with a hat that resembled an admiral's cap—white with a black peak and embroidered gold leaves—but worn at a modish angle.

Betty opened her car door. "You moving up front?"

Tony shook his head. "Good luck in there. Not that you'll need it."

Nell watched her saunter into the hotel before gingerly hitting the gas. Betty hadn't been kidding—whatever gas was still in the tank had to last for the rest of the month.

A week after the start of production on *The Big Sleep*, Bogie had moved out of Horn Avenue again and into the Beverly Hills Hotel, where Mayo had been calling him so incessantly that he'd had to tell the switchboard operators to stop putting her calls through. But even then, Nell hadn't believed the separation would hold until the morning Taplinger had asked her to draft a statement for the Associated Press announcing the separation of Mr. and Mrs. Humphrey Bogart after six years of marriage.

Nell turned onto Sunset and joined the traffic heading east. "What will you say to Hedda?"

"I sure wish Avery could be here with me."

"Me too, but the scenic art department is down to just him. He's working flat-out, seven days a week on *Three Strangers*. That's okay, though. You'll do a great job. So, again, you'll say to Hedda . . ."

Tony pulled himself forward, resting his chin near Nell's neck. "I got inspired by Kathryn—"

"No. Introduce yourself first, starting with your rank. That way, she knows you're Navy. Then your first and last name, so that she realizes you're Luke's brother. And *then* go into how you were inspired by Kathryn's suggestion of Hollywood helping to decorate the barracks at Pearl Harbor."

"Right. Then I tell her, 'I painted this portrait and I hope you like it.' I lift the blanket—'Hey presto!'—and make sure she gets a good, long gander at it. How many paintings have the Navy brass okayed?"

"Thirty. Be sure to mention the USO show that'll be accompanying her. She's real proud of that."

"And then I produce the note with Luke's name on it."

Nell turned north onto Fairfax, which would take them to Hollywood Boulevard, where Hedda kept her office in the Guaranty Building. Kathryn had thought Nell's idea was "wonderfully inspired," and had included it in her column three days later. Avery had finished the portrait the first morning of the three-night snuggle fiesta Howard Hawks had granted his two *Big Sleep* stars. Sure, this plan was batty as a belfry, and she'd be lucky to pull it off, but so far, so good.

"And what do you say if she asks how you know Luke'll be at Pearl Harbor?"

"That I'm just guessing it, based on my own Navy experience, which will be when I mention my injury. How am I gonna do that, though? Drop my pants and show her my peg leg?"

"Grimace and groan a little, as though you're trying hard *not* to show it so that she asks you what's wrong."

"Yeah, but what if she doesn't?"

"Improvise."

"Does that mean make it up as I go along?"

In several ways, Tony and Luke looked similar. And sometimes, he came out with a word or a phase exactly the same way Luke would have said it. But being around him had its pros and cons. The two of them were enough alike to fend off the worst of the pangs of missing Luke. It let her pretend, if only for a fleeting moment, that Luke was still close by. Other times, Tony would say something that reminded her these Valenti brothers weren't interchangeable at all.

"Yes," Nell replied, "play it by ear."

At the Ivar Avenue intersection, a battered Chevrolet truck, more rust than paint, pulled away from the curb out front of the Guaranty. Nell made a sharp left and pulled into the space before a Hollywood Boulevard streetcar blocked her. Yet another good omen, surely?

She got out of the car and opened the passenger door. The portrait measured twenty-six by twenty inches and was mounted on a simple frame, so it wasn't too heavy. "I'd tell you to break a leg," she winked at him "but given the circumstances . . ."

"I hope I can bring home the bacon."

"This from someone who faced Guadalcanal. Hedda will be duck soup in comparison." She walked him around the corner, held open the glass door, and hit the elevator call button. "I'll be right here when you get back."

\* \* \*

She hadn't sat behind the wheel for more than a minute before she was out of the car again, pacing the sidewalk.

Bogie had told her how cigarettes calmed him after going toe-to-toe during contract negotiations with Jack Warner or surviving a vicious tussle with Mayo. She could have done with a calming Lucky Strike, but it was too late to start smoking now.

Wasn't it?

She eyed the tobacco store on the south side of the boulevard. Nah, she decided. It would take a couple of packs just to get the hang of it.

And what would Luke think if he came back to find his sweetheart had turned into a cigarette fiend? She had a hunch that servicemen wanted to return to a home that hadn't changed while they'd been cooped up in submarines and foxholes, Sherman tanks and B-17 gun turrets.

It was Luke's spirit she missed the most. To be with him, hear him laugh, listen to him snore. Whenever she thought of those early days, she was shocked at her behavior, walking up to him so brazenly in Schwab's that day. She could hear her mother tsk-tsk. "Nice girls wait to be asked."

A chilly November breeze gusted out of the Hollywood Hills. She ought to have worn a warmer sweater than this springtime cardigan. She wrapped her arms around her waist and thought about getting back into the Plymouth.

How excited Betty had been this morning, flitting around the apartment, choosing provocative lingerie and alluring perfume. Nell didn't have the heart to tell her that Bogie didn't give two hoots if she wore French garter belts or a bargain-basement girdle from Newberry's. She doubted he'd notice if she sprayed herself with Coty Vertige or drugstore bilge water. He was so damn happy to have freed himself of the manacles of his marriage that she could have arrived at room 207 dressed in a potato sack and all he'd see was the girl of his dreams.

"She ordered me to come get you."

Nell whipped around.

Tony stood three feet away, his face taut with apprehension, his hands empty. "She happened to be looking out the window when we arrived."

Oh, crumbs. "The jig's up?"

"I wouldn't say that."

"What would you say?"

"The jig's up in the air."

. . .

Hedda's office looked like a cross between a city paper newsroom, a second-hand curio store, and a set designer's notion of what a Broadway star's backstage dressing room looked like—but with secretaries hammering away at typewriters like a pair of Rosie the Riveters at the Lockheed factory.

Hatboxes of all colors filled the west-facing wall. At each end was a stand with at least ten hats dangling from each limb. A wardrobe rack on wheels stood between them, packed with dresses and jackets on wooden hangers. Behind Hedda's desk stood shelving with piles of books, stacks of magazines, a scattering of award trophies, vases, Victorian figures, and a cluster of shabby ostrich feathers. The desk itself was a beat-up piece of junk that looked like it had been salvaged from a shipwreck. It was strewn with fan letters, notebooks, two empty bottles of Mucilage glue, a pickle jar of chewed pencils, and assorted lipsticks.

Hedda stayed seated and pretended to review a typewritten article.

Fine. If that's the way she insists we play it. "Hello, Hedda."

She made Nell wait four seconds before she deigned to look up. Avery's painting was propped up against the hat stands on the left. She cast a gnarled finger at it. "It's exorbitantly flattering."

Hedda hadn't invited either of them to take a seat, so Nell gripped the back of the nearest guest chair. "When I mentioned Kathryn's proposal, I didn't tell him what to paint, did I, Tony?" He shook his head. "But if it kicks off a slew of donations for Pearl Harbor, then that's what matters."

"You think yours is the first?" Hedda tipped the red pencil in her hand at a stack of three paintings against the wall behind her left shoulder.

"I'm sure those bubbleheads will be glad to have interesting art to look at instead of pipes and gauges and a rack eight inches above them."

"Believe me, those barracks are as plain as it gets," Tony said.

"The walls are gray. The linoleum is gray. Even the white sheets are gray."

Hedda arched a guarded eyebrow. "You've seen it?"

"Yes, ma'am." He shifted his weight onto his prosthetic, winced theatrically, then shifted it back again. "We stopped over there en route to Guadalcanal."

Hedda sat up straighter in her chair.

"I shipped out—" He cut himself off with a sharp inhale. "May I take a load off?" He knocked on his leg. "When the weather turns cold, my wound aches something terrible."

Hedda gestured toward one of the empty chairs. "What rank did you say you were?"

"Gunnery sergeant." He landed on the seat with a heavy whimper.

"It must have been dreadful."

"Better to look forward than back, ma'am. When I heard you'd taken up Kathryn Massey's suggestion, I thought to myself, now there's a cause that'll achieve some actual good. Hats off to you, Hedda Hopper—that's what I said." He turned to Nell. "Didn't I?"

"He did!" Nell exclaimed. "And so did I."

Hedda twirled the pencil around her fingers. "You got a lot of mileage out of our little incident."

That same pinched, overbearing simper emerged, the one that had made Nell want to slap her in the first place. "What I got was fired."

"But you were reinstated. No harm in the long run."

"Except that everyone thought I slapped you."

"And now you have more notoriety at Warners than you ever dreamed of. Quite frankly, I deserve a great, big thank-you."

Nell hated to admit it, but the gorgon had a valid point. Alas, this exchange had veered from the reason they were here.

"You're right, Hedda." *Tell her what she wants to hear.* "I hadn't thought about it in quite those terms." *She's the star of this scene; let her hog the spotlight.* "I do get more respect now." *And you're a lying crone from hell whose revenge backfired.* "So I guess I do owe you my heartfelt thanks." *Happy now?*

Nell needed a moment to swallow the bile rising in her throat, which Tony took as his cue. He reached into the side pocket of his jacket and held up the note Nell had written so that Hedda could see *Ensign Luke Valenti* on the envelope.

"I detect the stench of a favor request coming my way."

"But when you published the message from Ensign Vee to Nellsie Dee, you must have known who they were."

"I had my suspicions. But why not go through the usual channels?"

"He hasn't gotten any of the letters I've sent him."

Tony slid the envelope toward Hedda. She didn't pick it up. "What's Nell's message to her long-lost boyfriend got to do with you?"

"He's my brother."

Tony added the right amount of tenderness to his voice. His lower lip was trembling. Not enough for Hedda to see from her side of the desk, but Nell could. *My goodness, he actually means it.*

"Two brothers." Hedda drummed her nails on her desk blotter. "Both at war. One pays a steep price as the other presses on to fight the good fight."

"It could be a nice follow-up to your Serviceman of the Week squib." Nell pointed to Avery's portrait. "It would make a fitting photo."

"It would, at that," Hedda admitted. "My readers love to see me with regular servicemen in their uniforms."

"With the portrait in the middle of you two."

"Whoa!" Tony threw up his flattened palms. "Not so fast. I ain't so fond of getting my photo took." His face reddened with surprising speed. "Hedda Hopper's readers want to see Hedda Hopper, don't they? With this painting, they get two for the price of one. Sorry, but count me out."

Nell wondered if landing in the *L.A. Times* with someone as high-profile as Hedda might lead to questions Tony would rather not answer about a picture he hadn't painted.

"Perhaps Tony's right," Nell said. "Let your readers see how wonderful Tony's portrait is and read the story of the two Valenti brothers." She held the flattering portrait in front of her, counted to ten, then peeked over the top. "Will you take the note?"

"I'll need to know what it says."

Nell slid the painting through her fingers until it reached the carpet. Hedda stared back, unblinking. "I'd rather you didn't."

"I'm a prominent woman with much to lose if—"

"It's personal," Nell blurted out. "In fact, you could say it's slightly graphic." Nell gave that final word extra oomph. It was enough to send Hedda's eyebrows skyward.

"I see. Not so much a billet-doux as a billet do-it?"

Nell wished she blushed as easily as Tony. Instead, all she could manage was what she hoped would come across as a bashful pantomime of closing her eyes as she turned her face away.

"All right," Hedda said.

"Thank you!"

"It is a lovely portrait, I must admit."

"I know you're busy, so we'll be—"

"Not so fast." Of course there was a catch. Wasn't there always? "In return, you must tell me where I can find Bogie."

"I'm not sure why you think I'd know," Nell hedged.

"You're pals with Bogie, and you're Lauren Bacall's roommate. If anyone would know where Bogie is, it's you. I tried to snare him last week when he took part in that loathsome pro-Roosevelt radio broadcast with Bette, Tallulah, Judy, and Olivia, but he ducked out. He hasn't spoken publicly about the end of his marriage. That was three weeks ago, so it's about time he did."

*Please don't put me in this position, Hedda. All I want is to reach Luke before the end of the year. I'm so desperate that I'll even recruit you to help me. But don't force me to betray two of my closest friends. They deserve three days of uninterrupted bliss, don't they?*

"You'll find them on Stage Twenty at eight o'clock Monday morning," Nell said. "You can—"

"Howard Hawks has barred all press from the *Big Sleep* set."

Nell didn't need to feign surprise at this news. "He has?"

"I got Jaik to call all hotels within a ten-mile radius, but he's been stonewalled at every turn. You tell me, or this carnal mash note—" she pinched a corner of it and held up as though it had been dipped in leprosy "—goes in the trash."

*Think, Davenport, think! There must be a path through this minefield.*

"Just because I'm pals with someone and roomies with someone else doesn't mean I'm privy to every little detail. I can only think of one other person who'd know."

"Who's that?"

"The Battling Bogarts have a divorce to finalize. Mayo must know where he is."

Hedda turned the envelope around and stared at Luke's name for what felt like hours, then tossed it onto a messy pile of correspondence. "I've got a column to get out." She dismissed them with a flick of the wrists.


Neither of them said a word until they were sitting in the Plymouth. Tony spoke first. "When she told me that she was watching us, I thought our ship was sunk."

Nell inserted the key into the ignition. "Didn't you ever see *The Perils of Pauline*? Your ship's not sunk until the hull hits the seabed, you've run out of oxygen, and you're going blind. And even then, you can count on some smarty-pants screenwriter to get you out of the worst fix."

"Like telling her to call Mayo?"

"Cast the soon-to-be-ex-Mrs. Bogart as our villain."

"You were so cool, calm, and collected up there."

"Pure bluffing!" Nell released a wobbly laugh as she fired up the engine. "Which is why we're going to Don the Beachcomber a few blocks thataway. They've got a drink called the Missionary Downfall."

"Sounds strong."

"My socks could do with some knocking off."

She threw the car into a U-turn and rejoined the traffic along Hollywood Boulevard. Surely they had a pay phone at Don's so that she could leave a warning message for room 207 at the Beverly Hills Hotel.

## 38

Avery's plum-colored Studebaker was eight years older than Betty's Plymouth, but it was bigger, and therefore more likely to impress Tony's family. "How old did you say Carol is?" Nell asked Tony.

"Eleven going on twelve," Tony said, then added, "Or going on twenty-five, if she's anything like her mother."

"Good kid, is she?"

"Oh yeah. The type who has tons and tons of friends. Way more than I ever did."

The conversation on the drive to Union Station had been an effort. Even more so now that they were almost there. Nell scratched around to keep it going. "Speaking of friends, I've got to say, this friendship between you and Avery, I never saw it coming."

Tony had been fidgeting worse than a Mexican jumping bean the whole drive over. He spat out a chunk of the fingernail he'd been gnawing on. "It's been a long time since I made a new pal."

"We all need them."

"He and I just sit around and shoot the breeze, play a little dime-a-card poker, yak about broads and cars and baseball."

"He must think a lot of you. He was renting his house to those factory girls for a tidy sum."

Tony chuckled. "Yeah, but I'm only there now because he lost a double-or-nothing hand. And thank Christ, too. I was having a real tough time finding a place where me and Audrey and Carol could stay."

Nell suspected Avery had always been a loner but valued his newfound friendship, and had lost that round of poker on purpose. "And Hollis? How's he doing?"

Tony's left knee jiggled up and down. "I don't see much of him no more."

"How come?"

They drove a full city block before Tony spoke again. "Hollis was a changed man after that night he danced with Mary Astor. Full of piss and vinegar, he was. Later on, he had an awful setback with his gut. Can't keep anything down. Nothing solid, anyway. Probably on liquids for the rest of his life. It's really screwed with his head." Another city block passed. "I never thought I'd say this, but I'm one of the lucky ones."

Nell stole an admiring glance at her passenger. "I'm glad to hear you say that."

"We were both gunnery sergeants going into Guadalcanal. We both got ripped up real bad. Both ended up on the hospital ship in adjoining beds."

"Is that how you got to be pals?"

"That first week back to the mainland, we helped get each other through some damned bleak times. And then my leg got septic and the docs decided they had to chop it off to save me. He was there for me every moment, day or night. At that point he was doing pretty well . . ." Tony's voice faltered. He took a deep breath to steady himself. "All they had to do to keep me going was stick a wooden leg on me. Yeah, sure, it was hard, but I get on with my life now." Another heavy pause. "But Hollis is a different story." They approached a sign saying UNION STATION NEXT

*RIGHT.* He sat up straighter. "Thanks for doing this. I know you're busy with one thing and another."

Spread over fourteen soundstages, *Mildred Pierce* was one of the studio's prestige motion pictures for 1945, and Jack Warner was going all out to get his money's worth. Taplinger had also given Nell *Pride of the Marines*, in which John Garfield played a blind US Marine. The West Coast premiere of *Hollywood Canteen* had been set for the week before Christmas. Nell had more stories and angles than she had columnists to place them with.

But Tony hadn't seen his wife in over two years. He was so keen to impress her with California life that Nell couldn't say no when he'd asked for moral support. Especially after he'd gone out and bought a suit and matching snap-brim fedora.

Nell swung the car into the railway station parking lot. "Take all the time you need."

Tony gawped at her as though she'd run over his dog. "You ain't coming with me?"

"You don't want anyone crowding your family reunion."

Tony blinked as he absorbed her words. "But I do."

The waiting area concourse was the least congested Nell had seen it since Pearl Harbor. "Maybe we really are reaching the end of the war."

"Could be," Tony replied. "Audrey booked the Union Pacific without too much trouble."

And that meant that Nell could no longer claim that securing a reservation on a train, a bus, or a mule was impossible. "But aren't the papers saying how the Allies will have a tough fight pushing into Germany—"

She broke off when she saw Tony had sat himself down on a broad leather seat and was sitting hunched over his knees. She took the adjoining seat. "Nervous?"

"What's she gonna say?"

"About what?"

He rapped a knuckle on his artificial leg.

"I'd imagine she'll ask if you need any help with it."

"Not if she runs screaming from the room."

"Why would she—Tony! You haven't told her?"

He shook his head. "I hinted that my injuries were pretty bad. That recovering from them was going to take time, and until I was better, I couldn't travel." He hid his face in his palms. "I felt less than a man," he said softly. "Damaged goods."

Nell laid a gentle hand on his wilting shoulder. "Don't you think she'd rather have a damaged husband than no husband at all?"

"She's expecting the Tony she kissed goodbye two years ago."

"And what Tony is that?"

"The one who could fix anything, do anything, try anything. Now I can't even climb a ladder."

The first time Luke had described his brother to her, they'd been sharing a hot fudge sundae at C.C. Brown's. Luke had talked about how rapidly Tony's temper deteriorated after just one beer. The yelling, the insults, the willingness to throw the first punch. Nell had seen no sign of that stinker over the past year.

"Maybe she'll like this version better."

He reared back. "I don't even know if I can—y'know . . . perform."

"Listen to me, Gunnery Sergeant Valenti, as a woman, I can tell you that if Luke comes home from the war 'damaged goods,' as you put it, we'll find a way to make things work. And you will, too. In the bedroom and out of it." He stared at her with skeptical eyes. "She's going to be more upset that you didn't tell her what happened to you than she'll be about the injury itself."

"You think?"

"Guaranteed." She patted the back of his hand. "We'll ought to get a move on because we need to make a stop first."

"Where at?"

"The florist, you big dope." She helped him stand up. "After a two-year separation, you were going to greet your wife empty-handed? Honestly. Have you men learned nothing from the movies?"

---

The Union Pacific locomotive was pulling into platform six as Nell and Tony walked up the ramp. "Look for blonde hair."

"Audrey or Carol?"

"Both. Carol's the spitting image of her mom."

The disembarking passengers were the usual mix of travel-worn salesmen, trimly uniformed servicemen, and a smattering of fur-enshrouded wives, each with a mountain of matching luggage and a maid to keep track of it as the Red Caps piled their carts. It wasn't hard to spot a pair of bright yellow coifs heading toward them.

Audrey held her arms out, expecting Tony to run to her. When that didn't happen, Nell caught a tremor of uncertainty, and held back to let eleven-year-old Carol sprint ahead and throw herself into her father's arms.

While Tony made a grand and glorious fuss over his daughter, Nell approached Audrey. "Hello, I'm Nell."

Audrey's hair was yellow as a ripe banana with no dark roots. Her victory rolls couldn't have been easy to style on a moving train in a cramped bathroom. She smiled blankly as she accepted Nell's hand and shook it limply.

*She's got no idea who I am.* "I'm Luke's girlfriend."

Audrey gave a little start. "Ain't that a kick." She pumped Nell's hand more vigorously. "I always thought he was on the tutti-frutti side, if you know what I mean." Her eyes shifted past Nell to her husband. "How is he?"

Nell stepped aside. "Eager to see you."

\* \* \*

"Where are we now, Daddy?"

Tony spun around to face Carol in the back seat. "You've heard of General MacArthur, haven't you?

"The war hero?"

"Los Angeles named this park after him. Pretty, ain't it?"

"All these palm trees," Audrey said, "just like in the movies. And this weather." She fanned herself with her pocketbook. "When we left Brooklyn, it was less'n forty degrees."

There was that tone Nell had picked up on at the station. Slightly irritated. Slightly put out. Just enough to alert the people around her that she was peeved. Not that Nell blamed her. Tony had put Audrey and Carol in the back seat while he sat next to her up front.

"Why don't you tell Audrey and Carol about *Pride of the Marines?*"

"You're a Marine, Daddy?"

"No, sweetie. I work in the movies now."

Audrey stopped fanning. "You *what?*"

Good God, Tony, did you tell your wife nothing in your letters home? You've been looking after Humphrey Bogart's toupées for a whole year. He's a little touchy about people knowing he wears a rug, but that doesn't mean you couldn't share a few details.

"I'm in the publicity department at Warner Brothers," Nell put in, "and Tony's in hair and makeup."

"Antonio Emanuele Valenti!" A light fizziness filled Audrey's voice. "You've let the world know what you can do with a brush and scissors?"

"He's a whiz, isn't he?" Nell said. "Just ask Jane Wyman and Alexis Smith. We recently finished a movie about the Hollywood Canteen, and Mister Modest here worked on all kinds of people who made cameos."

"The Hollywood Canteen?" Carol piped up. "I read about that in *Motion Picture* magazine. Can we see it? Can we go in? Can I dance with Tyrone Power?"

Nell braked at the Western Avenue stoplight. "You have to be in uniform for that, but we can drive past it so that you can tell all your friends."

"That'd be swell."

As the light turned green, Nell stole a quick glance at Tony's knee. It had resumed its distracted jiggling.

"What about *Pride of the Marines*?" Audrey asked.

"That's the new John Garfield movie," Carol said. "I read about it in *Motion Picture*, too. He's a dreamboat. Will you be combing his hair, Daddy?"

Not long after Jack Warner had announced that they would film the memoirs of a Marine who had been blinded at Guadalcanal, Nell had mentioned to the picture's director that Tony Valenti in Hair and Makeup had served at Guadalcanal, had also suffered egregious loss, and might be a useful resource for realism and credibility. Delmer had wasted no time putting Tony on staff as one of the picture's technical advisors.

"Go on," Nell said, "tell them about it."

Nell steered Avery's DeSoto to the curb along the eastern side of Cahuenga Boulevard and braked. She wound down the window. "You see that big sign above the awning? It's made of rope on account of the place used to be a barn. Bette Davis and your pal, John Garfield, kept it that way because they knew so many of the boys would be coming off farms." It was also cheaper to convert it into a club if they kept most of the original fixtures, but Nell's little white lie made for a cozier story.

Audrey rummaged around her valise. "At our last Fourth of July barbeque, Enzo put the big cathedral radio in the kitchen window and we listened to a broadcast. 'Live from the famous Hollywood Canteen, with Kay Kyser and his orchestra.'" She produced a Box Brownie and handed it to Tony. "Take Carol across the street and get a photo of her out front." She waited until they had crossed Cahuenga.

"There was a time when Tony couldn't keep his hands off me. But now he's been treating me like I'm Sister Mary Berta from St. Athanasius. So what gives?"

Nell kept her eyes head ahead. "That's a question for Tony."

"Is it some glamour girl I can't compete with?"

"Oh, gosh no!" Tony's amputation wasn't Nell's story to tell, but it seemed like Audrey was owed at least some kind of explanation. Nell swung around. "When Tony told me you were coming, he couldn't have been more excited."

Audrey's furrows of worry relaxed a little. "That place he was in—is it a nuthouse?"

"Guadalcanal was tough on everybody. He's come through the worst of it, especially now that he's working at the studio. Tell me, did he do your hair behind closed doors so that nobody knew?"

Audrey's ear-to-ear beaming grin revealed the pretty girl Tony must have fallen for. "Ain't it crazy? A rugged man's man like him fixing hair. Everybody used to be so envious because I was good at it—or so they thought. I hadda nod and thank them. Of course, it all backfired on me after Tony went off to war. I had to do my own hair, and I was so outta practice. So I started brushing it back into a braid and said I was keeping it simple for the duration." She patted at her victory rolls. "I've been practicing since our train left New York."

A pair of sailors had joined Tony and Carol. The four of them were now taking pictures of each other in front of the *HOLLYWOOD CANTEEN* sign.

Nell said, "The head of Hair and Makeup at Warners told me Tony has been a godsend because of his work ethic. He told me that he can throw Tony into any situation."

"Those Valenti boys ain't nothing if not hardworking."

They watched the sailors hoist Carol onto their shoulders as Tony clicked.

"He wants us to move out here, don't he?"

Another question Nell shouldn't have to answer. "What has Tony been telling you in his letters home?"

Audrey shrugged. "He's written me all of three times since he shipped out."

Tony was shaking the sailors' hands goodbye now. He'd soon be back in the car.

"Tony has news he needs to tell you. It'll be as tough for him to say as it will be for you to hear. But when that time comes, he's going to need you to be a good wife."

"I am a good wife."

"Then just be yourself."

Carol opened the rear passenger door and climbed inside. "We met Ralph from Yonkers and his buddy, Milton from—where's Milton from, Daddy?"

"Kalamazoo." Tony rejoined Nell on the front seat, where he started singing. "I've got a gal in Kalamazoo-oo-oo—"

"Simmer down, Bing Crosby," Audrey said. "You've been found out."

"I've what?"

"This trip is a campaign to convince us to move here, permanent like."

Tony threw Nell a look. She threw up her hands. "Audrey worked it out by herself."

"Would it be so bad if I was?"

Audrey raised a noncommittal shoulder. "There are worse places a guy could drag his family." Tony threw Nell another look, and this time a trace of hope splashed across his face. "Luke has taken to living here real well."

"When was the last time you heard from Uncle Luke?" Carol asked.

Nell didn't answer right away. Audrey's first assumption, that Tony had found someone else, was now sowing seeds of doubt in Nell's own imagination.

What if Luke had met somebody? He could've gone home to Brooklyn on a weekend pass and bumped into some local girl who'd had a big crush on him. Okay, well, now you're being ridiculous. He made the effort to send those letters in code, didn't he? That's a lot of trouble to go for someone you're not serious about anymore. But I've received nothing in six months. What about Midway Island? Aren't there nurses? They're at Pearl Harbor. Tons of them.

"It's been months, hasn't it, Nell?" Tony prompted.

She blinked. "Not since April."

"Gee, honey, that's tough. And I oughta know. In four years, all I got from Ernest Hemingway here was three lousy letters." She had attempted to sound light and airy, but her words got caught on the barbed wire underpinning her point.

"You're going to love the house Tony has rented. It's a darling place in the heart of Hollywood."

"Sounds glamorous."

"It's cute," Tony said. "More to the point, available. Out here, the housing shortage has been nuts."

"Same in Brooklyn, what with the Navy Yard operating twenty-four hours a day. How did you find it?"

Oh, boy. Where to start explaining about Avery? "A guy at the movie studio. His tenants moved out."

Nell turned the ignition key. "You guys heard of Grauman's Chinese Theatre?"

"I have!" Carol sang out.

"How about we drive past to give you a sneak preview?"

\* \* \*

As they approached Grauman's, a delivery truck pulled out of a parking space out front of a lamp shop. Nell did a swift U-turn ahead of a downtown-bound streetcar and nabbed it. "How about

I take you to see the footprints and give Mommy and Daddy a chance to catch up?"

Carol peered out her car window at the milling crowds.

"Who's your favorite movie star?" Nell asked.

When the little girl failed to answer, Audrey prompted, "It's Shirley Temple, isn't it?"

Nell lowered her voice to a stage whisper. "Did you know that Shirley's footprints are there?"

"They are?"

"Uh-huh. Let's see how your feet compare." Nell turned to Audrey. "Where's that camera?"

She was already pulling it out of her purse. "Take your time."

With Carol's hand tucked in hers, Nell led the way across Hollywood Boulevard to the theater's forecourt, where Shirley's patch of cement lay sandwiched between Joan Crawford's and Jean Harlow's.

Carol looked up at Nell. "Shirley stood right here where I'm standing?" She got onto her knees and compared her hands to Shirley's. "They're so little."

"She was only about eight. How old are you?"

"Eleven."

Nell looked across the boulevard. Tony had joined Audrey in the back seat. They were facing each other. From what she could see, Tony was doing all the talking and Audrey was slowly nodding. *Go on. Tell her. She needs to know, and you should have done it months ago.* Audrey's head and shoulders gave a sharp jolt. *Oh boy, it's done.*

"Nell?" Carol's hands were still covering Shirley's. "Take a picture of me?" She cocked her head to one side and teamed it with a gappy smile as Nell snapped the Box Brownie.

"That's going to come out beautifully!"

When Nell looked across the street again, Tony and Audrey were locked in a tight embrace, their heads touching. She helped Carol to her feet. "Before we go back, let's find Judy Garland."

\* \* \*

Pulling into Avery's parking space outside the scenic art department that day, Nell had come up with an idea. Although it had been born of unhinged foolishness—the notion that Luke had met another girl—it was, in fact, a solid one. Momentous, even. And if there was one thing Hollywood appreciated, it was a momentous idea.

Taplinger had liked it when she'd pitched it to him. But, he'd reminded her, it was Bette Davis who had the final approval.

A six-foot potted ficus held open the door to the photographic studio. Its leaves brushed against Nell's shoulder as she rushed into the building. She found Bette dressed in a stiff suit of broadcloth with puffed sleeves. She had a small watch pinned to her chest and wore a gray-streaked wig backcombed several inches off her scalp.

"Not my most flattering look, is it?" she asked, spinning around. "But fitting for an eighteen-nineties Welsh schoolmarm."

"Publicity photos for *The Corn is Green?*" Nell asked.

"And some glamour ones later."

Nell took a seat on the tufted fainting couch Bette had been using as a prop. "Do you have a minute?"

Bette turned to the gentleman adjusting a camera stationed behind a twin pair of spotlights. "Scotty, dear, can you give me ten?"

He disappeared into the shadows.

"I have an idea," Nell said. "Taplinger's on board, but it needs your go-ahead."

"The smart-aleck wags might call me the Fifth Warner Brother, but I have very little power around here."

"You do at the Canteen."

Bette's face lit up. "Ah, well, that's different."

"Our *Hollywood Canteen* movie is opening on New Year's Eve, so what do you think about a live broadcast from the real

Canteen the week leading up to Christmas? With you hosting, we could put together a line-up of some of the Warner Brothers stars who make cameos to come on and do a bit. And maybe get Leo Forbstein to sling together a studio orchestra?"

Bette slapped Nell's knee. "That's inspired! We should recruit non-Warners stars so that the whole show doesn't seem like blatant advertising."

"If we can coax Armed Forces Radio to hook into the broadcast, it could also be a Christmas show for all the servicemen stationed around the world."

"Wonderful! I love it!"

Nell flopped against the back of the fainting couch like a Victorian lady whose corset had been bound too tight. There was an extra part of her plan she hadn't shared.

"It's such a gangbuster I'm jealous that I didn't think of it myself." Bette fingered the dark brooch pinned to the base of her throat. "I'll be at the *Hollywood Canteen* premiere on the twentieth, so let's shoot for the twenty-first. Do you think we could convince Bogart and Bacall to appear? After the hullabaloo *Have and Have Not* got at its New York premiere, those two alone would guarantee us a vast audience. But they're no vaudeville song-and-dance troupers, are they?"

"I've already thought of that."

Bette drew back, looking Nell over with renewed approval. "Of course you have."

\* \* \*

She found Bogie and Betty standing on the edge of the Philip Marlowe set, where they were preparing to film a scene in which their characters make a prank phone call to the local police station.

"Well, well, Davenport," Bogie said, after she had told them about the Christmas broadcast, "you're brimming with ideas these days."

Betty twirled the black felt beret she'd be wearing. "When's this happening?"

"December twenty-first."

"Sounds fun." She turned to Bogie. "We should persuade Emmeline to roster us on that night."

"I was hoping you'd participate," Nell said.

"Doing what?" Bogie scoffed. "My ten-pin juggling act doesn't come across too well on radio."

"But you performed on that USO tour. You must have done something when you got up on stage."

"Yeah. Embarrass myself."

"Did you sing?"

Another scoffing sound. "Right before I embarrassed myself."

"Could you make it through 'As Time Goes By'?"

Bogie laughed out loud. "You might as well have said 'O Sole Mio.'"

This was exactly the resistance Nell had been expecting. "Oh, sure." She elbowed Bogie in the ribs. "Giuseppe Verdi compared to Herman Hupfeld. Why, it's practically the same thing."

He sliced the air with a flattened palm. "There's no way I'm singing to a couple of million people. What about you, my precious little lemon drop?"

Betty stopped twirling her beret. "What about me?"

"You could sing 'How Little We Know.'"

"Fat chance. Getting through that song took me eleven takes."

Nell parked her butt on Marlowe's desk so that she was lower than either Bogie or Betty, to give them the impression that they were in charge. "'As Time Goes By' will forever be linked to you, so it's a perfect number for you to present."

"I will not sing it."

"How about reading it?" Bogie didn't shoot down the idea straight away, so Nell plowed forward. "Like it's a poem. If you shade those lyrics with a different slant, the listeners will hear them like they're brand new."

The left side of Bogie's mouth twitched as he chewed the inside of his cheek. Nell started counting to ten. If he hadn't spoken by the time she finished, she had another gambit up her sleeve. She got to eight before he said,

"You don't think it'll sound chintzy?"

"Not if the two of you do it together."

Nell looked at Betty, who looked at Bogie, who looked at Nell with a how-can-I-say-no pout.

"You could say alternate lines," Nell said. "Or verses. Anticipation over *To Have and Have Not* has turned you two into box-office dynamite. Joe and Jane Public will eat it up. Mention that you're making a second movie together and everybody wins."

Betty positioned her beret in place. "I, for one, think it's a great idea. I'm in."

Nell waited a moment, then asked Bogie. "And you?"

"I know when I'm beat."

## 39

Nell switched on the lights of the rehearsal studio she'd booked from six p.m. until eight. She set her handbag on the scruffy piano and handed Bogie and Betty the lyrics to "As Time Goes By" she had typed out. "There are thirty-two lines, which means you each get sixteen."

"Does that matter?" Betty asked. "It's not like anyone's keeping score."

"Darling," Bogie said, tapping the back of her hand with his lyrics, "Davenport's used to dealing with pompous movie-star egos who'd count up the number of lines."

"Oh. Well. In that case," Betty flicked away his lyrics with a manicured fingernail, "you're all on notice. When we open next month, I plan on becoming a full-scale movie star with all the trimmings: huge dressing room, a Swedish masseuse, and an astrologer, naturally, plus twice-daily tantrums and my own hairdresser. Newsflash: I'm stealing Tony. You'll have to find a new rug caretaker."

A comment like that from Mayo would have launched an all-afternoon screaming match. But it was the sort of wisecracking their *Have Not* characters bandied about as verbal foreplay.

"Want to flip to see who gets the first line?" Nell asked.

"Bogie should," Betty said. He went to protest, but she shut him down with a flattened palm to his face. "To the millions of listeners, he was the guy ordering his pianist to play the song that—gosh! Millions!" She cut herself off to rub her hands up and down her arms. "I got the heebie-jeebies."

"I keep telling her she'll have to brace herself when the movie opens."

"He's right," Nell said. "Eleven different newspapers want to know which train you'll be on at Grand Central."

"Oh my. It's all getting very real."

"Broadcasting to millions is about as real as it gets." Nell rattled her lyrics sheet. "Okay, so Bogie has the opening line. Betty, you have the 'kiss' line, and Bogie, you get the 'sigh' line. Then Betty for 'the fundamental things,' and back to Bogie for the last line of the verse. Let's do a run-through and see how it sounds. Forget the way Dooley sang it. Simply speak the words like it's a poem."

It wasn't until the fifth try that they found a natural rhythm, as though they were the only lovebirds in the world who knew this sonnet existed.

"Moving on to the second verse, the 'two lovers woo' line is Bogie's, which means Betty gets the 'I love you' line."

"That'll be easy." Betty made a rasping purr.

Hoagy Carmichael strode into the rehearsal room. "One of the grips told me I might find you here."

"How goes it at RKO?" Bogie asked, shaking his hand.

With his narrow face and long chin, Hoagy looked as though he should be six feet, but he was no taller than Bogie. Nell realized, for the first time, that Betty was taller than both men.

"Compared with *To Have and Have Not*, filming *Johnny Angel* with George Raft is like making do with roadside beans and franks when you're used to filet mignon. Oh brother, oh boy, oh my. He's every bit the handful Howard warned me about. He thinks it's still 1932 and they're making *Scarface*."

"Did he ask about *To Have and Have Not* with Bogie and Howard?" Betty asked.

"Not a chance." Hoagy let a well-timed moment pass by before adding, "So I told him in great detail just to piss him off." He noticed the sheets in their hands. "Am I interrupting?"

When Nell explained they were running through Bogie and Betty's bit for the Hollywood Canteen broadcast the following week, Hoagy suggested he play the song. Maybe it'll help bring out a mood." She feared he'd be a distraction, but when he played the melody softly, Bogie removed his necktie and Betty slipped off her shoes. Besides, he was Hoagy Carmichael. What was she going to do? Tell him to beat it?

*  *  *

With each pass, they nailed down the pace, the pauses, which words to emphasize, and where they could say a line together.

When they were done, Hoagy suggested getting a drink, but Bogie begged off. He and Betty had dinner plans with Howard and Slim at Romanoff's. After they had left, Hoagy asked if he could walk Nell back to her office.

As they passed a *Mildred Pierce* set on Stage Four, he said, "That one must keep you busy. Crawford's first movie for Warners based on a James M. Cain book, directed by Curtiz, music by Steiner. It's got all the ingredients."

"Yes, but that doesn't guarantee a popular cake," Nell replied. "*The Blue Bird* had Shirley Temple directed by Walter Lang with two million of Zanuck's money—and it laid an egg." The December sun had sunk behind the Hollywood Hills, turning the dusk sky a deep purple. Nell hadn't counted on the chill penetrating the air. She hugged her purse to her chest. "Ditto *Two-Faced Woman*. MGM had Garbo and Cukor, and that movie seems to have killed her career." The day's final, dim light drained from the sky. Whatever motive Hoagy had for suggesting this stroll, it wasn't to talk about box office flops. His casual amble had taken on a hesitant air as they approached the administration building. "This is me," she told him.

Hoagy uncrossed his arms. "Bogie's not who I came looking for."

"What's on your mind?"

"*To Have and Have Not* is my movie debut, so I want to capitalize on as much publicity as I can get."

"Sounds smart to me."

"My usual photographer went home to Maine for Thanksgiving, where he slipped on the ice and broke his kneecap. He's now literally The Man Who Came to Dinner. I feel bad for the poor bastard, but he's out of action for months. I figured you'd know who the best Warners photographer is."

"That would be Scotty Westbourne."

"Okay, but I can't just waltz in there unannounced and ask for him. Or can I?"

"Publicity shots come out of the picture's budget and need the approval of the producer. But Howard is neck-deep into *The Big Sleep*. As far as he's concerned, *Have Not* is in the rearview mirror. My infamy from slapping Hedda has opened many doors. I'll make a few inquiries."

"That'd be terrific, but don't go calling in any favors on my account."

Even in the fading light, his earnestness shone off him. "If one of us owes a favor, it's me." He broke into a grin. "I bet your family was super-duper impressed with that record we made."

It had been over two months since Nell had shipped off her recording, and one month since she had given up hoping for a response. "Scotty gets booked solid. Come inside with me and I'll give you the number to call. You won't need to fuss with hair and makeup and costumes, so maybe he can fit you in."

They stepped inside. "Just some nice headshots. He won't need more than an hour."

Nell paused as the door closed behind them. Why did the air smell of fresh paint and oil? And why has my desk disappeared under a mountain of framed paintings?

"What's all this?" Hoagy asked, following her over to her desk.

The top painting was a competent rendition of Santa Monica Pier at sunrise, the sand undisturbed by the squelching of a thousand bare toes. The name in the corner meant nothing to her. The second painting was of the Hollywood Hotel with its cochineal roof tiles.

A note was propped up against her telephone. The handwriting scrawled across the front—*Miss Nell Davenport, Publicity Dept, Warner Bros.*—confirmed her worst fear.

"I should have known better than to count my chickens."

She tore it open and read the contents out loud.

*"Dear Nell,*

*The Navy embraced the concept of my presenting the Pearl Harbor base with artwork to cheer up their stark barracks. And they loved the idea of the positive PR of your boyfriend seeing a portrait by his brother who has survived Guadalcanal. But when push came to shove, my entourage, plus the USO tour, had too much luggage."*

Hoagy snorted. "Too many goddamn hat boxes is more like it."

*"So the paintings have to stay behind. I haven't the time, so could you do me the hugest favor of returning them all? Thanks ever so.*

*I do have some good news! This Hollywood Canteen broadcast you've put together—Bravo to you for a wonderful idea! I shall trumpet it as often as I can in my column, as well as during my own broadcasts. I've also suggested to the brass that they play it over loudspeakers throughout the Pearl Harbor Navy base. Every sailor and serviceman will be listening!*

*I must away. So much to do before I set sail. But tell Luke's brother that I love his portrait so much that I'm keeping it and it now takes pride of place in my office.*

*Hedda*

Nell crushed the notepaper into a thick ball and catapulted it across the office. It hit the window with a dull whack and dropped out of sight. She swallowed the sob rising in her throat. "I'm paying for my crime."

"I was having breakfast with Walter Brennan at Du-par's when he read out Kathryn Massey's column. He said to me, 'Nobody slaps Hedda Hopper and gets away with it.'"

No portraits meant no note to Luke. Not that there was much chance the old cow would have passed it on anyway. What a fool she was to think she might have. The sob rose again, determined to erupt from her. "He's right."

"Hey, listen. I've thought of a fellow," Hoagy said, offering her his handkerchief. "He was college roommates with a trumpet player I know. He works on the *Lurline* now that it's a transport ship between here and Hawaii—"

"It's not about the damn paintings!" She hated sounding like a wailing harpy, but the last of her hope had drained out of her. Time had slipped through her fingers. She had failed Luke.

Nell rummaged through her handbag for a handkerchief and located one in time to stanch the tears. She didn't turn around until she felt her sorrow recede a little.

"I was the one who came up with sending these paintings to Pearl Harbor. They were an elaborate way to get word to my boyfriend. I need to contact him before a deadline expires at the end of the year. I convinced Hedda to take a note to him along with all these." She waved a wilting hand over the paintings now crowding her desk.

"You can't send him a V-mail?"

"He's hard to contact. We've communicated a few times, but only via a special code."

"A *code?*" Hoagy shook his head slowly. "Are you putting me on?"

"It's quite clever. You write a letter like normal, but you compose it in such a way that the reader only pays attention to every fifth word."

Hoagy slapped his thigh. "Bogie told me you were whip-smart, but that's prison-shiv smart."

A shaky laugh rattled out of Nell as she mopped her tears. "Today is December seventeenth. Short of stowing away on the next NATS airplane heading west, it's all too late now."

Hoagy picked up the stack of paintings on Nell's chair and transferred them to the adjacent desk. "Sit." She did, and he then rolled the chair out from behind it and positioned himself next to her. "I have an idea. It's a little crazy, though."

"You're looking at a desperate woman."

He propped his elbows on his knees and interlaced his fingers. "This concert at the Canteen is being broadcast throughout Armed Forces Radio, right? And that means your boyfriend will hear it, won't he?"

"He could. In theory, at least."

"What if we write a song together? Whatever message you need to get to him, we can weave it into the lyrics."

Nell's heartbeat quickened. "You're right. That's a crazy idea. Even if Luke hears the broadcast, how will he know to note every fifth word? And even if he does, how do you expect him to know which is the fifth word as it's being sung live to air?" She waved her hands around. "I've seen some nutty publicity stunts, but this one can't—"

"What if we call it 'Every Fifth Word'?"

Nell's protests dried up in her throat. "And put each important word at the end of each line?"

"Not unless you want to write the world's longest song. A better idea would be to make it the final word of each verse."

Nell's heart gave a little flutter. "It would make him think, wouldn't it?"

"Especially if he knows *you* are singing it."

Nell launched herself out of the chair and paced the floor. "Oh, no, no, no. That's too much."

"Says the girl who sang at Orry-Kelly's farewell party."

"It was in front of a hundred and fifty people. Armed Forces Radio reaches *millions*. It's all in a day's work for the Andrews Sisters, but the thought of it makes me break out in hives."

"If he knew you were singing, and if he knew the name of the song, he'd be paying very careful attention. You're in charge of PR for the project. Won't you be sending out a program? And wouldn't the Navy post it on bulletin boards?"

"I don't know. Would they?"

"They would if you include a suggestion. And in that program, you could say 'Nell Davenport singing a brand-new Hoagy Carmichael song called "Every Fifth Word."'"

The idea of writing a song with Hoagy Carmichael was nuttier than a bag of goobers, but Nell's head spun from the thought of singing into a microphone that would broadcast her voice all over the world. Jumping june bugs, could she really do it? Yes, she decided. I could if I knew Luke was listening.

After she had written out Scotty Westbourne's number and sent Hoagy on his way, she lifted the pile of paintings off her desk blotter and did a double-take: there sat an envelope containing a Western Union telegram.

Was it from Luke? Had he found a way to reach her? Was he

already at Pearl Harbor, safe and sound? Had he snuck into Western Union in Honolulu?

She ripped along the top of the envelope and unfolded the cable.

MOTHER AND I WILL BE DRIVING ROUTE 66 TO CALIFORNIA STOP
PLAN TO ARRIVE IN A FEW DAYS AND RETURN TO SOUTH BEND BY CHRISTMAS STOP
IT IS TIME YOU REJOINED THIS FAMILY STOP

## 40

Nell threw back her bed covers and swung her feet onto the floor. Six-twelve a.m. Three minutes before her alarm. Not that she needed the whole day to prepare, but "Expect the unexpected" was a practical rule to live by.

Throwing on a robe, she peeked into the hallway. If Betty's door was closed, she had slept at the apartment; if it was open, she had spent the night with Bogie.

It was open.

Not that Nell blamed her, but she missed their get-ready-for-work camaraderie: making breakfast, borrowing sweaters, sharing lipsticks, swapping studio gossip.

She carried her coffee to the small dining table to go through the evening's program. She had checked it a hundred times, but reading it helped soothe her jitters.

- Bette Davis – welcome speech
- Dorothy Lamour – singing "It Could Happen to You"
- Three Stooges – comedy routine

- Nelson Eddy – swing version of "Ah! Sweet Mystery of Life"
- Greenstreet and Lorre – satirical routine mixing dialogue from *The Maltese Falcon* and *Casablanca*
- Frances Langford – singing "I'm in the Mood for Love"
- Jack Benny and Martha Raye in comedy number – "Coffee Cups and Soap Bubbles" about washing dishes at the Hollywood Canteen and seeing none of the stars
- Keenan and Ed Wynn – comedic poem
- Cab Calloway – singing "I've Got the World on a String" and "Minnie the Moocher"
- Jimmy Cagney – harking back to the Great War with "Over There"
- Bogart and Bacall – reciting "As Time Goes By"
- Nell Davenport – singing "Every Fifth Word" written for tonight by Hoagy Carmichael, with Mr. Carmichael at the piano
- Ginger Rogers – singing "I'm Putting All My Eggs in One Basket"
- The Andrews Sisters – medley of "Boogie Woogie Bugle Boy" & "Don't Sit Under the Apple Tree" & "Bei Mir Bist Du Schön"
- Bette Davis – performing "They're Either Too Young or Too Old," followed by an appeal to buy war bonds, a raffle drawing in which one serviceman in the audience will win $25 worth of bonds. End with thank-you speech to all the servicemen around the world.

"A heck of a show, even if I do say so myself." With Betty gone more and more often, Nell had taken to talking to herself. Maybe it was time to think about getting a cat.

She reread the twelfth act: *Nell Davenport – singing "Every Fifth*

Word" written for tonight by Hoagy Carmichael, with Mr. Carmichael at the piano*. Even though this was her last opportunity to reach Luke, it was, at best, an outside chance. The thought of performing to an audience of millions alongside the Andrews Sisters, Ginger Rogers, and Nelson Eddy was enough to unglue her, and if she didn't have to participate, she might enjoy the evening.

In the plus column, writing "Every Fifth Word" had been a hoot. Hoagy had turned the task into a fun game. "Think of it as a verbal jigsaw puzzle, finding the right words that slot well together." It wasn't the easy task Hoagy had made it out to be, but after a few hours, they had a decent song. Whether or not Luke would hear it, she could go to sleep tonight knowing that she'd tried everything.

The doorbell rang. At six forty-five in the morning? It could only mean one thing: Western Union.

Nell opened the door to find a middle-aged man with a Friar Tuck haircut who had inserted himself into a uniform that might have fit him in high school. He held up two telegrams.

Only two? What a relief. She had told them to relay any telegrams prior to eight a.m. to the apartment. With twenty artists booked, Nell was willing to bet ten bucks that at least one of them would bail.

She handed over a generous tip—war or no war, a grown man like that shouldn't be biking around at this time of the morning—and returned to the kitchen table. The first telegram had been sent from the Christie Hotel a couple of blocks down from Grauman's Chinese.

I WILL BE LISTENING TO YOUR SONG TONIGHT STOP

A thoughtful gesture, but who was it from?

She told the telephone operator to connect her with the Christie. When a professionally cheerful voice came through, Nell asked if they recalled sending her the telegram.

"Why, sure," the woman replied. "We rarely send telegrams at five a.m."

"May I ask who the sender was?"

"He checked in yesterday afternoon. He's a sailor with a one-week shore leave. He was telling me how he'd been cooped up in a submarine for weeks on end."

A sailor? In a submarine? On shore leave? "Can you describe him to me?"

"Bright red hair and a ton of freckles. Irish, I expect."

The telephone felt heavier than a box of bowling balls. "Do you recall his name?"

"Lieutenant Burton Foyle."

Nell held her forehead in the palm of her hand. "Is he in his room right now?"

"No, ma'am. Those boys don't waste a minute. We call them BBBs: Burgers, Beers, and Broads. They run all over, getting their fill. And of course, some of them ask about the Hollywood Canteen. 'What time do the doors open?' 'Will I meet Rita Hayworth?'"

"Did Lieutenant Foyle ask about it?"

"He did. But I warned him they're doing some big broadcast there today. It's gonna be more crowded than Santa Monica Beach on Labor Day. He seemed determined, though."

"I'm working on that broadcast. It's possible that I could get him in ahead of the line. Did he say if he was returning to the hotel beforehand?"

"No, ma'am. I'm happy to take a message in case he does."

Nell left instructions to tell the security guard at the volunteer entrance to come fetch her the moment Lieutenant Foyle arrived.

Hawaii *and* a submarine? Such a specific coincidence couldn't be random. Was Foyle acting as Luke's messenger? The odds no longer felt quite so stacked against her.

She ripped open the second envelope and unfolded the telegram.

SPENT LAST NIGHT IN BARSTOW STOP
ARRIVE LOS ANGELES THIS AFTERNOON STOP
WILL PICK YOU UP AND HEAD STRAIGHT
HOME STOP
BE READY STOP

Well, fine. That's just peachy. I can't stop them, but I don't have to be here with my bags packed and my hands folded in my lap like a penitent nun. I've got a world-wide broadcast to run. I might not get home till late. Very late. Or even tomorrow morning. That bunk on the *Arabella* is mighty comfortable.

* * *

NBC Radio's broadcasting equipment took up a swath of floor space in the corner usually reserved for the coffee station. A labyrinth of cables snaked to the stage where Tommy Dorsey's orchestra was setting up. Bogart and Betty huddled near the hat check counter with Greenstreet and Lorre. None of them was smiling.

"And how are we all doing?" she asked.

"Why in God's name did I let you talk me into this?" Betty bawled. "It's okay for these three musketeers. They've had stage experience." She held two fingertips half an inch apart. "I'm *this* close to heading for the hills."

"Do that, my sweet," Bogie added, "and I'll beat you there."

"Oh, come on!" Nell protested. "Song lyrics will be a piece of cake compared to performing *The Petrified Forest* as a radio play, and you pulled that off without a hitch."

"This one's for the boys. I want to do it right."

"Bah!" Lorre said. "It'll be over before you know it."

Mention of the word 'singing' sent a shudder of anticipation mixed with dread through Nell. If she performed "Every Fifth Word" as a poem, too, she could speak with a little more deliberation to give Luke a better chance of catching the key words. And if she weren't following Bogie and Betty, she would have been tempted to make a last-minute switch. Too late! Get the lead out, Davenport, and don't look back.

Keenan and Ed Wynn appeared. As the five men gabbed, Nell pulled Betty aside to show her Foyle's telegram. "So if you see a redheaded sailor—"

"Send him in your direction?"

"If I'm not around, try your best to pry any details out of him."

Nell checked the clock above the entrance. The doors would be opening in less than five minutes.

*  *  *

She found Bette Davis pacing her office, looking over the main points of her opening speech. "Oh, Nell. Thank God it's you!"

"Just popping in to check that everything is all set."

"'I want to welcome everybody.'" She consulted the list in her hand. "'Servicemen, sailors, GIs, airmen, officers, Coast Guard, WACs, WAVEs, and WASPs.' I'd hate to leave out any group, but what if I've forgotten a someone?"

"You mean like merchant marines and the medical corps?"

"Aw, cripes." She scribbled in the two additions.

"What about the military police?"

"I should ditch the list altogether, shouldn't I?"

"I don't think of you as the easily frazzled type." Secretly, Nell was reassured to discover her so worked up. If Bette Davis could get anxious before a show like this, then her own nerves were more typical than she'd have guessed. She coaxed the paper from Bette's grip. "How about 'The brave, dedicated men and women serving in all military branches'?"

"A vast improvement." Bette slipped on the ivy-green jacket of her suit and handed Nell a gardenia to pin to her lapel.

"What about your closing speech?" Nell asked. "Any rough patches?"

Bette was looking past her to a beefy redhead with the shoulders of an ox. "You're Bette Davis."

"Quite right, Lieutenant," Bette said. "However, the dance hostesses, all of them younger and prettier than I, are thataway."

"I'm—I'm—" He shook his head like a wet dog. "Sorry. I'm not normally tongue-tied, but you're—you're—"

"And you," Nell said, stepping forward, "must be Burton Foyle." She extended her hand. "I'm Nell."

Foyle took in Nell for the first time. His lips curved into a thoughtful, almost brotherly smile. "You're exactly how he described you."

"Luke?" Her voice was barely above a whisper.

"I'll see you backstage." Bette checked her tiny gold watch. "You've got forty minutes. Thirty would be better." She left behind a cloud of gardenia-scented air.

"Tell me, Burton—"

"All the fellas call me Burt."

"Did you serve on the *Lanternfish* with Luke?"

Burt frowned. "You know about the *Lanternfish*?"

Oops. Fifteen seconds in and she had already spilled too much. He dug his hands into his pockets. "I wasn't on it."

"Were you part of the convoy?"

"Jeez Louise, how much do you know?"

"A half-educated guess. The telegram you sent—was it Luke's idea?"

Burt nodded. "Handbills about tonight's broadcast have been posted all over the Pearl Harbor naval base. Between this and Hedda Hopper's USO show, morale hasn't been this high in a long time. And boy, do we need it. Three years of war are wearing us down, so this one-two punch of rousing entertainment couldn't have come at a better time."

"We here on the home front have it easy compared to what you fellas go through. What makes it hard is not knowing where you are, and how you are."

"Limping across the Pacific keeps you out of touch. That's when you rely on your buddies."

"Like Luke?"

"Yep. He's a great guy. We were shared a Quonset hut on Mi—" He cut himself off.

Nell was tempted to say 'Midway,' but stopped herself. "I'm delighted to know Luke has made a good friend."

"You should've seen his face when he dropped himself onto my bunk. He had one of those handbills and was practically yelling at me. 'Look at this! My Nell's going to be singing on that big Hollywood Canteen broadcast!' When my shore leave came through and I finagled my way over here, he asked me to send you a telegram." Burt blushed almost as red as his hair. "If you go by the Navy rule book, I shouldn't have done it. But when a buddy asks a favor, you'd be a heel to say no, wouldn't you?"

"But one little telegram—?"

"All our correspondence must go via the proper channels. Especially for us on sea duty."

That last word almost died on his lips. He glowed bright red again. Someday, Luke would explain to her what all this secrecy was for. But for now, she had a live broadcast to run. Oh, cheese and crackers! That song. With this news of Luke, she'd been able to forget about what lay ahead for a few blissful minutes.

But to her astounding surprise, the prospect of stepping in front of that microphone no longer loomed over her. It wasn't going to be a cinch, but knowing Luke would be listening let her breathe a mite easier.

"Tell me," she said, "do you have a second-favorite movie star?"

A toothy grin stretched his freckles. "Ann Sheridan."

"You're in luck, sailor. How about we go out there and I'll introduce you?"

* * *

The Three Stooges arrived in the officers' lounge only minutes before their scheduled entrance, citing mechanical trouble with Moe's old Ford Coupe. Nell wasn't sure why they'd squished themselves into a two-door car, but they walked on stage as though they'd been taking an evening stroll and had dropped by to say hello.

Martha Raye had, ironically, spilled actual coffee on her striped dress while waiting to go on stage with Jack Benny to perform "Coffee Cups and Soap Bubbles," which Frank Loesser had written for them. Jack pretended to spill coffee on Martha during the number, causing five hundred servicemen to roar.

While Keenan and Ed Wynn were improvising rather than reciting their outrageous doggerel about life at boot camp, the security guard Nell had spoken to approached her, hesitation filling his face.

"Miss Davenport?"

"Thanks for tracking me down, but Lieutenant Foyle's already found me."

The Wynns screamed in unison, "Handstamp your oil lamp until you're damp and start to cramp all through boot camp!"

"I've got these two people at the volunteer entrance."

"Did you tell them the Hollywood Canteen is for servicemen only?"

"They insist on seeing you."

"Is Emmeline around? Perhaps she can—"

"The woman looks like you, plus thirty years."

Mother and Father were more resourceful than Nell had given them credit for. But great Caesar's ghost, could their timing be any worse? "Explain to my parents that we're in the middle—"

"Your father's been barking at me, insisting that you come outside. Right now."

Nell looked at her schedule. Next up was Cab Calloway singing two songs, then Cagney doing "Over There," and then Bogart and Bacall. Three minutes per song and thirty seconds of applause for each one meant she had fifteen minutes before she was due on stage.

Nell ran to Betty, who was throwing down Four Roses for Dutch courage. "My parents have shown up."

Betty started. "Here?"

"If I'm not back in time, ad-lib."

"Like what?"

Nell was already heading out the door. "Throw the boys the 'Do you know how to whistle?' line. Ask the ones at the front where they're from. That always works. And then ask if they kissed a girl goodbye and what her name is." She wasn't sure if Betty heard that last part because she had already left the room.

By the time she reached the rear entrance, Nell had given herself a pep talk. *Don't give in. Don't give an inch. Don't listen to their reasons or their rationales. And whatever you do, don't get in their car. You've got eleven minutes. Twelve, tops. Be firm. Be calm. Be tenacious.*

Pressing her notepad to her chest like armor, she stepped into the chilly December air.

They hadn't changed. Neither of them. Not a jot. Not in five whole years.

Mother still braided her mousey-brown hair into a single plait and looped it at the base of her neck. She still cut her own bangs in a blunt line across the middle of her forehead, and was still ignoring Nell's advice that she ought to let them grow an extra inch.

Father stood ramrod straight as though he were still a Great War doughboy presenting himself for inspection. He wore the same drab necktie he always wore, never any of the convivial alternatives Nell had given him for Christmas.

"There you are," he said. "We managed to find a parking space six blocks away, although who knows if the car will be there when we get back."

Okay, so she wasn't his favorite daughter right now—or ever, if it came to that—but after five years' absence, this was the greeting she got?

"Hello, Father. It's nice to see you."

"Nell, darling." Mother planted a kiss on Nell's cheek. She still smelled faintly of carbolic soap and the tang of Mrs. O'Leary's Health Syrup that Nell suspected Mother indulged in a little too often. "You're looking well."

"Thank you, Mother. But look, I'm very busy. We're broadcasting over the Armed Forces Radio."

"That can't be helped," Father said. "If we hit the road now, we can at least get clear of this circus of a town."

"I can't leave. And I'm running the show."

Mother blinked. "You? Running—" she flapped a hand toward the open door behind Nell "—all this?"

"The broadcast was my idea."

"But isn't your job to take notes like a secretary?"

"Didn't you get the letter explaining that I got promoted? It was with the record I sent you. Did you even listen to it?"

"It was secular music."

"On one side, yes. But on the other side I sang 'Amazing Grace.'"

Father made a point of consulting the pocket watch the Studebaker company had given him on the twenty-fifth anniversary of his hiring. "I don't care if it was Al Jolson singing to his mammy."

"It was me singing, Father. Me, your own daughter! And pretty darned well, too."

"Pride is one of the seven deadly sins, Nell."

"I sang 'Stardust,' written by Hoagy Carmichael, and he accompanied me on the piano."

"If that's supposed to impress us, it doesn't."

"Hoagy Carmichael . . ." Mother's voice had taken on a dreamy quality. "He wrote 'Skylark,' didn't he?"

"How would you know such a thing?" Father demanded.

"Gloria's daughter has a Helen Forrest record. She plays it whenever I'm over there helping with her bake sales for the orphanage." She turned to Nell. "And he wrote the song you sang on that record, too? I rather wish we hadn't thrown it in the trash."

Nell's heart thudded into the pit of her stomach. She should have known sending that package would be a waste of time and effort.

"I must get backstage." She inserted a sharp edge to her voice to ensure they were listening, "I go on right after Humphrey Bogart and Lauren Bacall."

"Go where?"

"I'm performing a song I've written with Hoagy Carmichael. You can stand out here in the cold, or you can come in and watch the show."

"Humphrey Bogart?" Mother peered through the open doorway. "He's in there?"

A sliver of hope shone through the cracks of Nell's desperation. "And after me is Ginger Rogers, then the Andrews Sisters, then Bette Davis. If you want to watch, then follow me. Or don't. It's your choice. But either way, I have to go."

Nell turned and strode inside without stopping to see if they followed. She was halfway to the stage before she mustered the courage to peek over her shoulder. The sight of her parents two steps behind her almost sucked the breath from her lungs.

A roar from the crowd went up as Jimmy Cagney strode onto the stage like the cocky George M. Cohan he'd played in *Yankee Doodle Dandy*. "Hiya, fellas!" He almost didn't need a microphone. "You all look swell in your uniforms and your big smiles. If I had a hat on right now, I'd take it off to the whole darned lot of you." The men started to applaud their appreciation but he waved them down. "The number I'm about to do harks back to the last time we Americans found ourselves in a war. I'm talking about the Great War, of course. We prevailed then, and we'll do it again, won't we, boys?"

The audience exploded into a din of applause, cheering, and whistling. As it began to die down, the orchestra played the introduction to "Over There." As Cagney sang about Johnnie getting his gun and taking it on the run, Nell started to say, "Pretty good, isn't—" but the thunderstruck expression on her father's face—part astonishment, part overwhelm, and part bewilderment—stole her voice out from under her.

Her entire life, Nell had never seen her father surprised. He had always been the embodiment of someone in full command of his surroundings, of his perspective, and of his thoughts. So she needed a moment to comprehend this slack-jawed, lip-quivering, almost misty-eyed man standing beside her now. Was he really so easily swayed by the sight of Jimmy Cagney?

But Nell didn't have a spare moment. Bogie and Betty were up next, then it was her turn.

Ingrid Bergman's smiling face appeared over Father's shoulder. Nell grabbed her arm. "Do me a big favor," she whispered into Ingrid's ear, "and play along."

Ingrid nodded.

"Mother, Father, I'd like you to meet Ingrid Bergman." She paused for a moment to let Ingrid's innate charm beguile them. "She'll keep you company while I'm on stage."

"Off you go," Ingrid said. "Leave your lovely parents in my care."

* * *

By the time Nell had slogged her way through the crowd and squeezed herself into the wings, Bogie and Betty had taken the stage.

"There you are." Hoagy had teamed a cranberry-red velvet bow tie with his tux. "No one knew where you were."

She checked her reflection in a large mirror hanging next to the light panel. "Last-minute hitch."

Hoagy tapped her shoulder with a silver hip flask and held it up for her to see HC engraved on the front. "In case you need a dose of liquid fortitude."

She slugged down a mouthful, swishing it around to get the full flavor before swallowing it. Betty was declaring how it was the same old story. That was the opening line to the last verse.

Nell would have loved a second sip. Or a third. It was difficult enough knowing Mother and Father would be watching her sing a sinfully heathen song, but if they detected even the slightest hint of drunkenness, that would be the end of everything.

That's not what I want. I just want them to accept that I'm happy here. That I'm not going back to South Bend with them tonight. Or any night.

She reached over to adjust Hoagy's bow tie, not that it needed straightening. "Break a leg out there."

"I break one, you break the other. Deal?"

On stage, Bogart and Betty chimed, "As time goes by" in unison. There was a brief pause, followed by an eruption from the audience that would have drowned out anything Hoagy might have said in response. The ovation was still filling the Canteen as the couple staggered into the wings.

"Thank God that's over!" Betty collapsed onto a hay bale.

"And now, ladies and gentlemen, and those of you who are AWOL," Bette said into the microphone, "let me ask: You guys know who Hoagy Carmichael is, don't you?" She got a tremendous cheer as a response. "Of course you do. You're no dummies. Well, he's written a new song especially for tonight. And to sing it for us, we've got a gal who's cute as a button. In fact, she's cute as a whole row of buttons. So, fellas, how about a big round of applause for Hoagy Carmichael and Miss Nell Davenport."

Hoagy took Nell's hand. It felt warm and reassuring. They stepped onto the stage, where the full force of the applause swamped her. She had worked at the Canteen countless times, but the air had never felt so full of testosterone.

It wasn't hard to locate her folks. Father was the only man not in uniform, his face the usual brick wall. Mother, wearing the drabbest outfit in the place, was listening to Ingrid, who was emphasizing each word with a finger poking the air. Was Ingrid's speech having a favorable impact? Nell couldn't be sure, but bless her for trying.

Hoagy struck the opening chord. She stepped up to the microphone and mentally crossed her fingers. *Please, Luke, be every bit as smart as I think you are.*

Hoagy was known for writing meandering lyrics that didn't adhere to the standard song structure. He thought nothing of following an eleven-word lyric with a five-word line, then a three-line chorus. His amorphous approach had made it easier to craft lyrics around their coded message, rather than crowbar it into a rigid framework.

They'd decided it might work best if they ensured the crucial word came at the end of each verse. That way, Nell could accentuate it in a way that Luke could catch. It wasn't too hard to rhyme "you talk" with "New York" and "delicate dance" with "inheritance." But would he be tuning in? Would the song's name —"Every Fifth Word"—be enough to prompt him to take notes? Would he notice how she stressed particular words?

*Bell Amiss White in New York inheritance deadline before end of year*

It was too late to worry about that. Her job was to sing as best she could and believe that the message would find its targeted ears.

The melody of the final line escalated from the D above middle C to the B next to high C and needed a lot of air. During rehearsals, she had hit the last note on key, but she'd also missed it enough times to not take it for granted. Especially in front of five hundred men, dozens of professional performers, millions of listeners—and her parents. She drew in a deep breath and closed her eyes.

The note came soaring out of her, clear and strong, and perfectly pitched.

The whooping and hollering joined the floor-stomping, heavy enough to vibrate the planks of the stage through her shoes and up her shins, becoming a tidal wave of acclaim that threatened to undo Nell entirely.

She scanned the cheering crowd as Hoagy stepped up beside her for their bow. Wait—what? Was she seeing what she thought she was seeing? Or was this a trick of the lights shining in her eyes?

Were Mother and Father *hugging*? Nell tried to recall the last time she'd seen them embrace each other in public like that. She guessed they must have once or twice, but she had no memory of it. Tears blurred her vision, but as she took her third and final bow, she could clearly make out one sight. And it was a marvel she never thought she'd see.

Father lifted his fist above his head and raised his thumb to the ceiling.

## 41

"Hey!" Betty yelled from the living room window. "Studebaker!"

Nell smoothed her tartan skirt and checked in the bathroom mirror that she had spilled nothing on her blouse. She wanted to be picture perfect; she owed them at least that much.

"Gosh, you look like your mom, don't you?"

"If you and Bogie hadn't cleared out after your number last night—"

"Correction, little Miss Scene Stealer." Betty let the curtain fall back into place. "You were swamped with so many admirers that we felt like a couple of plates of last week's chopped liver."

Nell picked up her hat and hatpin, but changed her mind. She didn't want to come across as though she'd spent two hours assembling herself—which she had.

Father was checking his watch when Nell and Betty walked outside. Good ol' Dad. Always with a schedule. Always with a plan. "You found the place okay?"

"Your instructions were thorough."

Mother made a tsking sound. "How you girls deal with this traffic is beyond me. I'd be a candidate for the madhouse."

"Mother, Father, I'd like you to meet my roommate, Betty Bacall."

"You're the actress, aren't you?" Father managed to say the word 'actress' without it sounding like a euphemism for 'whore.' It was only the sign Nell needed to know he was trying.

"She has a big movie coming out next month, co-starring with Humphrey Bogart." They didn't need to know that Betty, purposefully demure in her Peter Pan collar and tweed skirt, was also sleeping with him. "Even though you two don't go to the movies, trust me, you'll be hearing a lot about her."

"We'll see how the movie fares," Betty said, with a well-practiced aw-shucks tone.

"What did you think of Nell's performance last night?" Father asked. "Wasn't she grand?"

Nell clenched her teeth. *Do not cry. He's just paid me the first compliment in living memory. You can blubber about it later. For now, get a hold of yourself.* "Thanks, Father."

He looked at her as though he were seeing her for the first time—which, in a sad way, he was. "I like to think of myself as being man enough to admit when I'm wrong."

*And yet, in all my twenty-four years, I've never heard you say the words.*

"Listening to the record you sent could have saved us all those gas rations." He folded his arms across his chest. "I was being a pigheaded fool. This whole time I've been thinking about myself. And what was right for Hank Elliot. That poor young man—"

"I've squared things with Hank."

Elias Davenport was not used to being interrupted. Certainly not by any of his daughters, who'd been raised to know better. Nell's stomach clenched for the lecture that was coming, but the indignant stare melted away almost as quickly as it had boiled up. "You have?"

"We bumped into each other at the Canteen."

"And?" Mother asked, hope quivering her voice.

Nell gave off what she hoped came across as an airy shrug. "He said what happened is in the past, and that life is too short to hold grudges."

Mother and Father stared at Nell, then at each other.

"Especially these days," Betty said, filling the strained silence. "We don't know when we're going to see our loved ones again."

"It's true," Mother murmured. "So very true."

"At any rate," Father said, "I failed to factor in your feelings, Nell. Last night showed me there's a lot more to you than I ever stopped to consider. And I—well, I regret that."

"I guess we all have regrets, don't we, Father? But can I ask what it was about last night that changed your mind?"

"It was that song Cagney sang."

"'Over There'?"

"It took me straight back to my infantryman days during the last world war. Memories I haven't thought about in years assailed me from all directions. Then I got to thinking about those young fellows all around me. And how they were heading off into a terrible and bloody situation with nothing more than a lick of gumption and a dash of bravado. We didn't have entertainers to wave us goodbye, but they did. And who was one of the entertainers up there on stage sending them on their way with a smile and a song? My own flesh-and-blood daughter. It made me proud."

Father had never been the hugging-papa-bear type, and Nell doubted he was about to become one now. She stifled the urge to wrap her arms around him. "Thank you, Father. That means a lot to me."

"And here's another regret: I wish I hadn't smashed that record of yours into a million pieces. Your sisters deserve to hear what a marvelous voice you have."

"I have a confession." Mother raised her hand. "I put it on the gramophone before you got home."

Nell turned to her. "What did you think, Mother?"

"I'd be lying if I said I was unimpressed with how you sang."

*That's about as close to a compliment as I'm likely to get.* "I can't tell you how happy that makes me."

"The song you performed last night . . ." Father ran his thumb down his jawline, which refused to soften with age. "Those lyrics weren't the usual moon-croon-June-spoon mush. There wasn't even a chorus. Do popular musicians not bother with choruses anymore?"

"Hoagy and I set out to write a special song."

"If your objective was to impress me and your mother," Father said, "mission accomplished."

It hadn't been, of course, but it was the sort of accidental by-product that would allow Nell to bid her parents farewell without a tidal wave of regret threatening to drown her as they drove north up Reeves Drive and out of town.

Nell's arms ached again to embrace him, but she stifled the urge. Instead, she had to satisfy herself with grasping at his forearm. "I'm glad to hear it." She felt the muscles beneath his shirt sleeve tense up. As she released her grip, Father consulted his pocket watch.

"We ought to be leaving, Mother. Getting clear of this city alone will take us all morning. From what I can tell, it goes on and on."

A sky-blue Cadillac pulled into the driveway. The driver door swung open and Bogie stepped out. "I was hoping I wouldn't be too late. You must be Mr. and Mrs. Davenport." He extended his hand. "I'm Humphrey Bogart."

"You most certainly are!" It was the closest Nell's mother had ever come to twittering.

Bogie had dressed in one of his nattier suits, a charcoal-gray flannel double-breasted, and a snazzy necktie dotted with deep yellow buttercups. He rubbed his jawline as Father had done a few minutes earlier. Had he been lurking around the corner, waiting for the right opportunity to show up? "Today is a Friday. Betty and I have scenes to film for our new picture. I thought I'd swing by to see if the girls wanted a lift."

"That's mighty considerate of you, Mr. Bogart."

Bogie tilted his head toward Nell. "Did our girl of the moment tell you last night's broadcast was her idea? She's the reason the whole shebang was such a success."

"And here was I assuming she orchestrated the evening to impress us," Father said.

"And did she?"

"Yes," Father turned to Nell, "she did." *I don't understand why you want this life*, his eyes seemed to say, *but it's what you've chosen.* "Nell, my girl, walk us to the car, will you? We can say our goodbyes there." He and Nell's mother bid farewell to Betty and Bogie, and headed back to their car. At the curb, he said, "We still have an outstanding matter to settle."

"I know, I know," Nell replied. "I still owe you eleven hundred and seventy-five dollars. I'm paying you back as quickly as I can, but if you require a lump sum, I guess I could ask Mr. Bogart for a loan."

"This trip out here hasn't ended the way I thought it would, but I no longer feel how I did."

There was a time when Nell would have given anything to hear that she needn't pay back her debt. She had sometimes gone without lunch and had learned how to darn her own socks because sending those payments home had taken most of what little spending money she'd had.

"Thank you, Father." She took Mother's hand in hers. "Thank you both. But I skipped town like a cowardly rat. It's my debt to pay."

"But—"

"And I'd like to pay it."

She looked Father in the eye and willed herself not to blink until he relented.

"You'll do okay," he said. "I should have guessed you never really needed protection."

"Protection?" Nell frowned. "From what?"

"How's a father supposed to keep his daughter safe when she's all the way out here in California, two thousand miles closer to danger, closer to the Japs, closer to the war?"

Nell stared up at her father, blinking in the sharp morning light. All this time, those "You must come home now" letters hadn't been about pulling her back into the fold and burying her in a life she didn't want. They'd just wanted to *protect* her. God, she thought, if only I'd given them the chance to explain that. Maybe this trip and all the gas ration coupons hadn't been a waste, after all.

Father studied the apartment building, then looked at Bogart and Betty, then back at Nell. "It's time we hit the road," he said, then headed for the driver's side.

"Your father's not the only one who's proud of you," Mother whispered. "I'll never forget what I witnessed last night for as long as I live." She opened the passenger door and climbed inside. By the time she had closed it again, Father had released the brake. He waved and pulled away from the curb.

Bogie and Betty waited until the Studebaker had reached Wilshire Boulevard and turned left, and then Betty walked down to where Nell still stood at the curb. She rested a hand on Nell's back. "You okay?"

Nell kept her eyes on the corner her folks had disappeared around. "It never occurred to me that they might be okay with me living my life my way. It's such a relief to know that I haven't let them down."

"I wish I knew how that felt." Betty fired off a trenchant laugh. "It's not like *my* mother is impressed with this movie-actress racket. Let alone with my getting involved with some middle-aged coot twenty-five years my senior."

"Hey!" cried Bogie, coming up behind them. He elbowed Nell. "Have I hog-tied her like a heifer at a rodeo? Miss Bacall is free to walk away any time she wants. And you have to do what's right. And now," he said, turning to Betty, "I'm giving you five minutes before I head for the Hollywood Hills."

Betty disappeared inside the apartment, telling Nell that she'd grab her purse too.

Nell ran a finger down Bogie's jacket sleeve. "Is this new?"

"Last weekend."

"Looks expensive."

"Silverwoods."

"How very fancy of you, Mr. Bogart."

"I'm A-list now, and don't you forget it, missy."

"I'll do my best." Nell peered at the corner again, then looked back at Bogie. "They like to pile it on thick about how they don't go to the movies or care about movie stars—but trust me. They'll be dining out for years on the time they met Humphrey Bogart in Beverly Hills."

"In that case, it was money well spent."

"Thanks," she said quietly.

He shrugged off her gratitude. "We all have to do what's right."

\* \* \*

Each Christmas season, the city attached twenty-foot electric trees to the telephone poles running the length of Hollywood Boulevard. They reminded Nell of the annual Christmas display in Robertson's department store windows on Michigan Avenue back in South Bend, and she always enjoyed walking down the street the first weekend after they were put up.

The Cadillac was passing the Pig 'n Whistle Café next to the

Egyptian Theatre when Bogie said, "Do you think Luke caught the broadcast?"

"Who knows?" Nell said from the back seat. A Laurel and Hardy picture, *Nothing but Trouble*, was playing at the Egyptian. If Luke were around, they'd have gone to see it. "And if he did, did he figure out the message?"

"I've got to say, Davenport, that was a mighty clever stunt you pulled. Burying a message like that in a song out there for everybody to hear."

"Thanks, but it was mostly Hoagy's doing. Although I rhymed 'you hiss' with 'quite amiss,' and 'red wine' with 'deadline,' which I thought was pretty damn impressive. But still, it's a moot point if Luke didn't catch the show."

"You could always call that law firm in New York, couldn't you?" Bogie asked.

"That'd cost a fortune."

"Unless you have . . ." Bogie withdrew a roll of quarters from his jacket pocket and tossed them over his shoulder to her as he drove through Hollywood and Vine. "Three dollars' worth ought to be enough." He pulled up at the curb outside the Owl Drug Store. "Make it snappy."

Nell chose the middle of the three public phone booths that lined the eastern wall. She had been carrying around the details of Bell, Amiss, and White in her handbag for two long years in case Luke found a way to contact her. As the receptionist put through her call, Nell laid her feverish forehead against the cool wood paneling. A loud click echoed over the wire, then the sound of an older gent clearing his throat.

"This is Horace Bell."

"Mr. Bell!" Nell's voice shot up half an octave. "Nell Davenport calling from Los Angeles. I'm the one who wrote to you to explain that Luke Valenti was away at war and it would be hard to reach him by the deadline set down by Boris Osterhaus's will."

"Yes. I remember."

"I was wondering if, by any chance . . . has he—has Luke, I mean—" She stopped when she heard Bell chuckle.

"As I told Mr. Valenti, he cut it awfully fine."

"You . . . you've spoken to him?"

"Thirty minutes ago."

Nell dropped onto the narrow seat secured to the wall. "How did he sound?"

"Like he was calling from the dark side of the moon. A very poor connection, indeed. But sufficient for getting the job done."

The clank of dishes and the chatter of drugstore customers faded away. "Everything's fine, then?"

"There will be some papers to sign, but we can do that once Mr. Valenti leaves the service."

A chime filled Nell's ear. "This is the operator. Please deposit seventy-five cents for the next three minutes."

Nell looked down at her supply of coins. She only had one left. "Thank you, Mr. Bell. You don't know how relieved I am to—"

The line went dead.

* * *

Nell dropped into the rear of Bogie's Cadillac. Betty peered over the front seat "Do you need a Bromo-Seltzer?" she asked. "Smelling salts?"

"A shot of whiskey by the looks of it," Bogie said, "and here am I without my flask." He started the motor and threw the car into a U-turn.

Nell counted three electric Christmas trees passing by the window before she flung her arms out wide. "It worked." The words came out in a breathy whisper. "The whole crazy, cuckoo, cockamamie plan."

"Jesus!" Betty screamed. "Tell us everything."

"The lawyer in charge of Boris's estate told me he'd already spoken to Luke."

The thought that she could sing into a microphone in Los Angeles and have Luke hear her on a radio somewhere in Hawaii overwhelmed her. It had been the whole point, of course. It was why she and Hoagy had written that song, and why they'd called it "Every Fifth Word," and why she'd had to summon up every scrap of courage she possessed. But throughout it all, had she ever believed they could pull it off? No, she realized now. Not really.

"It's a Christmas miracle!" Betty reached into the back and ran a fingertip under Nell's right eye. It came away glistening with tears in the morning light.

Bogie turned right on Cahuenga and headed into the Hollywood Hills. "You have around fifteen minutes to mop yourself up. Got a handkerchief?"

Nell let herself fall back onto the seat and stared out the window. They passed the Santa Fe Trailways bus depot—the one she had arrived at five years before. She scarcely recognized the girl who'd stepped off the bus that day with her scuffed saddle shoes, the little suitcase crammed with whatever clothes had come to hand, and not a clue about what she would do next.

*He's out there. He's listening. And one day he'll come home. To me.*

There was no way to know when that day would come. And when it did, would he step off a train missing a limb like his brother? Or be overwhelmed with battle fatigue like Simon Kovner? She'd seen plenty of men like that sitting alone in cafés, or wandering along the streets with no particular place to go.

But if that was a bridge they needed to cross, it was far off in the future. For now, she had a home fire to keep burning. Not an actual fire, of course. Betty's apartment didn't even have a fireplace. But down deep inside her, until she could take him in her arms again. And when she did, she'd never let him go.

"It's awfully quiet back there," Bogie said. "You okay?"

"Better than okay." Nell wiped her hands across her wet cheeks. "I'm terrific. Let's get to work and make some movies."

**THE END**

(Keep turning for Author Note)

**Did you enjoy this book?**

**You can make a big difference.**

As an independent author, I don't have the financial muscle of a New York publisher supporting me. But I do have something much more powerful and effective, and it's something those publishers would kill to get their hands on: a committed and loyal bunch of readers. Honest reviews of my books help bring them to the notice of other readers. If you've enjoyed this book, I would be so grateful if you could spend just a couple of minutes leaving a review.

Thank you very much,

*Martin Turnbull*

# AUTHOR NOTE

All the song lyrics reproduced in this novel are in public domain.

Bacall really was Clark Gable's date at a dinner party at Howard and Slim Hawks' home while he was on leave. Bacall talks about it in her memoir, *By Myself*. I can only imagine what it must have been like to be a nineteen-year-old, fresh off the train from Brooklyn, and finding herself Gable's date for the night.

The fighting between the Battling Bogarts was legendary around Hollywood. To give you an idea of how bad they were, I found this quote from Peter Lorre, who was one of Bogie's closest friends: "Charlie Lederer (a writer) and I once made a bet of $100. I swore I could make Mayo and Bogart have a tremendous fight within 5 minutes, starting from scratch. I invited Mayo, Bogey and Lederer to my house one night. As I was walking through the bar carrying some drinks, I said, more or less to myself, 'General MacArthur.' That was all I said. Within 3 minutes Bogey was hitting her over the head with a glass and she was biting and scratching him. She was for MacArthur and he was violently against."

In November 1942, Bogie and Mayo embarked on a ten-week USO tour of Northern Africa and Italy, often playing two shows a day along with visits to hospitals. Bogart and Mayo, actor Don Cummings, and accordionist Ralph Hark called themselves The Filthy Four. At their first stop, in Dakar, Senegal, they performed to a huge audience on an outdoor stage where a local orchestra greeted them with twenty choruses of "As Time Goes By." Much to everybody's surprise—including their own—Bogie and Mayo got along beautifully under very trying circumstances, but reverted to their "Battling Bogarts" antagonism as soon as they arrived in New York. In reality, Lauren Bacall never visited the Bogart home (nicknamed *Sluggy Hollow*) on Horn Ave in West Hollywood while they were away.

At around the time Bogart and Mayo returned from their 10-week USO tour, it became known that no alcoholic beverages had been distilled since November 8, 1942. That's because a hundred gallons of alcohol were needed to make one 18-inch shell, and also because "it has been discovered that a better grade of butadiene is more economically made from alcohol than from other materials formerly used." Butadiene was also important in making synthetic rubber. Four hundred and twenty million gallons of whiskey were stored in bonded warehouses in the United States. But because of spills and evaporation, only 208 million of those gallons would be available for the duration of the war—and nobody knew how long the war would last.

The following quote gives us insight to what the real Humphrey Bogart was like, as compared to his screen persona: "Bogie had a 16mm projector and liked to run pictures at home. He liked to run *A Star Is Born* [with Gaynor and March] and cried bitterly every time. He associated himself with March's character (an alcoholic Hollywood star) and with his downfall and being unable to pull himself together. That was the only time I saw Bogie cry."

In real life, Lauren Bacall lowered her voice by reading out loud from *The Robe* until it was hoarse pretty much as I described in this novel—without, of course, the participation of the fictional Nell Davenport. The banks of searchlights combing the sky over the Hollywood Bowl happened in real life.

Bogie did wear a toupée during this time. Verita Thompson looked after them for him (among her other clients were Charles Boyer, Gary Cooper, Ray Milland, and George Raft). She was from Arizona, as mentioned in this book; however, she did not return there during the war. That plot development was my own invention.

Bette Davis caused a minor stir when she insisted that the Hollywood Canteen be integrated. Until then, it had been rare for whites and people of color to mix freely in public. Bette insisted that if Black servicemen were good enough to fight for freedom, then they were fully welcome at the Canteen. As far as I can tell, this mixing resulted in no violent incidents. Or at least none serious enough for anybody to report. At around that same time, the Billy Berg's nightclub at 1356 North Vine St. in Hollywood became the first interracial nightclub in Hollywood. I don't know for sure that they took the cue from Bette Davis, but the Canteen's refusal to separate the races must have been, I would imagine, the topic of great discussion in the Black community at the time, and reason for great hope that the brick wall of segregation might, at last, be dismantled.

Naturally, Lauren Bacall was given more preparation to perform "How Little We Know" in *To Have and Have Not* than the way I describe it in this book, but if you'd like to see how the number turned out, hop over YouTube.

By the way, studio executives didn't like the way she sang it, so they brought in a sixteen-year-old kid named Andy Williams—yes, *that* Andy Williams—to record the song and dub him over Bacall. In the end, they decided that even though Bacall didn't have the greatest singing voice, it was distinctive and therefore audiences would know this wasn't her, so they kept her voice in the final version.

Bogie and Hedda Hopper did travel on the same junket train to Kansas in late March 1939 for the premiere of *Dodge City*, but he never threw any of her belongings from the train.

The scene where Nell and Betty sneak into the preview of *To Have and Have Not* is partially true and partially of my own invention. Warner Bros. held two previews. A three-car motorcade with Jack Warner, Steve Trilling (who was second-in-command to Jack Warner), Charlie Einfeld (who worked in Warners publicity), and Howard and Slim Hawks made its way to the Huntington Park Warner Theatre south of downtown Los Angeles to watch the first one. That happened on or around June 5, 1944 (the day before D-Day), and is the one I depict in this novel. Hawks did not want Lauren to attend that one, but it went so well, he took her to the second preview held ten days later. Lauren later wrote about it, saying that she was not prepared for the audience's reaction—so much laughter, so much sheer enjoyment from strangers—and would have enjoyed it more if Bogie had been with her.

Orry-Kelly left Warner Bros. in 1944. I couldn't find an actual date, so I set the scene of his farewell party in June of that year. As far as I could see, the studio did not give him a farewell party, so that scene was my own invention.

The scene in Chapter 36 when Slim Hawks shares her secret about Howard's nerves I drew from both Lauren's and Slim's memoirs. Howard Hawks was a very stoic individual, and took his work seriously. During the first week of production on any new movie, he would frequently have to pull over en route to the studio and throw up into the gutter.

The scene in Chapter 25 where Bogie tells Nell about him and Bacall meeting up on Selma Avenue in Hollywood after work so that they could have some fleeting private time together actually happened. Bacall talks about it in her autobiography.

The USS *Lanternfish* submarine is my invention.

You can see Bogart's cameo in *Thank Your Lucky Stars* on YouTube.

You can see Joan Crawford's cameo in *Hollywood Canteen* on YouTube.

The ballerina who Tristan was finding a tutu for in Chapter 12 was a pre-MGM Cyd Charisse. You can see her 2½ minute dance on YouTube.

There's no need to look up Violet Beaudine's song "When My Boy Helps to Liberate Gay Paree" on YouTube. That title is my own invention.

# ALSO BY MARTIN TURNBULL

**The Hollywood Home Front trilogy**

A trilogy of novels set in World War II Hollywood

Book 1 - *All the Gin Joints*

Book 2 - *Thank Your Lucky Stars*

Book 3 - *You Must Remember This*

*Chasing Salomé*: a novel of 1920s Hollywood

*The Heart of the Lion*: a novel of Irving Thalberg's Hollywood

**The Hollywood's Garden of Allah novels**

Book 1 – *The Garden on Sunset*

Book 2 – *The Trouble with Scarlett*

Book 3 – *Citizen Hollywood*

Book 4 – *Searchlights and Shadows*

Book 5 – *Reds in the Beds*

Book 6 – *Twisted Boulevard*

Book 7 – *Tinseltown Confidential*

Book 8 – *City of Myths*

Book 9 – *Closing Credits*

**Rave reviews for Martin Turnbull's *Hollywood's Garden of Allah* series:**

**What a marvelous series!** I tore through all nine books in record time and plan to go back to the beginning and start over! Thank you so much for this grand treat!

**I loved this whole series,** I'm sorry it had to end, but the reading was worth it! One of the best book series I have ever read!

**If you start The Garden of Allah series from the beginning** you will be treated to not only a great story but an accurate history of Hollywood from the 1920's Silent Era through the mid-1950's. I highly recommend this series of books for your total enjoyment.

**I would give every one of the nine books more than 5 stars.** This was a wonderful series that I wish did not have to end. I LOVED reading this series! They were so well-written, thorough, detailed, and really really interesting. I would love to read more, as I enjoyed these characters so much, and loved learning about the development of the industry and the area.

**Martin Turnbull not only entertained me,** but he gave me a respect and love for movies, actors, actresses, writers, directors, studios, and everything that contributed to the development of our entertainment industry.

**What a great series of books!** Anyone who loves movie history has to read these. I really felt I was part of of the friendship with Marcus, Gwen, and Kathryn, and shared every emotional rollercoaster ride.

~oOo~

See the Hollywood's Garden of Allah novels
**on Martin Turnbull's website**.

~oOo~

**Be the first to hear about new books and other news - sign up to my mailing list - http://bit.ly/turnbullsignup**

(I promise (a) I won't fill your inbox with useless drivel you don't care about, (b) I won't email you very often, and (c) I'll never share your information with anyone. Ever.

# ACKNOWLEDGMENTS

My heartfelt thanks to the following:

My editor: Jennifer McIntyre for her keen eye, unfailing humor, and the willingness to debate every last letter and comma placement.

My thanks, also, to Susan Milner and Andie Paysinger for providing verisimilitude. I can only dream of these lives, but Susan and Andie lived it.

Steve Bingen, who provided me with detailed photos and maps of the Warner Bros. studio lot in Burbank, California.

John Luder, who provided me with many of the finer points of World War II and U.S. military details.

My beta readers: Vince Hans, David Fox, Beth Riches, Bradley Brady, and especially Steven Adkins and Gene Strange for their invaluable time, insight, feedback and advice in shaping this novel.

My proofreaders with the best eagle eyes in the biz: Bob Molinari, Susan Perkins, and Leigh Carter.

Book cover by Damonza

# ABOUT THE AUTHOR

A lifelong love of travel, history, and sharing his knowledge with others has led Martin Turnbull down a long path to authorship. Having made the move to the United States from Melbourne, Australia in the mid-90s, Martin staked his claim in the heart of Los Angeles. His background in travel allowed him to work as a private tour guide--showing off the alluring vistas, mansions, boulevards, and backlots of the Hollywood scene. With stints in local historical guiding with the Los Angeles Conservancy as well as time on the Warner Bros. movie lot, Martin found himself armed with the kind of knowledge that would fly off the very pages of his future works. As a longtime fan of Hollywood's golden era and old films, Martin decided it was time to marry his knowledge with his passions and breathe life back into this bygone world.

The product of his passions burst forth in the form of Hollywood's Garden of Allah novels, a series of historical fiction books set during the golden age of Hollywood: 1927-1959. Exploring the evolution of Hollywood's most famous and glamorous era through the lives of its residents, these stories take place both in and around the real-life Garden of Allah Hotel on iconic Sunset Boulevard. Although Martin's heart belongs to history, his energy remains in the present, continuing to put his passions on paper and beyond.

# CONNECT WITH MARTIN TURNBULL

**Website**

**Facebook**

**Blog**

**Goodreads**

**Amazon author page**

Be sure to check out the **Photo Blog** for vintage photos of Los Angeles and Hollywood on Martin's website: website: **MartinTurnbull.com**

~oOo~

**To hear about new books first, sign up to my mailing list -**

**http://bit.ly/turnbullsignup**

I won't fill your inbox with useless drivel or I email you too often or never share your information with anyone. Ever. (And you can unsubscribe at any time. No hard feelings.)

~oOo~

Made in United States
Orlando, FL
03 December 2023